Praise for Pa~~tricia Rice~~ and her
previous novel, *Blue Clouds*

A *Romantic Times* Top Pick

"Vastly entertaining . . . A wonderful combination of poignancy
and humor."
—*Romantic Times*

"A wickedly luscious novel filled with scintillating dialogue,
madcap characters, and a premise that shows what true
romance is all about. With her superb talent, Ms. Rice pens
remarkable tales that come across the pages in whatever
genre she writes."
—*Rendezvous*

"Absolutely stunning . . . Rice gives us *everything* we could want
in this 'to keep forever'—love, mystery, and adventure. . . .
Fantastic."
—*Bell, Book & Candle*

"[A] romance that snares the reader right from the start."
—*Library Journal*

"You can always count on Patricia Rice for an entertaining
story with just the right mix of romance, humor, and
emotion."
—*The Romantic Reader*

VOLCANO

Patricia Rice

FAWCETT GOLD MEDAL • NEW YORK

A Fawcett Gold Medal Book
Published by The Ballantine Publishing Group
Copyright © 1999 by Rice Enterprises, Inc.

www.randomhouse.com/BB/

Library of Congress Catalog Card Number: 99-90541

ISBN 0-449-00609-3

Manufactured in the United States of America

First Edition: August 1999

10   9   8   7   6   5   4   3   2   1

I cannot possibly begin to list all the people I wish to thank for being there when I needed them. You know who you are, and I love you all.

Still, I cannot resist adding that without Katherine Bernardi's pointing out what was obvious to everyone but me, and without Connie Rinehold's constant back-patting, I would probably have retreated to my accounting office to suck my thumb rather than finish this book. To them go the first annual "Charlie" awards!

❧ AUTHOR'S NOTE ❧

Although the island of St. Lucia, its drive-in volcano, the marvelous resort of Anse Chastenet, and the town of Soufrière exist in all the glory I have depicted, none of the inhabitants of this book remotely resemble any person living or dead—although we can always dream!

❧ ONE ❧

As the airplane circled the runway, Penelope's stomach clenched with panic. She'd never flown out of the country before, never dealt with the unanticipated complications of foreign travel alone. She'd never had such an important assignment, either, one that carried all her desperate hopes and prayers.

Given a choice, she'd take the security of the known any day. She blamed the unfairness of life for assigning the most important project of her career to a tiny island in the middle of the Caribbean, where she knew nothing and no one.

As the airplane wheels bumped on the runway, Penelope watched the tropical landscape fly by with an interest heightened by fear. She was such a damned coward. She should be thrilled at this opportunity.

She steadied her emotions by envisioning the interminable wait to file off the plane, the ordeal of negotiating the soulless terminal with thousands of strangers hurrying toward unknown destinations, and the cab ride to some faceless hotel like all the other hotels she'd ever known. Only then could she finally start the job that would establish her foothold in the career of her choice. She needed that partnership so desperately her teeth ached with it.

Her uneasiness arose from hunger and exhaustion and nothing more. If she could readjust her thinking and consider this as simply one more assignment in a string of successful assignments, she would be all right. She knew she was good. She might be an emotional basket case, but she had brains.

Carting her briefcase and overnight bag off the 747 into unknown territory, she just wished she could solve her growing anxiety along with her growling stomach. The initial gnawing had originated with her 6 A.M. arrival time without breakfast at the Miami terminal for international passengers. The line had been endless, offering no opportunity to grab a bite before boarding. The plane had sat on the tarmac for over an hour after that, so she'd missed her connection in Puerto Rico. She'd spent another hour standing in lines to book another flight, leaving her just enough time to run through an unfamiliar airport, without lunch. Naturally, neither of the flights had served meals. Surely her nervousness had more to do with an empty stomach and incompetent airlines than fear.

Heat slammed into her the instant she stepped down the plane stairs. No brief hike through weather-protected tunnels into an air-conditioned terminal on this underdeveloped island. Warily watching more seasoned passengers, Penelope followed them across the tarmac to a shaded walkway. The tropical sun glared off the pavement, and drooping palm trees shimmered behind the heat in the distance. Even coming from Miami, she could feel the difference.

Penelope skirted around the chattering passengers trailing along the walkway as if they had all day. Even in her low pumps, she still towered over most of the crowd. As a twelve-year-old, her height had utterly embarrassed her. She'd come to terms with it since then, but sometimes she still felt like that gawky teenager, especially when people stared.

She'd been warned her destination required a lengthy taxi journey to the other side of the island. She wanted to arrive before dinner, so she needed to hurry. But she was starving now. Would a restaurant be too much to hope for? Garbed in a man-tailored business suit meant for an office and not the tropics, Penelope felt moisture pooling beneath her shirt as she hurried toward the terminal.

Adjusting her horn-rimmed glasses as she entered the building, Penelope breathed a sigh of relief under the slow-moving fans cooling the high-ceilinged immigration office. The sight of half a dozen long lines ahead of her didn't help the gnawing in her stomach, but the consequences of Beth's accident had taught her patience. She was almost there. The hotel had promised an agent would meet her outside the gates. She wouldn't have to find her way alone after that. Setting her briefcase safely between her navy pumps, she tightened the pins in her upswept hair.

She knew how to find her way alone by now. Admittedly, she'd led a sheltered childhood in an upper-class environment, but she'd spent these last eight years since college making her own way in the world. Caught up in their divorce, her parents had never helped her. Besides, they were still disappointed that she hadn't married Zack and settled down back in Charlotte as Beth had. And she certainly didn't have any man holding her hand, pretending she was too helpless to manage these journeys alone. Zack had never forgiven her the day she'd gone back to Charlotte on her own, leaving him drunk in Daytona on spring break.

Looking around at the tourists crowding the room, Penelope summoned pity for the harried women with crying children clinging to their hands while their husbands juggled baggage and pretended competence. If those women had fooled themselves into believing their husbands would take care of everything, they would be sorely disappointed. Men couldn't do a blamed thing without a woman behind them.

As if confirming her opinion, the man at the head of her line searched frantically through the pockets in his expensive L.L. Bean traveling jacket while his wife held a crying baby and watched in bewilderment. Lost the passports, Penelope thought cynically.

The next man in line looked vaguely familiar. Wearing an expensive suit in contrast to the casually dressed tourists around them, he clutched a leather briefcase as he handed over his passport. Penelope frowned as she tried to figure out why a middle-aged, balding, burly man would look familiar until she realized he was one of PC&M's clients, a major contractor. Interesting that PC&M had acquired a new client here at the same time one of their contractors was moving in on the area. Could be some connection. Maybe the contractor had recommended PC&M to Anse Chastenet. That was how these good ol' boy networks worked. She mentally filed the knowledge for future use.

Shoring up her confidence, she decided that after a few more trips like this one, she'd be an experienced traveler, ready to specialize in Poindexter, Combs, and MacMillan's Caribbean accounts. Maybe then she could take the time to enjoy the exotic setting of the islands.

Right now, she worried about finding her suitcase, getting through customs, and locating her assigned agent. Then there would be the perilous journey to the hotel. Cadogan's guidebook hadn't called it perilous, but she could read between the lines. "Tortuous paths," "series of switchbacks," and "rough, potholed roads" meant any number of things, none of them pleasant in her current frame of mind. She didn't like situations she couldn't control.

Finally, her turn arrived. The agent gave her passport a cursory glance, stamped it, and motioned her away. Penelope had already watched the passengers ahead of her and knew they'd disappeared somewhere to the left. She couldn't see any signs to guide her, and the agent's heavily accented English reduced the possibility of asking questions. Gathering her courage, she shouldered her bag and trudged down another corridor.

At least the natives of St. Lucia were supposed to speak English. Her high-school Spanish and college French wouldn't hold up well in this nerve-racking environment. She'd known the islanders spoke a patois. She hadn't counted on their heavy accents converting their English into a foreign language. She prayed the hotel management had a better grasp of her native tongue or she'd be in for an uphill struggle in installing their software.

She saw no sign of the contractor in the crowd of tourists circling the baggage claim. He must have only brought his briefcase for a quick trip. Pity. She might have made some new connections here if he knew the area. Maybe another time.

Native porters hustled around them, practically grabbing the unloaded luggage from unsuspecting hands. Vowing to hang on to hers if only to avoid figuring out how to tip with the Caribbean equivalent of her American currency, Penelope trained her gaze on the carousel. Finding her wheeled travel case, she snatched it away from an eager porter and glanced around for the next step in this circus.

Customs. She still had to carry the bag through customs. She'd hoped they'd had the efficiency to inspect the bags while she'd waited in those interminable lines in the first room. She should have known better. Airports and efficiency were a contradiction in terms.

Resignedly listening to her stomach growl—she couldn't find so much as a vending machine in this barn—Penelope arrived in still another mob of harried tourists with crying toddlers. She eyed the children with suspicion and chose a different line. She didn't have time for thinking about children. Even her sister's had become alien creatures now that her brother-in-law had them. Considering her options right now, it was probably best if she kept things that way.

She transferred her attention to the line ahead of her. She couldn't decide what system the clerks used for inspecting baggage. A muscled man in a tank top, heavy mustache, and mirrored sunglasses she could swear was a drug dealer passed through with a wave of a hand. Teenage girls with pimply faces had their purses emptied.

Penelope's nerves teetered on edge as a tall man jostled her from behind, and another traveling alone eyed her with an interest she recognized only too well. She had contemplated removing her stiff, buttoned jacket, but she tugged it around her now. She pushed her glasses farther up her nose and checked to make certain her hair hadn't strayed from its knot. The glasses were more protective disguise than necessity. She'd bought them to correct her distance vision but discovered they aided her goal of emphasizing her intelligence, not her looks.

Ahead, the muscle-bound jock in the revealing red tank top handed his backpack to a porter, then leaned his shoulders against the far wall, apparently waiting for someone. She hated people who affected sunglasses inside, and she hated mirrored sunglasses even more. The men who wore them were inevitably egotistical asses. This one with his droopy mustache definitely looked like a drug dealer.

Uneasy, she checked her money belt and the pepper spray in her pocket.

The man in the mirrored glasses seemed to be staring at her. She hated this adolescent self-consciousness that struck her at the most inopportune times.

Forcing herself to look away, Penelope concentrated on her empty stomach instead of her jumpy nerves. Next time, she would pack food in her briefcase. She just couldn't believe any airline was so inconsiderate as to think passengers checking in at 6 A.M. could travel all day without food.

The man in the sunglasses was still lounging against the wall as she reached the desk. The clown probably thought he was hot stuff, showing off that bronzed-all-over look. To Penelope, it simply meant the man had nothing better to do but feed his vanity while developing skin cancer in tanning booths. He reminded her of Zack. Except by now, Zack probably had a beer belly and a bald head. This man proudly displayed his trim physique in low-cut jeans that emphasized slim hips and muscled thighs, and there was nothing balding about that headful of wind-blown chestnut hair.

He crossed his arms over his massive chest as the customs agent ordered her to open her suitcase. Cringing at the thought of revealing her undergarments and nightwear, Penelope bit her tongue and reluctantly unzipped the case. At least she'd had the forethought to put her more intimate items in the overnight bag.

She winced as the uniformed agent dangled a bra in one hand while rummaging through her clothes with the other. He couldn't have been ruder if he'd done it deliberately. Tired, starving, and nerves already frayed, Penelope contemplated the tongue-lashing he deserved. Before she could release it, the agent held up a plastic bag of suspicious white powder and yelled over his shoulder excitedly.

Stunned, she felt pure panic sweep through her, amplified by the gasps of people behind her. She knew what that white powder meant. So did everyone else. Her empty stomach knotted and nausea rose in her throat. Visions of foreign jails danced through her head. This couldn't be happening. She'd dozed off in the heat and was having a nightmare. There was no way that bag could have gotten into her suitcase—unless someone had planted it there.

Uniformed soldiers sprinted through the building, all shouting in the native patois, crystallizing the nightmare into reality. Dark skins, baleful expressions, and ominous automatic weapons spun the situation into a surreal hallucination. She couldn't understand a word anyone said. Although she recognized some of the French root of the dialect, none of the sounds made any sense. Only the anger and accusation in their voices penetrated.

Before Penelope realized the agent had asked her a question in English, the man in the tank top had elbowed his way through the crowd and caught her arm. She squealed and tried jerking away, but he squeezed her arm reassuringly. She was trembling too much to shake him off. Fainting appeared a very real possibility.

"Alonzo, what seems to be the trouble here? I've been waiting all day for my wife to arrive, and now you're holding up our honeymoon."

Penelope considered sinking right through the floor at the stranger's joshing tone, but the red haze of fear prevented anything except recognition of his clear Southern drawl and his obvious familiarity with the customs agent.

The agent replied in rapid-fire patois, and the man in the

sunglasses responded in the same language without hesitation. Penelope watched in astonishment as the stranger dismissed the plastic bag of white powder with a wave of his hand and a burst of sarcastic verbiage. With equally astonishing ease, he produced a wallet full of bills, displayed his passport, and slipped a few bills across the counter with it. "You know where to find us. I've got a taxi waiting," he said in English.

Leaving the customs agent literally holding the bag, the man in sunglasses grabbed Penelope's suitcase, and clasping her arm firmly, towed her out of the customs office toward the bright light of day.

Terrified, Penelope attempted to free herself from the stranger's hold. She had thought he would smell of sweat and suntan lotion, but he exuded the spicy fragrance of expensive aftershave. That didn't reassure her enough to allow his manhandling, although she had to wonder briefly if her knees wouldn't collapse under her should he release her.

"You can let me go now," she hissed as he maneuvered her outside into the hustle and bustle of people locating tour guides, porters, taxis, and rental cars. The concrete shed reminded her of a livestock consignment barn with all the inhabitants mooing in protest, but she didn't linger on that image. The hard hand scorching her through the sleeve of the raw silk jacket held her attention.

"Not until we get you out of here. Do you have someone meeting you?" He scanned the crowd with deliberate precision.

"The agent from Anse Chastenet," she told him reluctantly. She didn't know any way of escaping his hold unless she let him know she was expected. She should have been grateful for his aid in rescuing her from an impossible situation, but his hand on her arm terrified her almost as much as the sight of the drugs. What on earth had he said to get her away so easily? Who the hell was he? Mafia? CIA?

"Anse Chastenet, excellent, although I would have picked

you as the Jalousie Plantation type. There she is. Stand right here, don't move. I'll take care of her."

Penelope didn't like the way he said that, but he gave her no opportunity to protest. Carrying off the suitcase containing all her clothing, he approached a petite woman in a business suit with a gold name tag bearing the Anse Chastenet motif. The woman listened to his swift patois, responded in the same, smiled in Penelope's direction, and waved them off.

She couldn't believe it, not even after seeing it with her own eyes. Events had happened too fast. She couldn't collect her thoughts. But as her would-be rescuer grabbed her arm and hustled her down the pavement toward a line of taxis, Penelope had the distinct impression that she had just been kidnapped.

❧ TWO ❧

The long legs had Charlie's mouth watering. He'd picked out those legs from across the tarmac as they'd waltzed right past all the other passengers. Her briefcase and power suit were somewhat off-putting, but he'd been caught off guard by Jacobsen's arrival and needed a solution, fast. Business Suit would provide a better decoy than anyone else in the terminal.

Good thing he'd landed when he had and seen the old goat, or he would never have suspected Jacobsen had any connection with St. Lucia. Until he knew what his worst enemy was doing here, he'd opt for lying low and scoping out the territory.

If it wasn't for that prim jacket, uptight hairstyle, and abominable glasses, he'd figure Business Suit for a fashion model. She had the height for it. He judged she reached past his shoulder, and he stood six-five. That milk-white skin could stand a little sun and makeup, but the features behind those hideous glasses were picture perfect. He bet if she let down that thick knot of ebony hair, she would almost look like a real woman.

Charlie ignored the stirring of anticipation in his pants as he practically threw the recalcitrant female into the waiting van. She felt good in his hands, slim and incredibly soft. She smelled good too, some old-fashioned flowery fragrance that

10

aroused images of warm southern nights. A good jolly-rogering right now would suit him more than fine, but he wanted out of Vieux Fort first. Business Suit here wasn't the kind of female he would normally choose for a good time—hell, she was the kind he ran from faster than a crazed bull—but kidnapping a family of tourists hadn't appealed to his baser instincts.

"What in the world do you think you're doing?" she hissed as he shoved her over on the seat and climbed in beside her. The driver had already thrown her bags on top of Charlie's backpack and was closing the van doors.

"Getting you out of there," he hissed back. "You want those soldiers seeing us take off in different cars?"

That silenced her long enough for the van driver to climb into his seat and start the engine. Charlie wished he could make the man move faster, but in the islands, time was irrelevant. The driver would leave when he felt so inclined.

"I don't mean to be rude, but you'll get out when we're out of sight?" Business Suit asked anxiously as the cab joined the line of other vehicles inching from the airport.

He admired her control. Her hands trembled and her lips had lost their color, but she didn't give in to the usual hysterical female dramatics. Instead, she held her cool and spoke coherently, although he was wary of whatever female weapon she fingered in her pocket. Damned uptight career women thought every man they met wanted under their skirts. Of course, in the case of this particular female, she was probably right. She didn't precisely have a lush body so much as a tantalizing one, the kind men watched on TV but never saw in real life.

"Just think of me as the local chamber of commerce welcoming committee, assuring your visit to St. Lucia is safe and trouble free." Charlie glanced over his shoulder at the traffic behind him: all taxis and rental cars. Jacobsen hadn't seen him and had probably already left the airport. That didn't mean his disguise had fooled everyone. He could bribe an old friend like Alonzo into playacting, but he couldn't bribe an entire island.

"I'm not a drug dealer," she asserted now that his attention was elsewhere. "I never saw that bag of white stuff before."

"Yeah, yeah, that's what they all say." He ought to feel guilty for his little prank of asking Alonzo to plant that bag, but he didn't. Raul was more important than the little princess. Not so little, he amended, as she shifted and her long leg brushed his.

"I thank you for your assistance," she said stiffly, obviously offended by his rudeness. "I'm sure I could have straightened it out eventually on my own. I don't wish to keep you from your duties any longer. I must insist the driver let you out wherever it's convenient for you."

Charlie turned his head and glared at her in disbelief. Her wide round glasses framed unblinking brown eyes rimmed with thick black lashes. He would wonder what world she came from, but unfortunately, he knew. "Do you have any idea what the Vieux Fort jail looks like?" he asked.

Charlie didn't think she could turn any paler, but she did.

"I'm sure it wouldn't have come to that," she replied as stiffly as before. "I'm an American citizen. They would have called the consulate or whoever is in charge of these matters. It probably wasn't even drugs, just someone's bath powder."

"They wouldn't have bothered testing before they threw your sweet little tail in jail and forgot about you. They do things in their own time and their own way around here," he said without repentance. "They haven't had a magistrate in six months and cases are backed up the wazoo. The inmates are a bit miffed, if you catch my drift."

Charlie checked over the driver's shoulder to be certain they headed the right way. Once out of Vieux Fort, nothing but the narrow rural road gave evidence of civilization. She might even be grateful for his company when they hit some of those hairpin turns.

He'd appreciate a little gratitude about now, but his haughty companion obviously disdained his animal presence. Charlie shoved his mirrored glasses more firmly up on his nose and sank back in the seat.

"Surely you needn't accompany me any farther," she protested, but her shoulders sagged in defeat as the town outside the window vanished from view behind a banana forest.

Charlie smugly suspected she'd just realized the village they left behind was the only civilization around. That ought to scare the hell out of Miss Rich Bitch. His animosity toward her surprised him. Generally, he was a Good-Time Charlie around women.

"I'm going to Soufrière. Anse Chastenet is just down the road. This suits me fine." He tried to stretch his long legs out. The position brought his hip closer to hers. He grimaced as she scrunched against the window. Maybe if he tried charming her just a little bit . . . Hell, he'd never charmed a woman in his life. They took one look at his bulk and either crawled all over him or ran for their lives. This woman was the running kind.

Maybe she responded to reason. Charlie didn't think it very likely, not the way she inched away from him and gave him furtive looks as if she suspected he would pull out a machete and take off her scalp. A guy would think she'd never seen a man before. So maybe he didn't wear a slick Italian suit or those yuppie camp shorts or whatever she considered socially acceptable. That didn't make him a killer or a rapist. Lots of women liked his size. *Lots*.

Forget reasoning. He couldn't take a chance on telling her about Raul. He didn't know anything for certain except that he knew damned well Raul wouldn't abscond with his money. He and Raul had grown up together, protecting each other's backs. He'd trust Raul with his life, just as Raul must be trusting Charlie with his right now.

"I suppose offering a ride is the least I can do in exchange for your help," she said tentatively, turning toward him with fear still etching the corners of her eyes as she watched him through those awful glasses.

That was more like it. Settling more firmly into the seat and crossing his arms, he regarded her with no small degree of interest. After all, they'd be spending considerable time together, although she didn't realize that yet. "My name's Charlie Smith. What's yours?"

That brought a wry look from beneath sooty lashes. "Smith? Why not just call yourself Brown and make a joke of it?"

He scowled. "Because the name is Smith. I come from a long line of plain ordinary Smiths. I take it you don't follow football?"

She still seemed tense, and the skepticism hadn't faded from her eyes as she answered cautiously, "No, I don't. Should I recognize the name?"

"Probably not," he admitted, shrugging. "Not unless you follow college ball. I pulled a kneecap my senior year and never went on to the pros. I could have though," he added defensively. It was a bit of a sore point with him. He'd been one of the top contenders for the NFL draft. His life could have been filled with wine, women, and song. What made it worse was that he hadn't even ruined the knee playing ball. He'd done it falling off a damned roof. He glared at her. "Your turn."

Briefly, amusement curved her naturally red lips and banished the wary look from her eyes. "Penelope Albright; no comments, please. I'm bright, but I'm not a Penny."

"Yeah, I doubt you come that cheap," he offered pragmatically. He didn't spend much time around women wearing designer suits and real gold, but he recognized them when he saw them. "So, what are you doing in St. Lucia, Penelope? Laptops and briefcases aren't the normal tourist equipment."

"I'm a management specialist in computer software design. I'm here on business. And you? You seem fluent in the native tongue."

She spoke stiffly, but Charlie noted that her hand no longer clutched as tightly at the weapon in her pocket. Maybe he'd found the key to getting where he wanted. Women always loved to talk.

"I spent some time here in my misspent youth," he admitted. "I'm here on business too. I can't imagine anyone in Soufrière possessing a computer though. The electricity is erratic at best. Whose software are you designing?"

She returned to regarding him warily. "I respect client confidentiality. Is Soufrière very small, then?"

Well, that didn't get him any answers. Charlie shrugged. "It's a fishing village aspiring to be a tourist mecca. They sell arts and crafts to the few souls brave enough to wander that far. The tourists come for sun and water, and everything they want is at the resorts. Why risk getting ripped off by fast-talking hustlers outside their sheltered world?"

Little Miss Albright grimaced. "There are streets in Miami I can't walk down without fear of being hustled. I like nice, private little shops with prices clearly marked. I never learned to haggle."

He'd figured that. His mother had always turned up her nose at the village market. This conversation was getting him nowhere. Pointing out the window, he changed the subject. "There's a cocoa tree. Have you ever seen one?"

The driver obligingly slowed so they could observe the green pods. In accented English, he pointed out the banana plantation farther up the hill, and the mango trees along the road's edge.

The farther they drove, the more Penelope succumbed to the grandeur of the view, forgetting her fear. She admired the lush vegetation of the roadside and strained to determine one variety of tree from another. The natural spill of palm trees and bougainvillea down the mountainside captured her appreciation. It was as if she'd entered another world, a tropical jungle where none of the usual human hazards existed. The only people she saw were young children scrabbling in the dust along the roadside, and an occasional elderly man or woman watching the world go by from their front stoop. Mostly, the road wound through acres of vegetation, offering glimpses of the sea far below.

Even the man beside her no longer seemed quite as ominous. She could handle old college football players. They were a breed she knew well. If he'd planned to hurt her, he would have tried by now. She'd still like to smack those mirrored sunglasses off his handsome nose. She hated the way the glasses hid his eyes—and his thoughts.

"I'm surprised the area isn't more developed," she commented bravely. The bag of white stuff continued nagging at the back of her mind, but she strove for calm. She could think better if she was calm. "I thought all these Caribbean islands were wall-to-wall tourist havens."

"Competition is tough, and St. Lucia doesn't have the services other islands have developed. They're working on it. Castries, of course, is just what you've imagined. That's where most of the tourists go, because that's where the hotels are." He shrugged. "Down here, the water and electric systems are unpredictable. Sewers, nonexistent. They've experimented with using the volcano's natural heat for generating energy, but the government takes the cheapest bids, and the companies they hire don't have the experience necessary for the task. Like everything, money is the key. Myself, I'd hate seeing this end of the island turned into a Miami parking lot. I prefer it as it is."

Penelope nodded at a shack on stilts with chickens pecking in the shade beneath the porch. "You prefer seeing people grubbing for a living with no hope of making anything of themselves?"

Taking a deep breath, she finally released her grip on the pepper spray. He hadn't attacked her in any way, and it seemed a trifle irrational to fear a man who talked intelligently of the island economy. On the other hand, he'd been at the right place at the right time when that powder appeared in her suitcase, and dammit, he *looked* like a drug smuggler. Maybe he'd been waiting for that shipment.

She shifted away from him as Charlie rested his arm on the seat back to point out the window again. She couldn't read his expression through the glasses, but he pulled back slightly at her movement.

"Do you really think civilization is worth trading in that

view?" he demanded. "Fish are plentiful. Fruit hangs on trees in the front yard. Vegetables grow like weeds. What more can a man ask?"

"Maybe that's enough for a man," she answered scornfully, pointing at a line of colorful clothes drying in the sun, "but what about for a woman? They're still scrubbing clothes by hand. Are there hospitals where they can have their babies? Can their children get an education? What if a person likes reading and math better than fishing and weeding gardens? What opportunities does that person have? Civilization isn't all bad."

His muscled arm behind her increased her nervousness, but Penelope refused to acknowledge it. Some people just didn't understand the need for personal space. A smaller man might not have made her so uneasy, but his build was a trifle overpowering. Zack had been a boy when she dated him. Charlie Smith was definitely a full-grown, very possibly *dangerous* male.

Her unwelcome companion sat back. "Civilization isn't all bad, but people don't know where to draw the line. Schools and utilities are needed. Miles of hotels and parking lots are not. Anse Chastenet has the right idea. They've developed a nearly inaccessible area using architecture that blends in with the landscape and a minimum of cement. They've taken care not to harm the environment and to preserve the natural beauty of the area. It's primitive, perhaps, but it has everything a person should need."

Penelope couldn't believe he was giving this lecture, but she listened as he continued relentlessly.

"Golf courses and cutesy boutiques can be found anywhere in the world. Why ruin the natural beauty of the island, something that can be found in fewer and fewer places, for something that can be had everywhere else you go?"

"I'm not arguing." Penelope held up her hands in surrender. Not having seen Anse Chastenet, she could scarcely argue the point. She couldn't believe she was actually discussing social economics with a man who had practically

kidnapped and blackmailed her. He was too large, too masculine, too damned self-assured. He crowded her space,
usurped her control, and now he sat here conversing on vital
issues as if they'd known each other all their lives. In her experience, men didn't *do* that. Not with her, anyway.

She didn't think the combination of raw male sexuality and
stimulating discussion healthy for her state of mind, yet talk
was better than glaring silences that left her with nothing to
do but worry. "Admittedly, I like my creature comforts. And I
suspect ninety-nine percent of the people with the wealth to
travel here want the same. Doesn't the island have any other
economy besides tourism? I should think it would be simpler
to preserve the island's natural state if they could keep
tourists out."

"Farming is the only other economy, and it doesn't support
them. If you've ever lived on a farm, you know the uncer-
tainty of weather and markets. St. Lucia will have to develop
industries to supplement the tourist trade, but industries rely
on transportation and utilities, and they're just not available
yet."

Turning to stare at him, Penelope caught her own reflection
in his mirrored sunglasses—a reminder of just how little she
knew about this man.

Feeling anxious and awkward all over again, she forced her
attention back to the incredible vistas of sea on one side and
mountains in the distance. She had never seen such magnificent scenery, and rather than argue with her accidental escort,
she admired the explosion of flowers along the hillside,
hoping they might distract her.

But in the unair-conditioned van, Charlie Smith's expensive fragrance combined with his healthy male musk into a
heady odor she couldn't ignore. "It's like driving through
a natural conservatory," she said, controlling her nervousness with speech. Clasping her hands, she nodded at the
window. "Look at the philodendron climbing that tree. And
that looks like an anthurium growing in front of that house.

And bromeliads growing wild. I can't even grow those things in my apartment."

"Well, they'd have to build climate-controlled buildings here to grow apple trees and lilacs," he said dryly. "This is a tropical climate, after all. I never saw the point of houseplants anyway."

She should have kept her mouth shut. She'd never been able to converse reasonably with men on any level, intellectual or otherwise. "Men don't generally see the point of picking up dirty clothes until they need something to wear either," she replied, irritation prevailing over fear. "It's the difference between the species." Ignoring the big brute, Penelope focused on enjoying her first Caribbean experience.

Except that experience included a bag of white powder, police, and a glaringly male jock in a red muscle shirt and mustache. The incident in the airport had thoroughly shaken her. She didn't know where that white stuff had come from, but until she knew more, she had to focus on those things she could control. She could do anything she put her mind to. She had to. She had no one else to fall back on. If she failed at this assignment, she could lose everything she'd worked so hard to gain these last years. And she would fail Beth.

Beth, the obedient twin. Blind Beth. Penelope uttered a mental groan and closed her eyes tighter against the image of her beautiful, kindhearted sister wearing scars and dark glasses. The accident hadn't just destroyed her eyes, it had destroyed her marriage, her home, everything. John hadn't been able to cope with the disaster. He'd taken the kids and left, not even thinking of how that would affect Beth. He'd called it making things easier for her, and the court had agreed—a blind unemployed mother could scarcely take care of herself, and certainly not two rambunctious preschoolers. John had robbed Beth of what few expectations she'd had left.

Despite Beth's brave efforts to build a new life, she was wasting away before Penelope's eyes. The new doctor with his experimental procedures had returned a look of hope to Beth's face. Penelope knew her twin thought if she could see even partially again, get rid of the mind-bending pain, she could have her old life back. It wasn't a reasonable hope, but Penelope couldn't deny it to her. She just needed to provide money for the operation, and this job would do it. John certainly couldn't.

In any case, her sister's ex had finished the job that Zack and her father had begun of lowering Penelope's expectations of men.

Remembering her promises, she set her chin firmly. She would make partner and double her income. Maybe she couldn't save the world, but she could save her twin. She would have traveled to darkest Africa if that was what it took to get that money. She could certainly endure the man beside her for a little longer.

"I don't think different species can procreate," her companion said thoughtfully in response to her earlier remark. "I don't think a difference in priorities creates different species."

Penelope regarded him with hostility. "You'd argue over anything, wouldn't you?"

"Yes, ma'am," he replied cheerfully. "Especially when it makes your eyes get all glittery like that. I like the touch of color in your cheeks too. We'll get along just fine."

"We're not going to get along at all. You'll get out at Soufrière and we'll never see each other again. I appreciate your help back at the airport, but I don't owe you any more than that."

He tugged at his thick mustache as he looked down at her. "You don't really think those soldiers let you go scot-free, do you? They think you smuggled drugs. Just because I bribed old Alonzo doesn't mean they'll forget the whole incident. They've probably already called ahead. What do you think will happen if you let me off in town and waltz off on your own to an unprotected port where anyone could drop off drugs?"

Penelope stared at him in horror, all the reassuring platitudes she'd whispered to herself crumbling into dust, whipped by gusts of panic. "You should have let me go to the American consulate. They would have fixed things."

"There's no consulate in Vieux Fort or Soufrière. You're on your own out here. There's scarcely even any *Americans* out here. Anse Chastenet is a European hangout. Face it, lady, you're stuck with me."

"I most certainly am not!" she replied in horrified tones, struggling for control of her emotions as well as the situation. "I have business to conduct here. I can't have a two-hundred-pound gorilla trailing behind me. Who in heck do you think you are?"

"Two-twenty, actually," he replied with more cheer than she thought warranted. "I have business here too, but we're both better off if we pretend we're married. We can be Mr. and Mrs. Smith-Albright, if you prefer. Or we can stay with your name. I'd prefer not using my own."

She couldn't believe she was hearing this. It was too absurd to take seriously. Penelope twisted until her back rested against the window, restoring the distance between them. "You're obviously known here. Why bother with the charade?" she asked coldly. Did his presence have something to do with her? Maybe he was the police and he thought that white stuff was real! With a vigorous mental effort, she shoved that thought down. She had done nothing wrong.

"I'm only known if I make myself known," he replied calmly, not retreating. "I was a kid when I was here last."

"Who the devil are you, then? What are you doing here that you can't use your own name?" The image of a drug smuggler surfaced again.

Charlie leaned forward and tipped up her chin with his finger. "Just a businessman. Honest. And if word got out that I was here, it would lead to all manner of rumors. It's no big deal. Trust me."

Liar, con artist, thief, smuggler, or—maybe he was telling the truth. For all she knew, he was an eccentric millionaire interested in buying the island. She was no better at guessing games than at haggling. She had no more energy left for puzzles of any kind.

Jerking her head away, she shook her head in denial. "It's out of the question," she replied, choosing to view this logically, without the childish speculation of a bad TV movie. "I'm not some twenty-year-old fresh off the turnip truck. You can go to Soufrière or check in at Anse Chastenet or whatever you like, but not with me. I'll report you to the hotel management if you even so much as suggest it again."

"Darling, you're a hard nut to crack." He sat back and crossed his arms over his chest, giving her some breathing room. "But I got caught with an unexpected change of plans at the height of tourist season. There's no room at the inn. The cottages at Anse Chastenet are big enough for both of us."

Penelope gazed at the stranger's implacable expression with horror. "You're insane," she murmured. The nightmare hadn't ended, then; it had just taken on a new aspect, one hidden behind mirrored glasses.

"I can be very cooperative if you play the game." He shrugged. "Or I can report you to the authorities as a drug smuggler as soon as we arrive. Which would you prefer?"

"They wouldn't believe you," she announced firmly, but fear shivered down her spine at the thought. Bad TV movies flickered through her mind again. It was terribly convenient that the plastic bag had shown up when he was around to "rescue" her.

"Oh, but they will," he responded firmly. "You see, if I introduce myself, the authorities here will know who I am, but they don't know you. If I tell them I've learned you're meeting a drug shipment, who do you think they'll believe? How do you think I got you past Alonzo?"

Not only the partnership, but her entire career would be no more than a gleam in her eye if she ended up in a jail cell. Beth needed hope right now, and Penelope could give it to her only if she had money. The money depended on this job. And this job depended on her staying out of jail and getting her work done.

Still, she didn't submit willingly. "You're the one who doesn't want your name on the register," she reminded him. "Are you certain the authorities will like hearing you're in town?"

He didn't uncross his arms but his voice dripped ice. "You catch on quickly, pretty Penny. But I'm not the one they'll put in jail. I'm just a businessman looking to protect his interests. They didn't find drugs in my suitcase."

She gave his tank top a look of disdain. "I can see you're a businessman. Is surfing a moneymaker these days? And I'm not a drug smuggler. That stuff was planted there. I'm not even certain it was drugs."

"Believe me, it won't make any difference. Money talks louder than evidence. You can argue your case all you like from the inside of a jail cell. Or you can spend a pleasant few days in my company, no strings attached. I just need a roof over my head until I accomplish what I'm here to do."

Penelope smoldered. She detested gambling, for good reason. Her father had gambled away her family and their happiness. Since then, she'd learned to search for life's certainties. She had no intention of taking any chances with Beth's future.

She heartily suspected this callous jerk or his officer friend had planted the white powder on purpose, but could she take a chance and call his bluff? Poindexter, Combs, and Mac-Millan wouldn't appreciate bailing her out of a Caribbean jail on the day of her arrival if her gamble failed. She didn't think the management of Anse Chastenet would appreciate their expensive consultant landing in jail either. She very much suspected Mr. Charlie Smith wasn't bluffing on that point. There was something hard and uncompromising behind his mocking smile.

Damn, but she didn't like haggling. She wanted her facts all lined up in logical formation so she could make the correct decision. She knew instinctively this man beside her had no connection with logic or order in any form. He represented chaos, anarchy, and the devil himself. She quaked at the idea of sharing a cottage with him, however temporarily.

With a sigh of defeat, she realized she was neatly trapped. She had to do it. Dealing with one man was far preferable to dealing with foreign authorities and international law. A cottage wasn't as bad as a hotel room. There would be several rooms. She might not even have to see him at all. A man who looked like Charlie Smith didn't need to rape women. He could have any woman he liked. She just needed to survive his arrogance and imposing physical presence. Remembering what Beth endured with every passing day, Penelope thought she could handle this much. Heaven only knew, she'd put up with a lot worse from the stiff rumps at PC&M.

With resignation, she asked, "Why me? There must have been three hundred people on that plane. Why did you pick on me?"

"You were the only one who needed rescuing," he said smugly.

Penelope wanted to kick him. She thought better of it as she took note of the impressive bulge of his biceps. Glaring out the window at the scenery, she saw only her own reflection in the glass. This assignment had taken on all the pleasure of a wienie roast, with her as the wienie.

❧ THREE ❦

Penelope's frayed nerves reached a screaming crisis as they turned on the potholed dirt road into Anse Chastenet. She had expected primitive. She hadn't expected a treacherous mountain path that surely should be accessed only on the back of a donkey. That the taxi driver didn't put them out and make them walk gave her new respect for his tenacity. Unable to verbalize her appreciation, she just groaned and avoided looking over the edge of the road.

The man beside her chatted casually with the driver in the island patois, each pointing out sights of interest to the other. She gathered Mr. Smith hadn't been here in a while and the driver showed him the latest additions to the town below— from their thousand-foot vantage point on the mountainside. Penelope closed her eyes and prayed they would arrive sometime before the acid in her empty stomach ate through her insides.

She could swear the drive into the resort took longer than the drive from the airport. Her head pounded with all the decisions she must make before she reached the reception desk. The management would be surprised that she had brought along a "husband" on a business trip, especially since management had paid for that trip. She could take a chance and explain everything that had happened since her arrival, but the idea of relating that hideously embarrassing incident at

25

the airport overwhelmed her. If they called her employer or the authorities and questioned her story, it would embarrass her even more, and possibly cost her the assignment. PC&M wasn't the most understanding or considerate of employers. Her old self-consciousness and her weakened state of anxiety and hunger steered her down the path of least resistance.

The van finally halted, and Penelope held her eyes closed a second longer, forcing her knotted nerves into submission. She could just pretend the big oaf beside her didn't exist. Maybe he would disappear if she pretended long enough. All men had their Achilles' heels, and she was very good at finding and using them.

Instead of dealing with their luggage and driver as she had expected, her obnoxious companion insisted on helping her from the van and leading her down the stone-paved stairs to the reception area. Penelope threw a frantic look over her shoulder at her abandoned suitcases and the taxi. Waiting porters had gathered the luggage and struck up a conversation with the driver. No one seemed in any hurry.

With the air of a seasoned traveler, Charlie strode to the outside reception desk. Amazed at the realization that the resort didn't even have an enclosed lobby, Penelope gazed around at the natural beauty of the greenery, unintentionally handing Charlie the lead. Taking full advantage, he introduced himself as Charles Albright, and flirted with the clerks while they found Penelope's file. He turned and handed Penelope the free tropical drink brought over from the bar and grinned at her stunned look.

"You're supposed to look as if we're on our honeymoon, Miss Penny," he whispered. "The islanders are just as romantic about newlyweds as any soap opera–watching housewife at home. Smile and look love-struck."

"I'm here on a business assignment," she answered as sharply as she could without being heard at the desk. The presence of towering hibiscus behind her, the sound of the surf from below, and the island music from the bar distracted and disoriented her. She stood outside on a tropical patio, sipping an alcoholic concoction while checking into a hotel. Had she arrived here without Mr. Charlie Smith, she would have been enchanted. As it was, she felt more inclined to throw up. On her empty stomach, she wasn't certain if the latter was possible.

The resort manager approached to greet them, addressing her with pleasure and some degree of regard. A dapper Englishman of middle age, he wore the white slacks and open shirt of the tropics rather than the business suit of the States. Penelope straightened and assumed the reassuring professional demeanor that had won the respect of her clients, introducing Mr. Henwood to her "husband."

"You did not tell us this would be your honeymoon," the manager chided her. "We would have provided a special treat. It is a shame to work when you are newly wed."

Penelope glared at Charlie from beneath her lashes but plastered a smile on her face. "Charlie is a bit of a jokester. This is more of a second honeymoon than a first. He was scheduled to be out of town this week but surprised me by meeting me at the airport." There, that should satisfy any nosy authorities who might doubt their cover-up.

Charlie beamed in approval at her improvisation as the manager shook his hand and offered a round of drinks at the bar. To Penelope's relief, Charlie took a rain check. She had seen the wad of bills in his wallet earlier, but she swallowed her amazement as he paid for a week's meal plan in cash. No matter how much money she earned, she'd never learned to wield cash that casually. This man threw hundreds on the counter as if they were ones. Maybe he was a drug dealer after all.

That thought didn't improve her stomach, and her head pounded in sympathetic accord. She almost didn't care when Charlie signed them in, tipped the taxi driver, and strode ahead of the porter carrying their bags up the winding path to their assigned cottage. She didn't care about anything except three Excedrins and a hot meal.

Penelope could swear the interminable path climbed straight up the mountainside. It led them past magnificent ferns, frangipani trees, and what were almost certainly tree-high poinsettias, but the beauty didn't relieve her suffering. Her calves ached, her shoes rubbed, and she wanted to swear at the man whistling ahead of her, not showing an ounce of exertion.

She thought longingly of the sea pounding somewhere on the other side of the jungle. Perspiration streaked her brow. The irony of being surrounded by some of the world's most beautiful scenery while she was dying did not amuse her. She hoped Mr. Charlie Smith had to carry her coffin single-handedly down the hillside.

Penelope sighed in relief and collapsed on a step as the porter finally set their bags on the porch of one of the cottages and tangled with the recalcitrant door lock. She let her jackass of a companion carry in the luggage. She rather liked sitting here alone. It gave her a moment to gather her resources and admire the view. Of course, observing that the cottage seemed impossibly perched on the side of the mountain almost made her quiver, but she could get used to it. Looking down through palm trees and frangipani, she could see the ocean, and she smiled in pleasure. She really could come to like this place if it weren't for the beast of burden inside. Somehow, she had to discover his weak point.

The porter emerged whistling, apparently well paid. Penelope called on what remained of her strength and stood up again. She wondered if she could charge her employers for all these tips she wasn't paying. It would serve them right for not adequately preparing her for this assignment. Actually, she had some recollection that tips weren't required here. Oh, well.

Penelope crossed the weathered porch to admire the view from the railing. Chairs and a table beckoned the inhabitants to watch the sunset on the horizon while sipping a late-evening drink. A bird called from the treetop below, and Penelope caught sight of a bright blaze of yellow just before the creature landed on the railing beside her. She stared in amazement at the brazen little fellow staring back at her.

"Bananaquit," a voice from behind her explained. "Little beggars. He thinks you'll give him food."

He handed her a glass as he stood beside her. Champagne. Just what her stomach needed. Still, the idea of sipping champagne while admiring the tropical view was a tempting one. Penelope accepted the offered glass and took a sip without looking at him. Charlie Smith's physical presence was too overpowering as it was. She lifted her chin and let the sea breeze cool her brow.

He perched his hip against the railing and stared at her. "I feel as if I just fell off that turnip truck you mentioned and bumped my head in the process. Do you have any idea at all how beautiful you are like that? This is like a scene from one hell of a movie."

Startled, Penelope glanced at him. Big mistake. He'd removed his sunglasses, and intelligent blue eyes nearly fractured her already shaky composure. Beneath that droopy mustache, he almost looked serious, and the puzzlement in his expression did something to her already disturbed stomach. She quickly looked away. He scared her as much as the soldiers at the airport had. At least, she thought it was fear raising goose bumps up and down her arms.

"It's the setting." She tried keeping her voice cool and collected, but the trembling had returned. She definitely needed food. "I assume something about the Garden of Eden must always tempt the human race. If you're not going to shower yet, I think I will. I haven't had anything to eat all day and I'm about to die."

"You should have mentioned that earlier. They don't dine here until seven. Unless you want to go back into Soufrière, you'll have to settle for the basket of fruit inside."

Penelope stared at him in disbelief. No food? Surely she hadn't heard him right. "There are supposed to be three restaurants on the grounds," she informed him coldly.

The teeth beneath that thick mustache gleamed white and

strong. "The main dining room, the beach bar, and the grill. The last one closed at three. You can have afternoon tea at four, I suppose, if you're into little snacky things."

Even little snacky things sounded good at this point. Stalking into the cottage, Penelope halted inside with a jolt of horror.

The cottage was just one big room. With one big bed. The living area had two short willow couches padded with loose pillows, neither big enough for anyone but a child to sleep on. The walls consisted of wood louvers that could be lowered against rain, and little else. No privacy whatsoever except the wooded hillside beyond. Nowhere she could escape the big jerk who was no doubt grinning himself to death right this minute.

He'd known this would happen. She could kill him. But not right now. Right now she would eat one of the strange fruits in the basket to prevent fainting from starvation. Then she would take a calming shower and plan her attack.

Whatever the odd fruit she bit into was, it was juicy and sweet. Sipping her champagne and sucking on the juicy meat, Penelope explored the bathing facilities. No bath. All right, she could survive that. She preferred showers anyway. This one was big enough for ten people. The bathroom had everything a woman could ask for, from makeup mirror to hair dryer. And a door she could close and lock—thank heavens for small favors.

Setting her glass down on the vanity and washing off her hands, Penelope went in search of fresh clothing. Exhilaration unexpectedly swept through her, probably the result of champagne on an empty stomach. This was the most exotic place she'd ever seen. Champagne in midafternoon and tropical fruits for the asking, a view to die for, and the rest of the afternoon to relax and pull herself together. By the time she showered and had tea, she would know how to handle Mr. Football Player.

Carrying her clean clothes into the bathroom, she firmly shut the door, then stripped to her camisole and panties before pulling back the shower curtain to warm up the water. A tarantula marched across the tiles in greeting.

The last thin nerve holding her together snapped.

Screaming, Penelope jerked back the curtain, dashed for her toiletry bag, and whipped out a tiny can of hair spray. Hysterically, she aimed at the unseen creature behind the curtain, then screamed again as eight heavy legs inched over the tile ridge from shower to floor. It hung there delicately until she squirted it again. Waving all eight legs in concerted motion, it ambled along the ridge in her direction, undeterred by the spray.

Penelope bolted for the exit.

Before she reached the door, it crashed open, and blindly, she bounced off Charlie's massive chest. He grabbed her shoulders to prevent her falling, then dropped his hands as if he'd burned them. "What is it?" he demanded, glancing over her shoulder in obvious expectation of a boa constrictor, at least.

"T-tarantula!" Stuttering, Penelope pointed at the shower while easing toward the other room. She didn't care that she wore next to nothing. Without a tub, only the minuscule tile wall separated her from that hairy, fuzzy, long-legged creature. She figured it could devour her foot in one bite.

Charlie pushed past her, crossed the room, and jerked back the shower curtain without any concern for their safety. Maybe he thought those giant boots he called shoes could stomp a spider, but Penelope knew better. Inching farther away, she prepared to bolt.

"That's not a tarantula," he said in disgust, turning on a blast of water and sweeping the doomed creature into the downpour of the shower. "It's just a big spider. They eat bugs, not people."

Charlie turned and caught a full view of Miss Penelope standing there, gasping in terror, a bath towel barely concealing the skimpy underthings she wore beneath. She'd removed the awful glasses but hadn't taken her hair down yet. It escaped in wispy tendrils over skin so flawlessly smooth it could have been airbrushed like a *Playboy* centerfold. Despite her height, she had slender, delicate bones that made her look all legs and arms, probably because he couldn't see anything in between. Charlie wanted to see *everything* in between. A powerful wave of lust ripped through him, urging him to do something utterly idiotic like cuddling her in his arms and reassuring her that she would be safe with him.

She wouldn't be safe with him. The first thing he would do was lay her on the bed and pump into her so fast she wouldn't know what had hit her until it was all over. And then he'd use her for his own purposes. Finding Raul was more important than romancing a skittish blue blood like Miss Penelope Albright. She would scream bloody murder and have him arrested.

Obviously, *he* wasn't safe with *her*. But he'd better get used to it. He needed her as his cover. Steadying his rising impulses, Charlie clenched his teeth and tried to imagine her as a shrieking shrew from a TV sitcom instead of a flesh and blood woman.

"The spider's gone. I'm going down to the lobby to make a few phone calls." He waited for her to ease away from the door before heading out. He didn't dare risk touching her again. His heart still thumped erratically from the effect of her scream and the feel of all that female flesh in his arms. He didn't know where this sudden surge of protectiveness came from, and he didn't like it one bit. Women were for sex, nothing else. Not now, anyway. He had too many other things on his mind for hormones to intervene.

"The lobby?" she asked, darting a look toward the shower enclosure.

"There're no phones in the rooms," he explained patiently. Her head jerked up. "No phones?"

He almost grinned at that. "No phones, no TV, no room service without prior notice. This is a getaway vacation kind of place. Relax, soak up the sunshine, enjoy the scenery. Who needs all the rest?"

"I do," she answered sharply. "How am I supposed to call Miami?"

"Cable phone in the lobby." He liked making her eyes light with anger like that. It was safer for both of them.

"I see."

She apparently didn't like what she saw, but that was no concern of his. Having nothing else to say, Charlie departed, whistling.

Out of sight of her royal highness, he applied his brain to the problem at hand. Assuming Raul hadn't absconded with his money, he had to decide who would want to harm Raul as well as empty the bank account. They'd already purchased the land for the development, so the account currently had only start-up funds in it.

Charlie figured the money was only an added attraction. The thief had some other goal in mind. Charlie had deliberately set up the corporation so few people knew of his involvement. Raul had flown down here and acted in his place. He couldn't imagine anyone using the corporation to get at him unless his identity had leaked somewhere along the line.

If he made the further assumption that his identity remained unknown, then the target could only be Raul or the development. The latter seemed most likely. There were conservationists here who had protested any further encroachment on the rain forest. He sympathized with their cause and hadn't intended harming the environment, but fanatics didn't always listen. They assumed the corporation was a foreign entity with no knowledge of the delicate ecology. Still, Charlie couldn't believe they would be crazy enough to kidnap Raul and steal the money.

He knew there were other developers who coveted that land. Charlie had pulled a lot of strings and called in a lot of favors to get that particular site, one that would have highway access and utilities. Now that all the dirty work had been done, it would be just like someone of Jacobsen's ilk to decide to move in. Raul would have been in the way.

Charlie almost preferred to think Raul had absconded with the money. At least then he could believe his friend was alive.

Taking a seat at the phone table in the tiled, outdoor lobby, he punched in a few numbers and waited for the connection. He wished he could figure Jacobsen into the equation for certain. The man had lain low since Charlie had agreed to act as star witness against him for construction fraud, but it was mighty suspicious seeing him at the airport. The last he'd heard, Jacobsen's construction company was facing bankruptcy. The last project Jacobsen worked on had collapsed, injuring half a dozen good workers. Raul's brother had been one of them.

The call connected and his secretary answered, practically jumping on him through the telephone. "Mr. Smith! We've been waiting for you to call," she whispered in a tone that froze icicles in Charlie's veins. "There's a man outside waiting to serve papers on you. It has something to do with the St. Lucia project." She took a deep breath and added in muffled tones indicating she cupped the receiver with her hand, "They've put a lien on your bank accounts. We can't write any checks."

A trickle of perspiration crawled down Charlie's neck. This couldn't be happening, not now, not when he finally had it made. He had too many balls in the air. They'd all smash to the ground at once without those bank accounts. He'd just deposited the advance money for the Orlando project and bought supplies. The payroll was due. All those checks would bounce.

The only consolation Charlie could summon as he hung up the phone was that he'd found the connection. Jacobsen had planned his revenge well.

❧ FOUR ❧

"Trouble, Mr. Albright?"

Lost in thought, Charlie didn't immediately recognize the name, but sensing he was no longer alone, he looked up and decided he must be exuding high-energy vibrations for the busy manager of a resort to notice. Wondering if a cable call could be picked up by radio waves or tapped electronically, he forced a smile to his face and greeted Roger Henwood.

"Just business. Can a water taxi into Soufrière be arranged at this time of day?"

The Englishman nodded affably. "Of course. They'll run until dusk. Does your wife like the cottage?"

His wife. Right. He had to remember he was "married." "She loves the cottage, but the airlines didn't feed her and she's about to expire of hunger. I thought I'd take her into town."

Henwood beamed approval. "Of course. You can catch the water taxi down by the beach bar. Do you know how to find it?"

Getting directions he didn't need, Charlie took the steps back to the cottage. He didn't know why Henwood was hovering around him. He didn't know the man. Unless he'd somehow overheard the phone conversation, Henwood shouldn't know his real identity. It must have something to do with Penelope's business here. The resort manager was just going out of his way for the lady's benefit. Circumstances had made him suspicious of everyone, including Penelope. Paranoia didn't become him.

Charlie created a racket as he entered the cottage so he wouldn't catch his reluctant hostess in another precarious state of undress. He needed her cooperation. He had a rat's chance in hell of gaining it without blackmail, but he would do what he had to do.

He groaned inwardly as he caught Penelope brushing out her long black hair. He couldn't believe this woman allowed her hair to grow out like that. She struck him as one of those efficient businesswomen who had her hair clipped and styled at some fancy salon every week until she looked more like a man than a woman. But right now, she looked like some exotic tropical fantasy his sick mind had dreamed up to nail him to the floor.

She looked up, startled at his appearance but apparently unembarrassed by the spill of silken tresses over her blazer. Idly gathering her hair in her hand, she pinned it to the back of her head with a silver clip. The severe hairstyle emphasized the dramatic jut of her elegant cheekbones and nose. "I didn't expect you back. Don't you have business to tend to?"

"I do, but I need you for cover. I want to look like a typical bored tourist roaming the streets of Soufrière. Come with me and I'll feed you." Trying to ignore her, Charlie walked past her heavenly scents and into the bathroom to wash.

"I'm not about to make that trip into town again anytime soon," Penelope informed him coldly, over the sound of rushing water. If Mr. Charlie Smith thought she was the kind of tractable female who bent to every man's will, he might as well learn his lesson now. She'd seen what submissiveness had done to Beth and her mother.

He emerged from the bathroom dripping water and rubbing his face with a towel. Obviously, some demented part of her mind still had a fascination with muscular football player types because her heart pounded and skipped a beat at just the sight of that broad chest beneath the skimpy tank top. A dark curl of hair at the shirt's neckline stirred a kind of lust she hadn't known in years. How the hell did he think he could disguise himself as a typical tourist? He'd be lucky if people didn't ask for his autograph.

"We'll take a water taxi. It'll be fun. And you'll get fed a lot sooner. You can poke around in the craft shops while I talk to a few people."

Penelope gifted him with her best scornful look. "If you think anyone will believe you're a typical tourist, you have beans for brains. You look like the Caribbean equivalent of Mafia. If I judged by appearances alone, I'd say you planted that white stuff in my bags. Although I suppose any self-respecting drug dealer would wear something a little more decent than what you have on."

She would have bitten her tongue in dismay at her temerity, but his surprised glance at his clothes was too typically male and not the least like a dangerous drug dealer.

"What's wrong with what I'm wearing? It's cool and comfortable. Jeans go anywhere."

With just a tiny bit of delight in her sarcasm, Penelope pointed out the obvious. "You're staying at an expensive resort. Didn't you look around you at all? The men wear khakis or long shorts with Tommy Hilfigers or oxford shirts. They don't wear cowboy mustaches and mirrored glasses and look like football players."

She'd hoped a good shot at his ego would drive him off, but the damned man looked up with a grin and a bold gaze that swept over her own rather conservative attire.

"This is how a man dresses," he informed her, "and I'm a man and you're not, so I ought to know. While we're at it, it wouldn't hurt you to look more like a woman. Do you always wear jackets in tropical jungles, Miss Albright?"

"What I wear is of little concern to you. *I'm* not hiding my identity. I'm going down for tea. Have fun in town."

He stepped in front of her, blocking her path to the door. "Hold it just a minute, Miss Albright. We're in this together. I'll keep you out of the hands of the authorities if you'll help me keep a low profile. Give me a minute to change. I'll play the part of tourist according to your specifications if you'll lose that gawd-awful jacket. You'll cook out there on the water with that thing on." When she hesitated, he added, "Food, Miss Albright. Lots and lots of spicy seafood. I'll show you the best places. You want the real stuff, not the tourist stuff, don't you?"

Her stomach rumbled. Tiny little snacky things didn't sound quite as tempting as lots and lots of spicy seafood. She loved spicy seafood. "How long?" she asked suspiciously.

"Minutes. Mere minutes. Soufrière is just around the bend and the water taxi is fast. Make yourself comfortable for an outing, and I'll be right with you."

Make herself comfortable. Right. As he disappeared into the bathroom with his backpack, Penelope glared at the full-length mirror on the closet door. The unstructured white linen blazer and matching trousers were comfortable, but she suspected they wouldn't hold up long in a motorboat or roaming dirty streets. She knew the macho jerk hoped for tight shorts and halters, but she didn't own such things. She gave all that up when she gave up modeling after graduation. The only way she could make men look at her with any degree of respect was by hiding behind the same business suits they wore.

But she was on her first trip to the tropics, and she could afford to lighten up just a bit for the afternoon. She would save the linen for tomorrow when she started work.

By the time Charlie finished in the bathroom, she had donned a white above-the-knee culotte and a navy T-shirt. Mindful of sun damage, she carried a wide-brimmed hat and a loose white cover-up. That should be touristy enough. When she looked up to see how her escort had improved his appearance, her mouth dropped open.

He'd shaved his mustache. Good Lord, with that massive mustache gone, he looked like a young Sean Connery. Where in heaven's name had a hick football player earned a face with that much character?

Gulping, Penelope forced herself to look away from Charlie

Smith's handsome square jaw to his attire. The short-sleeved striped golf shirt didn't shout "designer," but it was far more suitable than the tank top. The baseball cap was hopeless, but she supposed he needed it to disguise that thick head of hair. The blue Dockers were probably his idea of dress-up clothes.

"I thought the mustache made a good disguise." He rubbed the bare space mournfully.

"It made you look like Mafia. Every cop in town would have followed you," she retorted.

Defensively, he slipped his mirrored sunglasses back on. "They could follow all they like. I haven't done anything illegal."

Penelope scowled at the glasses. "Not those things. They make you look like a motorcycle cop. They probably have something down at the gift shop you can wear."

"With a fancy price tag, no doubt," he grumbled. "I like these."

"If you find a single tourist in the entire town wearing anything like them, I'll buy dinner." Grabbing her handbag, Penelope marched out the door. For just a few minutes, he had almost fooled her into thinking they were a normal couple arguing over dress conventions. How could she forget that he had kidnapped and blackmailed her and probably set up the whole arrangement for some nefarious purpose of his own? She could only be grateful that he hadn't made any physical overtures. She would blast him with the pepper spray should he even try. His restraint was the only reason she didn't shove him over the cliff.

"I sure hope it's hunger that makes you so damned irritable," he complained as he hurried down the path after her. "There's nothing worse than a bitchy woman."

"Yeah, there is, it's a bossy man. You're ruining my first trip to the islands, jeopardizing my job, wreaking havoc with my privacy, and you're complaining about me? Up yours, Mr. Smith."

Charlie couldn't help it. He grinned. She had the elegant

lines of an expensive, high-class thoroughbred, and the mouth of a construction worker. Staying one step behind her, he watched the sway of that sassy rear in the short skirt. She might think she was covering up, but she couldn't see herself from behind. Whistling to himself at that thought, he happily followed in her long-legged footsteps.

"Black sand!" she exclaimed in wonderment as they reached the foot of the stairs and the crystalline crescent of beach curved before them. "I've never seen black sand. Look, it sparkles!"

The afternoon sun caught all the glistening volcanic facets, paving a diamond path between jungle and turquoise water. Charlie almost regretted not having the time to sprawl in the sand, catch the sun, and listen to the music of the waves. How long had it been since he'd had time to indulge in the simple pleasures with a gorgeous woman by his side? Too damned long. But if he didn't find Raul soon, he would be calling the beach his home.

"Lava flow," he responded curtly, ignoring the beckoning sand and aiming for the water taxi. "This is a volcanic island."

"They're *all* volcanic islands," she said crisply. "I don't remember hearing they all have black sand."

"This one got lucky." He caught her elbow and hurried her on as she tried to dawdle and admire the tropical setting.

"Is the volcano still active?" Her long-legged stride easily kept up with his.

"Bet your sweet britches it is. Smells like hell, if you're inclined to see what the devil has in store for us."

"Romantic sort, aren't you?"

Charlie snorted at the dryness of her comment. To pacify her, he stopped in the gift shop on the beach and purchased the shades she insisted on. The Ray-Bans cost two arms and three legs, and with his bank accounts closed, he should be conserving expenses, but what the heck. Maybe the fancy duds would hide him for a while.

Pulling on the dark glasses, he had the opportunity to discover the success of his disguise soon enough. He recognized the water taxi driver as the kid brother of an old friend of his. On his best tourist behavior, Charlie handed his "wife" into the boat, not lingering long over her elbow but climbing in after her with the skill of experience. If Miss Penny stiffened any more, she'd break. He maintained his distance as he took the narrow seat beside her. The driver didn't even look at him as he gave his directions. Maybe the sunglasses worked.

Charlie concentrated on his plans for Soufrière rather than on the woman beside him. St. Lucia wasn't the business world of Miami he'd operated in these last years. He couldn't disguise his identity for long. He had to accomplish as much as possible in the least amount of time. That didn't bode well for Lady Jane beside him.

Damn, but he couldn't stop thinking about her for two minutes at a time. He'd make it up to her later. Right now, he just wanted to pacify her so he didn't fall victim to her damned sharp tongue.

The boat roared around the sheltering curve of the seashore into the cove beyond. The two towering rock formations ahead framed a stunning view, but Charlie's concentration centered on the weathered village in the center of the cove. The wealth of the northern part of the island hadn't found its way down here yet. He and Raul had hoped to change that. If he didn't find Raul soon and get back to fight off Jacobsen's maneuvers, those plans would crumble into sand.

The taxi didn't bother docking but pulled up on the shore, leaving them to wade through the water. Admiring the flash of long legs as Penelope climbed out, Charlie thanked whatever gods there were for her intelligence in not wearing panty hose and high heels or something equally outrageous. She probably would have demanded he carry her ashore. As it was, she simply slipped off her sandals. He doused his tennis shoes in the water and didn't worry about them.

"Food," she demanded as soon as they reached shore.

Charlie admired the way she stalked right past the stares of the men and boys idling around the dock and shore. Surely she realized the ripple of excited chatter all around them had little to do with the arrival of new suckers for their wares and more to do with her looks. Hell, he didn't have to worry about anyone recognizing him. They didn't even notice his existence. All attention fastened on his companion's sleek long-legged looks.

"Don't talk to anyone, keep your eyes straight ahead and your feet moving," he ordered, steering her past the street vendors hawking their wares. "If you so much as make eye contact, we'll never get out of here."

She had the maneuver down pat. Charlie suspected she used the same attitude when walking past a construction site full of howling workers. For just a moment, he felt sympathy for her plight. But the moment didn't last long. She could handle herself. He'd best look to his own protection.

As they strolled up the shadowed street between narrow two- and three-story buildings jammed together like a medieval city, Charlie decided he liked walking beside Miss Penelope Albright. She didn't make him feel like a Gulliver giant who had to stoop to her level to carry on a conversation. She strode briskly beside him, matching him step for step.

In the interest of scientific experiment, Charlie increased his stride. Penelope increased hers accordingly, without any noticeable lessening of her questions on their surroundings. By the time they reached the restaurant, they were practically running, and she hadn't uttered a word of complaint.

Charlie glimpsed a decided glint of mischief in her eyes as he opened the door for her. The lady *liked* meeting his challenge. That should have scared the hell out of him, but his mind had already gone on to the next test.

The hole-in-the-wall restaurant had changed hands since his last visit, but the food was still delicious. Charlie watched in anticipation as his companion bit into the spicy seafood concoction he'd ordered for her. His mouth fell open in surprise as she closed her eyes and savored it with ecstasy. Who would have thought Miss Blue Blood could handle chili peppers? As she sampled the exotic plantains and cassava next, he wondered if he'd been hanging out with the wrong women all these years.

Not liking the path of his wayward thoughts, Charlie glanced impatiently at his watch. If he wanted to catch Jacques, he'd better do it soon.

"I'm going out the back door and down the alley," he whispered to get her attention away from the food. "There are craft shops all along the street by the shore. I'll meet you down there in about an hour."

Horrified at being abruptly deserted in a strange place where she knew nothing of the local customs, Penelope started to object, but Charlie merely left some odd bills on the table and walked out. For a brief moment she considered running after him, then common sense prevailed. She wasn't any safer with Charlie Smith than by herself. She had half a notion to go down to the dock, hire a water taxi, and leave him here alone. As far as she was concerned, if she never saw the man again, it would be too soon.

Penelope had second thoughts about that while she idled over the rest of her meal. The architecture of Soufrière was a fascinating blend of French, Spanish, and something definitely island original. But the houses were old and decaying, resembling the shabbier parts of Miami or New Orleans. Some of the inhabitants of the town were little better. With her height and looks, she was accustomed to people staring at her, but here she felt like a duck ripe for plucking.

When she couldn't linger any longer over the meal, Penelope thanked the cook behind the counter and sauntered out to the street, striving for a casual demeanor. She wondered how long it was before the sun set. The idea of walking these streets after dark didn't improve her sense of security. She was as big a coward as her ex–brother-in-law.

Taking a deep breath, she pulled her gauzy cover-up around her in an attempt to conceal her vulnerability, and aimed for the shops. At least there were a few tourists wandering around there. She hadn't expected an opportunity for shopping on this trip, but she didn't object when opportunity knocked. Maybe she could find something to make Beth smile. And she needed to take her niece and nephew something.

She passed up the volcanic beads and seashells and other tourist wares, wandering through the arts and crafts shops with more attention. She recognized some of the willow furniture from the cottage, and the fabric wall hangings with the bold designs. Settling on a textured sculpture of a native woman in knotted kerchief for Beth and some hand-carved wooden toys for the children, she breathed a sigh of relief that the prices were clearly stated in U.S. dollars and counted out her money.

"They rob you, miss," a sibilant voice whispered from somewhere near her elbow.

Glancing down, she saw a skeletally thin black man sitting in the shadows, polishing a bowl. Dark eyes glittered as he caught her gaze, then returned to his work.

Penelope really didn't care. She'd rather be robbed than argue. But something in the man's warning gave her pause, and daringly, she put back one of the toys. "I don't think I'll take two," she said tentatively.

The clerk or artist or whoever it was behind the counter looked surprised, then smiled again. "I give two, special price, one for half price of first."

Startled at how easy it was, Penelope laid out the bills, and with a bravery she hadn't known she possessed, offered half her savings to the man on the floor. He slipped the money hastily into his pocket without so much as looking up.

Quite foolishly proud of her minor accomplishment, Penelope picked her way back through the shops to the street and glanced at her watch. Charlie's hour was up.

Deciding it would be much more relaxing if she thought she were returning to the cottage alone, Penelope sauntered toward the dock where the water taxi had left them. She didn't know how one went about hiring a boat, but she'd figure it out. The water ride had been considerably more comfortable than the potholed road.

Noting the evening sun settling into the banks of clouds over the ocean, she hurried a little faster through the dusty street.

Before she reached the dock, a familiar hiss beckoned from beneath a wind-bent palm tree. Startled, she scanned the shadows, at last locating the man in a tattered shirt carrying his polished wooden bowls from strings around his neck. She suspected he was the same man from the shop, although how he had managed to get here before her, she couldn't imagine.

Just a little afraid, she hesitated, not going nearer but waiting to hear what he had to say.

"Your man, he got big trouble. You follow me."

And with that ominous statement, he rattled off down the road, leaving Penelope to follow if she dared.

❧ FIVE ❧

Slipping out the back of the restaurant, Charlie cut across the yard and down a side alley between two crumbling residences. He'd told Penelope an hour, but he suspected if he didn't return at the appointed time, his lady friend wouldn't mind in the least. She would probably hope that he'd fallen off a cliff and merrily go her own way. He'd been looking forward to the argument over that big double bed though. Even with his entire business collapsing around his ears, his mind was on sex.

Focus, Charlie.

He hurried past crumbling stone facades and weathered Creole-style buildings with wooden gingerbread and wrought-iron railings. Too many people knew him here. It had been ten years and he'd changed some, but he couldn't very well hide his size or color. The population here was predominantly black, so he looked like a tourist. But he walked streets most tourists didn't take.

Turning down a narrow alley, he encountered suspicious glares from the assortment of men and boys lounging against street corners and sitting on stoops. If it weren't for the hot Caribbean sun blazing down on them, he'd think he was in a Chicago slum. The pounding beat of a steel drum from one of the bars quickly dispelled that notion.

46

Charlie understood the insults muttered in patios but he ignored them. One advantage of his size was that most people didn't confront him physically. The disadvantage was that he didn't consider it fair play to grab the pip-squeaks by their shirt collars and wring them out. Picking on someone his own size was difficult when everyone was smaller.

Finding the house he sought, Charlie didn't bother knocking on the front door leading into a half-empty general dry-goods store. Stepping over the rusted hulk of a bicycle, he wended his way through a littered side alley and around the back.

The stench of rotting fish assaulted him from one side; the delicious odors of a spicy island gumbo wafted toward him from the other. Hoping he hadn't completely lost touch with his contacts here, Charlie stuck his head over the sagging half of a rear door and hollered, "Jacques!"

A small, curly-headed toddler with wide eyes appeared first, taking in his alien presence and scampering away. Then with a low muttering stream of indistinguishable invectives, a tall shadow advanced out of the dim interior. Hair braided in a multitude of thick dreadlocks, the bony silhouette loped into view.

"Captain! You come back!" he said in the lilting accents of the island. "Come in! Come in!"

His graying beard tapering to a point, his black skin stretched taut over his thin frame, Jacques appeared more apparition than human. But the strength of his hug was real enough. Charlie caught Jacques's skinny biceps in a tight squeeze and practically lifted his friend off the ground.

"You haven't changed any," he said dryly. "I'd rather wrestle an alligator."

Jacques emitted a high, thin cackle. "Life make me strong. Sit, sit. Antoinette will give you gumbo. You have had no gumbo until you have Antoinette's."

"Gone and got yourself married since I saw you last, have you?" Charlie took the seat offered at the rickety kitchen table and winked at the toddler peeking at him from behind a beaded curtain. He knew better than to get down to business as soon as he arrived. The chances of accomplishing anything before dusk were slim. Somehow, he would have to get word to his impatient lady. Releasing any fantasy of returning to that double bed and his irate companion, Charlie concentrated on the conversation.

They discussed local happenings over an enormous bowl of seafood accompanied by the local beer. Good thing he hadn't filled up earlier. By meal's end, Charlie bounced the toddler on his knee and had a better idea of island politics as they'd developed since he'd left. Jacques might parade his religious beliefs in public, petition the government to save the rain forests, and lead tourists on nature hikes like an aging hippie, but he had a shrewd understanding of what went on behind the scenes. He knew everything and everyone on this end of the island. And it was here that Raul had disappeared.

The sun lowered toward the sea as they took their drinks out on the back step and spoke quietly while Antoinette and the toddler slipped into the interior.

"So, what brings you back, my friend?" Jacques asked. "I hear you do big things in the States. You made friends with your papa, no?"

Charlie shrugged. "I never had any argument with Dad. It was just difficult visiting him over that distance. We developed his construction company once I got back there. It's doing fairly well now." Charlie crushed his beer can. "Dad died last year."

"Ahh, I am sorry to hear that. You come back now to tell your mama?"

Charlie uttered a harsh laugh. "Not likely. She already knows. She just never cared. No, I'm not here to see her. I'm looking for Raul."

Jacques gave him a shrewd look but did not comment. He and Jacques had known each other almost as long as Charlie had known Raul. Jacques had been a father figure for them both.

The older man nodded in understanding. "There is bad hoodoo in these parts now. Money is the root of all evil."

"Greed is the root of all evil. We're our own worst enemies. Who needs devils and demons when we have humans?"

Jacques glowered. "Don't you be preaching to me, mon. What can I do to help?"

Slowly, gathering his thoughts as he went, Charlie outlined the background of his enmity with Jacobsen, Raul's disappearance with the company money, the liens, and the papers halting the company's development project. As he reached this last, Jacques growled a guttural curse and threw his empty soft drink can at a yowling cat.

"You best go talk to your mama, boy. That man of hers has the hoodoo these days. He owns this half of the island."

"That's an exaggeration. Emile keeps expanding the plantation, but he's never had any interest in development. I think he'd like his own private island, but a good chunk of one makes him happy. His name never came up when we were developing the site."

"Things change. You talk to your mama. There's things out there you don't know 'bout. I start looking down here, but the spider spins its web from the top."

Charlie grimaced at the image. "I thank you for the help. Could I get you to put me up for the night? I've got to send a lady back where she belongs."

Jacques gave a wicked grin. "Don' worry. No problem."

The blazing red Caribbean sun had hit the blue bank of clouds on the horizon by the time Charlie hurried down the street toward town. He didn't like taking the main streets, where he might encounter someone familiar, but he'd left Penelope alone entirely too long. He didn't look forward to a ranting tirade; he didn't want to be responsible for anything happening to her either. He had this nagging feeling that leaving a beautiful snob like Penelope alone for any period of time could be an invitation for trouble.

Curse his wretched hormones. Why couldn't he have picked out a mousy female who would nod her head and look at him with dewy-eyed awe, obeying every word he said?

Of course, if Penelope had her way, she would do her best to look mousy. Wearing those damned horn-rimmed glasses with her hair all tied up in a knot would convince any casual onlooker, particularly when topped by those hideous jackets that concealed everything feminine about her. He should have kept his mouth shut about the jacket, but he had to get his kicks by showing her off to everybody on the damned island.

Pride goeth before a fall, he muttered to himself, just before someone slammed a telephone pole against the back of his head.

Penelope screamed as she saw Charlie topple like a tree in the street ahead. The dark figures clambering over his fallen body scampered into the shadows before she could reach him. Even the mysterious man she'd followed had somehow melted into the dusk. She didn't know how her informant could have known this would happen, and she didn't care right now. Fury overrode any sense of self-protection. There had to have been half a dozen men and a big stick to bring Charlie down from behind. Not that he probably didn't deserve it and that she hadn't considered it herself, but she'd always had contempt for cowardice.

By the time she kneeled beside him, Charlie was pushing up from the dusty street, shaking his head, and groaning.

"I should have known they couldn't hurt you by hitting you in the head," she murmured more in distress than disgust as she touched the bloody lump. She dug through her purse for the packet of moist napkins she always carried when traveling.

Not attempting to rise, he rested on one elbow and, nearly

cross-eyed, glared up at her. "What in hell are you doing back here? I thought I told you to stay near the beach."

"You told me you'd be back in an hour too. You tell me a lot of things. That doesn't necessarily mean any of them are true." She ignored his wince as she applied the towelette to the back of his head. It wasn't bleeding much and seemed more scrape than cut.

"Look, we've got to get out of here. Those thugs could come back any minute once they realize you didn't bring the cops with you." Pulling the towelette from her hand, he struggled to sit up.

"Any normal person would be nauseous, have a splitting headache, and be dizzy as all get out after a blow like that. Why would you want to be normal?" she asked sarcastically as he pushed to his feet.

"Any normal female would be weeping and carrying on and offering to take me back to rest my poor head on her pillow," Charlie countered, staggering slightly as he straightened. "Let's just accept that we're different. Come on, let's see if we can still catch that taxi. I want to get you out of here."

"Can you walk?" Penelope asked doubtfully, for the first time admitting a measure of fear, whether for herself or this man she couldn't quite determine. She glanced nervously at the narrow street, wondering who watched from the darkened doorways beneath overhanging balconies.

"I'll manage." Finding his balance, he proceeded onward with only a slight hitch in his gait. "I've been hit from behind by a two-fifty tackle and survived."

"I daresay you were wearing a helmet at the time," she reminded him.

Charlie glanced at her wryly. "You're enjoying this, aren't you? Did you hire those guys, just to teach me a lesson?"

"Well, I wish I'd thought of it, but I haven't learned my way around that quickly. I think it more likely some of those old chums you're hiding from hired them."

"Chums don't come after a guy with a tree. Did you see what the hell they hit me with?"

"A big stick," she said calmly, although her heart still raced and perspiration slithered down her back. "Shouldn't we call the police?"

"Unless you can identify them, it wouldn't do any good. The town's inhabitants don't normally attack tourists around here. They're smarter than that. Gives the place a bad name. It's me they were after. And I'd rather not let the police know I'm here."

Penelope made a noncommittal noise while mentally tallying all the reasons he wouldn't want the police to know of his presence. The list was far from reassuring, yet still she walked beside him and worried about his welfare instead of running as fast and far as she could. Maybe his incompetence at covert activities reassured her. She'd helped Zack out of his various scrapes throughout their college years. Maybe it was just habit, one she really ought to break.

They walked the rest of the way to the dock in silence. Penelope imagined Charlie's head hurt like hell so she obligingly kept her opinions to herself. By tomorrow, she would be back at the work she knew best, and he could fall into the ocean for all she cared. Somehow, they just had to struggle through the night ahead. With his head feeling like a pounding kettledrum, Charlie shouldn't present much problem. From the right perspective, she could almost feel grateful for his attackers.

"Oh, shit," he muttered as they reached the dock in time to watch the sun ease into the sea in a blaze so hot it should have produced steam.

Ignoring his profanity, Penelope watched the magnificent sunset with awe. The lapping of the waves at her feet, the cool sea breeze, and the tropical setting of riotous flowers and palms soothed her shattered nerves. She could almost wish they had those champagne glasses in hand now. With a little music and moonlight, she'd be completely lost. She might heartily dislike the big man beside her, but she wasn't immune to his masculine appeal, not in this setting apparently.

"The taxi's gone," he explained, pointing out the obvious if she'd just had the presence of mind to look.

Jerked back to reality, Penelope gazed at the deserted dock that had swarmed with people not half an hour before. Nighttime fell quickly in the Caribbean, and darkness shrouded the beach. "Won't it come back?" she asked tentatively, hoping he'd give the answer she wanted to hear. "It's probably making a run to the resort."

She couldn't see his exasperated look, but she felt it. "It's gone back to the resort, all right, and that's where it will stay. It doesn't run after dark."

"But what about all those other boats?" she asked in bewilderment. "Surely someone could take us around?" She couldn't believe she wouldn't be sleeping at the resort tonight. It wasn't all that late. She needed to be at work first thing in the morning. All her clothes and toiletries were back there, for heaven's sake. She certainly couldn't spend the night on the beach.

"Those are fishing boats, and all the fishermen have gone home to supper. They keep early hours. Come on. We'd best not stand around here gawking; those thugs might come back looking for us. Let's see if Jacques can provide us with transportation."

She was beyond exhausted as they trudged back into town. She'd been up before dawn, traveled a thousand miles, been accused of drug smuggling, kidnapped, and watched a mugging all in the course of one day. She just didn't have the strength for much more. If by *transportation* he meant another van ride down that treacherous excuse for a road, she would sleep in the streets first.

Silently cursing her lack of choice, she followed Charlie's lead. This was all his fault. Had she been on vacation, she might have considered this an adventure, but she wasn't, dammit all. She had her job to worry about. And Beth. The sooner she lost this great lummox, the better off she'd be. He was definitely what her mother called bad news. She remembered men like him at home, with the manners of gorillas and the social skills of apes—definitely bad news.

The lights of television sets flickered through shuttered windows as they passed by. Reggae music poured from a balcony above them. Lilting voices sang from doorstep to porch and back, but she couldn't see the speakers. Uneasy in this alien environment, she edged closer to Charlie's large presence.

He didn't take the opportunity offered to slide his arm around her, as many men would have. Now that she noticed, she realized he avoided touching her, thrusting her away quickly whenever circumstances forced them into contact. She thought that exceedingly curious considering the unmistakable look she'd caught in his eyes more than once. She'd been the recipient of that kind of look all her life. Men saw every woman as a challenge to their sexual prowess. This man was no different, except that he didn't take up the challenge.

She didn't have time to puzzle over the discovery. Charlie led the way down a narrow alley to someone's backyard and knocked softly on the back door of a two-story concrete block structure. No one answered.

Cursing, Charlie tried the door. A dead bolt held it firm. He rattled it louder, hoping to stir the inhabitants, but the lack of lights in the rooms above told their story. Jacques and Antoinette had left. Why?

Stumped, he crashed his shoulder against the door, hoping to shatter the old bolt, but Jacques knew how to protect his home. The bolt didn't give an inch, but Charlie's shoulder acquired an ache to match the one in his throbbing head.

"You can't break in!" his companion uttered in tones of horror.

"He promised me a place to sleep." Charlie knew he was being obstinate, but he couldn't believe his old friend had left him out in the cold like this. Something was wrong, but his aching head couldn't muddle it out right now. He could only manage one thought at a time, and the one uppermost at the moment was getting rid of this female before she got hurt. After that, he could take care of himself.

"You were going to sleep here?" she asked in disbelief.

"Yeah, I didn't figure that would disappoint you any." He wandered along the back of the house looking for a way in.

"Could your friend have left because he's expecting trouble?"

He hadn't realized she'd followed him. Damn, but the blow must have scrambled his brains more than he'd realized. She was right, of course. Jacques would have assumed Charlie would get the message when he came back and found the place empty. He'd just suffered one too many setbacks recently and thought the worst of everyone.

Word must still travel like lightning through the village. Someone must have recognized him. Maybe he hadn't left Jacobsen behind in Vieux Fort—could the man really be desperate enough to follow him?

Grimacing, Charlie considered his alternatives. To find Raul, he needed to get back into the interior, but that required transportation. If he produced his license and credit card, whoever sought him would know just what to look for and where.

Would they know about Penelope yet?

Damn, but she wasn't going to like what he was thinking one bit. Maybe he could soften her up a little, turn on the old Southern charm. Glancing down at the top of that lovely head of black hair, Charlie recognized the problem with that. He didn't want to just charm her. He wanted to tumble her into bed and not get up for a week.

Well, hell, he'd do that later. Right now, they had to get back to the resort and safety.

"Come on. I can still hot-wire a boat. With luck, I'll remember which one belongs to Jacques."

Noting the lights on in the corner grocery and deciding a

six-pack of beer would make a better sedative than aspirin, Charlie dragged his lagging companion after him. He could almost hear her high-society condemnation as he lifted the beer and strode out, listening for her hurried footsteps behind him. It would almost be easier if he thought she worked for Jacobsen. He really didn't need the scold bubbling on her lips. With luck, he could outdistance it.

Luck had deserted him, pitched him off the boat, and left him to drown. Penelope's long-legged stride brought her right up beside him, and to Charlie's amazement, she grabbed his unoccupied hand. He almost shook her off before he reconsidered. He wasn't the type to go around holding women's hands. He didn't possess an ounce of sentimentality. But her hand was slender and somehow erotic wrapped in his big fist. He kept it there.

"You're not really going to hot-wire a boat?" she asked anxiously, tripping along beside him in the darkness of the alley.

"Got any better suggestions?"

Since she remained silent, he assumed she didn't. He appreciated the silence. His head had a hard enough time hearing himself think through the pounding in his brains.

He left her standing lookout on the dock while he scoured the beach for a familiar fishing boat. No fancy rigs here, just skiffs with motors. He could steal any one of them without much trouble. He just knew he could pay Jacques back for any lost wages once he got out of here.

He settled for one that looked familiar, threw in the beer, pulled out the wires, got the motor running, and signaled for his lookout. She was already running down the sand toward him. Silhouetted in the moonlight, her figure was all long arms and legs. Good thing for him he was a breast man.

Unfortunately, his John Henry didn't recognize that fact. He ached in several places now, and picturing that bed waiting for them at the cottage intensified the one below his belt. He'd have to sleep on the porch with the mosquitoes to keep from having at her. The warmth of her trusting hand still burned against his palm. If she was as smart as he thought she was, she'd push him overboard halfway there. Men like him had no place anywhere near her.

"You know, you're the first man I've ever met who knows how to handle a situation without being told," she said thoughtfully as they roared around the curve of the shore.

After that, Charlie figured he'd better swim home.

❦ SIX ❧

Penelope remained silent as they chugged the boat to shore at the resort, climbed out, and hauled it far enough up the beach to stop the tide from taking it. She was exhausted, physically, mentally, and emotionally. She wanted to curl up somewhere and sleep for a week. Preferably not with Macho Charlie. But that wasn't the entire reason for her silence.

Warm salt water lapped at her bare toes. A slice of silver moon cut a swath across the black sand, breaking it into dancing diamonds. Palm trees dipped and swayed to the ocean breeze. And from somewhere amid the lights on the hill, calypso music drifted with a lilting tune she recognized but couldn't name.

She was standing in the midst of every woman's fantasy. Alone.

She discounted the football player slogging through the sand beside her, beer in hand. She'd had her fill of football players and their egos long ago. If she'd envisioned any man at all in this fantasy, it would be a tall, sophisticated gentleman, one who would whisper romantic words and offer a lover's toast with his champagne glass. Not an ox who bellowed orders, cursed under his breath, and preferred beer.

But she wasn't angry with Charlie. She was just—soppy sentimental, she supposed. She'd avoided dreams of marriage and kids in favor of a career. All her life she'd craved respect

58

for her brains and education, instead of her looks. She'd achieved that respect, sort of. She was well aware that men with half her abilities had been promoted to positions ahead of her. But she'd taken up golf—she hated golf—networked with the partners, and finally garnered this chance to earn the position she deserved. And she stood here now, in this exotic setting, wondering if it wouldn't be better dancing in the moonlight than worrying about corporate tax structures.

Stupid of her. The ocean and the trees would be here tomorrow, and next year, and the years after that. Beth's operation couldn't wait that long. Beth would never see an island beach beneath the moonlight. Even the operation wouldn't guarantee that much. It offered only hope that her eyes wouldn't deteriorate and the pain wouldn't worsen. Conceivably, someday, she might be healthy enough to dance to the island music.

"We need to rent a car."

The masculine voice startled Penelope as abruptly as if he'd awakened her. She glanced up at Charlie's broad silhouette, backlit by the moon as they reached the steps. Primitive of her to enjoy the view. His words jerked her fantasy back to reality.

Charlie caught her elbow and steered her up the stairs. She pulled her arm from his grasp.

"I need a car to get back into the interior," he explained carefully, as if to a two-year-old. "I don't want to show my license or use my credit card. They rent jeeps here. We can stop at the lobby and you can—"

"Put a jeep in my name so you can disappear with it? Don't tempt me. If I could afford it, I'd almost be willing to pay the price. But I can't, so forget it."

"Look, I've got money. I'll leave you all my credit cards, if that will make you happy. If I don't return, you can use them to cruise the Mediterranean. Or get a cash advance to pay for the jeep. Just don't use them in St. Lucia. Someone might recognize the name, and you may find yourself in more trouble than you can handle. I'm not certain what I've gotten myself into here."

"How very reassuring." Although tired, Penelope increased her pace up the hill. She wondered if weariness accounted for her lack of terror toward a man who hot-wired boats, needed someone like her for cover, and had murdering muggers after him. She definitely would not blame her inability to fear his presence on his good looks and masculine presence. That would be stupid.

The bottom line was that she had no business getting involved. She had too many problems of her own, and she certainly didn't need the problems of a total stranger. What she needed to do was figure out how to get this man out of her life. Now.

He grabbed her arm and pulled her into the shadows of a bougainvillea spilling over a retaining wall. "Look, a man's life is at stake. Do you think I enjoy begging?"

"If you're trying to instill guilt here," she said conversationally, "you might as well know I'm impervious to it."

Another couple descended the stone stairs carrying drinks and laughing. Penelope envied them their carefree gaiety. Why did she have to be the one tormented with other people's problems? Surely Charlie was exaggerating. Men were like that. She didn't want anyone's life depending on her. Beth's life was more than enough responsibility.

Charlie crowded closer, backing her against the wall and placing his hands on either side of her head as if he meant to kiss her. Penelope didn't consider calling for help. She wasn't afraid of him. Maybe she should have been, but perhaps because of her height, men had never physically molested her, and she'd never learned that kind of fear.

"Back off," she warned. "I won't be intimidated."

To his credit, Charlie immediately removed his hands. "You could go with me," he suggested.

"No, I can't," she said wearily. "I have a job to do. If I don't do it, I'll be unemployed."

"If I don't get a jeep, a man will be dead. I've got connections. I'll get you a new job."

"Is the Mafia paying well these days?" she asked in exasperation. "You practically kidnap me, blackmail me, maybe even set me up for drug charges, and I'm supposed to fall all over myself giving you anything you want? Why don't you just take your motorboat back to town and hot-wire a car?"

"Stealing from the poor is too easy." Sarcasm laced his voice as he turned away and started up the stairs. "I'd much rather scare women."

"I'm sure they have women in town."

Despite his anger and frustration, Charlie almost smiled at that. She was determined to get rid of him. For some insane reason, he was determined to stick to her like a burr. In this resort world, people traveled in pairs. Besides, if he drove a stolen car, the police would be on the lookout for him.

They trudged past the outside bar and restaurant. Laughter and the gentle clinking of glasses and silverware mixed with the lively calypso beat of a kettle band. He wondered if Miss Penelope could rumba. She'd look damned good on a dance floor.

One of these days he'd have time to find a lady who could do more than drink beer and talk sports. Admittedly, he wasn't likely to find one in the kinds of places he'd been hanging out, but he hadn't really been looking either. All he needed was a little fun now and then. Commitment was for women.

So, he wasn't considering commitment, just a good rumba or two. When he got back home, he'd forget all about it. The islands made a man a little crazy, bubbled the blood or something.

Charlie scanned the shadows around the cottage as they approached. He didn't think anyone could have traced him here yet, but he wasn't taking chances. A palmetto leaf danced lazily across the path. A bird called from the poinciana, then settled into silence. He should have left a light on. He wasn't used to this cloak-and-dagger stuff.

"Wait here," he ordered as they reached the porch. Miss Penny didn't seem in too much of a hurry to join him. She leaned over the railing and watched the moonlight on the ocean. He rattled at the door lock, distracted by a glimpse of long pale legs. Like a damned ostrich, he thought in frustration as the lock gave, she'd ignored every damned bait he'd offered. She might as well have her head in the sand.

He switched on the overhead, checked the closet and bathroom. Everything looked just as they'd left it. Good. If all went well, he could get some sleep and head out in the morning, with or without Miss P's permission. By tomorrow night, he'd be out of here.

Charlie returned to the porch. Penny wasn't looking at him. She would be even more furious in the morning when she discovered how desperate he was for that jeep. Someday he hoped he could make it up to her. To prove his point, he offered what he could.

"I'll go down to the bar. You go catch up on your beauty sleep."

She glared at him in disbelief, but turning on her heel, she stalked into the cottage. Before Charlie could drag his weary feet back down the path, she screamed.

Not again. Amusing himself with thoughts of "tarantulas" or other creepy crawlies, Charlie shoved open the louvered door and glanced across the dimly lit cottage.

Without turning to acknowledge his presence, Penelope pointed at the floor on the far side of the bed.

Okay, snake, maybe. At least she hadn't gone after it with hair spray this time. Snickering at that memory, Charlie sidled up beside her and looked over the bed.

"Oh, shit. Bat." He hated bats.

"Bat?" Apparently having the animal identified calmed her. She visibly relaxed and strained to watch the creature with curiosity. "It's tiny."

"It's lost. We need to get the damned thing out."

"Suggestions?" she asked dryly.

Most well-appointed hotel rooms did not come equipped

with brooms for sweeping out nocturnal visitors. Most didn't come equipped with bats either. Charlie didn't relish kicking the thing out between the louvers from which it had entered. Bat wings in his face had never amused him.

"We could just go to the bar and wait for it to leave," he suggested.

"There is no way in heaven or hell I'm traipsing down that mountain one more time tonight. I'll sleep with bats first."

As she flounced off to the bathroom and slammed the door, Charlie wondered if he ranked lower than bats as a bedmate. His mind had a one-track kink in it tonight.

Sighing with resignation, he searched the high-ceilinged room for a weapon.

After washing and changing, Penelope emerged from the bathroom to find Charlie sprawled across the double bed, posterior side up, mosquito netting draped around him, poking what appeared to be a tree limb at the floor.

"Shh, don't move. I've almost got him out."

There was something innately appealing about a large man sprawled across a bed, gently poking a furry critter to safety. Or maybe it was just his tight buns.

Obviously, exhaustion had exploded inside her head, turning her brains to dust.

"Got him!" Charlie leapt from the bed, tangled with the netting, and nearly collapsed through the louvered walls before locating the closure rod and snapping the blinds shut.

All right, so maybe even suspicious characters like him had been little boys once. That didn't mean they weren't evil. She wouldn't fall for that conquering male look of triumph. He'd pushed a baby bat out the window, not killed a mastodon.

"There's no air-conditioning," she pointed out prosaically. "We'll suffocate with the louvers closed."

"The wind comes from the other direction. He's not likely to cross a porch to get at us."

Penelope noted his glance dropping to her rose silk pajamas. She wore more now than she had earlier, but logic had little to do with the direction of the male mind. "You were going to the bar?" she reminded him.

"Oh, yeah. Well . . ."

She had no difficulty reading his regret as he glanced at the rumpled bed. If he was half as exhausted as she was, she would almost believe his thoughts were entirely on a good night's sleep. She knew better though. She'd never been quite that naive.

"Maybe you'll find a lonely fisherman's widow," she offered maliciously.

"Yeah, right. If they're anything like golf widows, forget it. I'm better off with a bottle of beer. Good night."

He slammed out.

Penelope listened to the crunch of his shoes against the gravel walk until the whisper of the tide below drowned him out. A puff of breeze lifted a strand of hair from her face. Why did she wish it were a man's hand instead?

She'd never felt this lonely in her life. She was accustomed to climbing into an empty bed every night. She used those minutes before sleep to line up the problems she must tackle the next day. Sometimes, they unraveled overnight and the solution presented itself when she woke. Having a man in her bed would only distract her.

She would not feel regret that she'd sent that bully out into the night.

A man who pushed a tiny bat out instead of killing it wasn't precisely a bully.

But near enough. Steeling herself, Penelope lined the sofa bolsters down the middle of the bed, switched off the light, and slipped beneath the mosquito netting. He'd taken the key with him. He would be back.

The sea had submerged the moon by the time Charlie traipsed back up the hill to the cottage. He'd had a hell of a time explaining to Henwood why he'd left his bride alone on their first romantic evening in the Caribbean. Mixing margaritas and beers hadn't been a smart idea, but it had distracted the man for a while.

And he'd secured the jeep. Fingering the keys in his pocket, Charlie slipped into the cottage as quietly as the obdurate lock would allow. He'd like to drive into the interior now, find Raul, and get home quickly. But driving island roads at night was the act of an insane man, particularly after ten years away. The forest would have reclaimed the roads he knew, and even the new ones tended to halt abruptly, buried under rock slides. Besides, he needed sleep.

His "bride" had curled up around her pillow in a waterfall of silken black hair and rose pajamas, resembling some exotic flower in the dim light. If he could just think of her in terms of objects, he could survive the night.

Eyeing the bolsters and the narrow space remaining on the bed with disfavor, Charlie jerked off his shirt and sat down to remove his shoes.

Penelope whimpered and stirred restlessly in her sleep.

Oh, hell, he'd be better off sleeping on the porch.

The problem was, despite all the grief they gave him, he really *liked* women. He wasn't much on commitment, maybe, but he liked having women around. He liked their soft scents, their dangling curls, the way their eyelashes fluttered. He liked holding their warm curves against him in the night. He even enjoyed finding feminine dainties strewn across his room. He didn't much enjoy their blather over coffee in the morning or their possessive instincts when they thought they had their claws in him, but up until that point, he really enjoyed himself.

Maybe that's why he'd chosen this hard-as-nails, nononsense tailored robot to appropriate. She wouldn't distract him like most women would. But then she had to go and put on pink silk pajamas. Admittedly, they were as tailored and boxy as her gawd-awful suit, but pink silk? Damn, his hands itched to touch.

He was too tired for this. He had to concentrate on finding Raul and getting back to the States and saving his company.

He dropped his shoes on the floor and unsnapped his pants. Glancing at the woman sleeping in the bed, he resisted pulling his trousers off. He'd be as uncomfortable as hell, but he didn't relish the scene she'd create otherwise. He didn't own any pajamas.

Intoxicating warmth enveloped her. Penelope buried her nose in her pillow. The alarm hadn't gone off. She could sleep a minute longer.

Sunlight flickered on her eyelids, but she ignored it. She loved the sound of waves lapping on the shore. She had a tape of nothing but water sounds.

But she wasn't at home, listening to a machine. Tropical warmth surrounded her. Well-being and contentment she hadn't known in years surged through her. She could conquer whole new worlds like this.

A masculine snort near her ear shattered the illusion.

Springing awake, Penelope discovered she was snagged in the trap of a muscular arm. A very naked, very broad chest pressed against her back. She wouldn't think about what her bottom curved against. The snore in her ear was sufficient distraction.

She jerked her elbow backward. "Let go of me!" she hissed as she connected with a taut midriff instead of soft belly.

"Oomph."

She tensed as a wide hand flattened against her stomach, hesitated, then drifted ever so slightly upward. She elbowed him again.

"Arghh," he groaned sleepily.

He rolled over, releasing her. She jumped from the bed and immediately tangled with the mosquito netting. Ignoring the snicker behind her, she swatted at the netting until she had it over her head. Damned man, he had no *right*. . . .

She slammed into the bathroom. When she emerged half an hour later, showered, wearing her linen pantsuit, he was gone.

* * *

"Smith and Son," Sherry chirped into the phone as she examined a nail she'd broken in the filing cabinet. "Mr. Smith isn't in. May I take a message?" she answered automatically to the question on the other end. Charlie was never in, even when he was here. He didn't like being interrupted during his few hours in the office. In the year since she'd had the job, she'd become quite expert at knowing which callers she could handle on her own, which messages to jot down on her pink memo slips for Charlie to follow up, and which calls to divert directly to her boss, whether he liked it or not. She was rather proud of her accomplishment. It hadn't helped her much these last two days.

"It's urgent. I must speak with him this moment. Can you not put me through to his cellular?"

The lilting Caribbean accent alerted her. Dropping the file, she grabbed a pencil. "Mr. Smith is unavailable. Is that you, Raul?" The man with the subpoena hadn't returned yet this morning, but Sherry still spoke furtively, afraid the walls might have ears.

"Tell him not to come to St. Lucia. Do you understand? Don' come to St. Lucia."

Horrified, Sherry tried to untangle her thoughts and her tongue and keep the construction foreman on the line. The phone went dead before she could stutter out a single word.

Shaken by the ominous tone of his warning, Sherry stared at the buttons on her phone. Who did she call now? Old Mr. Smith was dead. Charlie was incommunicado. The company's best foreman had disappeared into the jungle and just called from out of nowhere. What should she do now?

Biting her bottom lip, she picked up her nail file and thought about it.

❧ SEVEN ❧

Anticipating the tropical treat of fresh juice on the veranda in the warmth of a Caribbean February sun, Penelope ignored the niggling concern over Charlie's whereabouts. If she had any luck at all, he'd stolen a jeep and disappeared from her life forever. She could immerse herself in the world of accounting software she knew so well and not be disturbed by unruly thoughts of imposing men and life passing her by. It would have been nice if she'd been sent to a singles' resort where she might at least have dallied with some interesting young engineer or lawyer.

That wistful thought shocked her sufficiently to force her to look around for other objects to concentrate on.

Following the waitress to a table overlooking the beach below, Penelope noted a small crowd forming in the cove where they'd left the boat. She wouldn't think a fishing boat was worthy of that much interest, even on a private beach.

Watching the crowd from the safety of the high veranda occupied her thoughts as she waited for someone to return with a menu. Two of the black men gesticulating vehemently on the beach wore the white shorts and shirts of resort employees. Several others wore cutoffs and T-shirts. She couldn't precisely place them as staff, but the resort had a variety of maintenance employees and occasionally allowed local artisans to set up booths on the beach. She watched as

Mr. Henwood hurried across the sand to join them, accompanied by a man in what appeared to be a khaki uniform. Police?

Liquid panic shot through her veins, fed by memories of yesterday at the airport.

The men below were looking at the boat, not knocking on her door, she reminded herself as she calmly accepted the menu and pretended to peruse it. But Charlie's warnings about catastrophic prison conditions on the island played a horror film through her mind.

Maybe the uniform was for security employees.

That thought evaporated with the arrival of a motorboat bearing an official-looking insignia and occupied by uniformed men. It might not be Miami Vice, but from this distance, the boat gave a good imitation.

Penelope clenched her fingers around her juice glass and tried not to panic. It was just a fishing boat, for heaven's sake. If Charlie had taken the wrong boat, he could pay the owner rent for its use, if that was the problem. Where was Charlie? He could explain.

Charlie. Horror washed over her as she stared down at the vignette playing before her eyes. Had something happened to Charlie?

And where the hell had that concern come from?

She suffered a moment's unreasonable dismay before the object of her fear sauntered from behind the beach umbrella stand at some signal from Mr. Henwood. She would recognize her roommate's hulking shoulders in that red muscle shirt anywhere. The damned man dressed like a pig. He probably rode a Harley. No, she mentally corrected herself. Good ol' boys like Charlie Smith drove battered red pickup trucks with "No Fear" stickers in the window.

Her horror and fear turned to disgust. A man like that *would* poke his nose in where it didn't belong, like a gawking voyeur at an accident scene. Rude, crude, and uncouth.

As if he'd heard her thoughts, Charlie glanced up the hill in her direction. Penelope imagined him straining to see her, and she had the foolish urge to duck from sight. He couldn't possibly pick her out from the other diners.

To her dismay, she saw him speak intensely with Henwood and the policeman, pound the slightly built manager on the back—probably enough to make him wince—and saunter off in the direction of the beach stairs. And her.

She would not panic. She had no reason to panic. She would sit here and eat a civilized breakfast like any rational person on a lovely day like this. Then she would introduce herself to the office staff and go to work. Perfectly logical, sane, and safe.

Until the disruptive force with the improbable name of Charlie Smith swept onto the veranda.

Heads swiveled as he muscled his way past tables of decently dressed couples. Waitresses in their triple-knotted head scarves stopped and gawked as he winked in their direction. He swiped a glass of juice as he passed the juice bar, sprawled in the chair across from her, threw back the juice, glanced around, and, discovering a coffeepot, got up and helped himself. On a second thought, he carried the pot to the table and poured Penelope some.

"Act calm," he ordered as he poured. "Drink your coffee while I talk." He returned to his chair, swigged from his cup, and grimaced. He hadn't shaved, and the stubble of the beard darkened his angular jaw in a manner Penelope wanted to label "criminal," but her libido yelled "sexy!"

For a moment, Penelope had the dizzying sensation that Charlie's bronzed shoulders and piercing blue eyes had obliterated her surroundings. Shaking her head, she forced her gaze away from the mountain of masculinity across from her. She had to get out of here.

Charlie caught her hand and pressed it to the table as she started to rise.

"No. Listen. There's a body in the boat we brought in last night."

Oh, God, this couldn't be happening. Penelope sank back into her seat and stared at him, willing herself not to believe.

Tension tightened the muscles of his unshaven jaw. The blue of his eyes had frosted into ice. He exuded fury. Not fear. Fury. He held her pinned with his glare.

"An old man, a harmless one. He played in the streets for coins. But Michel knew everyone, heard everything. He helped me out more than once when I was a kid. Jacques looked out for him when he could. Now Jacques has disappeared and Michel is dead. I've got to find Raul and get out of here before something else happens."

Penelope wanted to ask him who Raul was but she had a sneaking suspicion it was the man whose life was purportedly in danger, the one she didn't want to hear about. The rest of Charlie's words alarmed her enough: an old man who had helped him out. Penelope let the words wash over her, tried not to let them sink in. But instinct, intuition, some sixth sense she hadn't known she possessed screamed warnings. "An old man?" she questioned. "Tall, skinny? Carved bowls?"

Charlie's eyes narrowed. "You saw him? When?"

"He warned me about the muggers last night. He led me to you. Do you think . . . ?"

"Hell, yes." Looking suddenly pale beneath his tan, Charlie gulped the rest of his coffee, and glanced down at the beach where the police had laid the body on the sand. "Grab the bread. We're getting out of here." He shoved several rolls into a napkin and stood up.

"What do you mean, *we*?" She wasn't certain whether to be scared or furious. That gentle old man hadn't deserved to die. He'd done nothing. How had he gotten into the fishing boat?

Charlie caught her arm, dragged her to her feet, and handed her the remaining baguette from the basket. "I told Henwood last night I had only a few days on the island, and offered to pay your expenses. I told you they're a romantic lot here. He waived the fee and offered you the day off, especially after I gave him some information about a couple of new engineers who could help him with the perennial waste-water problem."

He tugged her through the rapidly filling restaurant. Embarrassed by the scene he was creating, Penelope hurried to keep up with him.

"What do you need me for?" she hissed as they reached the path outside.

"Protective coloration. A white man driving alone out here is automatically suspicious. One wearing a baseball hat and squiring a female is a tourist. It would help if I was sunburned, but otherwise, I can play lost tourist real well."

"I can't!" she protested as she ran to keep up with him. She'd thought herself in good shape, but she was already panting in the uphill race. Maybe it was the altitude. "I've got a job and a family to get back to."

He swiveled and glared back at her. "You're married?"

"No!" She should have said yes. Damn, that was stupid. But he unnerved her so thoroughly, she couldn't think. "My sister is blind. She can get around pretty well, but she's not used to being left alone for long."

He returned to his race up the hillside. "This should only take a day or so. One of my employees is missing and I have to find him before whoever murdered Michel does. The island is only nineteen miles across. There are only so many places he can hide."

Remembering the mountainous trip here, Penelope wondered if that was nineteen miles up and down or as the crow flies. She suspected she didn't want to know.

"Look, I don't see any reason why I should accompany you. You'll travel faster without me. Just go your own way, and I won't tell anyone about you." She swore as her heeled sandals caught on a rock and twisted. They were almost at the cottage, thank heavens. She could scarcely catch her breath.

Charlie snorted. "The dust wouldn't have settled behind me before you'd be telling the cops how I blackmailed and kidnapped you. They'd have search parties after me all over the damned island. Forget it. We're going together." He caught her hand as she halted, pulling her up the porch stairs. "Pack an overnight bag. Include insect spray and soap. And for Pete's sake, change into jeans and tennis shoes. This isn't a cruise ship."

Penelope stared at him in horror as he threw her suitcase on the bed and began heaving clothing and toiletries into his backpack.

When she didn't move, Charlie propped his wide hands on his hips and stepped in front of her. Her breath shortened even more at his imposing proximity.

"They *murdered* Michel," he reminded her. When she still didn't respond, his mouth tightened in impatience. "They saw us together. They dumped Michel in that boat, on that beach, for a reason. They're telling us they know where we're staying, and warning us to back off." He glared at her blank look of incomprehension. "They're not just after me now. They're after both of us."

Penelope's knees nearly crumpled. "They're after *me*? What have I done?"

"Kept me from getting killed." Abruptly, he swung around and returned to packing.

This couldn't be happening. In blind terror, Penelope stumbled to the closet and reached for her khakis. She didn't own jeans.

She would lose her job. Beth wouldn't get her operation.

She could get killed out there.

"I can't believe I'm doing this," Penelope muttered as the pink jeep with its candy-striped awning bumped down a dirt road that looked as if it might fall off the side of the mountain at any given moment. The view was phenomenal, if she didn't think about falling into it. The lush fronds of banana trees vied with the frothy foam of fern trees and the brilliant scarlet of poinciana to pave a path of greenery straight down to the vivid blue of the sea below. If she had been watching it on TV, she would have been overwhelmed by the beauty. Instead, she clung to the seat and prayed.

She'd stripped off the loose linen shirt she'd worn to protect her skin from the blazing sun. The jungle provided shade and enough humidity that even her square-necked T-shirt clung to her back. If the maniac in the driver's seat would only stop to allow a quick dip in a mountain stream or just a moment of peace where she could enjoy a breeze, she might relax. As it was, her perspiration was as much from fear as from heat.

Maybe she should tell him she was the world's biggest coward, that she was more hindrance than help, that he should just put her on a plane back to civilization.

He wouldn't listen.

The jeep finally rumbled to a halt in front of a crude cabin propped on stilts. Had it not been surrounded by towering cocoa trees and the thick leaves of a local vegetable vine, the cabin would have resembled some of the worst housing in Miami's slums. But amid the luxurious vegetation, it merely appeared quaint.

"We're blamed lucky nobody out here carries shotguns," Charlie muttered as he unfolded his big frame from the small seat and stepped out. "I'd shoot anything looking like this if I were them."

Since he'd been complaining about the pink jeep since they'd climbed into it, Penelope didn't question his grumbling. Charlie Smith made a surly companion when his mind was focused on something. She'd given up asking him anything after the first few minutes in his company.

A goat ambled from beneath the house but no other sign of life appeared. She would have liked to ask if Charlie was lost and looking for directions or if this had been their destination all along, but she merely stayed seated and enjoyed the respite from their breakneck pace. Her companion looked slightly miffed that she didn't respond, but he shrugged his massive shoulders and sauntered toward the cottage. Maybe if she gave him the silent treatment long enough, he'd put her out at the airport.

As he approached the cottage, a large mocha-colored woman filled the doorway, her flowered cotton dress swirling around her legs, barely missing a rooster that darted from behind her. "Charlie?" she called, in a voice entirely too high for a woman her size. "Charlie!" she squealed as her visitor ran up the path.

"Monica! You haven't changed a bit."

Penelope watched in mild astonishment as her chestnut-haired football player of a companion nearly disappeared into the woman's embrace. They hugged and pounded on each other as if long-lost pals. A whispered inquiry apparently reminded Charlie that he wasn't alone, and he briefly gestured in the jeep's direction. Penelope couldn't hear his explanation, but the woman grinned broadly and waved. Politely, she waved back, but she didn't budge from the jeep. She wasn't moving until she got to the airport. She'd given up on the idea of Anse Chastenet. Maybe her employers would understand if she told them of the murder.

Maybe not. Oh, well. She still wasn't getting out.

She sat stonily with arms crossed as Charlie and Monica held a hurried discussion in patois. The woman looked angry and frightened as Charlie talked. Anger apparently won out. She gesticulated and replied furiously, scaring the goat into the jungle and the rooster into hiding under the porch. More than once she pointed up the mountain, until Penelope feared she was telling Charlie they had to travel even farther up the treacherous road. She would climb out and hike back to civilization, if that was the case.

Finally, after another round of hugs, Charlie waved farewell and loped back toward the jeep. Penelope didn't want anything to do with the deceitful bastard, but she couldn't help noticing the worried frown between his thick eyebrows. If she were the imaginative type, she'd think she read real anxiety in the tightening of his unshaven jaw as he started the jeep again. But she wasn't imaginative. She wasn't even curious. She would simply sit here until he put her out.

He threw her a quick look as he shifted the jeep into reverse and swung it around to head back down the mountain.

"I always thought women talked too much. Can I count on the silent treatment lasting much longer?"

She hadn't thought he'd even noticed. "Far be it from me to intrude upon your weighty conversation with yourself. Just consider me part of the hardware."

He snorted and turned his attention back to the road. "The hardware I know about has a useful function. Other than looking good, what's yours?"

He couldn't have found a better means of slapping her. All her life she'd worked toward being useful, something more functional than a pretty face on a magazine cover. She scorned men who wanted to use her as a trophy piece on their arms. She shoved her brains and knowledge into every conceivable corner of her life until people expected her to have all the answers. And now this muscle-bound punk was comparing her to a hood ornament.

"I don't pack picnic lunches and flirt with the natives, if that's your meaning," she replied stiffly.

"All right, you don't cook and you don't sew. So what else can you do? You can talk, can't you? Or must we discuss the theory of relativity before you unbend?"

Penelope cast him a curious glance but she couldn't tell anything from his square jaw. "You *want* me to ask questions?" she asked incredulously.

"Yeah. I'm used to women chattering. Makes me nervous when they shut up."

"It makes you nervous when they shut up," she repeated flatly. "We're running from a murderer, driving like maniacs on roads that could collapse if a bird lands on them, and my silence makes you nervous. Forgive me if I don't laugh."

"Look, I didn't mean to get you into this, all right? I thought I'd just get in and out with nobody the wiser. I haven't been back here in ten years. Nobody should have recognized me. There's something going on here that I can't explain. But I've got to find Raul. You wouldn't leave your sister if she were in trouble, would you?"

"I *have* left my sister and she's in trouble," Penelope

asserted. "That's why I've got to get back as soon as possible. That's why this job is so blamed important to me. And you've gone and ruined everything. What makes your plans more important than mine?" Because she couldn't hold out any longer, she added, "And who the devil is Raul?"

He shoved his hand through windblown hair and gave her a suspicious look. Apparently losing some internal argument, he explained. "I own a construction business and Raul's my foreman. He's disappeared with the project funds. Maybe he just got drunk and wandered off, but I have to *know*." He didn't explain further but threw her an anxious glance. "I'll do what I can to make it up to you once I find Raul. But if either of us gets killed, we can't help anybody. So let's just do what we can to keep each other alive until we get back to civilization. Why does your sister need an operation?"

"She was in a car accident that caused nerve damage in her face. She's developing painful blood clots and her vision is deteriorating. She needs an experimental operation her insurance won't pay for. Our parents went through a messy divorce and what assets they have left are tied up. So it's up to me to come up with the money."

She didn't know why she'd rattled on like that. If she had some odd notion that he would take pity on her and let her go home, she was out of luck. The information about his foreman explained more than she wanted to know about his desperation, and she sensed he hadn't told her the half of it.

Charlie nodded grimly and swung the jeep onto a paved highway, or what passed for a paved highway in these parts.

"All right. This shouldn't take more than a day or two. Once we find Raul, he can tell me who's behind whatever's going on. Then you can go back and do your job and everything will be just fine. If not, I'll take care of things. I've got connections all over Miami. You'll keep your job or I'll find you a better one, and your sister will get whatever she needs. Just help me out a little here. We're heading back into civilization and I need your cooperation."

"Yeah, right, like I believe you." Penelope sat back in the

seat and crossed her arms. She could repeat a litany of broken
promises she'd heard from men, starting way back in kinder-
garten when her father had promised to take them to Disney-
land, and continuing right up to her employers, who'd told her
she'd have a corner office within five years. "Do all men think
women are fools?"

Charlie reached into his hip pocket and wiggled out his
wallet. He threw it in her lap. "Keep it. It's got my credit cards
and my ATM card. You can run a credit report, empty my
bank account, run up my American Express, whatever. I don't
give a damn. Money isn't worth shit. It's a pity you haven't
figured that out yet. Women never do."

"That's because women have to work three times as hard to
earn it," she responded angrily. "Our fathers don't conve-
niently leave us their businesses or connect us to their old-
boy networks. Male-dominated companies don't promote or
encourage us. We have to fight for every damned penny we
make. So don't give me that 'money is shit' line. It's only shit
to people who eat it for breakfast."

He flashed a row of white even teeth as he grinned. "That's
more like it. I knew you had brains, Miss Penny. Let's apply
them to getting out of here. We're off to visit a volcano. Hold
your nose."

He swung the jeep down another sharp turn, narrowly
missing a police car.

❧ EIGHT ❦

Ignoring the island police, Charlie gunned the putt-putting engine of the sissy jeep down the road to the island's biggest tourist attraction. Damn, but he couldn't believe the resort didn't have something with a little more oomph to it.

He pressed the gas harder. Raul's grandmother had said Raul had been hanging out with his second cousin Pedro lately. If he had to follow the convoluted vines of his friend's island relatives for information, it could take him years.

Shooting a sideways glance at his terrified companion, Charlie eased up on the gas. She clung to the jeep as if he meant to personally dump her on the side of the road. At least she'd ditched that bulky flowing thing she'd been wearing so he could have a view to admire. She was a little too slender for his tastes—those thin, long bones reminded him of a greyhound. He could get used to it though, if she'd let that long black hair down. It was like thick silk. He wanted to dig his fingers into it.

That was not a thought conducive to intelligent conversation. He had to keep her talking so she looked less like a kidnap victim and more like a wife. That's who he'd told the police she was. He'd also used her name instead of his. He'd vaguely recognized a couple of the older officers investigating Michel's murder, but the younger ones wouldn't know him from Adam. He prayed the older ones had forgotten him too. He didn't want word of his visit getting back to his mother.

He didn't want to think about his mother right now either. That was an old, dead argument, one he'd gone beyond. "Focus on Raul," he muttered as he swung the jeep into the parking lot. *Get Raul back, then go after that bastard, Jacobsen, and his liens.* The company couldn't run long without money. His employees had to get paid. There were plenty of topics to chew on without bringing in his mother.

The famous St. Lucia "drive-in" volcano didn't have many visitors this morning, thank goodness. Turning off the ignition, Charlie saluted the security guard drifting out to take his money. The place crawled with guards in uniforms, none of them looking particularly eager to do anything more than eye Penelope with appreciation. Charlie resisted the urge to cover up her skimpy T-shirt again.

The guy taking his money beamed as Charlie spoke to him in patois. Maybe he shouldn't do that. Knowing the language didn't fit with the image of tourist. Damn, but he wasn't any good at this spy business. He was a damned contractor, not a cop who knew how to protect himself.

Penelope still sat cross-armed in the jeep, sulking. He'd never known a woman who could look elegant as she sulked. He ought to leave her here and see how she liked it when the jeep crawled with beggars trading cheap gewgaws for anything they could lay their hands on. She'd end up half-naked and covered in malachite necklaces.

"Are you coming out or do I have to haul you?" he asked in his most polite tones, bending down to see beneath the wretched striped awning.

"I see no reason why I must accompany you on whatever nefarious business you're pursuing. I'll assume you're not here to admire the view." She glared straight ahead at the pitted gravel road and the gray blot on the landscape that was the outskirts of the volcano.

He might not want to believe she worked for Jacobsen, but he wasn't taking chances by leaving her alone. He opened the low-slung door. "We're tourists, remember? We're here to see the volcano. Come on. I've got to speak with one of the guides. You'll have something to talk about when you go home. This place is advertised as the world's only drive-in volcano, although I wouldn't advise driving over the part that bubbles."

"It bubbles?"

Ha! He'd finally caught her attention. Taking advantage, Charlie caught her elbow and helped her out. He couldn't get used to having a woman standing nearly shoulder to shoulder with him. There couldn't be too many men in this world who would appreciate her height as much as he did.

He didn't want to contemplate where that thought came from or where it led. Miss Penelope Albright was way out of his league. He wasn't much into the country club social scene, ballroom dancing, and monkey suits. Give him a wide-screen TV, a Dolphins game, and a beer. Miss Penny would die a thousand deaths before stepping inside his favorite bar. He'd suffocate in the rarefied atmosphere of her golf club.

"It's a live volcano," he reminded her as he guided her toward the steaming gray hell they called a tourist attraction in these parts.

"It could explode?" she asked warily, treading delicately through the ruts.

"Nah, probably not. It lets off enough steam on the surface so it doesn't build up." Keeping his eyes open for Pedro, Charlie steered her toward the safer edge of the bubbling, steaming morass.

"You said the beach was caused by a volcanic explosion," she reminded him.

Damn, when he wanted her to shut up, she wouldn't. Wasn't that just like a woman? Scanning the dark-skinned guides collecting tips from tourists, he wanted to ignore her, but remembering the part he played, he grudgingly answered. "The last time it exploded, this place was a mountain. The explosion took out the whole side. That's lava we traveled on getting in here."

Spotting Pedro, Charlie released Penelope's elbow. "Stay right here. Don't wander off. That stuff down there is treacherous. It's swallowed grown men."

He trotted off, leaving her near the only guardrail. In the States, the place would be a liability hazard so high they'd have the whole area cordoned off. Here, a person could walk right into the volcano if they were stupid enough.

"*Bõzhu,* Pedro!" Charlie shouted as he neared his goal. He was taking chances again, but Monica had told him Pedro and Raul had been barhopping together. He didn't know Raul's cousin well, but he had to start somewhere. If he'd known a private detective on the island, he would have hired one. He'd just have to move quickly and pray hard.

Pedro looked momentarily puzzled at a T-shirted tourist in a baseball cap yelling his name and a greeting in patois. Recognition briefly crossed the guide's face as Charlie doffed the cap and sunglasses. He instantly pokered up and glanced furtively over his shoulder in the direction of the forest.

"Don't you dare run," Charlie warned in a whisper as he approached. He reached for his wallet, remembered he'd given it to Penny, cursed, and pulled out the cash from his pocket. "Pretend I'm just asking you to be our guide. Walk with me back to my wife and pretend you're giving your usual spiel."

Pedro nodded nervously and fell in step with him. He shoved the bills into his pocket as he walked. "You should not be here," he whispered harshly. "It is dangerous."

"I'll be damned if I'll leave Raul out to dry. Where is he?"

"Don' know. He go into jungle and not come back."

"If that's all it is, then why do you say it's dangerous for me? Monica says Raul's been talking to you. You must know something."

They reached Penelope's side and Charlie offered brief introductions. Pedro gesticulated grandly at the gray bubbling cracks of mud beyond the guardrail. In a low voice, he continued their conversation. "Ask your papa," he said scornfully. "Ask the man. Better, just go and not come back. There are forces here you cannot control."

"Bullshit." Charlie strode along the railing, pretending to point out things of interest. He was aware of Penelope's inquiring glance, but she followed without a word. "The only forces are man-made ones. I want to know what man, when, and how."

"Ask your papa," Pedro repeated stubbornly.

"He's not my damned father!" Charlie bit his tongue and curbed his temper before speaking again. "I don't want to see the old goat. What's he got to do with anything? He never worked a day in his life and he's not about to start now."

Pedro shrugged. "If you say. Then go home. Forget Raul. Forget this island. Make beautiful babies and be happy."

Charlie ignored Penelope's unfeminine snort. "I won't forget Raul and I've got too much money tied up in this island to walk away. Give me something concrete, Pedro."

The guide gestured toward the edge of the volcano. "There is no concrete in Soufrière. We live on molten lava. Go, and don' come back."

Shoving his hands in his pockets, Pedro walked away, leaving them to stare at the steaming maw of boiling mud beneath them.

Penelope twitched her shoulders and stepped back first. "What was that bit about your father?"

Charlie didn't know whether to be exasperated or relieved that she had settled on this topic instead of the more deadly one. Pedro had just asserted their lives were in danger, and she asked about his damned father. Women!

"He's not my father," he repeated, catching her arm and steering her toward the car. Now what in hell would he do? Jacques was in hiding. Monica could tell him nothing. Pedro wouldn't. Michel was dead. Where did he go next?

"Okay, he's not your father. Who is he, then?" She trailed along obediently.

Charlie liked the way she fit beside him. Maybe they could

find some common ground back in the States. "You like football?"

She jerked her arm loose, halted, and glared at him. So much for that theory.

Not knowing where else to turn, Charlie ran his hand through his hair and stared down at her. Sort of down. Her nose wasn't much below his and it was pointed so far upward right now they could play Eskimo. He briefly contemplated the wide mouth below her uppity nose, wondered how those moist lips would feel against his, but heroically, he resisted that too. He couldn't let his thoughts stray at a time like this. "I just asked. You don't have to look at me as if I'd insulted your honor."

"I *detest* football," she replied in a tone so cold it should have frosted the volcano.

"Yeah, I kinda figured. You and my mother ought to get along real fine. Come on. I'm not getting anywhere as a tourist. Let's see what happens if I play it straight." Without touching her, Charlie swung on his heel and marched toward the jeep.

Hell, if he found Raul alive, he'd murder him for putting him through this ordeal.

With no idea of where they were going or why, Penelope admired the scenery and tried to ignore the tense man in the driver's seat. He swore every time an approaching car forced him to slow and take the pulloffs on the narrow road. He definitely hadn't developed the islanders' laid-back "don't worry, be happy" attitude.

She frowned as a foreign sports car didn't yield the right-of-way but forced them off the road where there was no pulloff. The man behind the wheel looked as angry as Charlie. She caught only a glimpse, but she thought it was the contractor she'd seen in the airport. PC&M clients tended to be overbearing power-trippers. The man's glare as he passed surprised her. Had he recognized her? Surely not. She was much too low on the totem pole to deal with the firm's big clients. Maybe she'd imagined it. Charlie was too busy trying to keep the jeep out of the mud to notice.

To Penelope's surprise, Charlie jerked the jeep down a private drive equipped with a seven-foot wrought-iron gate laboriously painted white and tipped with gold. Surely it wasn't gold leaf. Nobody outside Versailles used real gold leaf anymore. She couldn't read the significance of the scrolled insignia as Charlie drove through. Maybe this was some historic landmark. She vaguely remembered reading that Josephine Bonaparte had been born or grew up on this island. Maybe this was her estate.

The drive curved through a landscaped forest of every tropical tree known to mankind. A waterfall splashed merrily into a flowing stream lined with exotic flowers. Shrubbery spilled red and gold blossoms across their path. Ingeniously tended vines crept up trees and over arches, blending water with grass and pavement and trees, painting a landscape of elaborate lushness. Penelope wanted to tell Charlie to halt the car and let her breathe it all in.

The grim clenching of his unshaven jaw warned her to keep her mouth shut.

She swallowed the words on the tip of her tongue as a mansion rose above the shrubbery around the curve ahead.

Her family dated back to the founding of Savannah. Her grandparents had migrated to Charlotte and owned cotton mills and acreage when Charlotte was little more than a hole in the road. The enormous house she'd grown up in had increased in value until it was worth more than everything her father had ever earned in his life. She'd grown up in and around the Charlotte version of historic mansions. She'd seen nothing like this one.

Trying not to gape as Charlie insouciantly parked the candy-striped jeep in front of the main stairs, Penelope climbed out with all the grace she could muster under the circumstances. She could swear the steps were marble. Maybe this *was* Josephine's estate. If so, where were the tourist parking lots and the guides collecting tickets?

The door swung open before they could knock. A tall black man in white uniform stared down his nose at them as they approached. Maybe it was a fancy French hotel. Had to be French. She'd never seen such a rude servant in her life except at a French restaurant she'd visited in New Orleans.

"Alphonso, we have bags in the car." Charlie gestured toward the backpack and carry-on they'd hastily packed that morning. "Bring us a couple of Bloody Marys and tell Mother we're in the solarium."

Without an ounce of awe or graciousness, Charlie dug his fingers into Penelope's upper arm, and towed her in the direction of a glass-enclosed area off what had to be a banquet room on their right. Penelope barely glimpsed an enormous antique crystal chandelier and an acre of gleaming mahogany before he jerked her into the sunroom.

"Mother?" she whispered harshly as Charlie dropped her arm and stood, hands in pockets, glaring out the tinted window at the vast expanse of tropical landscape. At least he'd changed out of his muscle shirt, but the Dolphins T-shirt wasn't much better. Out of spite, she reached up and pulled off his baseball cap. Thick chestnut hair tumbled loose over his forehead, and he brushed it off his face without a backward glance. The heavy stubble of his beard made him look downright dangerous.

He glanced at one of the delicate chairs gracing the walls, shrugged, and began pacing in the center of the room. "Yeah," he grunted. "Don't make anything of it."

Mother. His *mother* lived here. This beer-drinking, muscle-bound, grunting bear of a man had lived *here*, in a mansion grander than any king's.

My God. Penelope sank into the flowered cushions of an antique wrought-iron couch. She'd grown up shopping in antique stores. She knew the costliness of that marble-topped table. That gilded lamp. One didn't buy things like these. One inherited them. Charlie with his football-player physique towered over the delicate pieces as awkwardly as an elephant in a flower garden. She wondered how many of the priceless treasures he'd broken as a child, and could almost feel sorry for him.

She hadn't had sufficient time to swallow the enormity of this discovery before she heard hurried feet tapping in the room beyond. The gait was odd, as if a third foot dragged between each normal tap.

"Charlie!" a high, sweet voice called excitedly.

Utterly unnerved already, Penelope turned to catch a glimpse of a mother who could sound so young and eager to a son so gruff and cold. Instead, she saw a girl years younger than herself. Shocked, not quite understanding the relationship here, she didn't immediately notice the cane hidden by the flowing Laura Ashley dress. Not until Charlie hurried forward and caught the girl as she stumbled on a narrow step into the solarium did Penelope realize the dragging noise she'd heard was the new arrival's left foot. Disease had distorted her leg and left her limping.

"Tammy!" Smiling at last, Charlie swept the girl off the floor and swung her around. "I thought you'd be off to university by now. Good God, you've grown into a gorgeous female."

Instead of beaming in approval at this praise, she pounded Charlie across his broad back with her cane. "You ingrate! You beast! You never write. You never call. I should hate you! Where have you been all this time? Put me down, you great lummox."

Penelope considered cheering and clapping, but not knowing the score in advance, she politely refrained and watched with interest.

Charlie tenderly deposited his slight burden on the tile floor and grinned. "You greet me like that and ask why I don't call? Give me one good reason why I should."

To his obvious surprise, Tammy burst into tears. "You know why, you awful man."

Biting her lip, wondering if she should disappear into the woodwork, Penelope eyed Charlie. He seemed sincerely at a loss. He wasn't precisely a smooth-talking charmer who would whisper sweet words in a child's ear and depart. Taking pity on him, she rose from the couch and crossed the room.

"I don't think he's any more awful than most men," she said thoughtfully, standing between the pair. "They're all insensitive louts."

The girl's head jerked up, and wide, tear-moistened blue eyes stared. With a jolt, Penelope saw the resemblance between the girl and the man beside her. Swinging her gaze from one to the other, she looked into identical blue eyes framed by inquiring thick brows. Surely he couldn't be old enough to be the girl's father. "Introductions, please?" she asked frostily.

"After that, you want me to introduce you?" With a frown that wrinkled his whole forehead, Charlie looked both disapproving and wary at the same time.

"All right, don't." Swinging around, Penelope held out her hand. "I'm Penelope Albright, kidnap victim. How do you do?"

The girl brightened immediately. She held out a delicately boned hand. "I'm Tammy St. Philippe, sister of the Abominable Beast. Did Charlie really rescue you from kidnappers?"

Throwing a triumphant look over her shoulder, Penelope smiled. "No, he's the kidnapper. I'm counting on someone rational to save me."

The tears cleared immediately and Tammy beamed. "How romantic! Charlie's in love at last. I'm so happy for you."

Penelope's flush and Charlie's embarrassed protests ended the instant a regal voice echoed down the hall.

"Tamara Louise, don't you dare speak to that horrible boy until I get my hands on him!"

Charlie answered Penelope's questioning glance with a shrug. "My mother."

❧ NINE ❦

"Charles, don't you dare sit in that chair. It's Louis Quatorze."

Wearing gauzy floral silk, Vivian swept in, waving her ringed fingers in Charlie's direction as he touched one of her gilded chairs. He jerked his hand away.

"Where *have* you been and who is this with you?"

He'd known better than to come here. Gratefully accepting the drinks the butler produced, Charlie made the introductions. Penelope looked more stunned than impressed. Someday he would ponder on whether he'd truly picked her out because he liked her looks or to outsnob his mother.

Vivian had always possessed social aspirations higher than her financial status. Now that she'd achieved both, she wielded them ruthlessly.

"Tamara, show Miss Albright to the gold guest room. Charles, you may have your old room." She gestured with a long-boned hand toward the door. "You'll wish to freshen up before dinner, Miss Albright. We have our main meal of the day at two." Apparently considering her guest dismissed, she turned her artfully tinted blond coiffure toward her son. "Charles, you will remain and explain your prolonged absence."

"I'm not planning on remaining anywhere, Mother. I just needed to talk with Emile for a minute. Penelope." He waited until she'd turned inquiringly. "We'll stay for dinner and return to the hotel," he lied. They sure as hell couldn't return to the hotel anytime soon. "Don't make yourself too comfortable."

He couldn't read Penny's expression. She had entirely too much in common with his mother. She possessed the same commanding presence and elegant beauty, although his mother's imperious manners had been hard earned at a late date, while Penelope had been born to them.

Penelope nodded with all the graciousness of a Southern woman of her class. And he knew class when he saw it. Penelope screamed of it, from her long white fingertips with their expensive French manicure to her delicately arched feet shod in Italian espadrilles. No Nikes for Penelope, no sirree. She fit right in here as he never would, not that he wanted to. High society gave him a world-class pain in the ass.

She wore tortoiseshell sunglasses that hid any curiosity she might have expressed. Was that concern he saw? He was grasping at straws. When he didn't say anything else, she turned and followed in his half sister's limping path. Charlie tore his hungry gaze away from the gentle sway of Penelope's khaki-clad hips.

"Well?" his mother asked imperiously. "I deserve some explanation of your behavior."

"I've been busy." He really didn't need this now. He shouldn't have come here. There was a damned good reason he'd left this ice palace and never returned.

But he needed help finding Raul, and his stepfather was one of the most powerful men on the island.

"You've been busy." The sarcasm in his mother's voice was unmistakable. "For ten years you've been too busy to visit your mother."

"I sent cards," he said defensively. "It's a long trip down here. I've been building a business. I wouldn't have come here now if I'd known I had to listen to a lecture."

"A lecture?" She raised her carefully groomed eyebrows.

"I ask what you've been doing and that's a lecture? Should I say nothing? You would prefer I smile politely at your latest floozy, pat my hair, and let you go off again without a word?"

"She's not a floozy." Desperately, Charlie shoved his hands into his pockets and stalked up and down the sunroom, not an easy task for a man his size in a room cluttered with fragile antiques. He felt like Gulliver in Lilliput, always had in this place. "She's an extremely intelligent businesswoman who graciously agreed to accompany me here."

His mother sniffed. "Then she's definitely a step above your usual type. I assume your father's influence hasn't affected you as much as I feared."

"Ma, don't get into that now. He's dead. Let him rest." She stiffened at his use of the word *ma*, but he gave her credit for holding her tongue for a change. They were sniffing around each other like two bull terriers seeking boundaries. He'd staked his territory long ago, but his mother had never recognized it.

"You're looking well," she said blandly.

Charlie shot her an impatient look. "Cut the crap. I sent you cards. I don't get out of Miami much. You're the one who chose to live out here in the middle of nowhere. Don't complain if I can't come visit on any regular basis."

"You're the one who chose to work with your father's redneck construction crew instead of staying and enjoying the kind of life Emile can offer. You could be building hotels in Castries right now if that was what you wanted."

"I'm building hotels in Miami, hospitals in Ft. Lauderdale, and a resort in Orlando, so don't sneer down your nose at my father's company. We built it ourselves, without any help from Emile or his handouts." Damn, but he hadn't wanted to get into this old argument. Whoever had said you couldn't come home again knew what he was talking about. He was a grown man with mature business relationships, but his mother reduced him to an awkward adolescent within minutes.

As if realizing the path they followed would degenerate quickly, his mother pulled back on the reins. "I'm happy to hear you're doing well. Perhaps you could tell us a little more over dinner. Why don't you freshen up and join us for cocktails?"

Charlie swirled the remains of his Bloody Mary. "I'm not much into fancy drinks, but thanks anyway. I'll go check on Penelope."

He strode out with his brain buzzing dangerously from just the one drink. He needed to keep his head on his shoulders to deal with Emile. He'd never liked the man. He was willing to admit that his mother's marriage to Emile immediately after her divorce—even though his parents had been separated for over a year—had warped his opinions, but age hadn't improved the relationship. Emile had wealth, a jet-setting sophistication, and an aristocratic heritage that Charlie's father had never possessed and never desired. Charlie had never understood his mother's craving for the artificial life Emile offered. Surely she knew by now that her second husband was a womanizer. Charlie had never told her that was the reason he'd left in the first place—when he'd discovered Emile's little love nest in Vieux Fort—but she must have guessed.

He didn't want to get into any of it now. They were all consenting adults, living their own lives to the best of their abilities. He just wanted to find Raul and get the hell out of here.

He knocked on the door of the gold guest room. Leave it to his hypocritical mother to place Penelope in the room next to Tammy's instead of next to his. If he were really sleeping with Miss Penny, the minor nuisance of bed location would scarcely stop him.

She opened the door cautiously and gazed at him without expression. Charlie nearly had lung spasms looking into those dark eyes. Even the long sooty lashes couldn't conceal the interest with which she studied him. The sun had tinted her cheeks a delicate rose against the cool white of her complexion, and Charlie had the daunting desire to kiss the pale freckles dotting her nose. His other desires weren't quite so innocent, and he stepped back, out of the intoxicating cloud of her scent.

"I'm just checking to see if everything's all right. I apologize for my mother's lack of hospitality. I make her angry."

"I can see that." Her voice was somehow cool and soft at the same time, gentle as a stroke across his brow.

How the hell did she do that? Feeling like the awkward teenager he once had been, Charlie plunged on. "Let me clean up and I'll come back and get you. I'm sorry I didn't prepare you for this charade. Don't worry about what you're wearing. We won't be here long enough for it to matter."

"I brought a change of clothes. I'll be fine. It's better than a jungle."

He thought he detected amusement this time. He hadn't thought his prim accountant knew the meaning of amusement. He gave her a sharp look, but not even the hint of a smile lingered on her wide lips. She never wore lipstick, didn't need it, but he would wager she carried it somewhere. She was too much like his mother, and his mother wouldn't be caught dead without it.

His mother had redecorated his old room in some kind of flowered cotton material in purple and pink. Shuddering at the ruffled pillow shams on the poster bed, he flung down his backpack, pulled out a clean shirt, and headed for the shower. Women! Why couldn't they leave perfectly respectable rooms alone? What was the compulsion to feather their nests with every conceivable twig and string within reach?

Catching his thoughts wandering to what Penelope might keep in her apartment, Charlie scowled, scrubbed, and after toweling dry, hastily shaved and ran a comb through his hair. He checked the mirror again and decided his hair needed a trim. He supposed he'd hear about that before dinner was through. His mother needed to get a life now that her children were grown.

Worried about Tammy's presence here when she should have been at school somewhere, he threw everything back in his bag, checked the mirror again, and headed for Penelope's room. He had packed only wrinkle-free shirts, but his mother had always hated knits, and he figured Penelope would disapprove too.

Penelope opened the door wearing a jade green sheath that stopped just above her knees. Charlie thought even this shapeless garment would be an improvement over her usual masculine attire, if she hadn't covered it up with a flowing sheer thing longer than the dress. Where in hell she got all these weird cover-ups was beyond him, but this one appeared to match the dress. She looked as if she were prepared for dinner with the president. *This* was what she'd packed for an overnight stay in the jungle?

Every single sentence he thought to utter was inappropriate. She still wasn't wearing her damned hair down, although it would have looked dramatic against the gauzy green. Damn, but he couldn't believe he was criticizing a woman's dress. Usually, he was more interested in undressing them. Maybe that was the problem: He couldn't undress this one.

"How the hell did you get all that in that little bag?" he finally demanded.

"It rolls up in a ball like a swimsuit." She shrugged and stepped out of the room, brushing past him when he didn't move out of her way.

"It rolls up in a ball. . . . Hell, it's some kind of knit?" he asked incredulously, falling into step with her.

"Probably. I don't know. I travel a lot and I buy things that don't need ironing."

He could scarcely believe his ears. A woman who didn't know what kind of clothes she was wearing. Amazing. Now that he looked, she wasn't wearing any dangly ornaments in her ears or baubles around her neck either. No fuss, no muss. Maybe he should have hung out with rich, beautiful women more often. They didn't need ornamentation.

Nah, that wasn't it. He'd dated beautiful women before.

Most of them spent half their lives in front of mirrors. They put lipstick on before bed. Charlie risked a hasty glance at Penelope's mouth. She was wearing something glossy, but it was scarcely noticeable. She'd powdered her nose and covered the freckles though.

Raul. Get his mind back to Raul. This idiotic fascination with a woman who thought him lower than toadstools had to be some kind of denial technique. Raul could be dead. He didn't want to believe it—so he looked for lipstick on a woman's mouth.

Charlie steered Penelope to the sitting room next to the family dining room. The house had more damned places to eat and stand and sit than he could count. But there weren't enough to avoid his family.

Emile waited there alone. Tall, dignified, with silver-gray hair Charlie figured a stylist tinted and cut, his stepfather looked as if he'd just stepped out of some expensive men's fashion magazine from a plate labeled "distinguished statesman." The red ascot was the only deviation from the norm. Emile had always affected an ascot. Considering he spent most of his time in a tropical country where air-conditioning was sparse, Charlie figured his stepfather had ice in his veins.

"It's been a long time, Charles." Emile nodded graciously in Charlie's direction, then immediately turned all his masculine attention to Penelope.

As Emile appraised Penelope, Charlie fought the primitive urge to shove his stepfather's eyes back in their sockets. Instead, he draped his arm possessively over Penelope's shoulders.

"Penelope, my stepfather, Emile St. Philippe." To Charlie's relief, he heard Tamara's cane tapping down the hallway. Deliberately ignoring the startled look in Penelope's eyes, Charlie pushed her in his sister's direction. "I need a word with Emile. Why don't you ask Tamara to show you her seashell collection."

Her spine stiffened, and he could almost hear the protests grinding through that transparent mind of hers. Then she gave him a swift look, softened, and with a wicked gleam, patted his cheek.

"I do so love seashells, darling. You just go have your old boring man talk. Tamara and I will have a lovely time without you."

Spiked, tackled, and brought low, Charlie grinned in appreciation of her sarcasm. Unable to resist the final play, he patted her on the rear as she passed by.

Unseen from Emile's direction, she shot him a glare that should have pierced and wounded, and warned of retaliation in the immediate future. Lord, but he loved a good fight. His blood was pumping in anticipation already. As Penelope reached Tammy and led her from the room, Charlie turned his attention back to his stepfather.

"Lovely woman. Do you know her family?" Emile was still following Penelope's path as she glided out the door. He swirled his martini as he watched.

Charlie had considered punching Emile out the day he'd discovered his stepfather's love nest. Out of respect for his mother, he'd resisted. But so help him God, if the man laid a single finger on Penelope, any semblance of respect flew out the window. He'd bury the creep.

"No one you would know, I'm certain," he responded coldly. "And that's not why I'm here. How much do you know about the new construction in Soufrière?"

With the women out of sight, Emile reluctantly returned his attention to his stepson. "That piece of swamp on the south side? I thought the project abandoned."

The man would have to live with his head in the sand not to know more than that. The island was a tiny place. Everyone knew everything that went on, without need of a daily newspaper. Every detail of the construction project would have been hashed and rehashed by the local grapevine. The pro–rain forest, antidevelopment people had staged protests for months. The local government had fought over who would handle the water/sewer arrangements. Townspeople had demanded low-cost housing. Real estate people had demanded modern construction suitable for sale to rich tourists. Everyone had an opinion.

"Emile, I am no longer twelve years old. You don't own this property without income to maintain it. I made it a point to know the basis of that income. You may never have worked a day in your life, but you own large percentages of every major construction firm on this island. You damned well know what's going on in your own backyard."

Emile shrugged the shoulders of his elegant silk coat and sipped from his martini before responding. "I invest my money where it receives the best return. My financial advisers handle that sort of thing. Should you have need of advice, I'd be happy to give you their names. They're quite good. Beyond that, I know nothing more than there's a mud hole where there used to be forest."

Why the hell had he thought he could talk to the man? Just because he could talk to Miami bankers, international acquisition managers, temperamental architects, and rough construction crews didn't mean he could talk to Emile. But he knew instinctively that no man pretended ignorance without reason.

"You remember Raul Joseph, don't you? We used to play soccer together in high school."

Emile wrinkled his smooth brow in thought. "One of those natives you insisted on befriending? I don't know why you wouldn't attend the private school I arranged for you. You would have made much more valuable acquaintances."

Hell, this was going nowhere. Here less than an hour and he was already regressing into the same arguments they'd had when he was thirteen. He knew better than to come here. Where the hell would he turn now? He'd counted on Jacques putting him in touch with the right people. He hadn't counted on Jacques being married and protecting his family by disappearing.

Shit. Charlie glared in frustration at his imperturbable stepfather. "This isn't productive. I'm looking for an old friend. If I don't find him, I'm likely to get extremely angry.

I'm not a pimply teenage boy any longer. I have money, influence, and a means of wielding both. If you want to duke it out over power tables, so be it. It would be a damned sight easier if you'd just tell me what you know."

Looking thoughtful, Emile drifted toward the wet bar. "You still haven't learned finesse, have you? I could have taught you that, but you insisted on breaking your mother's heart by returning to your father and the trailer park you grew up in. There really isn't much we have to say to each other after all these years, is there?"

"For my mother's sake, I'd hoped so. If you loved her at all, you would make some effort to cooperate, but you never loved her, did you? Why the hell did you marry her in the first place? She scarcely came from one of the 'best' families."

Tamara chose that moment to return to the room, with Penelope in tow. His lovely half sister lit the room with her golden smile. Slender, blithe, as sweet as she was beautiful, Tamara had always been the dove of peace in this nest of wolves. She had his mother's startling blue eyes but her father's silken blond hair.

In that instant, Charlie answered his own question. In her greed and ambition for the good life, his mother had spent every penny his father had paid her in support and used her position as interior decorator to the wealthy to work her way into what passed for Miami society. She must have used the oldest trick in the book to nail Emile's hide to the wall. He could remember Tamara being born within a year of his mother's remarriage. Less than a year. As an eleven-year-old, he'd been more disgruntled by the nuisance of the infant than interested in counting months. He didn't need to count them now. Emile had married his mother because she was pregnant. And he'd probably been furious that she hadn't borne him a son. Tamara's deformed leg must have quadrupled his fury.

Charlie couldn't believe he hadn't seen it earlier. Damn, but teenagers were blind, selfish idiots.

Fighting other nasty thoughts, Charlie turned and took

both beautiful women on his arms. "Ladies, a stroll on the terrace before dinner?"

He'd never get anything out of Emile. Charlie had learned his blue-collar attitude from his formative years, and he'd never adopted the proper respect for his so-called "betters." He'd never be the perfect son.

Maybe he should start looking for Emile's lovers. On an island this small, they shouldn't be difficult to find. The stories they could tell might be useful.

❧ TEN ❧

"Father looks angry," Tammy whispered to Charlie as they stepped into the garden. "What did you say to him?"

"How the h . . . How can you tell that?"

Tammy smiled at her brother's attempt at polite language. Charlie had always pretended to despise her in front of his friends when he was a kid, but he'd always stood up for her. He'd pounded one of his schoolmates into the ground the day he'd found the creep making fun of her leg. She'd always thought of her half brother as a hero, even when he'd been hiding from her so he wouldn't have to take her into town with him. She prayed her childish beliefs weren't too far wrong. She needed a hero right now.

"The muscle beside his eye twitches when he's angry. I always get out of his way when that happens. What did you say to him?" Tammy liked Penelope, but she wished the other woman would disappear so she could talk to Charlie alone.

"We just don't get along," Charlie said dismissively. "Now tell me why you aren't in school. I thought you always wanted to be a nurse."

A nurse—like her father would allow that. She'd outgrown childish daydreams years ago. "They think I'm too delicate," she answered defensively. "I'm perfectly capable of taking care of myself. That's why you've got to help me."

She was afraid she sounded desperate. If she'd learned

nothing else about men, it was that they retreated quickly around anyone who sounded desperate. She tried smiling reassuringly, but she thought her mouth might have wavered a little. Charlie was staring at her as if she'd grown three heads.

"Don't look at me like that, Charlie. I'm twenty years old, old enough to be on my own. Do you want me to marry one of those insufferable jerks Father brings home for my inspection? Can you imagine how much money he must be offering to make them even consider someone like me?"

"What a lovely waterfall!" Penelope exclaimed from Charlie's other side. "I'll just wander over and look at it while you and your sister catch up on old times."

Tammy knew she liked Penelope for a reason. She beamed approvingly at this suggestion.

Charlie grabbed Penelope's arm and held on tight. "No, you don't. You're damned well staying here and translating for me. I don't talk womanspeak so well. Is she saying what I think she's saying?"

Tammy wanted to punch the lout. Why in the world had she thought the fatheaded jerk would understand? He never had. He'd just bullied people who made her cry, and in her silly hero worship, she'd thought that meant he understood her pain. He didn't. He just reacted like any outraged male.

"Tamara, let me apologize for your brother," Penelope said stiffly, halting their progress around the terrace. "I've known him only a couple of days, so if there's any hint of sensitivity in his nature, I haven't had time to discover it. I don't want to intrude on a family quarrel, but I'd be happy to help if you need someone to talk to."

Tammy fought the tears burning her eyes. She was a weakling. She'd always known that. She cried over TV shows, for heaven's sake. And now she was crying because Charlie hadn't found a true love at last. Stupid of her to think he had. He'd certainly never had any example to follow. Or maybe she was crying in frustration. It didn't matter. She could see through the patio doors that her mother had finally arrived. It was time for dinner. And then Charlie would run as fast as his feet could carry him.

"Thank you, Penelope. I appreciate the offer. If you could persuade Charlie to linger longer than dinner, I might take you up on that. Otherwise, I'm sorry you won't be my new sister-in-law. I didn't know Charlie had really resorted to kidnapping these days."

Releasing Charlie's arm, Tammy carefully walked toward the house, trying not to drag her leg too badly. She wasn't too tired, so she thought she carried it off pretty well.

Behind her, she could hear Charlie and Penelope arguing. She almost smiled. At least Charlie had found a woman who would stand up to him. She could remember the airheads he used to bring home. They'd practically licked his feet. The relationship would probably never last, but she'd like to admire it for the time being. Maybe she could learn a thing or two about standing up for herself.

The conversation over dinner was inevitably stilted. Tammy wished she could tune out the pain of it. Her mother tried desperately to persuade Charlie to stay, stooping as low as outright bribery. Charlie ignored her. He had his mind focused on Raul's construction project in the village. Tammy didn't understand his digs at Emile, but they were getting under her father's skin. Emile always appeared implacably cool, but she knew her father too well. He had a terrible temper, a cold one that simmered until he wreaked revenge on whoever had thwarted him. Charlie was playing with fire.

She wasn't entirely certain of Penelope's part in this drama. She admired the way Charlie's friend held herself aloof, politely speaking when spoken to, displaying the manners that reflected her upbringing, but Tammy sensed an undercurrent there that she couldn't tap. Being left on the outside of activities all her life, she'd learned to be observant. Penelope hid anger beneath her pleasant demeanor, but Tammy didn't think it was a destructive anger.

A boom in the distance rattled the dinnerware. Charlie started out of his seat, but Emile merely waved his fork in dismissal. "They're repairing that rock slide on the highway. It's nothing."

Tammy wondered why Charlie didn't look as if he believed him, but she had more important worries on her mind. She appreciated Penelope's attempts to make peace between Charlie and their mother. Penelope knew how to handle polite conversation in ways that Charlie in his male contrariness did not. Eventually, even Charlie fell victim to her soft insistence on diverting the topic to more neutral grounds.

"I'm not an engineer, but I think studies have been done proving the heat of the volcano could provide sufficient energy for this half of the island," Charlie responded to Penelope's questioning. "But you've got to understand the island mentality. The water company alone employs more people than they can use. If they didn't hire these people politicians push down their throats, management would lose their jobs. Only, with all the people on the payroll, they don't have money to buy equipment to keep them productive. If you think politics are bad in Miami, you ought to hang around here for a while."

"It's not just the politicians at fault," Tammy reminded him gently. "There are power brokers behind them who pull the strings. But unlike the States, there is less money and less distance between the puppets and the puppeteers, so the results are more noticeable." Tammy basked in Charlie's startled but approving look at her comment. At least somebody around here noticed she was not only an adult, but one with brains.

"You have no idea what you're talking about, Tamara," Emile intruded gruffly. "You would do better to concentrate on where you and your mother would like to go shopping next week. Paris? New York? Or is that too cold?"

Tammy thought Penelope's jaw would drop to her chest at this response. Heartened by the possibility that the attitude in the States might actually be as enlightened as she hoped, she smiled at her father. "Miami, Papa, I would like to shop in Miami."

"Nonsense. Italy is warm this time of year. What do you think, dear? Rome for the spring fashions?"

Emile addressed the inquiry to his wife, but Tammy saw the smoldering fury in the look he sent Charlie. She hadn't intended to target Charlie with her request. She'd just been following the path she'd tentatively constructed to freedom. She threw Charlie a helpless look of apology, but he appeared oblivious to the nuances of the conversation.

"You ought to let her visit me in Miami. They have some nice shops, and I can show her around. Or Mom could. She knows the place as well as I do, although it's changed some since she was there."

Bless Charlie's blind little heart. He was offering everything she wanted to hear, and everything her father wouldn't allow. Tammy didn't understand the whole of it, but she understood her father's need to control. Her mother had given up trying to return to her old home years ago. Emile wouldn't consider it.

Desperately, Tammy tried to think of some way to divert the inevitable explosion to follow, but she hungered for Charlie's offer too much to think clearly. She stuttered, and Penelope stepped into the gap for her.

"I'd love to show you the newest places," she offered quietly. "And my sister would love to meet you. We're twins, but she's always been a homebody. One would think that sharing identical genes and environment, we would think alike, but nothing could be further from the truth."

Wow! That was a great diversion. It had even thrown Charlie for a loop. Tammy bit back her laughter as he looked at Penelope with astonishment and maybe even a little admiration. She'd love to throw these two together, but she still had her own plans in mind, dangerous ones.

Tammy still couldn't believe Charlie was actually here. It was like manna from heaven. Raul had told her that Charlie was behind the development, but she hadn't believed he'd ever return to the island. She'd been counting on Raul to help her out, but Charlie was better yet. Charlie could fight Emile on more even ground than Raul could, should it come to that.

"We're taking the yacht into Castries for drinks with a few friends later this evening," her mother announced as the last dessert plate was cleared. "We'd be delighted to have you accompany us. Have you seen much of Castries, Penelope?"

"No, and I would love to some other time. I'm afraid I have a job here, however, and I really need to get back to work in the morning."

Tammy thought Penelope might skewer Charlie with the pointedness of her look, but Charlie deliberately ignored her. She would kick her brother under the table but she needed his help too much to antagonize him. Rising, she deflected the conversation to her own purposes.

"I have some supplies I want to take down to the church. It would be lovely if you could take me, Charlie. I hate bothering Alphonso."

"Alphonso will take you," Emile declared, also rising. "Charles has already made it clear he has business elsewhere." He directed his next shot at Charlie. "I suggest you return to Miami, where you know what's good for you and what's not. You're out of your league here."

He strode off without looking back.

"We really must be going, Mom. Maybe I'll have time to look in on you before I leave again." Charlie hugged his mother and kissed her cheek.

Tammy hadn't realized how much her mother had shrunk over the years. She'd always thought of Vivian St. Philippe as an elegant, statuesque beauty who drifted through society with ease. She could see now that she was merely a woman torn by her family and battered by circumstance, no matter how comfortable her surroundings. Unfortunately, she didn't have time to pity her mother. She had her own life to live now, and she wasn't letting this opportunity escape.

"If you'll send Alphonso for their bags, Mother," Tammy said lightly, hoping no one could see the river of desperation coursing through her, "I'll walk Penelope and Charlie to their car. Have you seen their jeep? It's the quaintest little thing, just like a little toy. I saw it from my window. Maybe Papa could get one like it for me. I'd love to have my own car."

That would raise enough arguments to divert any suspicion. She could drive with her left foot. She didn't need the right. But her parents wouldn't hear of it. Hiding impatience, she smiled through her mother's weak protest, caught Charlie's arm, and tugged him toward the terrace.

"All right, baby sister," Charlie hissed as they reached the corner of the house, out of hearing of anyone but Penelope. "What the *hell* is going on here?"

"I'm practically a *prisoner*," she bleated, hating the sound of her own voice but unable to control it now that freedom could be minutes away. "They're smothering me. They won't let me go off to school, they won't let me drive, they won't let me go anywhere without them or one of the servants. I can't stand it anymore. How am I going to have my own life if my mother's tied to me by an umbilical cord?"

"And what do you want me to do about it?" Charlie asked incredulously. "Penny was only kidding about the kidnapping. I'm not any good at underhandedness."

Penelope snorted beside him but held her tongue.

"Take me with you. Put me on a plane out of here. I don't even have my own money. I've tried *everything*, but it's hopeless. You're my only chance. Raul promised to help, but he's disappeared. I don't know what else to do."

Charlie instantly stiffened. Glancing behind them, he pulled her farther into the shrubbery, where spying eyes couldn't see them. Tammy noticed Penelope lingered near a dangling orchid, within hearing distance but guarding their privacy from anyone walking down the path.

"Have you seen Raul?" Charlie demanded. "I'm looking for him."

Tammy bit her quivering lip. She hadn't wanted to face all the possible causes of Raul's disappearance. She'd thought he'd just grown tired of her. He was a man of the world, closer to her brother's age than her own. She didn't have much to offer. But she couldn't ignore the possibilities. . . .

Fighting tears, she turned her face up to Charlie. "I thought he'd gone back to Miami. I love him, Charlie. You've got to help me find him. You don't think Papa would hurt him, do you?"

She didn't want to believe her father would hurt anyone, but she was afraid he'd kill Raul if he knew what they'd done. Raul couldn't exactly be classified as wealthy, aristocratic, or from the best of families. He wasn't even entirely white.

The cold shock on Charlie's face verified her worst fears.

❧ ELEVEN ❧

"Damn, but I'll kill the bastard. You're nothing but a baby. He had no right. . . ."

Penelope wrapped her fingers around Charlie's thick biceps and squeezed, hard. She didn't figure she'd caused any pain, but she surprised him enough to shut him up. "Twenty is not a baby. Shut up, Charlie, before you make things worse."

She swung a sympathetic gaze toward Tammy. "Look, I have some idea of what you're going through, but you'll have to put your own needs aside for a while. Raul is missing. That's the main concern here. Help Charlie find him. Then we can move on to the next step."

Tears clung to Tammy's eyelashes, and her bottom lip quivered. She looked prepared for a physical blow, but at Penelope's words, she straightened her shoulders and nodded. She gave Charlie a tentative glance, but her voice was steady. "Raul has a hut at the back of those acres his cousin used to farm. It's in the forest and kind of covered with vines. It's not much, but people left him alone there. He was hassled constantly when he stayed on the site."

"The tree house!" Charlie exclaimed. "I can't believe he's built another tree house. The man has shit for brains."

He would have stalked toward the car right there and then, but Penelope dug her fingers in. She could tell Charlie didn't like being held back. It was about time someone taught him how it felt. "Your sister?" she reminded him.

Charlie shifted awkwardly from one foot to the other. He could scarcely look Tammy in the face. Penelope smothered a grin. Men were so damned transparent. "I assume the island doesn't offer a large choice of men?" she prompted him.

He regarded her warily but nodded. Tammy pouted and started to speak, but Penelope cut her off.

"I don't encourage running away, but perhaps some arrangement could be made? My sister and I have a guest room, if that will help."

Both Tammy and Charlie regarded her with matching suspicion and hope. Penelope felt like a harpooned porpoise, caught and inextricably trapped. "I really don't want to hurt your mother. Is she as helpless as she seems?"

Tammy jumped on that one. "Yes. She's argued and argued but Father won't let her go to Miami and won't listen when she stands up for me. Not that she stands up for me often," she finished sulkily.

"Look, Raul could be in some danger. I've got to find him before it gets dark. I haven't got time to plan your escape, Tammy, and I'm not certain I approve, in any event. Raul's too damned old for you."

Penelope could see the anger flaring in Charlie's eyes, but he knew nothing about vulnerable, lovesick young girls. She did. "That isn't the point right now. The point is whether we should help Tammy start a life of her own. Can you help put her through school if she goes to the States?"

She could almost see his relief at this sensible suggestion, one he could control with money and a minimal amount of emotional involvement.

"Yeah, I can swing it, if I can get back in time to save my business," he added ominously. "It's the wrong time of year for starting school though," he pointed out.

"Do you think Raul is in some danger?" Tammy asked, ignoring his objection.

Charlie shrugged, but Penelope knew the answer to that.

He wouldn't be tearing the island apart as he was if he didn't fear for Raul's life. His sister wasn't a fool either.

Eyes blazing, Tammy limped toward the drive. "Take me with you. If Father has hurt Raul in any way, I never want to see him again. I can help, Charlie. Let's go."

Charlie wavered. Penelope could see his confusion. She didn't think he was much used to dealing with family, and certainly not with his kid sister, one who wasn't a child anymore. He had too many problems on his mind to take on a new one. She gave him credit for not throwing a tantrum and refusing outright. He wanted to do what was best. He just didn't know what it was.

Neither did she, but Tamara was apparently taking the matter out of their hands. She had already disappeared around the corner of the house, in the direction of the jeep. "Let's go, Charlie," Penelope whispered. "She's a grown woman, whether you recognize it or not. She has every right to get in that car and go where she wants."

"But this is a hell of a way of doing it," he protested, striding hurriedly after Tammy.

"Then we'll send her back if she has a change of heart. This is an island, remember. She can't go far."

He nodded and took a deep breath. "All right. We'll take her into town, drop her off at a friend's. I can call my mother later and tell her Tammy's all right."

Penelope knew it wouldn't be quite that easy, but this wasn't her family. Now that Charlie wasn't undercover, he could drop her off at the resort and she could go back to work. Her conscience sighed with relief. The rest of her plummeted into some weird hole she could almost label disappointment. How had her life become so boring that she actually enjoyed being kidnapped by a lunkheaded ex–football player?

As they rounded the corner of the house, they encountered Vivian in white gloves and heels standing stalwartly beside Alphonso and a gleaming Mercedes. Shoulders drooping, spine curved in defeat, Tammy waited beside her mother. She didn't even glance up as Penelope and Charlie appeared.

"Bear with me," Charlie whispered, squeezing her arm. Striding confidently forward, he hugged his mother and checked the back of the jeep to make certain their luggage was loaded. Penelope lagged uncertainly behind. Tammy wouldn't meet her eyes.

"I'm taking Penny back to the resort. Got your bathing suit, kid? You can teach Penny to snorkel until I get back."

"Tamara cannot possibly—"

Charlie cut his mother short. "She's a grown woman, Mother. You can't baby-sit her forever. Penny and I will be there. What can happen? You know the resort. We'll dine on the terrace, listen to the band, and be back here before midnight. Nothing to it."

Vivian looked less certain. She glanced at her daughter, who had tear streaks down her face. "Well, but I think I should send Alphonso with her. And she's to come home before ten. Those roads are quite treacherous, and they're worse at night." She shot the candy-striped jeep a disapproving look. "And since I'm going into town anyway, she can travel with me. You're much better off taking a water taxi to the resort."

"Whatever you say, Ma," Charlie said, deliberately goading his mother. He chucked his sister under the chin. "If you're going in with Ma, I'm going to make a little side trip. We'll meet you at the dock around five, okay?"

Penelope heard the warning in his voice. So did Tammy. She looked up uncertainly, searched Charlie's face, then nodded.

"Good girl. Buy yourself some dancing shoes while you're in town. I'm in the mood to rumba."

Rumba. The man could rumba. Penelope stared at him in incredulity as he strode around the car and opened the door for her. She'd like to see this big football player of a man on the dance floor, moving to the music. Actually, she could. The image was totally devastating. Now that she was released from any thought of danger, her mind had taken flight.

After she climbed in the car, Charlie leaned under the

awning and grinned at her. "If we find Raul, we'll rumba all night. Remember your dance lessons, Miss Penny?"

He didn't give her time to answer. As the Mercedes rolled down the drive and out of sight, he jogged around the jeep and leapt into the seat, spewing restless energy from every pore.

"Let's get this show on the road. I should have known the bastard would hole up in the woods. He's probably watching for those damned disappearing parrots. We'll probably find Jacques there too."

Penelope didn't think that very likely, but it was no longer her concern. Cautiously, she reminded him, "Since you don't need me any longer, you could drop me off in town. I can take the water taxi back."

His jaw set stubbornly as he shifted into gear. "It's easier if I go up the mountain first. I want to see that hut in daylight." The jeep putt-putted slowly through the settling dust of the Mercedes. The other car was long out of sight. "Besides, we're still on our honeymoon, remember? Wouldn't you like to see what remains of the rain forest? We have some nearly extinct parrots flitting around in there. I can't promise you'll see them, but we can look."

Put that way, she could almost rationalize the side trip. She might never have another opportunity to see the island from the standpoint of a native. She could spend years flying in and out of airports, trapped in hotels, and never see the real countryside. Why not take this one chance to see something new and exotic?

She slid down in her seat and scowled as she realized she was actually trusting a man who had kidnapped her. Just because he had family problems like everyone else on the planet didn't make him any less dangerous.

"Why were we wasting time slinking around when you could have asked your family for help in the first place?" she demanded. "Didn't you intend to visit them?"

"Raul was more important." He glared at the road ahead and hit the gas. The jeep didn't noticeably accelerate. "Besides, you saw what they're like. Even if Emile knew anything, he wouldn't tell me. And if Raul has been fooling around with Tammy, then he was playing with fire for certain. I can't believe that jerk. I was about to make him *partner*, dammit. I *trusted* the man."

"Then if you trust him enough to make him a partner, why shouldn't Tammy trust him?" she asked, reasonably enough, she thought.

He cursed colorfully, hung on to the steering wheel as a tire hit a crater and the car bounced crazily, then he swung the vehicle up a narrow gravel road. The ensuing silence hung heavily between them. Finally, Charlie cut her a glare.

"His mother's the Caribbean equivalent of a *mestiza*, all right? And he doesn't know who his father is, although chances are real good the man was more white than Raul's mother. It's not exactly the American family, okay?"

"Yeah, right." Penelope crossed her arms and watched the road ahead. "You sound just like your stepfather."

"She's my baby *sister*! You think I want her to endure the kind of heartache a match like that can bring? Even if he were richer than Croesus, and lord knows, Raul's nowhere near that working for me, what do you think her life would be like back in Miami?"

"I think that's something she has to figure out for herself. It's none of your damned business. It's not as if you've taken any interest in her over—" Penelope screamed at the gaping maw opening ahead. "*Stop!* My God, Charlie—"

Cursing, Charlie slammed the brakes and swung the wheel violently toward the uphill side of the road. The tires squealed in protest, the jeep reeled out of control, then smashed to a rest against the trunk of a cocoa tree. In front of them, a washed-out section of the road crumbled down the hillside into the valley far below.

Stunned, Charlie reached over and brushed a tumbled lock of black hair off Penelope's pale cheek. He'd seen her jerk forward, but it had happened too fast. He couldn't see blood. "Penny, you okay?"

She blinked but continued staring at the missing road on his side of the vehicle. "We could have gone right down the side of the mountain."

He figured it was some kind of shock reaction. He was having a hard time taking it all in too. He just wanted to make certain she was all right before he thought about it. "Maybe we'd better get out of this thing. Can you open your door?"

Penelope pushed the handle of the passenger door, but the door hit solid ground, leaving only a narrow crack. "I can probably climb over," she whispered.

Charlie looked at the road on his side. Mere inches separated the jeep from the ravine that had once been road. They rested at a precarious angle on the edge of nothingness. "Maybe you'd better try that," he said carefully. He didn't think she was entirely aware of the danger of their position yet. He'd just have to pray the jeep didn't shift as she climbed out. She might make it. He didn't think he would.

He watched as she wrapped her fingers around the tree trunk outside the door and eased herself up and out. The way she moved, he thought she was probably bruised and more than a little shaken. He'd never meant to hurt her. He regretted everything he'd done since he'd first laid eyes on her. He acted without thinking too damned often. If they lived to get out of this, he'd see she got safely back to her job. He'd have everyone he knew send commendations to her damned stuffy employers. And he knew lots of people.

That didn't repair the damage already done, but it gave him impetus enough to want to survive. As Penelope swung her leg over the side, the jeep tilted dangerously. Charlie pushed her from the car and leapt over the seat after her.

She fell in a thicket of weeds as he wrapped his arms around the tree trunk. The gravel beneath the jeep slipped a little more, and rocks tumbled and bounced off trees and boulders far below. He was a little out of practice at acrobatics, but he swung over the door, clinging to the tree as the jeep began its gradual descent into the ravine. He continued clinging as the jeep slid out from under him.

"My God, Charlie!" Penelope screamed, finally wakening from her daze. "It's going to fall!"

"It's okay. I'm okay." Trying not to breathe too hard, he eased his feet to the ground and steadied himself against the tree. Not too hard. The tree could follow the jeep. Shakily, he pried his fingers loose from the bark and fell beside Penelope, a few yards from the crumbling roadway. "We're all in one piece," he reassured himself aloud.

The jeep caught on a jagged edge, teetered, then succumbed to gravity. Silently, they watched it slip into the crevasse, flip over, and tumble hood over trunk down the mountain. Presumably, it disappeared into the canopy of trees below. Charlie didn't have the incentive to stand up and look.

"I think I'll sit here for a little while," Penelope said thoughtfully from beside him.

She didn't sound like the woman he knew. He threw her a cautious glance. She still looked perilously pale. Even her lips had lost color. She sat rigidly in the weed patch, her fingers clenched around the purse in her lap. She still wore that clingy green stuff from dinner. The sheath had slipped well up her thighs and the gauzy jacket had a rip in it. Her sheer panty hose had torn into ladders wide enough to put her foot through. She didn't seem to be looking at anything but the brilliant blue sky on the far side of what remained of the road.

If he thought it would do any good, he would wrap her in his arms and comfort her, but she didn't look like the type who would willingly weep on his shoulder. He wasn't much used to comforting women anyway.

"I'd better check, make certain no one else went over the edge before us." He didn't know how he would do that either, but it seemed like the thing to do.

"Tamara!" she uttered, finally jolting from her stupor. "Did your mother come this way?"

Feeling a little better now that those dark eyes had regained a semblance of life, Charlie smoothed another tumbled lock from Penelope's cheek. He liked doing that. She'd lost several pins, and the heavy mass was in danger of tilting as precariously as the jeep. For whatever inane reason, her dishevelment seemed to ease their differences. "No, they took the main road down. They're fine."

She nodded. He didn't think she'd even noticed his touch. He contemplated pulling out the remaining pins and burying his face in the silken mass of her hair, but that might wake her up a little too abruptly. He'd best go do something heroic. Or stupid. He couldn't just sit here, twiddling his thumbs.

Gingerly, Charlie stood up, clinging to a more stable tree for support until he was certain his feet wouldn't tumble out from under him. Testing the ground ahead, he worked his way toward the ravine. He grabbed a vine, tugged to verify its safety, and used it for a safety rope as he edged closer.

"Damn," he muttered.

Penelope jerked her head up and stared in incredulity at the sight of Charlie hanging over the edge of the ravine.

"What the hell are you doing?" she whispered. She couldn't seem to raise her voice. Maybe she feared the mountain would crumble if she spoke too loud.

"Our bags are right there on that damned ledge."

Their bags. She hadn't even thought about them. Glancing down at her once elegant skirt, she shuddered. "Forget them. They're not worth your life."

"You know what?" he asked thoughtfully, ignoring her request.

"Tell me when you get back here," she urged.

"I don't think the road just washed away."

She stared as he bent to examine something over the side of the fallen road. "Charlie, don't do this to me. Get back here immediately."

Gingerly clinging to rocks, he turned to face her again, his heavy eyebrows pulled into an ominous frown.

"I think that explosion earlier was someone blowing out the road with dynamite."

❧ TWELVE ❧

Dynamite! Penelope gripped her elbows as she tried to pull her mind back from the precipice they'd almost dived over. Surely no one would deliberately set explosives. . . .

"Charlie, don't do this to me," she shouted as he peered over the edge again. "Get back from there." Nerves stretched taut, Penelope gritted her chattering teeth as Charlie hung there, examining some idiot dent in the rocks. Men had utterly no sense of danger.

Charlie pulled up a few rocks and inched backward to safer ground. "I can smell traces of explosives, and these rocks are still hot."

"All right, we'll call the police. Just get away from that damned ravine." She couldn't believe she was worrying over the jerk. If it hadn't been for him, they wouldn't be in this predicament. But he was her best route out of here now. "We'd better put up some kind of warning so no one else comes around this curve and falls in."

Shoving the rocks into his pocket, Charlie stood and dusted himself off as he glanced up and down the road. "This is mostly a farm road. Only the people who live here travel it. I'll pull some saplings across and stick a flag on them."

Penelope didn't complain when he commandeered what remained of her jacket for "flags." She just wanted out of here as swiftly as was humanly possible, before she started thinking of all the implications of exploding roads. She wanted a hot shower and a cool bed. She wanted peace and quiet. She wanted her life back.

She shook her head in amazement as Charlie literally pulled trees up by the roots and positioned them across the road. She couldn't imagine too many people with the casual strength to just rip trees out of the ground.

Although he'd torn his shirt climbing out of the jeep and compounded the damage with his feats of strength, he had the decency to keep the damned thing on. His shoulders strained the seams as he wrenched the trees out of the loose dirt, but at least she didn't have to see him half-naked. She'd thought she'd grown out of her adolescent lust for muscles, but obviously something in her psyche remained unresolved on that particular matter.

She took a deep breath and attempted to calm her racing heart as Charlie finished his task and headed back in her direction. She prided herself on her logical mind. It was time to apply it. "Why would anyone blow up a road?" she asked in what she considered a calm voice.

Charlie wouldn't look her in the eye. He shrugged his big football player shoulders and tied the last flag on a high tree branch. Suspicion raised its ugly head. There was a hell of a lot more going on here than a missing foreman.

Ignoring her question, Charlie narrowed his eyes against the sun and gazed up the hillside. "We're not too far from Raul's old home-place. Let's check that out as long as we're here. Then we'll catch a ride from the other side."

Maybe she was too calm. Maybe she should have hysterics. Maybe she should scream and rage and curse until he agreed to put her on the next bus or whatever into town. Maybe she should have her head examined.

Acknowledging the uselessness of that thought, Penelope resignedly pulled herself up, considered the ravages of her torn dress, and shrugged. "Sure, let's make this a game of one-upmanship. Whatever you can do, I can do better. In sandals. And stockings."

A sexy, totally disarming grin crossed Charlie's face as he looked her up and down. "I don't want you to do what I can do. I want you for something entirely different."

His casual comment hit Penelope with the same breathless feeling as if he had slammed her to the ground and jumped on her. She couldn't believe she was even thinking about sex, under the circumstances, but she didn't think she'd mistaken the smoky look in Charlie's eyes. He wanted *her*.

"Come on, it's an easy climb. Tourists do it all the time." He caught her hand and tugged her forward.

So, they were both shaken and not quite in their right minds. And maybe there was this electric thing popping and fizzing between them occasionally. He was just copping the usual male attitude and making it into something it wasn't to distract her. She certainly had no intention of doing anything stupid with this great ape. She'd long ago determined she wouldn't settle for anything less than a relationship that at least hinted of a future, and Charlie Smith had absolutely nothing to offer in that department.

But his big hand engulfing hers was reassuring as they strode over the rough terrain. He held back vines and crushed roots to clear a path for her as if they really were on a casual outing. In his own rough way, Charlie played the role of gentleman well. The mind-bending part was that she was beginning to accept him as he was. She, who never associated with anything less than a sensitive nineties man in a pinstripe suit and white collar, had accepted that this man didn't fit the mold, and—she didn't want to change him.

She must have hit her head on the windshield. He was arrogant, overbearing, selfish, and single-minded, like all men. Most of the time she wanted to smack him. But he damned well knew what he wanted to do and how to do it and did it without complaint—crushing all in his path. She had to admire his determination.

As the route they took veered into rough wagon tracks and crudely tilled fields, Penelope dropped the subject. She didn't know who would dynamite a road or why. She didn't want to know what Charlie was involved in that his foreman would take cover in the jungle for protection. She would just play tourist and admire this sight of the interior that she would never have seen had she stayed at the resort.

They clambered over rotting trees and through weeded tracks between rocky fields. The farms here had no giant combines and equipment sheds as they did back home. It looked as if some of them were still worked by mules. Considering the up-and-down terrain, she could understand the difficulty. The only thing these farmers had in their favor was the climate. Long seasons and plentiful water created garden jungles. Lush greenery covered the poor soil. Penelope couldn't be entirely certain whether they were weeds or vegetables, but the vines were plentiful.

Her espadrilles were covered with mud and soaked through by the time they reached the edge of the forest. Too mountainous for farming, this area of rain forest clung to the earth just as it had centuries ago. Trunks shot straight up to the canopy of leaves overhead. Vines crawled over the trunks. But the thickness of the shade prevented any dense underbrush. They had to watch for rocks and roots sticking from the ground, but the walk wasn't nearly as treacherous as she had feared.

Of course, if Raul came back here with any frequency, he could have cleared the brush, but she couldn't detect anything resembling an actual man-made path. She prayed Charlie knew where he was going.

As they climbed deeper into the interior, Penelope cast him an anxious glance. He hadn't said a word in forever. She could see tension knotting the muscles along his jaw. The hand clasping hers squeezed so tight at times, she thought he'd crush the bones. In spite of that tight hold, she figured he'd forgotten her existence. She supposed if someone had blown up the only road to Raul's hideout, he had some right to be concerned. Things didn't look good for Charlie's foreman. Or Charlie.

She wondered briefly over Tammy's comment about her father. Surely a civilized man like Emile St. Philippe wouldn't stoop to murdering someone to keep him away from his daughter. Men like that arranged business deals, had people like Raul fired or trapped by the law or any of a dozen different half-legal stratagems used daily to remove obstacles in the way of the powerful. They didn't, however, usually resort to outright murder.

But Charlie said Raul had disappeared and that wasn't normal. Penelope prayed, for his sake, that Raul had merely gone into hiding. It just struck her that if Charlie was so confident of finding his friend on this island, anyone could.

"The tree house used to be right around here somewhere," Charlie muttered. "There was a big clearing. . . ."

"How many years ago?" Penelope scoffed. "It could have grown over."

"Maybe, but I think there was bare rock right under it." Cautiously, he shoved aside tree branches, searching for a memory.

"I may not be a contractor, but it seems to me that building on bare rock might present a problem."

"Not to Raul. And not for this kind of construction. There are no utilities up here. It would just be a shack. . . ."

He froze between two trees, and Penelope nearly walked into his back. Biting her lip in irritation, she stood on her toes and peered over his shoulder.

At first, she saw nothing but a small glade in the midst of towering fern trees. As she turned her focus from the greenery to the small open space, she discovered the reason for Charlie's silence.

Black ashes. Already sprouting vines and weed, they looked more a smear of dark rock than anything significant.

She considered holding Charlie back, telling him it was better to go on and assume these were the remains of someone's campfire. But even as she considered it, she knew it was not only a stupid thought, a denial, but it was impossible to carry out. Wild bulls wouldn't stop Charlie now.

He surged forward, swatting aside leaves and branches, his

jaw so tense she thought he'd break it. Reluctantly, she followed in his wake.

Up close, she could see the charred remains of stout timbers, bits of broken glass, and scorched metal. Charlie circled
the overgrown perimeter, picking up a broken tree limb and
poking at the logs. Apparently deciding it was safe, he strode
through the charcoal into the center and began heaving timbers aside. Penelope didn't follow.

She knew the instant he discovered what she had feared.
He bellowed a roar of anguish so gut-wrenching, tears sprang
to her eyes.

Reaching down, Charlie flung aside a beam large enough
to be physically impossible to move. Penelope caught a
gleam of white, the flutter of tattered cloth, and a glimpse of
something shiny before Charlie closed his fingers around it,
and ripped it from whatever held it down.

Moaning, he gripped the piece of gold and twisted it in the
sun. Penelope thought she saw tears glittering in his eyes before he shoved the damaging evidence into his pocket.
Cursing fluently, Charlie abruptly heaved a loose rock across
the clearing.

On a rampage now, he kicked a charred log until it ca-
reened through the grass, flung more timbers from the pile,
and roared futile curses at the sky. Not acknowledging Penelope's existence, he bellowed with primal rage, and whirl-
ing around, slammed his fists repeatedly into the nearest tree
trunk.

Penelope thought she'd fall apart watching his raw anguish. She had strong memories of grief so great she'd
wanted to destroy something, anything, but she'd never given
vent to it. Her unspoken despair had torn her apart, and
continued to rip her to shreds through years of helplessness.
Charlie's outburst seemed indecent in comparison. She couldn't
bear it.

Tears flooding her eyes and streaming down her cheeks,
Penelope wedged between Charlie and his target. His hands
were already bleeding from the blows. He didn't seem aware

of her presence. She recognized the howling emptiness in his eyes.

Bitterly, she smacked her fists against his iron-hewed chest.

"Stop it! Stop it this instant, Charlie." She couldn't describe what she wanted stopped if her life depended on it. She just knew he was tearing her to pieces. Out here, in this primitive jungle with no one watching, she didn't have to maintain her stoicism. She smashed her fist against him until she had his attention.

"Get out of my way, Penelope," he warned in a voice torn with grief. He shoved aside her puny blows and tried to step around her.

"No, I won't! I can't. Not until you . . . Charlie!" she screamed as he dug his fingers into her hair and jerked her head back.

She stared into the bitterness blinding his eyes. She wasn't certain he was even seeing her.

"He's dead, pretty Penny. They killed him. Because of me. I've killed my best friend. Do you understand? Do you have any idea—"

She pounded futilely on his shoulders. "Yes, I do! I know precisely how you feel. Worse. A million times worse. You can't even begin to—"

He cut her off by lifting her into his arms and burying his face against her neck. His arms nearly strangled the life from her as his powerful shoulders shook with grief and rage.

Penelope slid her hands around his back and held him, willing him the strength she used to fight back her own tears. She'd not thought herself capable of empathy, but Charlie's pain shot straight through to her heart and resonated with the pain already there.

Abruptly, he raised his head and glared at her as if she possessed something he had to have and would take by any means. Penelope stared back, captured by the raw misery behind his challenging look.

Without warning, he dipped his head and covered her mouth with his.

Devastating flames swept down her throat, igniting an inferno in the dried kindling of her lower regions. Penelope dug her fingers into Charlie's shirt and hung on as his mouth ravished hers. He showed no mercy but staked his claim and mined it thoroughly, leaving her gasping and weak-kneed. And hot. So hot she could rip her clothes off right now. Rip them off and fling herself into his arms. His naked arms, preferably.

Punishing fingers gripped her breast and kneaded. Vaguely, Penelope recognized that Charlie's embrace might be the only reason she was still upright. Her tongue met his, and his hold tightened, slid to her hips, crushed her against him.

Charlie's fingers bit into her buttocks as he rocked their hips together. Penelope whimpered beneath his mouth, not with terror, but with desire, with the volcanic rush of mindless need racing through her veins. All the frustration, the pent-up tension, exploded, freeing her from the box of propriety she'd lived in for so long. She released his shirt and grabbed his shoulders.

Charlie shoved her against a tree and returned to plundering her breasts. Insane with a desire she'd never known, not knowing how to cope with it, Penelope raised her legs and wrapped them around him, demanding he continue to hold her. Her skirt slid upward until it reached her waist.

Charlie effortlessly took her weight, and muttering something obscene against her mouth, bit her lip. He slid his hands up her thighs until strong fingers brushed against the crotch of her torn panty hose. No longer caring how she looked or what she did, Penelope surged against him, and he dug his fingers deeper, pushing, exploring until she squirmed with desperation and the first quaking signals of total surrender.

A squawk screeched past their ears. Red and green feathers stirred the air so close they jumped with surprise. Another squawk and flap of wings intruded, jolting them back to earth.

"His nest must be in this tree," Charlie muttered through

clenched teeth, unable to release the moment entirely, unable to bear parting from the escape she offered. Her heat and scent surrounded him. He had only to unzip his pants and lose himself inside her. All the blood in his body had surged to his loins, leaving nothing in his brain. He wanted it that way. He wanted the mindless release of sex, the conquering plunge, the sheathing shelter of her woman's body. In some vague part of his mind he hoped he could release all his anger and grief into her, bury his guilt and fears deep inside her womb, and come out whole again.

The blasted squawking parrot diving at his head knocked him back to reality.

Still aching with unquenched desire, Charlie reluctantly released Penelope's hips and let her legs slide back to the ground. He cupped her breasts, and she shuddered with the same passion flowing through him. She averted her eyes as he studied her, but she couldn't disguise the flush of pink across her cheeks. Her embarrassment nearly undid him.

Obviously, he had very strange reactions to death. He brushed her cheek with his raw knuckles and kissed her forehead. The damned parrot screamed its fury overhead.

"I lost my head; I apologize. I'm not sorry, but you deserve better." Needing some crutch of sanity, Charlie gripped her hand as he stepped away.

She still didn't look at him, but she didn't pull her hand away either. "We both overreacted, I guess."

He didn't want her looking ashamed. He wanted the Valkyrie back, screaming him to his senses. Only he hadn't returned to his senses; he'd dragged her down into hell with him. For that, he was sorry. The ache in his heart swelled as the enormity of Raul's death hit him again. He'd killed his best friend and nearly raped an innocent woman. Maybe his mother wasn't far wrong. He was an uncivilized gorilla.

Tears streaked the dust on Penelope's cheeks. She wasn't crying entirely for him, he suspected. "What did you mean, that you knew how I felt, only a million times worse?"

She dropped his hand and wiped at her eyes as she walked

away. "Never mind. How do we get out of here? We need to notify the police. Tammy will be waiting for us."

She'd slammed the lid closed on her emotions again. The porcupine had returned. He'd like to shake her. He'd like to do a damned sight more. Mostly, he wanted to jog her back to the woman of passion who'd wrapped her legs around him and demanded satisfaction.

With his best friend's murdered body a charred skeleton in the jungle, passion was the last thing he needed right now. There was a time for caution, and a time for revenge.

"Tammy," he groaned as another thought struck him. "What the hell will I tell Tammy?"

He flushed at Penelope's look of surprise. So, maybe he wasn't entirely an insensitive clod. She didn't need to know that. He answered her last question curtly. "We have to follow the ridge down to the road. We can hitch from there. This isn't Miami."

He sounded like a Nazi jerk, but his balls still ached, his head spun with memories of Raul, and a manic voice inside him screamed for justice.

Maybe he could develop a split personality to accommodate all the splintering parts of his soul.

❧ THIRTEEN ❧

They caught a ride in the back of a farm truck hauling chickens to market. Feathers flew as the birds protested behind their wooden bars, but Penelope bumped along without complaint, figuring each squawk and feather brought her that much closer to civilization and that much closer to leaving the morose man leaning against the opposite side of the truck, wrists propped on knees.

She didn't need bones in the jungle, dead street hustlers, and international intrigue in her life. She definitely didn't need Charlie's pain or that moment of electricity between them. If she concentrated on any of this at all, she would run screaming to the airport or swim for home. She didn't have that option. She had a job to do, and she would focus on it much more easily with Charlie out of the picture.

Surely he would go home now. He didn't need her any longer. Maybe he would meet his sister at the dock and the two of them could take a water taxi to the airport. She didn't know how she'd explain the loss of the jeep and her supposed husband to Mr. Henwood. The resort manager would probably think she'd killed her louse of a spouse and pushed him over a cliff in the car.

She'd never gotten her kicks from excitement before. Penelope glanced at Charlie, but he had crossed his arms over his knees and buried his face against them. Surely her odd reluctance to lose the adrenaline-induced pace of the last few days had nothing to do with Charlie. It must be relief from boredom. Spending twelve-hour days at a desk so she could drag home a paycheck, pay the bills, and stuff the remainder in a savings account might not be very exciting, but surely she could find something less dangerous than Charlie Smith's company.

Still, she couldn't rationalize that explosive kiss. She'd never done anything like that in her life. She didn't even *like* sex—but a howling banshee inside her head warned she'd never had sex with Charlie Smith before. Shutting out banshees while fighting the memory of two dead men was a difficult juggling act.

As the truck rattled to a stop at Soufrière's version of a farmer's market, Charlie lifted his head, blinked, scanned their surroundings, and scowled.

Leaping down from the flatbed, he held out his hand to Penelope. "Come on, let's get out of here. I think we may be a lot better off if we're not seen."

She took his hand to climb down, then released it immediately as if she'd held a burning brand. "Don't be ridiculous." She spoke more sharply than she'd intended. "We need to go to the police, and we agreed to meet Tammy at five. It's past that now."

Aware of the stares their white faces and rumpled clothing attracted, she hurried toward the narrow path she figured was a street that might lead into the town center.

Charlie grabbed her wrist and pulled her toward an alleyway between two narrow houses. "From the looks of those vines, Raul's been dead for over a week. That dynamite could have been meant for us."

"Don't be ridiculous," Penelope protested again, mostly because she didn't want to believe him. Dynamite and murder happened only on TV news, not to her. There had to be some rational explanation. She had only Charlie's word for most of it, after all. She'd have to be insane to take his word for anything. She wanted to get back to the hotel and a hot shower and her safe, sane accounting environment, away from Charlie Smith and the banshee screaming louder in her head every time he touched her. "No one knew we'd be taking that road."

"Anyone who knew I was here looking for Raul could figure I would take that road sooner or later." He pulled her deeper into the darkness of the trash-strewn alley.

"Well, we can't very well lurk in shadows forever. Let's go to the police." Penelope tried to twist her wrist from his grip, but Charlie paid no attention to her efforts. He was busy peering into the yards on the other side of the houses. She shouldn't let him do this to her. Couldn't.

"Jacques lives not too far from here. I need to see if he's back. I'll trust Jacques over the police any day."

"He ran away when you needed him," she scoffed. "Fat big help he is."

"He was protecting his family. He'll be back. Come on, there's no one out there right now. We can get across these yards and go in the back way."

"I don't want to. I want to go back to the hotel. I need a shower. Charlie . . ."

Ignoring all her protests, he yanked her into someone's littered backyard, through a broken fence, across a vegetable plot, and zigzagged through more fences and empty lots, until he reached the shrubbery surrounding a more secluded home. Pushing underneath a brilliant purple bougainvillea, he stopped and waited at the edge of the next open space.

"Charlie, this is nuts," she whispered in desperation. "I haven't played hide-and-seek since I was a kid, and I was never any good at it."

"Look, I'm sorry I got you into this. I'll try to get you out. Just be quiet and let me think."

Heart beating unsteadily, Penelope waited. She didn't know which she feared more, Charlie or his mysterious enemies. She just had this wild idea that if she could get back to the resort, everything would be normal again. That idea was fading as rapidly as the setting sun. Even now, shadows spread beneath the bushes and between the houses where they hid. She could hear laughter floating through a distant window. The house Charlie studied remained ominously quiet and dark.

"Wait here."

He released her wrist and eased from beneath the bougainvillea branches. Penelope considered following him if for no other reason than that she didn't like being left behind. But if there were murderers waiting in that house, she didn't want to encounter them. This was all Charlie's fault. Let him deal with them.

She picked up a beer bottle lying near her feet and watched intently as Charlie's silhouette slid between the shadows and toward the back door. He was still her safest transportation out of here.

A warbling whistle startled her into almost dropping the bottle until she realized it came from Charlie. Swell. Now he had secret signals.

The back door popped open, and a head topped by Rastafarian braids peered out.

"Get yourself in here, mon, before you get your brains blown out!"

Charlie turned and signaled for Penelope. She contemplated running in the opposite direction. As far as she was concerned, if this was Jacques, he was more terrifying than anyone else they had encountered all day. Reluctantly, she slipped from beneath the bush, still carrying the beer bottle.

The back door had already closed. No light shone from within. Charlie grabbed her arm again and pulled her forward. "Interesting souvenir," he commented grimly as his fingers brushed the bottle.

She dropped it and glared at him, for all the good it did. "Is this where I get to go home?"

He didn't answer, but she figured the hug he gave her was answer enough. It was one of those "Sure, honey, whatever you say" hugs that men used when they didn't have the right answer but wanted her to shut up anyway. She considered taking a large bite out of his shoulder to compensate, but she was too rattled to do more than follow.

Inside, Jacques waited for them at the Formica kitchen table. To Penelope's utter surprise, Tammy waited for them too.

Charlie's half sister looked up with relief and a degree of wariness. "Thank goodness! I thought you'd fallen off the mountain. Did you find Raul?"

Penelope bit her lip and glanced at Charlie. They hadn't discussed this. Maybe Charlie was certain that was Raul up there, but they didn't have positive identification.

She could see Charlie's hesitation and held her breath. Surely he wouldn't blurt it out like this and break Tammy's heart.

"The shack's gone," he finally admitted. "I didn't find him."

Penelope let out her breath. The damned man continually surprised her.

"Gone? What do you mean, gone? It was there two weeks ago. He had it all fixed up. . . ." Tammy shut up beneath her brother's withering glare. Everyone in the room could guess why Raul had fixed up the shack and under what circumstances she had seen it.

Jacques waded into the ripples of silence. "Get yourself and your ladies from here, mon. Sell that land and don' come back. You don' need this."

Penelope watched in fascination as the two men exchanged glances. She had the oddest feeling that Jacques knew what Charlie had found up on the mountain.

"I'm not leaving," Charlie insisted. "Get us to the airport and I can get Tammy and Penelope out of here. They can take your family too, if you want. But I'm staying."

"You crazy, mon. There nothing you can do. Go home where you belong," Jacques insisted, though his protests had lost their luster beneath Charlie's determination.

"I can't go home yet." Penelope tried to be reasonable in the wake of Charlie's sudden desire to be rid of her. "I've got work to do. I have nothing to do with whatever's going on.

Just get me back to the hotel, and I'll be happy." She didn't want to whine. She just wanted her sane life back.

"I'm not going until we find Raul." Tammy crossed her arms in imitation of her brother.

"Jacques?" Charlie waited, but the demand was in his voice.

"If you stay, those around you are in danger too. The stakes are much too high."

The man's singsong voice could have been repeating some pleasant island refrain if one didn't listen to the words. Maybe she shouldn't listen to the words. But if Raul was really dead, if someone had killed him and—she'd rather not think of this—tried to kill Charlie by blowing up a road, then the stakes were pretty darned high indeed.

"What if Tammy goes back to the house? No one will know she's involved." Charlie sounded slightly desperate.

"I had to run away from Mama when you weren't at the dock," Tammy replied coolly. "I'm not going back. They'd never let me out again. I want to help find Raul."

Charlie dug his hands into his hair and tugged. Penelope could almost feel sorry for him if she didn't have the resentful notion that this was all his fault. Since she didn't know precisely what was going on, she could refuse to help. Or she could sort out the problem, solve it, and get back to work.

"Perhaps it's time that we clarify a few things here," she declared in resignation. She'd brought worse meetings to order in her time. "What, precisely, are we in danger from? Does anyone know?"

Jacques sat back in his chair, unwilling to offer more.

Charlie tossed her a quick, jerky glance after she said "we," then continued digging his hand into his hair, not looking at anyone. Penelope wanted to smack him, but one didn't smack people one hardly knew. She'd nearly had sex with the man, but she didn't know him. She wondered if she really knew herself. What had possessed her to say "we," as if she was actually working with him? Damn, but she was losing her mind. Or her usual set of principles.

She lifted a questioning eyebrow in Tammy's direction.

"It's got something to do with that land Raul was clearing," Tammy answered boldly. "They blew up the trailer he used as an office. They shot at his truck. Someone wanted him out of there." She threw a swift look to Jacques. "I'd say it was the naturalists who don't want more development, but guns and explosives aren't their usual style."

Jacques frowned but didn't contradict her. "There are bad men all over. You never should have come here."

"You're Raul's friend," Tammy said defensively. "I had to go somewhere."

Penelope kicked Charlie beneath the table. His head shot up and he glared, red-eyed, at her.

"Who wants the land, Charlie? Did anyone else bid on it?"

"The Resort Foundation," he said with a sigh. "They're behind most of the development in Castries. They're turning the place into a concrete carnival. The naturalists don't have any money. They couldn't bid on a palm tree."

"Would the Resort Foundation use violence?" If she couldn't get information out of them any other way, she'd pull it through their noses. She'd never seen such a taciturn lot.

"No," Tammy said adamantly.

"Yes," Charlie replied at the same time.

"Daddy owns part of that company," Tammy said indignantly. "They're perfectly proper. Don't be ridiculous, Charlie."

"Stockholders are not part of a company." Wearily, Charlie slid back in the chair. "Management makes the decisions. The management of the Resort Foundation would string up their own mothers if they got in the way of making money."

"Sell to them and go home," Jacques advised.

"I'll be damned if I will!" Charlie pounded the table, rattling the empty glasses. "This town needs houses, not amusement parks and concrete palaces for tourists. And if they had anything to do with Raul's disappearance, I'll have them nailed to the damned wall before this is over."

"And how do you plan to prove they're behind anything?" Penelope asked, quite reasonably, she thought. "Maybe the neighbors object to a subdivision. Maybe you've got street gangs who haven't anything better to do than blow up things." She knew that wasn't quite as reasonable, but she egged Charlie on. She had to get something sensible out of him.

"How in hell do I know? I'll just start moving heavy machinery in and post guards on the perimeter to shoot anyone who gets near. Sooner or later I'll have them."

Penelope couldn't quite determine if the silence following that declaration was shock or agreement. She just knew Charlie danced on a dangerous edge right now, and he wasn't in any mood for reason.

"Fine, then. Live behind barbed wire. What about your family? If these people are desperate enough to do something to Raul, who do you think they'll pick on next? The guy behind barbed wire or his innocent, unprotected family?"

"Dammit!" He smacked the table again and glared at her. "What do *you* suggest?"

"Finding out who's behind the Resort Foundation, who has the power, who has the ability, who has the strongest desire and motive to commit acts of violence." She kept skirting around Raul's death for Tammy's sake, but it was getting harder and harder.

Jacques looked at her with new respect. "Who can do this? These people are not from here. They know nothing of the island but the money."

"A corporation has to be registered somewhere. It just takes a little digging. If you want to avoid whatever the island calls a courthouse, you could use a computer and modem."

Charlie straightened and looked more alert. "Find the major stockholders, board of directors, and top management. Is that possible?"

Penelope shrugged. "Can't say unless I try." She couldn't believe she'd said that. She didn't want to try. She had to start work tomorrow. She didn't have time for massive computer searches.

"That's it, then. We'll go back to the hotel and get your laptop."

Charlie was half out of his chair before Jacques halted his escape.

"No, mon, do you not remember Michel? He was a warning. They know where you stay. They will be waiting. You cannot go back there."

Penelope stared at him, speechless. She had to go back. She had no clothes. She needed that job. Where would she go?

Charlie dropped back into his chair. "Help me get the women to the airport. The resort can ship Penelope's things back to Miami later. Where can I get a computer around here?"

"And what would you know about computers?" Penelope asked with disdain. "I bet you have a bookkeeper or secretary who handles computer entries."

Charlie shrugged. "So, I'll learn. It can't be all that difficult."

"I'm not going without Raul," Tammy repeated stubbornly. "If you stay, I stay."

Penelope had about reached the point where she'd agree to leave on the first flight out if that was the only way she could get a bath, but the memory of that poor old man held her back. It shouldn't take her long to poke around the Internet and come up with something. She had contacts. She could network a little.

She had this wide-screen vision of cornering the villain in cyberspace and Charlie riding to the capture on horseback, six-guns firing. She needed sleep.

"All right. Let's do it this way. Get me a computer with a modem and Internet software. I know the island has an Internet server because I connected with it before I came out here. I'll need a telephone hookup." She looked at Charlie's little sister. She couldn't let the girl sit here in anticipation of Raul driving into town when this was over. It wasn't going to happen. Distraction was needed. "Tammy, I hesitate to ask this, but my sister is expecting me home in a few days. She's blind. She fares pretty well on her own, but she can't pick up groceries by herself. And it's possible some of the information I dig out will need confirmation from court records.

Chances are that we'll find most of these guys operate out of Miami. Do you think . . . ?"

Tammy's eyes widened in surprise. "You want me to help dig out the records? And look after your sister?"

"She won't appreciate the 'looking after' part," Penelope said wryly. "She thinks she's doing just fine on her own."

"And she probably is." Tammy sprang to the defense of a woman she didn't even know. "But she's probably worried about you. Have you called?"

"My cell phone doesn't have an international connection. I'll send her e-mail just as soon as I get that computer."

Charlie ran his hand over his face and looked back and forth between the two women. "Does this mean one of you is staying and the other is going?"

"Men." Penelope shrugged. "They're a little dense sometimes."

Tammy's eyes were shining as they fell on her half brother. "I've got my passport in my purse. How will you get me out of here?"

Charlie groaned and turned to Jacques for guidance. "One's better than nothing, I guess. You got a boat?"

"I have a boat," Jacques agreed. He turned a serious gaze to Penelope. "You would do well to go with her, miss. This is no computer game."

"I doubt your bad guys have the know-how to trace my modem. Who's to know where I am if I sit behind a computer all day? You could stick me in an office anywhere and no one would ever notice."

Slumped in his chair, arms crossed, Charlie snorted loudly at this last but didn't comment.

"But I want a bath," she warned him. "And some clothes."

"That, I can promise you." Slamming his feet back to the floor, Charlie stood up. "Come on, Jacques, let's get Princess Tamara Louise out of here before the evil witch finds her. Her ugly stepsister can just blow off the dragons if they show up while we're gone."

Penelope wished she had something to throw at him. Better yet, she wished she'd sliced out her tongue with a dull knife.

First thing she would do when she got home was have her head examined.

❧ FOURTEEN ❧

Hands full, Charlie slipped through Jacques's moonlit garden. A faint light glittered behind wooden shutters, but it held no guarantee that anyone waited inside. Penelope was quite capable of changing her mind and running as fast as she could in the opposite direction.

Her managerial analysis of their situation earlier had thoroughly impressed him. Now that Penelope had thrown in her lot with his, he had to admit that beautiful head on her shoulders had brains.

He also had to admit that her "we" earlier had darn near brought him to his knees. He'd thought he had lost everything when he found Raul's body. But Penny offered to fill some of the emptiness. It might be only a temporary repair, but it had prevented him from ripping the whole town apart with his bare hands.

He didn't have much experience with women of intelligence though, so he didn't know how long this "partnership" would last. The construction business didn't cater to women, not the kind of women he enjoyed anyway. If he hung around her much longer, he might have to reconsider his personal prejudice against both society women and career robots.

Damn, but she'd felt powerful in his arms earlier. It was a wonder she hadn't run right there and then. He wouldn't have blamed her. He'd sure as hell scared himself.

But if she was still here, if she really meant it about helping him, he would do his best to behave. He couldn't afford to lose any more help, and certainly not the kind of high-tech maneuvering Penelope offered. He didn't want to scare her off.

He couldn't figure out how in heck to get in the house without doing just that though. Would she recognize his whistle as Jacques had?

He tried it. A night bird hooted somewhere in reply. He waited, with the damned bougainvillea vines scratching his neck. A shadow passed across the shutters. A moment later, the back door opened a crack.

He dashed across the yard, slipped inside the house, shut the door, bolted it, dropped all his packages, and in an excess of zeal, grabbed the gorgeous woman waiting for him and kissed her soundly on the mouth. Utter heaven.

She froze and backed away instantly. Charlie let her go. After all his promises to himself, he'd gone and done what he'd just sworn he wouldn't do, but he didn't regret it. In the dim light, she looked surprised and beautiful, not shocked or disgusted. Maybe Miss Penny just wasn't used to a man grabbing and kissing her. He was an optimist by nature. Besides, he really liked the idea of having a beautiful woman waiting up for him. It assuaged some of the ache of loneliness left by Raul's death.

Her gaze dipped to the bundles scattered across the floor. "What did you do, rob a bank?"

"Burlap is easier to carry up a mountainside than suitcases. Most of your things should be in there somewhere." Charlie stopped to inspect what she'd done to herself in his absence. She'd availed herself of Jacques's shower, obviously. Her long thick hair hung down her back in a heavy sheet of black satin, still damp around the edges. She wore some bright red muumuulike thing that must have belonged to Jacques's wife, confirming that Penelope could look good in a sack. Damn, but she managed to look exquisite and graceful and all those delicate things a female should be, while concealing a mind that could cut a man off at the balls.

"Up a mountainside? What did you do?" She seemed genuinely puzzled as she sorted through the packages.

"Took the boat to that deserted cove on the other side of the ridge from the resort. The path over the ridge isn't particularly well laid out, and I didn't want to be seen from the beach. So I reached the cabin from behind."

Her head shot up and she stared at him through luminous eyes. Charlie would give his life savings if he could keep that expression forever, but right now, he was tired, hungry, and more vulnerable than he'd been in his life. Even his father's death hadn't left him this empty. He'd had time to prepare for his dad's dying. Raul was too damned young. So maybe he wasn't thinking straight when he saw admiration in her eyes.

"You climbed over that ridge behind the cabin?" she asked incredulously. "You must be mad."

"Yeah, that's what all the women say. Did Jacques leave anything to eat? I'm starved."

Returning to the resort had not only been insane, but stupid. He'd just had an idiotic notion that she'd appreciate having some of her things, and he'd wanted to show his gratitude for her help. Silly of him.

"Jacques's wife left a seafood concoction in the refrigerator." She pounced on the laptop case, pulled it from the bundle of clothes, and carried it to the table, essentially forgetting his existence. So, she was a computer whiz and not a cook. He could accept that. It wasn't as if he were going to marry her or anything.

"Don't make yourself too comfortable. We've got to get out of here as soon as I get something in my stomach." Charlie rooted through the refrigerator, blessed Jacques for keeping beer on hand, found the casserole, and lugged it to the stove.

"Get out of here? Why? I'm asleep on my feet as it is.

We've got everything we need here. This couldn't take more than a day or so."

Charlie tuned out the incredulity and pain in her voice. He'd put her through hell today. "It looked like someone sifted through the cottage in our absence. If they're onto us, it's not safe here. Everyone on the damned island knows Jacques is a friend of mine. I'm hoping if someone really wants to kill me, they'll think I went off the cliff with the car, but there's no guarantee. I tried to leave the cottage looking as if we'd only taken a few days' worth of stuff with us, but how many people take laptops on their honeymoon?" He spooned the casserole into a pan and turned up the heat.

"Computer geeks," Penelope answered, as she reached around him, removed the pan, and added water to cover the bottom, to prevent scorching. "I can't do anything without electricity and a good phone connection. My battery barely lasts two hours at a time and it's probably not charged up." She slapped the pan back on the stove.

"Charge it up now."

"That could take all night. Couldn't we just take a boat to Castries and find another hotel room?"

"They check passports up there. And that would be putting ourselves right in the Foundation's hands." Charlie stirred at the mess in the pan. He bordered on the edge of exhaustion himself, but the charred remains in that jungle cabin ate at his gut. He would have his revenge. His whole damned business could go down the tubes, but he'd get his hands around the neck of Raul's murderer.

"Do you think Jacques got Tammy to the airport all right?" She wilted wearily into a chair at the table after plugging in the laptop.

"Yeah, they'll be fine. I've got friends in Vieux Fort who will take care of things. Tammy will be winging her way to your sister in no time. You might want to e-mail a warning. I don't know if we'll be near a telephone in the morning."

"Yeah, I remember your friends," she said sarcastically,

opening the computer and hitting a few buttons. "I hope that wasn't real cocaine in the bag."

Charlie shrugged and tested the casserole for warmth. "Who knows? It's a good ruse for holding undesirables until they can really nail them. This isn't precisely the good old U.S. of A."

"Undesirables." She snorted inelegantly and tapped away at the keyboard. "Do you really think it's this Foundation that's behind things? Or do you have any other suspects?"

She asked it innocently enough. Charlie couldn't see her face clearly in the dim light as she worked over the computer. But he knew what she was asking. "As far as I'm aware, the Foundation is made up of outsiders. There might be a few local stockholders, but all my contacts with them have been through Miami and European businessmen. Emile has lived here all his life. I've never seen him do more than play golf and tennis and occasionally talk to his lawyers and accountants, but he knows every damned person on this island. It wouldn't take him long to find Raul's hiding place."

"Especially if he had someone follow Tammy," she answered enigmatically, still not looking up.

"I don't know how in hell she got out there," Charlie muttered, removing the pan from the stove and taking it to the table. He found a fork in a drawer and carried his beer over too.

Penelope looked up and frowned at his crude table setting, but she had the wisdom not to comment. Instead, she pulled out a cord, got up, and strode directly to the kitchen phone. She'd apparently researched her surroundings thoroughly while she waited. Charlie watched as she unhooked the phone and plugged in the computer. He hoped to hell she knew what she was doing.

"Raul probably met her somewhere and took her back there in a jeep," she commented idly. "She's not precisely a cripple, you realize. She can walk. It's just tedious going. Can't doctors do anything for her?"

"Doctors have operated. My mother has taken her to physi-

cal therapists. They've done all that is humanly possible."
Charlie answered all the other questions probably floating
around Miss Penelope's active mind. "She wouldn't be walking at all if they hadn't. It was some kind of birth defect. They
couldn't have done anything to prevent it."

"How badly will they take her running away? And is there
any way she can get word to them to tell them she's safe? No
matter what you may suspect your stepfather of, he has a right
to know his daughter is safe."

"She can call when she gets there." Charlie ran his hand
over his face and shoved in another forkful of food. He wasn't
hungry anymore. He just needed sleep. "Can you investigate
Emile the same way you can look up the Foundation?"

She shrugged. "The Foundation probably has a network
of computers with a name that software can find with luck,
patience, and hard work. Personal computers don't have
names. My software won't reach his computer unless your
stepfather has a connection with the Foundation's or some
other network."

That made about as much sense as the financial statements
his accountant prepared, Charlie decided wearily. He understood the bare bones necessary to get by. Maybe he should
have spent more of his college years on financial courses. At
the time, he'd thought them strictly the territory of knock-
kneed nerds. He'd known he'd be going into his father's company and never thought accounting and computers necessary
for hard hats and hammers. The stupidity of youth.

"Yeah, well, check it out however you can. As far as I'm
concerned, Emile is capable of ordering Raul murdered for
just looking at Tammy. He probably has his sights on raising
grandkids with aristocratic titles he can leave his money to.
The man's a snob of the worst sort." He scraped his pot and
carried it to the sink.

"That wouldn't explain the problems at the land site." Penelope hit a button, sat back, and watched the screen. "The
server here is slow. Searching could take awhile."

After running water in the pot, Charlie turned and leaned

against the cabinet to watch her. Miss Penny wasn't wasting much time looking at him. She stared at the computer screen. "You sure you're up for this? It's too late to get off the island tonight, but I could put you on a plane tomorrow night." He had to ask. He wasn't entirely certain he would live up to his word if she decided to leave, but he really needed to know she was staying voluntarily.

She tilted her head and looked at him sideways, her long hair spilling over one shoulder. "I'm not an environmentalist. I don't have time for causes. But I still have a conscience. If that old man died for helping us, I want the culprits caught. And if I can prevent this place from being turned into another hotel parking lot, I'm willing to expend a little effort. My main problem is my job. I can't afford to lose it."

She still didn't fully comprehend the danger, Charlie realized. This was all like a TV movie to her. Two men die, a car crashes over a mountainside, and none of it related to her. He'd like to keep it that way. "I told you, I've got connections in Miami. If you work for real assholes, I'll get you a better place."

"Yeah, right. I asked you before, how well does the Mafia pay?" She slammed the computer shut and began gathering up the phone cord. "Let's just get this over quickly and let me see if I can wiggle out of the problem. Maybe I came down with a bad case of dysentery while cruising the outback."

"Better find some comfortable clothes. Without a jeep, we'll have to hike out."

Groaning, she stretched and arched her aching back and glared at him. Charlie ignored the look. He'd much rather watch the press of her breasts against the red fabric. A new hunger rumbled through him, but this one he'd have to deny.

"I didn't bring hiking shoes," she reminded him, abruptly righting herself and turning away to examine the contents of the sacks he'd brought.

The way she avoided his eyes, he'd wager she felt the electricity too. They'd been together every minute for almost two days now. And his practically attacking her this afternoon hadn't helped. If she were his usual type, he'd just take her up to bed and they could work off some of the tension. Unfortunately, a woman like Penelope would probably punch him in the face first. He wasn't up to that right now.

"I'm gonna shower while you dress. Be ready in ten minutes." A cold shower ought to do the trick. It would wake him up, if nothing else.

Following behind Charlie, Penelope slung the strap of her padded laptop case over her shoulder and clutched her sack of clothing in the opposite hand as they slipped past the edge of town and along the road into the interior. Dogs howled wherever they passed. A few curtains opened and dropped in darkened windows. One or two night owls staggered out of their alleys to watch them, but no one spoke. She could almost sense the innocence of this town, the lack of crime and greed that corrupted the cities back home. Which made the crimes she'd seen all the more sinister. They didn't bode well for the future.

"I trust you have some definite goal in mind," she whispered in exasperation as Charlie turned off the paved road onto what appeared to be little more than a goat path.

"Jacques has friends. One of them is in the States right now. We'll borrow her place for a while."

"Does it have a telephone?" she demanded. From the looks of the rustling trees on either side of the path and the thickness of the undergrowth, she wouldn't bet on it.

"We can hope. The place is littered with telephone lines. I can always rig something up."

Penelope watched Charlie's narrow hips and heavy backpack precede her up the rocky path as if he didn't have a tired bone in his body. She hadn't exercised this much since her cheerleader days in college. She wanted to curl into a ball and fall asleep right here. Instead, she focused on his words. "You can rig up a telephone?"

"No big deal. I can steal electricity too, if we need it. You've got your talents, I've got mine."

"Oh, great, you can steal electricity and telephones. Those are talents to be commended," she answered dryly. She watched her step carefully, fearful she would stumble and fall and never get up again.

"Invading other people's networks is a commendable talent?"

He had her there. "It is where I come from," she muttered.

"Ditto here." He shooed a curious goat from their path. "Sometimes things go wrong on a job site and emergency action is required. I make amends later. That's more than some companies can say."

That's more than she could say. How did one make amends for invading privacy? It wasn't a talent she was proud of, but she'd learned it back in college and occasionally found it useful. She'd caught the partners unaware more than once. It was the only way she'd ever conquer their all-male ranks.

She didn't know how far they'd walked. A million miles at least, she surmised. All uphill. Her shoes rubbed, her legs ached, and she couldn't keep her eyes open. She was stumbling by the time Charlie halted ahead of her.

"Wake up, we're almost there," he whispered, catching her by the shoulder and holding her upright.

He possessed all the strength she'd never had. She wanted to lean into him and sleep right here. She'd never known leaning on someone could feel so good. She burrowed her nose against his shoulder as she slumped unconsciously into his embrace. "Almost, as in I can fall forward and hit the bed?" she mumbled into his shirt.

She heard the grin in his voice. "Something like that."

Without further warning, Charlie swept her up in his arms and carried her down an overgrown path with leaves smacking them in the face every step of the way.

"Prince Charming," she yawned as she cuddled her bundles in her arms. It didn't seem the least bit strange to be riding along in Charlie's arms. She really must be out of it.

"Wicked stepsister," he retaliated, dropping her feet to the ground in front of a shack built into the hillside with the use of stilts.

Too tired to examine their surroundings more closely, Penelope followed him up the rickety stairs. A rooster crowed a warning from beneath the house.

Not bothering to search for the lights as he shoved open the unlocked door, Charlie steered her inside and toward the back room. "This way, Sleeping Beauty. Don't let the bedbugs bite."

With that reassuring thought, he pushed her onto a mosquito-netted bed and departed.

Unprotestingly, Penelope merely curled up on the sagging mattress beneath the heavy netting, closed her eyes, and, swearing to get even in the morning, slept.

She didn't wake when Charlie collapsed on the bed beside her.

Somewhere around dawn, Penelope woke and remembered the name of the angry man she'd seen leaving Emile's estate. Jacobsen. His name was Jacobsen, and he was a big-time contractor. She'd have to remember to tell Charlie.

❧ FIFTEEN ❧

"Go there and *die*," Penelope muttered into her pillow as the hand resting on her breast took on a life of its own.

Her head wasn't ready to awaken, but the rest of her was already aroused and responding to the large male body wrapped around hers. She'd hoped he would just politely roll away on his own. *Polite* wasn't in Charlie's vocabulary.

The hand lingered, playing a tempting tune along sensitive nerve endings. She had too much self-respect to do this. She had nothing whatsoever in common with Mr. Charlie Smith except this overcharged sexual energy that had come out of nowhere. She didn't want to know what sex with Charlie Smith was like. She wanted to solve his problem—which had somehow become her problem too—and get out of here.

She refused to listen to the awakening voice whispering inside her head that said she'd never know what sex with Charlie was like until she tried it.

Scrambling out from beneath the covers, and batting back the mosquito netting, she escaped the trap of bed and man and her own repressed longings.

Charlie watched her go with a lot more than regret. He wasn't a kid who needed instant gratification. He could deal with a morning erection without dying of it. But he wanted a lot more from Penelope than physical gratification. What he really wanted was to take the comfort she offered and forget the horrors of the real world for just a few minutes. Maybe then he could face the day with the strength he needed.

He'd never wanted a woman for that reason before.

Shaking his head at the mess his mind had become, Charlie crawled out of the sagging bed and looked around as he'd been too tired to do last night.

Jacques hadn't led him astray. The place was sparsely furnished but well tended. The bed and a wicker chest were the only furniture in the room, but they were well made, clean, and more respectable than some places he'd occupied in his misspent youth. Miss Penny should have appreciated the clean sheets, if she'd been awake enough to notice.

Hearing her in the shower, he stumbled into the main room. An apartment-size electric stove, a sink above a single cabinet, and a table apparently made of tree trunks with polished boards for a top indicated the kitchen area. A hammock hanging from the timbered ceiling and the island version of a futon marked the living quarters. After a careful inspection, he discovered the telephone hiding beneath a towering stack of cotton fabric. Whoever owned the place sewed for a living.

Rummaging through a cabinet nailed to the wall, he located coffee and a metal pot. He had the coffee boiling by the time his new chief operating officer appeared from the minuscule bathroom.

She had all that thick black hair loosely clipped into a stack that Charlie hoped would topple at any moment. Without any forethought on his part, his gaze dropped to the perfect breast he'd held in his hand so briefly that morning. She'd covered it with a loose linen camp shirt, but even through the pockets, he could see that she hadn't harnessed herself in one of her damned bras. Maybe, just maybe, Miss Penny was loosening up.

He shouldn't care. He'd known her type back in college, the sorority girls with their preppy clothes and their noses stuck in the air. They'd wiggle under a successful football player eagerly enough, but not one with a busted knee and no prospects. At the time, he'd been putting himself through school on a scholarship and whatever he could earn in his father's struggling construction company. He'd driven an old Plymouth that the cheerleaders laughed at, worn Sears jeans and Goodwill shirts they'd pried off his back and paid their own money to replace with designer duds. He'd thought it funny while he was riding high on NFL prospects. He hadn't appreciated their condescension after the knee incident. Maybe he'd just grown surly with age.

Penelope Albright was no different from those college cheerleaders. She'd already stated her opinion of his choice of clothes and sunglasses. He could just imagine her opinion of his vintage GTO. She was the kind who dated the frat boys, the ones with BMWs and Tommy Hilfiger jeans. Just because they were trapped together in this foreign setting wouldn't change her attitude any. He had too many other concerns at the moment to burn his fingers on a woman like that.

Just acknowledging that she had the power to burn him wrenched at Charlie's gut. He'd stay well away from Miss Penelope from now on. If he'd seen the hammock last night, he would have slept in it. It was safer that way.

She eyed him warily as she sipped the coffee he handed her. "Telephone?"

He almost had to smile at her one-track mind. At least he didn't have to listen to a tirade on all his faults. He'd credit her with that much. "Behind the futon, underneath the stack of cloth. I'll move the table over there so you can set your computer on it."

She nodded and scanned the cabin much as he'd done earlier. "Nice. Food?"

If he wasn't so damned worried, he'd enjoy this. A woman who didn't chatter first thing in the morning. Amazing. "Cereal and goat's milk." She wrinkled her nose without replying, and he grinned. His opinion, expressed more succinctly. "Toast and guava jam."

She nodded in approval. "If you're offering to cook, I accept. Set up the table, and I'll get to work."

She was relegating him to beast of burden. It had happened

often enough for him to recognize the attitude. Right now, he really didn't care. She was doing what he wanted her to do. He'd willingly play the part of ape-man for a while, if that's what it took to find Raul's murderer.

"Is there some way of notifying the police about the cabin in the rain forest?" she asked absently as he hauled the table across the room.

"Is there some point?" he asked with more acidity than she deserved.

"Identifying the body for certain. Tammy has to be told, but it doesn't seem right without more proof."

"He was wearing the watch I gave him last Christmas. How much more proof do you want?" Charlie slammed the table, ashamed of his ill humor but unable to tone it down. He didn't want to believe he'd lost Raul. Raul was his right hand. Raul was the turtle to Charlie's rabbit. Many a time Raul's slower pace had forced Charlie to stop and think things through more clearly, saving him untold amounts of time and money. Who the hell would he rely on now?

Penelope didn't flinch at his tone. "The watch could have been stolen. You owe it to Raul and to Tammy to verify that the remains are his. And to bury them."

"Damn, see if I offer you any more coffee," he muttered, unburying the phone and tracking the line to its source.

"What's coffee got to do with it?" she asked in genuine puzzlement.

"Turns the motor on, apparently. Here, give me your modem cord. Maybe if you get to work you'll shut up."

She shut up without further prompting. Throwing him the phone cord, she went in search of an electrical outlet. The cabin apparently had two: the one to the stove and another behind the futon. Charlie mentally groaned as he glanced up to see her bent over the back of the sofa, looking for the plug. She'd chosen shorts for a change, fitted ones. A backside like that deserved a place in the *Playboy* Hall of Fame.

Unaware of the flight his mind had taken, Penelope slid

back into the seat and opened the laptop, sufficient reminder that he had his own job to do.

He couldn't spend the day watching her work. Toasting the bread in the skillet with some lard from the cupboard, he flipped the pieces onto a plate, left the plate beside Penelope, and ambled off in pursuit of eggs. He'd seen hens in the yard.

By the time he'd fried the eggs, she'd finished her first piece of toast and gone through a second cup of coffee. She also had the tiny piece of junk she called a printer spitting out paper.

He handed her more toast. "What's that?" Slapping an egg on his bread, folding it into a sandwich, and biting a chunk out of it, Charlie reached for the paper as it fell out.

"List of the Foundation's board of directors. Frequently, major stockholders are on the board. I'll start looking them up next." She watched him with a quizzical expression as he read through the list.

Charlie nearly swallowed his egg sandwich whole. "Don't bother with the others. Start with Emile and this Sam Jacobsen." Jacobsen! He should have known.

Penelope glanced up at him with an odd expression. "Why did you choose Jacobsen?"

He didn't like the way she asked that. Now wasn't the time to remember she'd arrived on the same flight as Jacobsen. Coincidence, or not? "I'll answer that if you tell me why you asked," he replied with suspicion.

She looked a little startled at his vehemence. "I just asked because last night I remembered his name. He's a client of my employer. I saw him at the airport and again yesterday, leaving your stepfather's estate."

Hit from two directions, Charlie didn't know which way to turn. Penny knew Jacobsen but didn't work for him. Jacobsen was at Emile's—just before the explosion. This didn't look healthy at all. Did he really want to believe Jacobsen killed Raul?

Penelope's expectant look forced Charlie out of his wallow of grief and confusion. He shrugged. "I'm helping someone sue Jacobsen, he hates my guts, and he's returned the favor by serving papers on me that have closed down all my bank accounts. I've got a payroll to meet next week, and if I don't, all the men working on the hotel in Orlando will walk. I imagine he figures I'll sell the St. Lucia land to get the cash to keep my company running." Charlie's brain ticked quickly. "If we can put Jacobsen together with Emile . . ."

Nibbling at her toast, Penelope punched a few more keys on the computer. "Credit records. Sometimes there are balance sheets attached."

She ate as the machine did its job. Diverted by her toy, Charlie took the seat beside her. He liked learning things hands-on. He had too much energy to sit still for long, staring at any kind of screen: computer, TV, or otherwise. But the gobbledygook scrolling across the laptop contained an array of information he'd like to grab with his hands and haul off the screen. Instead, it jabbered slowly into the printer.

While she waited for the machine to print, she hit some more keys, flipped through a few more on-screen pages, and Emile's name appeared across the top. Charlie widened his eyes as he scanned quickly through the information scrolling before him.

"Damn, but I should have taken computer courses in college. I wasted three years reading Dickens and fiddling with math problems and never learned one thing of any use except the Dolphins' old plays."

Finishing her toast, Penelope unconsciously sucked a smear of jam off her finger, then wiped her hands on a napkin before reaching for the paper falling from the printer. "College has essentially become a playground for kids who don't know what to do with themselves," she answered absently, scanning the printed page in her hand. "Most of the jobs in our current economy can't even be taught in college. Why they don't wise up and start apprenticeship training is beyond my understanding."

Forgetting the paper she handed to him, Charlie stared at

her with incredulity. "I thought all you preppy types believe a college education is essential."

She blinked, shrugged, then returned to reading. "Who needs a college education to lay bricks? A good course on accounting and bookkeeping, maybe contract law, could put someone with technical training into business, provided he'd learned what he should have in high school. College teaches theory, not practical basics. It gives kids time to grow up and maybe learn a little more than they did in high school. Maybe. But when I graduated from accounting school, I couldn't even balance a ledger. I'd never *seen* a ledger. But I had a computer and could use one. Theory is helpful; practice is everything."

"My God, where have you been all my life?" he muttered as he read through the next pages falling from the printer. "Even my father wanted to disown me when I didn't graduate. I wasn't learning anything useful. I was earning a business degree, can you imagine? I took *marketing*. Did that class ever teach me how to go out and hobnob with the movers and shakers? How to make word of mouth sell? Not in this lifetime."

He laid the papers out on the table, pulling out the ones he recognized as balance sheets and laying them on top. "All right, so this shows that both Emile and Jacobsen own percentages of the Resort Foundation. What's that prove?"

"Not any more than we already guessed." She rearranged the stacks. "But this shows Jacobsen is in a heap of financial trouble. And he owes Emile's corporations, big-time." She pulled out another sheet. "He also owes several of the other board members. Are you sure I shouldn't look them up too? A lot of them look European, so it may not be as easy," she added thoughtfully.

Charlie sat back and shuffled through the stack on Jacobsen. "So, we've proved Jacobsen is a desperate man. Where does that get us?"

She turned her beautiful brown eyes in his direction. "You realize Samuel Jacobsen is a big client of PC&M's."

"PC&M?" Charlie could have fallen straight through the beckoning fields of her eyes except he heard the ring of warning in her voice.

"My employer." Her voice had taken on a flatness he didn't recognize. "They do the bookkeeping for Jacobsen's companies, as well as financial statements and taxes."

He wanted to kiss her. "You mean, you could—"

She cut him off. "I'd lose my job. That's confidential information. I'd lose my license as well. I could be fired just for digging into his background like this."

That had been too lucky a break. He should have known it. "What if he had Michel and Raul murdered?"

"Then the authorities would have to subpoena the information." She glanced down at the screen, hit a message light, and opened her e-mail. "Beth got my note about Tamara." Penelope frowned and glanced down at her watch. "It's almost noon here. What time did Tammy's flight arrive?"

"Dawn. I had my pilot take her in. Why, what's wrong?" Charlie jerked the screen around so he could read it. "Damn," he swore. "Where the hell is she?"

"Not with Beth," she answered dryly. "Pilot? You have your own pilot?"

He read the message again. No Tamara. "Florida is a big state. It was taking too long to get from job to job. So I got a plane. Now I can fly crews in and out as I need them." He couldn't look away from the screen. Where had the damned idiot gone?

"Maybe you could call your pilot?"

"He'll have hit the sack by now after flying in the middle of the night. I can leave a message on his machine. Turn this thing off so I can hook up the phone again."

"Give me his name and number; I'll have Beth do it. She'll need to be our Miami connection."

Charlie glared at her. "I thought you said your sister was blind. How's she reading this damned thing?"

Penelope shrugged. "Voice monitor. There are limitations,

but one of the guys I went to college with is on the high-tech edge of these things. Beth tests his software."

With a snort of disbelief, Charlie gave her the number and lurched to his feet to pace the room. He didn't need this now. Damn Tamara . . . He would wring her neck.

"Charlie."

The alarm mixed with worry in Penelope's voice swung Charlie around. "What?"

She stared at the screen. "I just got another message from Beth. She says someone is trying to crack my firewall."

"What?" He tried not to yell, but that made no sense at all.

"I use my PC at home to network with the firm's computers. I've installed the newest software that keeps hackers like me out. Someone's trying to break through it. It shrieks a warning. Beth wants to know what to do next." A frown creased Penelope's forehead as she looked up at him. "I don't have that firewall on this machine yet. They may know everything I've looked up this morning."

"Can they trace it?" Charlie demanded.

"If I were them, I'd damned well be hunting me down right now. They'll know I'm on the island server. I have no idea if the St. Lucia telephone system can sustain a wiretap, but if they have police connections, they can probably trace us through the server number."

"Hell, shut that thing down and let's get out of here. If *I've* got police connections, you know damned well Emile does."

"Give me a minute. I want Beth to delete the network software. I don't want them after her too."

Charlie stared in dismay at the vulnerable nape of Penelope's slender white neck as she bent over the laptop. She'd stuck that neck out because of him, and now he had three women in danger.

Maybe he ought to sell the damned land and cut his losses while he could.

Before he could follow that thought, Penelope was standing in front of him, her eyes nearly on a level with his.

"I've got the address for Beth's ex in my e-mail file. He's

a bastard of the worst degree, but he's a cop. He can find Tamara and keep Beth safe. It will do him good to be useful. And we need the cops on our side, Charlie."

He heard the warning in her voice, but he also heard the commitment. He'd never heard a more beautiful sound in his life. Miss Nose-in-the-Air Careerwoman was with him on this, even though it might cost her her precious job.

Without giving it a second thought, Charlie wrapped Penelope in his arms and kissed her. The minute his lips touched hers, he forgot to think at all.

❧ SIXTEEN ❧

Penelope slid her hands around Charlie's broad T-shirted back, as if she'd done it a thousand times before. Charlie might not know the meaning of the word *cautious*, but he had a good grasp on *gentle*. His mouth seduced her with gentleness, plied her with lovely, mind-bending kisses until she no longer wondered at her insanity but offered him what he wanted.

The instant she parted her lips and his tongue touched hers, a shudder swept through him and he tightened his grip around her waist. The pressure warned Penelope she was playing too deep, that it was time to back away, but she ignored the warning she'd obeyed so often these last few years. Charlie's muscles rippling beneath her palms felt too good, too right, and the mouth covering hers obliterated any other thought. He kissed her as if he meant it, as if he wanted just this intimacy and nothing more, as if he really cared enough to hold her and kiss her and cherish her without demanding more than she had to offer. And she fell for it, hook, line, and sinker.

Lifting his head, Charlie gazed into her eyes with as much amazement as she felt. "My God," he whispered. Apparently unable to formulate a more complete sentence, he lowered his head toward hers again.

Penelope's fingers gripped his back, torn between holding him closer and pushing him away. But the decision was ripped from her as he caught sight of something outside the window and swiftly dropped his hands.

"Cops! Grab your computer. They can't know we're here, but it's just a matter of time. . . ." Cursing under his breath, he began pulling telephone and electrical cords and throwing them in her direction.

Glancing out the window, Penelope caught sight of a uniformed officer on a motor scooter slowly rolling by on the dirt road outside. She dropped to the futon and hurriedly shut down the program. Heart beating so fast she figured she'd fall on her face if she stood up again, she forced herself to calm down. "What are they doing? Patrolling?"

"If they're looking for us, they've got a list of Jacques's naturalist friends. They've been a thorn in the government's side for years. But it doesn't look like the cops are in a hurry to get out and beat the bushes yet. What are they going to charge us with anyway? Existing?" Charlie stalked to the back room. Still cursing, he shoved clothes into their bags and backpack.

Obviously, men recovered from earthshaking kisses faster than women. Or the earth hadn't moved for him as it had for her. Her fingers actually shook as she shoved the laptop into its case. Maybe she'd refrained from sex too long and this was the result. If so, she'd damned well better get it out of her system before she began thinking it meant anything.

Love on the run, she thought grimly as she draped the strap over her shoulder and hurried to grab her sack of clothing from Charlie. She should have had a sensible backpack too, but stumbling through jungles hadn't been on her itinerary.

"Where do we go now?" she asked in exasperation as he checked out the wide front window. "We can't get anything done if we keep picking up and running."

Charlie glanced around the neat little room with a half-crooked smile that nearly took her breath away, then fixed her with a look that shook her clear down to her shoes. "Yeah, I was just beginning to like this place. I could have stayed awhile longer."

Which didn't answer her stated question but certainly answered one or two others. He wouldn't have stopped at kissing. She should have known. She had known; she'd just fooled herself into thinking otherwise. Damn the man. Women probably fell all over him. It meant nothing to him. She'd better keep that thought firmly planted in the forefront of her mind, right after staying alive.

"Let's just get out of here, okay?" she demanded anxiously.

"Righto, it's into the hills we go. Pity they burned Raul's shack." He shifted his backpack, snagged the laptop from Penelope's shoulder, and hooked it over his own. "Out the back window, my fair lady. Got your climbing shoes on?"

She didn't own climbing shoes. She wore the cheap Keds she'd intended to wear for walking on the beach. But they were better than heels. With a sigh, Penelope threw her sack of clothing through the window and followed him out under the camouflage of a fern tree. Charlie's hands catching her waist and helping her down didn't ease her jumbled thoughts, only increased her awareness. She had a sudden mental image of Charlie's impressive chest, naked and leaning over her. Just the image took her breath away. She'd probably faint if it ever became reality.

Get a grip, she muttered to herself as she trudged in Charlie's footsteps through the thick greenery behind the house. Maybe she was in a state of denial. Thinking of sex was her mind's way of avoiding the danger they could be in. She really hadn't tapped into fear yet. She simply couldn't believe this was a life-threatening situation. But two men were dead, their jeep had been wrecked, and Tammy had disappeared. And someone had tried to breach her firewall. Now she knew she was in trouble.

They had to take only a few steps before the cottage disappeared entirely behind the curtain of trees and vines. Penelope prayed Charlie knew where he was going, because any sign of civilization disappeared along with the cottage.

"Do you think we should head back to Miami?" she asked tentatively. From this angle, she could see no more than his broad back. She hadn't learned to read him yet, but she judged by the way he was stomping down the undergrowth that he wasn't in an amiable mood.

"I need to be in two places. Hell, I need Raul." He shut up again, ripping a massive vine out of his way and forging a path of his own through what could be someone's backyard, as far as she could tell.

"Beth will start looking for Tammy. She's learned to really manipulate the computer and telephones. If John gets my message, he can help. It's not much, but it's better than nothing until we get there," she offered.

"If she's done this on purpose, I'll strangle her myself."

That wasn't helpful. Penelope threw Charlie's broad shoulders a scornful look. That was the problem with men his size. They thought brute strength would solve everything. Her stomach did a little jig at the fleeting thought of just what men of his size could do, but she didn't linger there. "Maybe she'll check in with Beth before long. We've got to figure out what to do next. We can't play Tarzan and Jane forever."

He threw her a look over his shoulder that involved a lifted eyebrow and a half smirk she should have kicked him for, but Penelope allowed him his little nonsense. He had reason to be half out of his mind.

"This Tarzan has no more fondness for jungle than Jane," he admitted, turning back to the task at hand and beating his way through banana leaves. "If I knew who on the island is on Jacobsen's payroll, I might make some progress."

"If that's all it takes, we just need to search for his local bank account. I doubt he pays vandals and murderers by check, but I wouldn't think he'd be stupid enough to send cash through the mail. Someone has to be taking drafts from a bank account here."

"And I suppose you can locate his bank account with that little box."

Penelope shrugged even if he couldn't see her. "I can create whole new identities with this 'little box.' I'm amazed that authorities haven't caught on to what can be done out there in cyberspace. I've known kids who can break into banks, past the most sophisticated of firewalls. I probably can't do that, but I bet the island bank has a standard software package I can get through without much problem."

He stopped and looked back at her. "Could you empty Jacobsen's bank accounts?"

"Here, easily. Back there? With a lot of work." Penelope shifted her sack to the other hand and glared at him. "But I won't."

She almost thought she saw admiration in his expression before he returned to hiking ahead of her.

"I'm gonna have to get me someone like you when I get back," he announced without preliminaries.

"Good luck. It'll cost you," she muttered. "And the authorities eventually catch on, so if you have crime in mind, be prepared to pay the price."

"Crime isn't what I have in mind at all." He didn't elaborate but studied a telephone pole emerging in the field ahead. "They usually keep extra wire out here in case of emergency."

The jump from crime to wire took a minute, but Penelope followed the path of his thoughts as easily as she did his path through the undergrowth. She stared upward at the low wires crossing the forest into the open field beyond. Civilization was never far away in this place. She should be grateful. The speculative look in Charlie's eyes wiped away any thought of gratitude.

"We can't camp out here in the middle of nowhere," she protested. "I don't care how many wires you can run or how much electricity you can steal. I'm losing my job because of you, Charlie Smith; I'll not become a criminal."

"I bet you don't even cheat on your income taxes." He shot her a rueful look and continued their march to nowhere.

"That's the way I was brought up," she replied stiffly.

"You don't mind stealing information but you stop short of cheating. I wonder just how far your shield of integrity and honor goes."

"What do you mean?" she asked testily.

"Nothing. Nothing at all. I'm just not used to dealing with women who won't scheme and lie to get what they want. It seems to come with the territory."

"You're a pig, you know that, Charlie? Why don't you just lead me to the nearest road and I'll take my chances on finding my own way out of here."

To her utter surprise, he turned and grabbed her shoulders, hugging them soundly. "Not a chance, baby. It's you and me against the world. Come on, I know where to go."

"What are you doing here?" Having opened the door, Beth couldn't very well slam it in the face of the man standing on the other side, but she would have liked to. Even though she couldn't see him, she'd know John's presence a mile away.

"I got Penny's message. She says there's some kind of trouble and asked me to stop by."

"Well, as you can see," Beth said this last word sarcastically, "I'm perfectly fine. You can go on about your business."

"Don't you even want to ask about the kids?"

She could almost swear she heard bitterness in his voice. What right did *he* have to be bitter? "I don't want to *have* to ask about the kids. I want them here with me, *telling* me how they are. And if you can't manage that much, then you could at least volunteer the information. I shouldn't have to ask."

"Then I'm volunteering. Will you get out of my way so I can come in or do I have to do it from out here?"

She didn't want to let him in. She didn't want him watching her tapping around a room stripped bare for her sake. Penelope, bless her heart, had stored all her lovely furniture and moved them into this apartment furnished for the handicapped—the physically challenged, she amended. All the counters and tables were built without sharp edges and fixed in place so no one could move them and catch her unaware. She hated it, hated knowing she needed the help, hated knowing Penelope had given up her own life, hated herself for not having the courage to just die and make everyone happier. Most of all, she hated her ex-husband for talking at her with pity behind his words.

Turning her back on John as he entered and closed the door, she returned to the computer table. "A friend of Penelope's is missing and now I can't reach Penny either. I think she's in some kind of trouble, but she's out in the middle of a jungle on an island, with no means of communication. I'm worried about her."

"If she's managed to reach both of us, then she's not without communication. I wouldn't worry about that sister of yours. She could raze the jungle in a single day if she needed to. Who's the friend and where's she missing from?"

Beth bent her head over the keyboard rather than let him see the flush on her cheeks as he stood behind her. She'd started dating John right out of high school. He was the only lover she'd ever known. And her physical reaction to him hadn't changed despite all the obstacles between them. Unfortunately, his had the instant she'd gone blind.

"She's a twenty-year-old kid who was supposed to have arrived at the airport this morning. I've left a message with the pilot of her private plane, but he hasn't returned it yet. I'm trying to track down someone at the airport to verify that the flight arrived." She held the information her Braille printer had transcribed from Penelope's e-mail with the pilot's name and number.

John reached over her shoulder and appropriated the phone and her notes. At six feet, he had a long reach. Beth held her breath and rolled the office chair out of his way. She didn't have much room between desk and console, and he didn't acknowledge her personal space. He propped his hip against her desk and hit the dial buttons.

She honestly thought her teeth would chatter as she listened to him in action. She'd always admired his competence in solving problems. It had taken years before she realized that there were some problems he solved by not facing them. He could hammer a nail or find a crook, but he couldn't deal with her emotional needs. After the accident, he couldn't deal with her at all.

He jotted down a number, hung up, and dialed again. In moments, she heard him repeating the time of arrival and jotting it down, then checking on passengers and flight plans. When he hung up, he had everything she'd been scrambling all over creation for.

"The plane arrived at 6:10 A.M., pilot and one passenger, a Tamara St. Philippe, checked through customs on schedule. I'll have headquarters check the taxi stand. You say this is the pilot's number? I'll have someone go out there and wake him up."

"You don't have to do this," she said resentfully, jerking the paper from his hand. "I'm not completely helpless. I checked the number in the directory, and I have a friend going over there now."

She heard the brush of his shirtsleeves as he crossed his arms over his chest. "All right, then explain what Penny meant about someone cracking your firewall." She could see his shadow glancing around at the eggshell paint of the apartment walls. "I don't see any cracked walls. Is it back in the bedrooms?"

"The computer firewall," Beth answered irritably. "Someone's trying to hack Penny's computer. She's afraid that someone may come here. I have no idea what she's up to or why anyone would want to break into her computer. There's nothing here that a hacker couldn't find in a dozen other places."

"Well, then, I guess we'd better find out. DeeDee has a dance rehearsal at four. We'd better get on it."

Beth wanted to cry hysterically and smack him at the same time. He thought he could just waltz back in here and take over her life again. Damn Penelope. She'd had no business calling on John. Beth didn't want him here. She'd just begun to learn to cope without him. She didn't want to be reminded of how good it felt to work alongside him. She'd never been alone in her life until the accident.

She had plenty of time to get used to being alone again after he left.

"Penelope forwarded some information she'd dug up on a man named Jacobsen," she said with a sigh. "Maybe we should start there."

❧ SEVENTEEN ❧

Penelope glanced up from the laptop and, shielding her eyes from the hot sun, checked on the man pounding at the shingles of a tottering, stilt-legged shack. Charlie's hammering had taken on the aspect of jungle drums as the day wore on. She could almost read the escalating tension in the viciousness of his blows.

He'd stripped off his shirt, and sweat glistened over bronzed skin and hard muscle. She was almost grateful that he'd chosen to take his frustrations out on the roof instead of her. Almost. A niggling imp inside her wondered how it would feel with all that naked flesh concentrated on her and not the roof. She gulped as he reached for another nail, and she glimpsed the pelt of hair narrowing down his taut abdomen. She was ready to melt like hot wax, and the sun had nothing whatsoever to do with it.

Reluctantly, she turned her attention back to the shade and the rickety table holding her laptop. Charlie had run wires for the telephone hookup from the pole, but the electricity came from the shack he worked on now. True to his word, he was paying for their borrowed utilities by repairing the roof. She didn't know how he intended to pay the telephone company, but since all her calls so far were local, she wasn't worrying about it.

They'd attracted a string of uninvited guests as the day

wore on. Apparently Jacques's local environmental group was small but close-knit. As soon as she and Charlie had arrived at this shack deep in the interior, word had gone out as if spread by jungle drums, or Charlie's hammering. The house itself was apparently owned by a relative of one of the group, but Jacques had assured Charlie the police knew nothing of it.

All day Jacques's friends had drifted in and out to check on their progress. One had possessed the forethought to bring her a ream of typing paper. She hadn't exactly worked her way through it yet. The information they sought was elusive. Jacobsen hid his trail well, but she was making progress. As Jacques's friends had observed, the Resort Foundation had connections to every major resort in the Caribbean, few of them environmentally friendly.

Resolutely, she tried to set aside the prejudices of the people encouraging her efforts, but she had to admit they had a point. The world didn't need still another concrete monument to greed and selfishness. The island harbored a rare beauty too seldom found in this day and age. She had difficulty balancing the beauty of nature with poverty and her own profit-oriented mind-set, but she could see the protesters' concerns. She'd hate to watch the rain forest destroyed for golf courses, and the wild beaches turned into lines of artificial grass huts and beach umbrellas for yet another hotel. She'd heard the rain forest provided oxygen, and rare plants that could someday make medicines that would save lives. It might even hold a cure for Beth. That was a bottom line she could understand.

So she worked her way through the web of Jacobsen's holdings while Charlie pounded the tar out of the roof. At least the woman who owned the shack would have a sturdier home when all was said and done. All Penelope would have to show for her day's efforts was a stack of papers with bank accounts, properties, and lots and lots of names. A roof was more constructive.

Searching the background on some of those names left her

more than a little uneasy. She'd heard tales of the Russian Mafia, but she'd thought them alarmist and of no interest to sunny Miami. But Jacobsen had an unending source of funds from two people who definitely had Russian passports. That didn't necessarily mean anything, but the potential for criminal money-laundering gave her the jitters.

Charlie nailed the final shingle to the roof as the sun began its slide behind the rock formations below. Too weary to sit still any longer, Penelope shut down the laptop and wandered over to watch him climb down. She regretted it immediately. Even though he'd thrown on a shirt, Charlie—standing this close, exuding healthy male sweat—rumbled her insides more than lack of food.

Eyes shadowed, he heaved his tools onto the front porch. "Ready to go?"

"Go?" He'd kept up a steady conversation with the various people drifting in and out all day, but she'd not followed the patois.

"Marcos found a place for us to stay for the night. It's safer if we keep moving, and you'll like it better than the jungle."

From the way he said that, Penelope had her doubts, but they had nothing to do with their accommodations and everything to do with the man accompanying her to them. Somehow, she had the impression that he hadn't completely worked out his frustrations on the roof.

"You are *insane*," Penelope muttered as they slipped inside the luxurious cottage nestled between hibiscus and privacy hedges in the isolated back acres of Jalousie Plantation.

Charlie checked the drapes, determined they were closed, and flipped a light switch. "And here I thought I was being extremely clever. Goes to prove it's all semantics." He admired the huge bed with its floral comforter, then peeked behind the shade at the steaming Jacuzzi in the pool lights outside. The oleander hid it nicely.

"Security will probably arrest us before dawn." She

dropped her laptop on the gleaming mahogany desk and glanced with interest at the kitchenette.

"Marcos *is* security," Charlie reminded her. "I thought after a day in the jungle, you'd appreciate a few of the comforts of home." He surveyed the bathroom, checked all the windows to determine how well the shrubbery hid their privacy, and deciding they were safe for the moment, flung his backpack in the closet. "Why don't we take a break and sample the Jacuzzi and some of this wine?" He picked through the basket of cheese and fruit on the counter, wondering if Marcos had provided that too.

Penelope stood mulishly in the center of the room, looking around as if she suspected assassins to jump out from behind the fancy dresser. He'd hauled her through wooden shacks, rain forests, and banana jungles and she hadn't uttered a word of complaint. He took her somewhere fancy, and she froze like a Popsicle. Maybe she suspected he had an ulterior motive.

Hell, he did have an ulterior motive. Sighing, Charlie stripped off his shirt and headed for the shower. "I imagine that desk has all you need. I wrote down the access code Marcos gave me. If we keep switching identities, we should stay one step ahead of any trace they have out."

She didn't look at him. She did that a lot. Charlie was beginning to think he was so ugly she was repulsed. He'd caught himself checking mirrors a couple of times to be certain he hadn't developed some kind of fungus. Jacobsen had already made him feel like a fool. Raul's death had shaken his confidence and undermined the world as he knew it. And now Miss Penny was succeeding in decimating what remained of his male pride. Maybe he ought to just wriggle on his belly to the shower.

"Your environmentalist friends trust you," she said softly.

Charlie froze and turned to watch her with suspicion. "They trust Jacques."

She busied herself plugging in the laptop. "They know who you are," she argued. "And even though you represent the enemy, they're more willing to trust you than your step-father or the other development companies on the island. That says a great deal."

All right, so maybe he wasn't lower than a snake's belly, but why had she bothered to admit it? He didn't figure that raised him any higher in her eyes. He shrugged. "They're just looking for justice."

She nodded and flipped on a switch. She hadn't sat down but stood fiddling with the wires as if prepared to bolt at the first alarm. Finally, she looked up at him.

Charlie had forgotten he'd removed his shirt until he saw her eyes widen. If his ego were in full gear, he'd almost believe he saw appreciation behind those long lashes before they lowered. He guessed they'd spent most of their more private moments in darkness, so she probably hadn't seen much of him. With Penelope, he couldn't tell if he scared her half to death or if she really liked what she saw. At least, with her height, she didn't make him feel like a randy bull beside a terrified heifer. He balled his shirt up in his fist and headed for the shower, out of the electrically charged air between them.

"You've just lost your friend, your business is in danger of going under, and you spent the day fixing up a shack in a backwater town that could offer you no more than a good meal. Maybe they've got reason to trust you."

Charlie stopped as if he'd hit a brick wall. He didn't turn around this time. He didn't trust himself or what he heard in her voice. "What else was I supposed to do? You're the computer dynamo. They provided you with what you needed. I just kept busy." In the world he knew, women expected men to hammer and nail. And in the world Penelope hailed from, women thought men who hammered and nailed were little better than trained apes. He wasn't sure where she was going with this.

"Have it your way. I told Beth I'd meet her in a chat room at seven. I'd better sign on."

He didn't hear coldness in her voice. Charlie supposed that was a step in the right direction. He strode briskly to the shower before she could divert him again. He didn't know what the hell a "chat" room was, but the immense amount of information she'd generated impressed him enough to want to be there when she got back from cyberspace.

Holding her breath so she didn't sigh outright, Penelope slid into the desk chair in front of her computer. If she could just concentrate on her task and not the half-naked man who'd left the room, she might be able to get out of here tonight and back to work in the morning. She couldn't remember any man who'd ever rattled her so badly. Even Zack hadn't looked that impressive with his shirt off. Zack had been only twenty. She really should have looked at a few more men since then.

But she'd spent her time since college in corporate offices and hadn't found a single man in a pinstripe suit who'd rattled her breathless like Charlie did. Maybe she should have taken a few of them home to see if it was just the neckties that put her off. Maybe she had this latent gene that required primitive men. Maybe she needed a good night's sleep.

Beth wasn't there when she reached the agreed-upon chat room. Penelope didn't like leaving the computer modem hooked up for long periods of time, but there was no point in turning it off only to go back in again. The island phones weren't all that reliable. She'd have to wait.

But waiting left her mind unoccupied. Mental images of Charlie working in the hot sun, pounding shingles on an old roof while relying on her to find the information he needed jarred her sense of place in the world. She *knew* men like Charlie: football players who sat in front of the TV and drank beer all night watching sports, men who thought women should be barefoot, pregnant, and in the kitchen. She knew men who wore suits and still thought women were for bedrooms and not boardrooms. Just because they hadn't encountered any televisions or sports on the island didn't mean Charlie had changed his spots. And she'd seen him poker up every time she avoided anything resembling a physical advance. He didn't handle rejection well. Still, he seemed to be relying on her more than any man ever had. He assumed she could do what he could not, and he accepted it. She wasn't certain how to take that.

Beth's greeting appeared below hers on the screen, and with relief, Penelope returned her attention to the problem at hand.

After a long shower and shave guaranteed to drag out the time until Penelope had climbed into bed, Charlie returned to the main room, wearing the thick bathrobe the resort provided. A dim bedside light revealed plump empty pillows and no shiny spill of black hair. He panicked until he sought the desk and saw the shadow of the laptop. She wouldn't leave without her computer.

Odd how hope could soar when everything was against him. If he had an ounce of sense, he'd be afraid something had happened to his efficient comrade-in-arms. Instead, he strode to the draperies and checked the Jacuzzi.

And smiled. She was there, head and neck resting on a pool pillow, pale arms floating beneath the bubbling water in complete relaxation. He'd packed her swimsuit and knew better than to expect anything *too* revealing, but still, he liked the looks of this setting.

Carrying the wine and two glasses outside, he set them on a poolside table and poured. "What did your sister find out?" he asked casually, leaning over to hand her one.

Charlie's heart nearly leapt through his skin when he saw her look up at him with shadowed eyes. Maybe he'd better put his trunks on. Originally, he'd planned on getting dressed and going out again, but finding her out here had given him different ideas. Her look of wariness and hope, now combined with a tantalizing glimpse of sexual awareness as her gaze flitted to his chest, captivated him. Carefully, he dropped to the pool's edge and dunked his legs into the warm water.

"Raul was alive two days ago," she stated flatly.

Her words slapped him more forcefully than her hand could. "Alive? That's impossible. There were vines over that body. . . ." Adrenaline triggered his heart into pounding erratically. "How does she know?"

The pool lights illuminated Penelope's face from below, hiding her eyes, but he could hear the wariness in her voice.

"Raul called your office and warned you not to come to St. Lucia, according to your secretary. I assume your secretary would recognize his voice?"

"Sherry?" Charlie tried to think, but exultation pounded through his veins. Sherry had no reason to lie, probably didn't have the brains to lie. That meant that the body in the jungle was not his best friend. Raul might still be alive. Why had he disappeared without contacting him? Remembering Tammy, he fought his suspicions.

"Sherry's been with us a year. She's an airhead, but she ought to know his voice." He forced his thoughts along more sensible channels. "What about Tamara? Have they found her?"

"She checked in, says she's fine; she's looking for Raul. John couldn't trace the call. She was very reluctant to say anything to him." Penelope pushed the pillow away and sat up straight. "If Raul is alive, who does that body belong to? And is Jacobsen really dangerous, then? Maybe some homeless person just burned the hut down. Maybe there's nothing going on here at all. Maybe Raul is the crook."

Penelope's movement drew Charlie's attention back to the pool. He didn't want to think about Raul being a crook. He wanted to focus on the way the water churned Penelope's curves into a wavering illusion in the pool light. The red strips that were her modest two-piece suit beneath the bubbling water taunted him. Her suggestions needled, but he brushed the pinpricks aside. He had to believe Tammy and Raul were safe. The relief made him a little light-headed. Computer hackers seemed far away under these conditions. He could afford to relax a little, revamp his plans, go after Jacobsen in a more organized manner. In the morning.

By morning, Penelope would think she could hie herself back around the coast to her infernal job, and never see him again. He couldn't let that happen. Not yet. It still wasn't safe. Besides, they needed to take this moment a little further to see where it led.

Without replying, Charlie unbelted the robe and slid into the silky warmth of the water.

He didn't give her time to gasp. He did what had worked so well earlier. He caught her by surprise and kissed her.

Oh, God, she tasted wonderful. Her tongue tasted of sweet chardonnay and her breath carried the scent of mint. The sweetness combined with the delectable moisture of her eager response drained all the blood straight from Charlie's head to his groin and he nearly passed out. Her fingers glided over his skin and every hair shot up with the electricity of the contact.

Groaning, he slid his hands around her bare back and settled her firmly in his lap. She stiffened at the contact with his arousal, but he lifted her higher and continued his explorations of the moist cave of her mouth. Gradually, she relaxed enough to wrap her arms around his neck and accept the pleasure of their joined lips.

Charlie luxuriated in the ease of their mating, the hungry kisses, the silken touches beneath the water, the desire bubbling as hot and powerful as the whirlpool around them. Penelope clung and melted as thoroughly as he did.

Until he hooked his fingers in her swimsuit top and freed her breasts.

She didn't exactly freeze, but she pulled back, fighting the stroke of his hand.

"Charlie, we have nothing in common," she whispered into his ear.

"Probably not," he agreed. He would have agreed with a bullfrog right now. His hand held the most delicious curve of pillowed softness he'd ever known. Not too large, not too small, just enough to fill his palm. Her soft moan as he stroked her fed his need. He couldn't have released her if his life depended on it. So he agreed with her. She was probably right. She usually was.

"I don't do this anymore," she murmured against his ear as his hand kneaded her breast and plucked her nipple. "It's not profitable without commitment."

"This isn't about profit. This is about us." Ignoring her absurd argument, Charlie reached for the last scrap of material between them.

She nearly leapt out of his arms as his fingers slid beneath the spandex and touched her where she boiled as hot and furious as the volcano that had formed this island.

So much for argument. He drew off her swimsuit bottom, and she kicked it adrift as her frantic kisses covered his chest.

❧ EIGHTEEN ❧

Penelope floated in his arms. Water slid down their chests, bubbled around their thighs, pumped into the air pockets where flesh rubbed flesh. Charlie held her so his arousal merely teased, and frustration steamed through her. She had about as much control as the volcano.

Penelope clawed at Charlie's shoulders, caught his lip with her teeth, thrust her tongue into the heat of his mouth, but still he wouldn't lower her. Instead, he raised her higher until his teeth nibbled at her nipple, and she cried out.

She'd never lost her head before. Never. But she was losing it now. She writhed in his hold, pressing her breast deeper into his mouth but not succeeding in reaching the part of him she needed most. She dug her fingers into his hair, slid her tongue into his ear, bit his earlobe until he shivered as much as she did, but still, his strength held her captive.

"Charlie!" she heard herself pleading. She never pleaded. She didn't like sex. She didn't want this. But parts of her throbbed as they never had before, and she knew of no other relief.

"We have nothing in common," he reminded her, kissing the corner of her mouth as his hand played havoc where his lips had been just moments before.

Her breasts ached beyond belief, but her lower parts ached more. "Charlie, don't do this," she whispered.

177

"Don't do what?" His hand slid down, parting her lower lips. "This?"

"Oh, God, Charlie, please," she moaned, hating herself for moaning, but she couldn't stop now. She was too close to shattering. He was too close to prevent it. She slid her hands down his chest, wrapped her fingers in the hair there, and urged her hips closer to his.

"Please what, pretty Penny? Tell me. I don't want to do the wrong thing. Remember, we have nothing in common."

She would kill him. When this was all over, she would shove a knife between his ribs. But it wasn't knives she wanted shoved right now. Prying one hand between them, she sought his arousal.

Now he was the one groaning. Good. Two could play this game.

Except he was so *big*. He surged and bucked against her, and she lost him as she grabbed for balance. Her fingers dug into his wide shoulders as she suddenly started sliding downward.

"Penny!" he groaned in sheer agony. "I didn't come prepared for this."

He tried to haul her away, but she wasn't having any of it. Kneeling over him now, she could feel the thrust of his arousal where he'd opened her and left her empty. One more stroke . . .

The primal cry ripping from Charlie's throat as Penelope thrust downward echoed her own cry as his thickness filled her.

She tried to back away, but it was far too late. Charlie's big hands caught her hips, steadied her, easing her downward as he shifted upward. In one sudden surge, he parted her completely, until he was so firmly embedded, there was no knowing beginning or end.

"Charlie," she whispered as he began to move, but she had nothing to say. Their bodies said it all.

He touched her in places she'd never been touched, aroused her in ways she'd never known possible. His hands were everywhere, stroking, urging, caressing, demanding until she was insane with need for more, to feel the same inside as out. He rocked with her, gently at first, letting her adjust until the frenzy within them grew too great. His fingers dug into her hips then, holding her, guiding her as he took over the pace.

Penelope swallowed her screams as she lost control. Charlie pounded her with as much force as the nails he'd driven earlier that day, but she knew no pain, only a devastating ride toward the edge of no return. She dangled on the peak, clutching at thin air, gasping for breath, until Charlie slid his hand between them and pushed her over the edge.

He fell with her. She felt him fall, felt him hanging on to her, calling her name, riding with her as they tumbled, weightless, into the depths. Penelope clung to him all the way down, sheltered in his embrace.

For the first time in her life, all the parts of her came together as one whole woman.

He could sleep for a week, just float off on this cloud of water, wrapped in silken flesh, more contented than he'd ever dreamed possible. She'd wiped out his mind, erased his will, reduced him to sensitive nerve endings and nothing more.

He registered every creamy curve, every satin tendril plastered against his shoulders and arms as Penelope's soft weight rested against him. Her heart beat in time with his where her breasts pressed into his chest. No one could convince him that they weren't made for each other. No one. Ever. Not while his mind boiled with the liquid fire of their lovemaking anyway.

Gradually, reason returned. They'd have to climb out of the pool or risk boiling like lobsters. With huge effort, Charlie located his feet and the bottom of the pool and heaved upward, carrying Penelope with him.

She stirred against him but didn't protest as he locked her legs over his arm and pulled her free of the water. The balmy night air caressed their overheated skin, and he was glad he hadn't bothered with the air-conditioning. The shock would have woken them too abruptly. He leaned over and caught the terry robe with his fingertips. She pulled it around her as he carried her the few steps into their room. He liked shielding her in his arms like this, taking care of her. That scared him. This woman of steel didn't need his or any other man's protection. But tonight, she'd been all soft femininity in his arms. He could handle that.

Charlie wanted to collapse in the bed beside her as he laid Penelope on the sheets, wrapped in terry cloth, but his mind was clicking again.

He heard her murmured protest as he wandered off in search of a towel instead of climbing in beside her. That wasn't all he hunted for. He needed the wallet he had given her. Besides his credit cards and identification, it contained the only packages of protection he possessed. He hadn't exactly come to St. Lucia with sex in mind.

The more he woke up, the more he couldn't understand what had happened. Yeah, he'd had sex in mind from the moment he'd first laid eyes on Penelope. He'd gone out to the pool with a vague idea of seducing her. But he'd had some fuzzy image of leading her into bed, sensibly asking where his wallet was, and taking it from there. There hadn't been a damned thing sensible about anything they'd done.

That alone was scary as hell. He'd had lots of women. It wasn't any big deal. He'd take them to his place, fix them some spaghetti, have a good time, and, feeling much better, he'd take them home the next day and not give them another thought. That was sensible. He had a drawer full of condoms. That was sensible. Not looking for more than a release of sexual tension was sensible. Having sex with a woman who was the antithesis of everything he'd ever wanted in a woman was *not* sensible. Having it in a Jacuzzi without protection was the next best thing to insane.

Imagining Penelope Albright swollen with his child aroused images that gave him cold chills.

With a shiver, Charlie stalked barefoot through the suite.

He'd damned well buy an entire box of condoms first thing in the morning.

By the time he found what he was looking for, he'd dried off sufficiently to climb into bed beside her. By then, Penelope was sound asleep, and he had no need of the foil packages he shoved under his pillow. Cursing softly, he peeled away the robe and hauled her against him, relaxing in the warmth radiating from her bare skin. Finally, he'd stripped the starch out of her. Now, if he could just persuade her to stay that way . . .

Sunlight sneaked between the slats of the wooden blinds and crept around the edges of the window before Penelope woke the next day. Disoriented, she lay beneath the terrycloth robe she'd pulled over her as she woke. She never slept naked. She was naked now. And so was the big man lying on his side next to her. Very naked. Without a sheet. She didn't dare open her eyes. Feeling his body heat was sufficient.

She ached as she hadn't ached in years. But she felt more wonderfully relaxed than she ever had in her life. Physical well-being flooded through her as she stretched, and cautiously, she replayed her memory of last night.

The kissing part she could handle. Charlie was a fantastic kisser. She would wish he'd wake and do it again right now if it weren't for where kissing inevitably led. Penelope forced herself to stop and think it over again before pushing the panic button.

He was big, there was no getting around that. She grinned briefly to herself. She *had* gotten around that. She'd been narrow and small, and he'd felt like a damned telephone pole shoving against her, just as Zack had. But everything after that had been different. She'd adjusted to his thickness, taken him inside her, and it hadn't hurt. It had gone far beyond not hurting. It had been marvelous, as explosive as the books had promised it would be, more powerful than her imagination had ever anticipated, not that she had much imagination, she admitted.

And now Charlie was snoring beside her. Penelope opened her eyes to slits, trying to accept that those muscled shoulders and narrow hips belonged to a man who had turned her world upside down. If he rolled over right now, she would probably panic and run. She didn't *know* this man. They were the next best thing to strangers. And he had taken her to the moon and back.

Shaken, she eased toward the edge of the bed. She'd made love with a construction worker, a man she hadn't even dated. They hadn't used protection, for heaven's sake! Her mind flew to that thought and clung there hysterically. How could she do that to herself? He could have given her anything. . . .

Not Charlie. Penelope relaxed a little as she slipped from the bed without his noticing. Maybe she didn't know Charlie well, but she thought maybe she knew him that much. Charlie might not be the most imaginative or sensitive of men, but he would never have walked naked out to that pool last night if he'd carried any communicable diseases. His truthfulness was a trifle misplaced upon occasion, but he had principles of a sort.

She grabbed her clothes and carried them to the shower. Now all she had to worry about was getting pregnant. She didn't consider that much of a problem. As many times as she and Zack had done it without protection, she figured she was safe. After the first few times when she and Zack had lived in terror but nothing had happened, it had almost become a joke between them. She had been damned lucky.

Scrubbing her hair with shampoo, Penelope thrust aside her foolish worries. Once wouldn't hurt. Charlie would be going off on his own now, and she had to get back to business. There was no room in either of their lives for any kind of relationship, no matter how much that small piece of her wanted it. She had Beth to worry about. He had Raul and Tammy. Going to bed wouldn't solve either of their problems.

She shrieked as a large shape shoved aside the shower curtain and stepped in.

"Charlie!" Foolishly, she crossed her arms over her soapy breasts as he loomed over her.

Lifting his eyebrows, he contemplated her crossed arms with dead seriousness. "You only reveal yourself in moonlight?" he asked without inflection.

Water pelted down his shoulder and arm as he reached for her. He hadn't combed his hair before entering the shower, but water quickly plastered it to the side of his head. Penelope could see the bristles of his beard as he pulled her closer.

"Charlie, not again," she whispered. "We can't."

"You have a good reason why not?" he asked with a degree of interest that apparently involved the soap on her breasts more than her words.

"I don't like sex," she whispered in what she knew now was a ridiculous defense.

Lifting his gaze from her breasts, he quirked an eyebrow. "You don't like sex," he repeated solemnly. "Tell me, when was the last time you had sex?"

He smeared circles in the foam, and Penelope quivered. He was doing it to her again, turning her mind to mush. She leaned back against the cool tiles and he stepped closer, until his arousal pressed firmly against her belly.

"I don't like men." That wasn't what she meant, but she couldn't think straight with all that masculinity pressing her against the wall.

"Since when? Since the jock in college?"

She expected laughter, but when she glanced up, he was beaming with delight and a very definite smirk of male arrogance. The warm water splashed off his wide shoulders, streaking through the soap covering her and running in rivulets through the flattened hair on his chest. The tiles at her back were no longer cool. The effect of his grin and his body bubbled through what remained of her brain.

"Protection," she managed to whimper. She knew she was whimpering. His fingers had turned her breasts into wild creatures demanding instant nurturing, and the hollow in her belly had opened so wide, she thought it would devour her from the inside out. She instinctively rose to her toes, offering herself as a target for his heat-seeking missile. She'd uttered her last intelligent word, and her mind had deteriorated to purple metaphors.

Charlie unfolded his fist and offered her the package within. "I remembered."

Gratefully, Penelope grabbed the foil, tore it open, and with trembling hands, smoothed it over his erection. It didn't help that Charlie groaned the entire time she worked at it.

"We're gonna have to come up with a better solution in the future," he muttered, sliding his hands to her buttocks and lifting.

Penelope scarcely heard him. Grabbing his shoulders, she covered his beard-stubbled face with kisses until he caught her mouth with his and pressed her solidly against the wall. His tongue thrust relentlessly between her teeth, robbing her of breath and all ability to reason.

He swallowed her cry as he thrust into her. Water and shampoo ran down her face as she leaned her head back, lifted her hips, and wrapped her legs around him. He took her weight and used it against her, prying her thighs wide as he drove into her, lifting her higher, taking her further, until she soared and he remained rooted to the ground, giving and giving until she could take no more.

As she floated back to the ground with the last spasms of her contractions, Charlie exploded inside her, holding her still with his arms around her back and her head on his shoulders as he filled her, until they both melted and slid down beneath the pelting water.

"Don't go," he demanded as Penelope tried to stir into a more comfortable position.

How could she stay?

Weeping through the pounding water, she kissed him until his great body shuddered against her.

❧ NINETEEN ❧

"I have to get back to work, Charlie!" Wearing a tailored polyester dress that swept about her knees, her wet hair gathered in a thick French braid, Penelope paced up and down the suite. "I've done everything for you that I can. Now I have to salvage my job."

"You all but declare Jacobsen is dealing with the Russian Mafia, that he and my stepfather own equal shares of the Foundation, that in all probability they're in cahoots, and you want me to walk off and leave you here? What the hell do you think I am?" Firmly planted in front of the door, Charlie watched her with growing fury.

"A sensible man with better things to do than baby-sit a grown woman!"

"I don't call sending you home where you'll be safe baby-sitting. I call it sensible. And I sure as hell gave you credit for more intelligence than to pull this stunt." He crossed his arms over his chest. "I told you they *searched* that cabin. They know who you are. They didn't murder Michel because they didn't like his looks. It was a warning. And we ignored that warning. Now we have to deal with it."

She flung up her arms in exasperation and finally turned to look at him. "Charlie, you just don't *understand*. Beth's insurance doesn't cover the operation. The only way I can earn enough money to pay for it is to make partner. The only way I can make partner is to show them I can carry out assignments like this one and acquire new clients. If I do this right, I could expand into Castries and all over the Caribbean. I can't let this opportunity slip through my hands."

"Your damned *life* could slip through your hands! I'm sending you home and that's the end of it."

"You wouldn't send me home if I were Raul," she pointed out caustically. "This is one of those *men* things, isn't it?"

"If you were Raul, you'd have the sense to go home," he grumbled. "That's probably where he is right now. Now let's get going before the day security guard comes around and catches us."

"Charlie, let's get something straight here." Penelope planted herself in front of him, hands on hips. "My father inherited a fortune and expected my mother to stay at home and let him 'take care' of her. She never learned to take care of herself—until he gambled their money right into the ground. All my sister wanted to do was raise kids. She married an up-and-coming young lawyer, had two kids, and lost both husband and kids when she lost her ability to see and her husband decided he'd rather play cop. Now she's helpless." She stabbed his chest with her finger. "I not only learn from my experience, but the experiences of others. The only person I can rely on is myself. If I think it's safe to return to the resort, then I'll return to the resort. You have nothing whatsoever to say about it."

He regarded her grimly. "You finished?"

At her decisive nod, he lifted his backpack. "Then let's go."

Penelope regarded him suspiciously, but with no other choice of action, she shouldered her laptop and picked up her sack of clothing and followed him out.

They'd walked in the back way from Soufrière. In daylight, they looked conspicuous cutting across barbered lawns and golf cart paths, carrying their luggage. Penelope gazed at the acres of English green lawn, tennis courts, and shuttle bus roads, and wondered if this was another of the Foundation's resorts. She couldn't remember seeing the name on the list, but it looked like the kind of place Charlie complained about.

Well, to each his own, she supposed, shifting the heavy laptop. Before she could adjust the strap, Charlie reached over and took it from her, heaving it over his shoulder.

"I can carry it," she hissed, trying not to attract attention from the tourists wandering past.

He shrugged. "So can I. Just think of me as your packhorse."

She wished she could. If she could just picture him as a thickheaded, muscle-bound jock as she had that first day, she could excuse what she had done with him as a moment of irrationality and go on with her life. Apparently the sex had gone to her brain, however, and now she saw him as some kind of leader, a man capable of making intelligent, rational decisions that affected hundreds of lives and acting on them with firmness. She could almost see him as a corporate executive commanding a payroll of thousands. He had that kind of power and decisiveness. He had taken over her life and the lives of everyone around him these past few days.

Which was all nonsense and a product of sunstroke and sex. She just wanted to shape him into the kind of man she thought she ought to be making love to, not the kind of man he really was—a male chauvinist pig like every other jock. If he were the kind of man she imagined, he'd be downright dangerous.

They stopped and bought breakfast in Soufrière like any other tourists wandering the booths along the waterfront. Penelope tried to look for shady characters or anyone following them, but she saw nothing but the fishmongers hawking their wares and the kids dodging in and out between the idle shoppers, selling their malachite necklaces. The sun shone benevolently on the waves lapping the shore. How could anyone believe in danger in a setting like this? She'd be perfectly safe in the isolation of the resort, feeding software into PCs and teaching the staff how to use it.

"There's the taxi now. Come on." Charlie grabbed her elbow and steered her hurriedly toward the dock.

For a moment, Penelope felt as if she'd been thrown back to that first day when he'd practically kidnapped her off the plane. She dragged her feet until she realized the water taxi was the easiest way back to the resort. They weren't strangers anymore. Charlie understood she had to get back to work. He might disagree, but he understood. Now that she'd established her priorities, he would respect them. She thought.

Just so there was no misunderstanding, Penelope announced the name of the resort as her destination before climbing into the fishing boat and taking the seat on the far side of the pail of fish bait. She didn't like it when Charlie followed her in, but he probably had things back at the cabin he needed to collect. And maybe he had the old-fashioned notion of "seeing her home." That was kind of sweet. Actually, she was relieved. She didn't like the idea of walking in on any more bats or tarantulas. She could get used to having a man around to handle some of life's more trying aspects.

As the boat roared into the deepening water of the cove, Charlie pulled his baseball cap over his eyes and fished in his pocket for the wallet he'd retrieved from her purse. Now that they were parting ways, it was only sensible to let him have his wallet back. She hadn't objected to his prying in her purse to get it. After all, he'd done it for her own good at the time.

"Here's a hundred if you can get us into Vieux Fort before noon." Charlie waved the bill and shouted over the roar of the boat's motor.

Eyes widening, Penelope stared at him in shock. "That's way out of the way! The resort is just around the coast a little. Why can't you drop me off there first?"

"Because we're not going there." Slapping his mirrored sunglasses on his nose, Charlie leaned back and rested his elbows against the rear seat as the boat changed direction for the southernmost point of the island.

"Don't be ridiculous." Penelope jerked out her purse. She didn't carry hundred-dollar bills, but she still had most of her traveler's checks. If that's what it took, two could play this game.

She rummaged through the contents of her normally well-organized purse. Calculator, Kleenex, cosmetics case . . . Where the hell was her wallet?

Panicking, she started tossing the contents on her lap, one by one. No wallet. No passport. No money. No identification. This couldn't be happening. She'd held on to her purse through crashing cars and jungles and midnight flights from the police. No one could have stolen her wallet.

Except Charlie.

Stomach tightening in an all too familiar knot, she turned and glared at the man beside her basking casually in the sun. "Where's my wallet?" she demanded.

"In a safe place," he answered calmly, not even lifting his head to look at her.

She'd only hurt her hand if she punched him. Too furious to speak, too furious to even consider consequences, Penelope abandoned any thought of propriety, lifted the pail of fish bait, and dumped the slimy contents over his fat head.

Charlie yelped and slid backward. She pounced on his backpack.

The boat slopped water over the side as it tipped back and forth. The driver shouted at her. Penelope didn't care. She damned well wouldn't let this man, any man, get the better of her.

She upended the backpack in the bottom of the boat. Jockey shorts, jeans, socks, and T-shirts tumbled out. She grabbed his shaving case and ripped it open. Nothing. She ran her hand over the bottom of the bag, searching for zippers or other openings. Nothing.

The more frantically she behaved, the more Charlie calmed down. After dipping a dirty shirt in the water to wipe his face, he jerked the pack from her grasp and began stowing his gear. "I said a safe place. Backpacks can get stolen."

Fear gripped Penelope's insides, the kind of paralyzing fear she'd known right after Beth's accident, when she'd been helpless to do anything but watch her twin fight death. Clenching her fists and trying to disguise her panic, Penelope spoke carefully. "I'll never forgive you for this, Charlie. Never. You have no right at all to do this to me."

"I got you into this, and I'll get you out," he stated calmly. "I'd rather you hated me alive than loved me dead."

"I more than hate you, Charlie Smith," she spat. "I loathe, despise, abhor, and detest you. And you still can't stop me. As soon as we get back to Miami, I'll turn around and buy a ticket back."

He looked at her with interest. "Did they teach you all those fancy words in college? Maybe I missed a few things. But that still doesn't make you any smarter than me."

She didn't like the way he said that. Maybe she'd been a little hasty in declaring her intentions. Maybe she should have waited until she had her passport in her hands before she opened her big mouth.

Maybe she ought to just give it up and rob a bank for her sister's operation.

Gloomily staring out at the beautiful crystalline water she had yet to play in, Penelope didn't say another word.

Charlie didn't waste his time worrying about his companion's silence. The fish bait was an interesting new routine, but he'd lived with a lot worse than the smell of fish. If she could stand the stink, so could he. That he'd gotten so far under her skin she could explode that readily was the interesting point, but he didn't have time to explore the implications.

He'd already decided to ignore his niggling suspicions about Raul and concentrate on a plan to save his company and maybe uncover Jacobsen. Penelope's silence gave him time to refine his plan. She did "frosty" real well, but he figured he could defrost her when the time was right. Of course, from the looks of it, the time wouldn't be right until he took care of this job fixation of hers.

As they arrived in Vieux Fort and climbed onto the dock, Charlie kept a sharp lookout on his unwilling companion even as he hastily splashed in the water to remove the worst of the lingering stink. He didn't want Penelope running off and getting into who-knows-what trouble while his back was turned. But she watched him bathe and followed him without comment as he sought a land taxi. He'd give her credit for common sense as well as intelligence. She couldn't go anywhere without a passport or money.

At the airport he bypassed the lines of tourists in the terminal by heading directly toward the ramshackle hangar where his plane was stored. His pilot and a customs inspector were already waiting when they arrived.

"I've brought another passenger, Jim," Charlie announced casually, producing his passport and Penelope's from his pocket and handing them over. Penelope's eyes dripped icy disdain as the inspector marked the books and handed them back to Charlie. He could hear her diatribe on that now.

"Weather's fine. No problem." Jim hitched their bags into the small plane's luggage compartment.

Penelope's silence was working on his nerves, but Charlie wasn't about to admit that to anyone. He handed her into the plane, and she jerked free of his hold as soon as her feet hit the deck. She was already buckled up by the time he climbed in.

All right, so he liked hearing her talk. She never rattled on about subjects of no interest to him. She always had something intelligent to say. Of course, he probably didn't want to hear the topics rolling around in that powerful mind of hers right now. They probably had to do with international kidnapping and the police. So he was better served by her silence. He just wished she understood a little better. He could use her insight on the best way to get the liens off his bank accounts.

Well, he had lawyers who could handle that. He'd have to concentrate on tracking down the connections between Jacobsen and his unlimited sources of income. That looked like the fastest way of putting the man out of commission. Charlie wasn't a cop. He couldn't identify the murdered man in Raul's shack any more than he could find Michel's murderer.

But he'd passed on all the information in his possession to the island police before they'd left this morning. They would have to handle their fair share of the burden while he tracked down the parts important to him.

Raul was his first goal. He only hoped his partner was being his usual cautious self by not imparting information unless he knew he was safe. Maybe that information implicated Emile, and Raul didn't feel safe telling it to Charlie. He'd rather believe that than think Raul was hiding something. But Raul had hid his relationship with Tammy. This wasn't productive. He had to find Tammy.

Finding Tammy meant meeting Penelope's sister and her cop ex–brother-in-law.

As the plane sailed over brilliant aqua waters, Charlie contemplated that little scene. Was Penelope's sister the stick-her-nose-in-the-air type? She probably wore little pearl necklaces and fancy flowy dresses. Just because Penelope's twin was blind didn't mean she'd forgotten her upbringing. He assumed they lived in one of those uptown condos with all the gleaming appliances and views of the skyline, cluttered with the delicate antiques a man couldn't sit on to save his soul. The sister would hear him blundering into her expensive Chinese vases or whatnot and figure Penelope had been having a little R&R with the stableboy.

Charlie slumped in his seat and rubbed his aching forehead. He knew better than to let his thoughts wander in that direction. Most of it was his own damned fault. He could put on a fancy suit and designer tie and drive up in a BMW— naw, he couldn't stoop that low, maybe a Corvette—but he just didn't see any future in it. He was a blue-collar kind of guy and he intended to stay that way. He had season tickets to the Dolphins games, not the opera. He didn't fit into Penelope's world any better than she fit into his.

But the sex sure was damned good.

He cast Penelope a sidelong glance, but she sat rigidly staring out the window. Well, he could kiss the sex good-bye. She'd sooner shove a knife down his throat than her tongue right now. Why the hell couldn't women see what was right before their noses? Did she really think he'd leave her on the island to get kidnapped by thugs? Jacobsen could have seen her going into Emile's with him. Would he recognize her?

Shit. Charlie stared out his own window, but he couldn't deny the hunger eating at him, gnawing at his innards and opening a hole bigger than the state of Kansas. He liked having Penelope at his side, working with him instead of against him. Hell, he'd even liked it when she'd been digging into him with those barbs of hers. He'd already figured out she was hard and crusty on the outside, but pure molten lava inside. Maybe other men were put off by the tough exterior, but the combination excited him. He liked a challenge.

He liked the way they bounced ideas back and forth and reached the same conclusion. He liked the way one silky black tendril always escaped her pins and caressed her throat, and the way she absently shoved it aside with manicured fingers. He even liked it that she cared enough for how she looked to have her nails manicured, and that she had them painted with clear polish instead of clown red.

And if he got off on the subject of how well he liked the way she responded to him in bed, he'd be harder than a rock and twice as uncomfortable.

She was right. They had absolutely nothing in common, except sex.

Remembering the Jacuzzi, Charlie sighed. Nothing in common, maybe, but a little extra something neither of them had planned on.

What the hell would he do if he'd gotten her pregnant?

❧ TWENTY ❧

Charlie was studying the computer printouts she'd given him as if they were a puzzle he could piece together. Penelope tried to focus on the blue-green sea below, but the sight had become a little monotonous. She'd left her supply of books back in the cottage. She had nothing else to occupy her mind but the man in the other seat. She could scarcely ignore someone who—just by his presence—made her hot all over.

"There's not much on these Russian guys, is there?" Charlie commented, holding aside the two sheets with the foreign names on top while he studied another stack of paper.

"There wouldn't be unless they'd applied for citizenship or jobs," she responded reluctantly. "Since their income is apparently from offshore investments, they don't even have social security numbers. Officially, I guess they're classified as tourists."

"But they've been living in the U.S. for almost a year." Charlie pointed at the date on the papers.

She didn't know why she was talking to him. He didn't deserve a second more of her time. But she was bored and he offered a challenge to her mind and she was a sucker. "Their address is one of the hotels on the Foundation list. As long as they stay clear of the law, there's apparently nothing wrong with that."

194

"So there's no way of connecting them with Jacobsen, other than they own stock in the same corporation?"

"They can't open bank accounts without social security numbers, so no, there's no personal connection to the funds. But if you'll look, Jacobsen's account receives regular deposits that correspond to withdrawals from the Foundation's island account. And the Russians are signatories on that account. They could be laundering money through the resorts and the Foundation into the pockets of individual owners. The United States requires banks to file forms on anyone depositing over ten thousand in cash, but if the cash from illegal operations is deposited in banks on the islands, there's no means of tracing the source of income."

"But not all the owners of the Foundation are receiving these checks. I don't see any in Emile's account."

"I don't claim to understand the minds of criminals. The Foundation could be a perfectly legitimate investment company, with only a few of the owners operating a scam. Or the whole thing could be legitimate. Maybe the Foundation is paying Jacobsen for construction projects."

"Jacobsen's construction company has been closed down until all the suits against it are settled. One of his buildings collapsed during construction, killing several men. He doesn't have the cash to cover the suits and the costs he's already incurred, and the company he was working for pulled the contract. For all intents and purposes, he's dead in the water. What project can they be paying him for?"

Penelope made the mistake of looking Charlie in the eyes. Searing intelligence and justifiable anger stared back at her. His eyes were as crystalline blue as the sky above, contrasting handsomely with the sun-scorched color of his skin, but it was the intelligence bowling her over. She wanted him to be just another jock. She could brush off a jock. She had the sudden premonition it wouldn't be quite so easy to brush off this man. He'd already thrown off the label she had used as a protective shield. She didn't want to imagine what he could do if he decided to expose her weaknesses.

"He could have started another company," she replied in her best crisp business voice. "Men like that file bankruptcy under one corporate name, leave their creditors hanging, and simply start over in a new company. PC&M handles clients who have done that, although they usually give more credible reasons for the new corporation."

"I don't suppose you could tap into their files and verify that's what they've done, could you?" he asked without much hope.

"That's a matter of public record. I can do that without violating client confidentiality, although using PC&M records would be a lot faster." Finally recovering some of her senses, Penelope glared at him. "Why should I?"

He shrugged. "In the interest of justice, maybe? Would you let Michel's murderer go free just to get even with me?"

Damn, he was good. Penelope turned her attention back to the window. "Jacobsen wouldn't have personally murdered the poor man. He would have hired someone. Chances are, they'll never find the real murderer."

"We know who's signing the checks," he reminded her. "If the Foundation is involved, those two Russians and a lawyer on the island are the only ones permitted to write checks out of the account. One of them had to have hired the murderer."

"A lawyer." She sighed with distaste. "Maybe we should set John on this angle of the case too. His mind should be contorted enough to follow the legal implications."

"If he has a law degree, why the hell is he a cop?" Charlie didn't really care what the answer was to that, he simply wanted to keep her talking. He was tired of his own thoughts chasing around and around and going nowhere, and he didn't like the pensive expression on Penelope's face. He had this bewildering need to make her happy, and no clue whatsoever of how to do it.

Penelope shrugged and didn't look at him. "You'll have to ask him. I think he had some kind of breakdown after Beth's accident. The driver of the car that ran into us was drunk and out of control, and he fled the scene. The police never caught him, and John simply couldn't live with that. Maybe he figured there were more crooks who never got caught than ones who weren't prosecuted."

"Us?" The desultory conversation took a sharp right turn, and Charlie jerked his head up to watch her. "You were in the accident?"

"I was driving the car."

Penelope spoke in a dead, flat voice that spoke of years of acceptance and guilt. Charlie's gut wrenched in pain. He wanted to hug her and offer what consolation he could, but she was far beyond that now, and, awkwardly, he realized his hug would inevitably turn to something else.

"But it wasn't your fault," he reminded her.

"I was the one who wanted her to go with me. She'd been baking Christmas cookies and singing carols with the kids. I dragged her out of the house to see the marvelous gown I'd found in a designer shop. It was going to be her Christmas present if she liked it. I should have just bought the damned thing and wrapped it up."

"And you've been blaming yourself for this for how long?" he asked quietly.

"Two years this past Christmas," she said bitterly. "Can you imagine what their Christmas was like that year? The kids were three and four at the time. The entire family spent the holiday in the hospital, watching Beth breathe, for fear if they stopped watching, she'd die. John gave the kids their gifts in shopping bags, in the waiting room."

Thoroughly helpless in the face of her grief, Charlie reached over and took her hand. "It wasn't your fault, Penny," he whispered. "It was fate, or God, or the stars, or whatever you want to call it. Not you. It happens every day, to people everywhere. Maybe your lives were too perfect and needed shaking up. We can't sit around trying to undo the past. We can only go forward."

She gulped and turned her face away, and he knew she was fighting sobs. He reached over and fished in her purse to produce the package of tissues she kept there. "It's okay. Cry if you want. Jesus, you have reason enough to cry. Just quit blaming yourself, all right? You didn't do it. The drunk did. And I think I can kind of understand why your brother-in-law went off the deep end and became a cop. I'd want to catch the bastard too."

She nodded and rubbed at her eyes with the Kleenex. "That's what I told Beth, but she wouldn't believe me. She thinks he always wanted to be a cop and that she made him miserable by expecting him to be a lawyer." Penelope gave a weepy laugh. "Beth blames herself for everything. She thinks it was her fault for running out on the kids to go play with me. And of course, it's her fault that John can't even bear to look at her anymore. I guess it runs in the family. And I don't know why I'm telling you any of this."

With relief, Charlie settled back in his seat. She was returning to the Penelope he knew. "It's good to know the dynamics of the family I'll be barging into. What about your folks? Who do they blame?"

That had her twisting in her seat and staring suspiciously at him. "Barging into? Why should you have anything at all to do with my family?"

He couldn't resist that one. He'd take anger over tears any day, and he knew just how to get under Miss Penny's remarkably thin skin. Lifting his eyebrows, he let his gaze slide from her lovely breasts down to her all too slender waistline.

"Aside from the fact that you could right now be carrying my child . . ." He waited for a burst of outrage, but she merely froze and glared. "My sister is supposed to be moving in with you. I suppose as a responsible brother, I should know what kind of family she's getting mixed up with."

"Coming from someone who hasn't seen his sister or mother for ten years, I think it's just a trifle too late to assume responsibility now. I suspect Tamara is perfectly capable of reaching her own conclusions without your aid."

"Are you ashamed to introduce me to your family?" He'd intended to needle her, but his own underlying concerns escaped in the question.

She sniffed and stuck her nose up in the air before returning to staring out the window. "They've met jocks before. It wouldn't kill them."

Too bad murder was illegal. After all they'd been through, she'd reduced him to the role of packhorse again.

Of course, knowing Penelope, it was probably some kind of defense mechanism because he was getting too close. He wasn't much on psychology, but with Penelope he had amazing insight. He recognized the purpose of her barbed-wire barriers. She wasn't just shutting *him* out. She shut out anything wearing pants.

The question here was, how badly did he want to break through those barriers?

Slumping in his seat and glaring at the papers in his hands, Charlie hated himself for even considering the question. He liked things simple and uncomplicated.

It wasn't as if he were afraid of commitment. He'd always intended to marry someday, have 2.3 kids, build a house in the suburbs, and own an RV. He'd kind of pictured a wife with big blond hair and bounteous breasts, but that was because that was the kind of woman he usually took home with him from bars. He hadn't troubled to think further than that, since any such commitment was destined for the distant future.

But it was possible the future had arrived. He mentally cringed at the thought. If fate chose Penelope Albright to be the mother of his first child, fate had a warped sense of humor. He could no more imagine Penelope in a house in the suburbs than he could imagine her with 2.3 kids. Or an RV. Hell, he couldn't even imagine her watching a game on TV. Or riding in his GTO.

So. They were approaching the twenty-first century. People didn't have to marry just because they produced offspring. He could see visiting his kid with miniature footballs, taking him to a game, arranging birthday parties at Chuck E. Cheese's. He could start a trust fund for the kid's college education. Penelope was a sensible sort. She'd understand that kind of arrangement a lot better than marriage to a redneck like him.

What he couldn't understand was this wayward trek his mind had taken on a child that was probably less than a minuscule possibility. Why the hell had he focused on that one tiny mistake and blown it into such proportions? He had enough on his plate right now without looking for more.

Disgruntled, Charlie closed his eyes and leaned back in the seat. If he didn't know better, he'd think he was looking for reasons to see Penelope after this was all over.

As if she'd heard some inkling of his thoughts, Penelope whispered almost to herself, "I'm going back to work, Charlie, and you can't stop me."

Sleepily, Charlie wondered how PC&M treated pregnant partners.

As Charlie steered her past Miami's sprawling airport terminal and toward the parking lot, Penelope decided she could learn to enjoy the benefits of private plane travel. She hated the endless lines and crowded halls of that damned terminal. Charlie's method of operation was much less stressful. Now, if only he had a limousine waiting . . .

No such luck, of course. They crossed the lines of traffic at the baggage pickup and hurried into the winter gloom of late afternoon.

"I could take a taxi home," she offered hopefully, catching sight of one standing empty, its driver leaning against the hood in anticipation of an arriving passenger.

"Give it up, Penny. You're not going back to St. Lucia until we find out what's going on."

He'd been rude and abrupt ever since they'd arrived. One would think *she* was the cause of all his problems. Penelope tried to jerk her arm out of his grasp, but he held her easily. "What are you planning to do? Lock me up somewhere?"

"I'm just taking you home right now. I'll work out the rest later."

Well, she could handle that. She needed to see how Beth was doing. She'd been feeling guilty about shoving John on her. Now that she was home, she could make John go away again. In the morning, she'd have to find some way of straightening out the mess with PC&M. Maybe if she bought her own ticket back to St. Lucia . . .

Charlie stopped at a mile-long midnight-blue car with side fins, gleaming chrome wire wheels, and white sidewall tires. Penelope stared at the behemoth with incredulity as he unlocked the trunk and threw in their baggage.

"*That's* your car?" She couldn't bite her tongue fast enough. The question just escaped without thought.

"Sixty-five GTO," he grunted, slamming the trunk.

"It's an *antique*." Her tongue had obviously taken control of her brain. She kept digging herself deeper. Admiringly, she slid her hand over the chrome trim. "Is it all original?"

"All GTO parts anyway." He regarded her warily. "You rather I take you home in a taxi?"

She jerked her head up in surprise. "Why? What kind of engine does it have? It will get us there, won't it?"

He unlocked the door on her side and held it open for her. "Just like the song, it's got three deuces and a 389. We'll get there all right."

"You listen to rock oldies?" she asked in disbelief as he slid in on the driver's side, then swore she'd bite her tongue off before using it again.

"Wasn't a whole lot else to listen to growing up in the boondocks. Couldn't buy my own collections, so I listened to my mother's. It wasn't all bad stuff."

Penelope could see the tension in Charlie's shoulders as he started the car. He really, really didn't like rejection. She could puncture his ego until he sagged with holes right now. Oddly enough, after everything he'd done, she still couldn't summon the killer instinct necessary to puncture this man. The aging GTO had turned her into putty.

"Beth and I used to hold sock hops for the neighborhood," she admitted softly. "We thought we'd been deprived by being born too late."

He backed the car out without looking at her. "Yeah?" he asked disinterestedly.

Maybe she should let it go. He had kidnapped her twice, probably cost her her job, and he didn't deserve a moment of her time. But some kind of crazy bond had formed between them these last few days, and she had this weird need to hold on to it. Maybe knowing even a big man like Charlie had his vulnerabilities affected her somehow. "We won talent contests with our *Saturday Night Fever* dance routine. That's a little later than the sixties rock you had, but we listened avidly to the oldies stations to make up new routines. I recognize the GTO song. I've just never seen a GTO."

The muscles of his broad shoulders relaxed a fraction. "It was my father's first car. He kept it in the garage after it died, and I tinkered with it in college until I got it running again. They just don't make 'em like this anymore."

"There could be a reason for that," she said wryly. "It must eat a gallon of gas every four feet."

Charlie grinned. "You ought to see the gas tank. But I've got a VW bug that will eat road all day without a fill-up. I figure it balances out."

"Has anyone ever told you that you're certifiable?" So much for holding her tongue.

He shrugged. "Can you tell the difference between any of those cars up there in front of us? They all look alike. What do you think ever became of the auto designers who dreamed up all the different models back then?"

"They got more practical?" she suggested.

"I don't see why practical has to be boring." He eased the car into gear as they hit the highway.

"I'm afraid to ask what the hotel project you're building looks like." Penelope gasped as they flew past a line of cars.

"Architect designs them. I just build them. But if I ever build my own house . . ."

He cut off that thought and Penelope cast him a quizzical look, but she didn't inquire further. She didn't want to know what kind of house this man would build. That would be admitting too much personal interest.

Still, she couldn't help noticing how skillfully he handled

the massive car, in and out of traffic, barely resting one hand over the wheel. He'd probably learned to drive from old movies.

"Well, you certainly can't disguise who you are driving in this thing. Everyone will know it's you for a mile around."

To Penelope's surprise, Charlie muttered a foul expletive and aimed the car for the exit lane, miles from her turnoff.

"What?" she demanded, instinctively glancing at the traffic behind them. In the growing mist, she could see little more than headlights.

"I can't take you home in this. They'll know right where we are."

He gunned the engine and sped down the ramp into the streets of one of Miami's poorer sections of town.

❦ TWENTY-ONE ❦

"What if something happens to your car?" Penelope asked in concern as they rattled down a quiet residential street in a smoke-belching, aging Ford Escort he'd borrowed from one of his men.

"Rick won't let anything happen to it. Besides, who would even look twice at a car that old? It's just a car. Will you keep your eye on the road and tell me where to turn next?"

Charlie didn't like the look on Penelope's face as she swiveled to stare out the window. The early evening gloom prevented him from seeing her clearly, but he was learning to read body language. He judged she'd just come up with an idea he wouldn't like.

"There's a strip shopping center on the next corner. Pull in there," she ordered.

"Why? You planning on taking back exotic souvenirs from the corner drugstore?" He eased the rattling car over the gutter into the parking lot, fearful the Escort's muffler would fall off if he hit a bump too hard.

That comment earned him a scathing look. "All my souvenirs are in the cottage. The kids will be disappointed. But that's not what we're after." She pointed at the brightly lit drugstore. "They rent medical equipment in there."

Charlie found a space in front and parked. "You're picking up a spare walking cane for your sister on the way home?

Come on, Penny, what gives?" He was damned glad he'd changed his shirt at the airport. The stench still clung, but at least he wouldn't knock any store clerks over.

"You don't want to be recognized, right?" She slid out of the car without waiting for him to open the door. Charlie admired her long legs with a sigh. She hadn't had time to get a tan and she didn't wear stockings, but she didn't need to either. Those legs belonged in a Hall of Fame somewhere, right along with her posterior.

"They could be watching your place, waiting for us to show up," he admitted. "I'm not much at skulduggery, but I can figure that much."

"And you don't think they'd notice someone built like you walking into my apartment building?" She strode briskly across the lot.

"Like you blend into the woodwork," he muttered, watching her sway.

"Exactly." Without any further explanation, she headed purposefully down the aisle of medical equipment to the rental counter.

Charlie stood back and watched as she ordered a wheelchair, grabbed a large scarf off another counter, added a packaged lap blanket, and turned in a thoughtful circle, searching for something else. Finally deciding on a baseball cap and a plastic fold-up raincoat, she added them to her collection, then turned to him expectantly as the clerk began totaling the bill.

Of course—he had the money. He didn't know what the hell he was paying for besides his own temerity in stealing her wallet, but he pulled out the bills. His cash supply was running low. He wondered if he could still access his bank accounts. If the bad guys could follow bank transactions as Penelope did, he'd have to be wary of giving too much away.

Outside, she demanded the keys to the car.

Charlie flung their purchases into the backseat and maneuvered the chair into the trunk as she struggled with the raincoat and cap. "What do you think I am, anyway? A real sucker?"

She smacked his arm hard enough to actually make him wince. Obviously, he'd had that one coming for a long time. The fish bait evidently hadn't been enough. But he could forgive her anything for the way she looked now, with her braid falling through the back of the cap. Maybe she liked baseball.

"I'm perfecting the disguise." She twirled to show off her coat. "Wheelchair-bound invalids don't normally drive. You did intend to go up to my apartment with me, didn't you?"

Crossing his arms, Charlie studied her in the wavering light of a dying overhead lamp. She radiated sincerity—and tension. She could very well be operating on nerves alone by now. It kind of scared him, wondering what had been going on in that formidable mind of hers as she sulked, but he'd have to trust her. Who the hell else could he trust?

He handed her the keys. "Wheelchair-bound?" he asked patiently.

She climbed in and started the car, waiting for him to fold up and wriggle into the low front seat. "We live in a building designed for the physically challenged. If I wheel you inside in a chair, no one will even look twice. It's perfect. Not that I believe anyone will be watching," she amended hastily.

"You just enjoy playing Halloween." Charlie frowned, though he had to admit she had a point. If anyone was watching, they wouldn't pay much attention to a battered Escort delivering a wheelchair patient.

The mention of Halloween reminded him of something else though. If he was not mistaken, tomorrow was Valentine's Day. As they drove through the narrow streets, he contemplated that minor problem. Should he buy flowers for a lover, or ex-lover, who might conk him over the head with them? Candy would be downright messy in that scenario. Maybe he should forget the idea entirely and hope she would too. But damn, he wanted to keep those doors open, those bridges unburned. He wanted back in her bed. He was damned close to wanting a hell of a lot more.

That realization didn't ease his sudden tension as they pulled into the handicapped lot and parked. He studied the unassuming building sprawling before him. Not precisely the fashionable condo he'd pictured Penelope living in, but he'd forgotten the blind sister part. So, she had a conscience. That didn't make her any less a socialite. Or her family any more accepting of a construction worker.

Efficiently, she whipped out the wheelchair as Charlie slumped in the front seat of the car, doing nothing. He didn't like doing nothing. He liked being the one in charge. Obviously, so did Penelope. He'd never had that problem before. Most women wanted him to handle everything. He wasn't at all certain he could adapt.

With efficiency, she settled him in the chair, covered his lap with the blanket, and threw the scarf over his shoulders. "Slump," she whispered. "You look as if all you need is a battle-ax in hand to go to war."

Charlie didn't think her plastic raincoat and baseball cap disguised her greatly either, but someone looking for a striking model and seeing a sloppy nurse pushing a wheelchair might not notice. He kind of liked watching her braid bounce through the cap, but he couldn't turn around to admire her properly as she shoved the chair up the ramp and down the walk toward the entrance.

"I'm too heavy for you," he protested as she grunted pushing the chair over the sill.

"It's a cheap chair. It'll do for now. I just don't know how we'll get you out of here on your own later." She punched in her security code and the doors opened to the elevator bank.

Charlie had been contemplating that, but he didn't think she'd appreciate his thoughts, so he kept them to himself as they entered the elevator and zoomed upward.

"We should have called first," she whispered as they departed the elevator on the top floor and rolled down the hall. "We'll scare Beth half to death."

"Not if she's anything like you," he muttered in disgruntlement. He really didn't like this helpless role. He wadded the stupid blanket in his fists and pulled off his hat as they rolled to a stop. Hell of a way to meet a woman's family.

Penelope unlocked the dead bolt, and he nodded approvingly at her security measures.

The door swung open on a tall man, legs akimbo in shooting stance, holding a deadly looking gun between his palms and aiming it in their direction. Charlie wondered if the wheelchair would prevent his being blown away by gunfire.

"John, honest to Pete, put that gun down. Do you think burglars have keys?" Penelope shoved the chair over the sill and slammed the door behind her.

Sighing with relief, Charlie junked the invalid crap and stood up. He felt much better once he towered a few inches higher than the jerk with the gun. The other man had a cop's stern, hard-boned face and a streak of gray through his dark hair. "Beth's ex, I assume?" he asked dryly.

As the cop sheepishly returned his weapon to his side, Charlie glanced over the man's shoulder. The main room apparently occupied the entire front half of the apartment. Gleaming pine floors unmarred by rugs emphasized the spaciousness. Plain sturdy furniture marked the living, dining, and study areas—furniture he could sit in without fear of crushing it into splinters. Real furniture with wood and leather and big pillows. Charlie approved wholeheartedly of Penelope's interior decoration.

As he accepted introductions to John Matthews, Penelope's ex–brother-in-law, Charlie caught a glimpse of two heads of glossy dark curls peering around the corner from the bedrooms.

"Deedee, Sean, come out here, you scalawags!" Penelope cried in delight, dropping all propriety by ignoring her guests and turning toward the children.

In an instant, two tall, beautiful children erupted from the hall to leap into Penelope's arms. Behind them walked a woman identical to Penelope in many ways, but not the same at all, Charlie decided. Where Penny's face was all taut angles and striking curves, this woman's face had a softness to it that rendered it more pretty than dramatic. He could see lines of pain etching the skin around her mouth, and wrinkles of worry creasing her forehead.

Then her empty gaze turned in his direction, and Charlie felt the impact of the same sharp intelligence in her features that he'd discerned in Penelope's. He rolled his shoulders uncomfortably beneath his T-shirt.

"Charlie Smith?" she asked dryly when Penelope didn't leap to make the introductions. Her voice was much softer and not as authoritative as Penelope's, but she got her point across just as effectively.

"Yes, ma'am." Charlie reached for his cap, remembered he'd already removed it—not that she'd notice—and stood there like an awkward lump. He had the social skills of a rhinoceros, he decided.

Penelope whispered something in the children's ears, and they immediately popped to attention, standing at Charlie's feet and gazing up at him in awe.

"My sister, Bethany, and her children, Deirdre and Sean," she introduced them proudly.

Charlie couldn't reach over the heads of the children to shake Beth's hand, so taking a deep breath, he dropped down to their height and held out his hand to them. "Good to meet you, Deirdre and Sean."

They looked at his big paw for a moment, studied his face a little longer, then, giggling, both grabbed his hand and pulled. Charlie nearly tumbled on his face.

"All right, kids, that did it. Go get your coats. We're heading home." Firmly, John took a child in each hand and shoved them toward the back rooms.

Both Penelope and Beth were giggling, but they pokered up as soon as Charlie straightened and glared at them. He caught a gleam in the cop's eye too, but it disappeared quickly as John shrugged.

"The women taught them that. They think it's funny. I apologize for them."

"For the women, or the kids?" Charlie asked dryly.

John's stern face cracked a grin. "I make no apology for the women. They're not my responsibility."

"Right, and we all know how seriously you take responsibility, John. You can go home now. Thank you for stopping in while I was gone." Penelope spoke with an acidity that Charlie had never heard her use before.

John's grin instantly evaporated. "Unfortunately, it's not quite that easy. You've stumbled across a dangerous situation. I had to call in the FBI."

"You *what*?" Penelope exclaimed.

Charlie held his silence and even Penelope shut up as the children tumbled from the back room carrying their jackets and pulling them on. He watched John stoop to help the kids with a tenderness surprising from a man who a moment ago looked as if he could have shot twenty villains at twenty paces. Watching the curly dark heads dipping and giggling as small arms twitched into jackets, Charlie felt suddenly adrift. What did he know of kids? Here he'd been complacently counting his 2.3 progeny, and he didn't know hell about raising them.

He cast a sidelong glance at Penelope. Her expression was almost worshipful as she knelt to retrieve a lost scarf and wrap it around the youngest one's neck. It wasn't cold enough out for scarves, but apparently the kid liked them. She— Deedee, he thought she was called—grinned with a gap-toothed smile, tucked the scarf end inside her windbreaker, then pressed a sloppy kiss on her aunt's cheek. Charlie melted.

He wanted that for himself. He wanted the gap-toothed smiles, the sloppy kisses, the silly giggles. Most of all, he wanted the woman with the worshipful expression. She loved those kids. She'd walk on water for those kids. *That* was the kind of woman he wanted.

Damn, but he was wandering weird paths again. He had a business to salvage, a sister to find, and a murderer to catch.

He had no right contemplating beautiful women and giggling children, particularly not this beautiful woman.

Before he shooed the children out the door, John caught Charlie's eye. "Beth has the information. Talk to her and get back to me in the morning." John sent Penelope a wary glance but continued speaking to Charlie. "I'd feel better if you stayed with them tonight. We'll talk about security tomorrow."

Charlie would have laughed at Penelope's expression as the door closed behind her ex–brother-in-law, but he had too much sympathy for her plight. He'd really gone in too deep this time, and he'd pulled her in after him.

"I don't suppose I could get a cup of coffee before the argument begins?" he asked without hope, eyeing the pillowed sofa with longing. It had been a damned long day. He really needed more fortification than coffee.

"John left his beer in the refrigerator. Would you prefer that?" Beth asked sympathetically, already heading toward the kitchen.

Yeah, he would, but he had a feeling that he didn't need his wits muddled any more than they already were right now. "Thanks, but better not. Have you heard from Tammy?"

"I'll get it, Beth." Coming back to life, Penelope started after her sister. "You catch us up on what's happening."

Beth didn't argue. Charlie had a feeling that this twin seldom argued. Somewhere along the way, the sisters had definitely developed different identities, intentionally or not.

She gestured toward the living area. "Won't you have a seat, Mr. Smith?"

Beth's cautious gait as she took the recliner explained the heavy furniture, Charlie thought as he sank into the comfortable cushions. She didn't want chairs that were easily moved. Maybe the apartment wasn't Penelope's decor. He'd like to get a look at her bedroom. It was probably all pink frills and lace. Damn, but he was too tired for this.

"Tammy's with Raul," Beth reassured him once he was settled. "He apparently likes to get away by himself"—she

raised an inquiring eyebrow but Charlie didn't respond—
"and he told Tammy about his hideaways."

Charlie tried to disguise his relief with a frown, but Beth
couldn't see it. She smiled at him as if she'd picked up his vibrations. Dealing with an all-too-perceptive blind woman
might be worse than tackling frosty Penelope.

"They won't tell us where they're hiding," she continued.
"Raul's a bit paranoid, I think. He doesn't trust us, and he's on
edge trying to figure out how to protect your sister. I guess he
figures he can do it better than anyone."

"Raul's got caution down to an art form." Charlie prayed
that's all it was. He didn't want to have to start wondering
how safe Tammy was with Raul.

The scent of coffee drifted in from the kitchen area, and
Charlie sniffed it appreciatively. Maybe caffeine would slap
him back to normal. Dealing with two identically gorgeous
women was akin to having his head squeezed between iron
bookends. A man couldn't think like this. He watched Penelope moving around on the other side of the counter, and
that relaxed him more than anything. He didn't want her out
of his sight. "Will Raul call back? If I can talk to him, we'll
work something out."

"He's to call at nine tomorrow morning. We didn't know
what time you'd be here." Beth tilted her head toward the
kitchen. "Pen, I've got some homemade bread and muffins in
there. You might want to put some ham on a plate and bring
them out."

"Aye, aye, mama-san," Penelope called in a resigned tone.

Beth grinned as she turned back to Charlie. "She hates
kitchens. When we quit modeling, I couldn't wait to get my
hands on food. Pen willingly eats it, but she'll just as willingly eat dry crackers rather than cook."

"I'd kind of figured that out for myself." Charlie glanced
toward Penelope, who was carefully arranging a coffee tray
with thick creamy mugs and sturdy pewter sugar and cream
containers. None of this bone china and crystal stuff, he
noted approvingly, although the setting looked atrociously

expensive and not at all like the Wal-Mart containers on his own table. "If you don't mind my asking, how did the two of you turn out so different?"

"Who says we're different?" she asked challengingly.

Charlie shot her an impatient look. "I'm not as dumb as I look, Mrs. Matthews. You took the wife-and-mother route; Penny took the career approach. You enjoy feathering nests. Penny prefers hunting and gathering. You're both beautiful, intelligent women, but she prefers hiding her beauty and you prefer hiding your intelligence. Am I getting warm?"

Beth tilted her stylish shoulder-cut hair and regarded him with interest. "Call me Beth, Mr. Smith. I suspect we'll be getting to know each other a lot better." She turned in her sister's direction, but Penelope was rattling in the refrigerator and not paying attention to them. "I can't give you an instant replay of where we diverged, but it probably had something to do with our love affairs in college. I married the man I loved. Penny learned her beau had clay feet. It's kind of slanted our points of view ever since."

Charlie didn't want to know about Penny's other lovers. Obviously, what few she'd had hadn't tried to please her. That was probably his appeal, he decided. He was the first man who'd shown her a good time.

That inflated his ego but didn't make him any happier.

Penelope finally appeared, carrying a tray with coffee and a plate of bread and ham slices. "No parsley garnishes or homemade relishes, sorry. I'm not Martha Stewart." She dropped the tray onto a sturdy round coffee table between them. "Now, spill it, Beth. What does the FBI have to do with anything?"

She poured the steaming coffee into the thick mugs but spoke with the command of a CEO at the head of a boardroom. Charlie watched her impatiently brush her thick braid off her shoulder and almost lost track of the conversation. How in hell could he concentrate when his brains had sunk below his belt?

"John's working with the DA's office these days. He found

your Russians in an FBI suspect file. They've compiled a case of circumstantial evidence that implicates their connections with the Russian mob, but they don't have enough to charge them. John sent the FBI the information you forwarded. They have an agent on the way to the islands now. I don't think your friends will be very happy when their records are turned over to the government."

Charlie experienced a sinking sensation in his gut. "Let me guess. Jacobsen knows I was in St. Lucia and that I'm probably responsible for the FBI probe. He knows I was with Penelope. He's traced Penelope back here." He threw Penny a look asking for verification. "He wouldn't have much trouble doing that, would he?"

She shrugged but he could see the uneasiness in her eyes. "If he has Internet connections, he can look up my name in an instant. There aren't too many Penelope Albrights in the country."

Charlie clenched his fist around the mug. "Then Jacobsen and friends have two choices: They can assume the FBI is on to them and run, or they can try to find out just how much evidence we turned over."

"It's all in the computer," Penelope murmured nervously.

"And both computers are here," Charlie finished for her. "I think it's time you ladies took a vacation."

He ignored the hand clasp the sisters exchanged. This time, *he* was in charge, and he was getting them the hell out of here.

❧ TWENTY-TWO ❧

Beth listened in fascination as Penelope bridled at Charlie's orders. She'd never actually understood the meaning of the word *bridled* until she saw her sister's silhouette outlined against the lamplight. Penny's head jerked back and her chin shot up as if someone had stuffed a bit in her mouth.

"Get out, Charlie," Penelope responded with what Beth thought admirable control. "You have no authority to tell us what to do. We're perfectly capable of taking care of ourselves. Go look for Raul."

"I'm damned well not budging until this is over."

Beth would have termed the tone of Charlie's reply mulish, had she not caught a hint of something else behind his words. She could almost swear that Penny's words had hurt that great mountain of man as much as if she'd slapped him.

She didn't know why she sympathized with Charlie, other than that she hadn't adopted her sister's belief that all men were jerks. Of course, she didn't work with them all day as Penny did. But Beth had the ability to see beyond their bluff and bluster. She wished she didn't. It would be much easier if she could just say to hell with them all, but she couldn't. She had a son of her own. She knew better.

"Penny, I think we'd better listen to Mr. Smith," Beth said quietly, leaping into the conversation before Charlie could stick another foot in his mouth. She thought he might be the kind of man accustomed to people jumping at his commands. She didn't know why she thought that. Penelope had described him as a muscle-bound beach bum. But appearances were deceiving, as she knew only too well.

"Call me Charlie, or I'll think you're talking about my dad," he reminded her. "I'm glad one of you has her thinking cap on."

Dumb, Charlie, Beth wanted to say, but she'd learned to hold her tongue better than Penelope. Before her twin could explode, she stood up between them. "Remind me to give you lessons in tact sometime, Charlie. Could this discussion wait until morning when we're all not so tired?"

"Beth, go on to bed," Penelope insisted with concern. "I can handle Charlie."

"Yeah, she can handle me real good."

From the shadowy movement, Beth guessed Charlie had leaned back on the sofa and crossed his arms. She could almost hear the lascivious grin in his voice.

If she weren't so exasperated with his behavior, she would have grinned. No one had ever talked to Penelope like that. Most men were scared to death of her and tiptoed around her with absurd caution. Charlie Smith behaved like an engaging elephant, fearlessly stomping wherever he chose. She suspected he might have more brains than an elephant and knew darn well whose toes he stomped and why.

"I'm not going to bed until the two of you agree to behave like adults instead of quarreling children." She turned toward Penelope. "If there's any danger here, we need all the help we can get. I'm not too swift at dodging gunmen and kidnappers." She shouldn't dump the guilt on her sister, but she was too tired to look for anything more effective. Dealing with John these last few days had drained what little energy she possessed.

Beth heard an intake of breath and the rustle of fabric as Penelope stiffened, then sagged in surrender. Once upon a time, she'd been able to read her twin's expressions like a book. Now she recognized her breathing patterns. Penny would do anything she asked. Beth wouldn't take such outrageous advantage of her except that this was for her sister's own good. Charlie Smith seemed like the kind of man who would look out for Penny, and if the chemistry between these two was any indication, her twin sister found Charlie more interesting than any other man in her life.

"We're in a secured building," Penelope reminded them, putting up one final struggle. "What can anyone do? Charlie has business of his own to tend to. We can't ask him to baby-sit us."

"If the agent has just flown to the islands, they might not be looking for us here yet, but my home is the first place they'll go when they do." The amusement disappeared from Charlie's voice as he focused his attention on Penelope, ignoring Beth between them.

Beth approved. Too many people thought they either had to touch her constantly to show they weren't bothered by her handicap, or behaved as if she were part of the furniture. Apparently, Charlie simply had eyes for no one but Penelope. A man like Charlie could drive away Penelope's obsessive worries about the operation, give her something else to think about for a change. There was no point in both of them suffering for what couldn't be changed.

"Then you'll stay here tonight," Beth said decisively. "I had John set up a cot in the spare room for Tammy. We've been using the room for storage, so I must apologize for its condition." Judging his size from the shadow in front of her, she looked at Charlie with a measure of doubt. "I'm not certain you'll fit on the cot though."

She heard the shrug in Charlie's reply. "I can sleep on the sofa. It's no big deal."

She knew the instant his attention returned to Penelope. Beth thought she'd faint if John ever focused on her that way. The electricity was almost palpable.

"The sofa is too narrow for you," Penelope replied tiredly. "Beth, go on to bed. We'll work it out." Her chin stuck out again. "But I'm going back to work in the morning."

"We'll talk about it then," Beth reminded her. "And maybe we should set a chair or something in front of the door, just in case."

"I don't think they're the type to break down doors," Charlie said gently, stepping from her path so she didn't have to maneuver around him. "Just don't answer the phone. I suspect terrorism is more up their alley."

Beth threw a half smile in his direction and nodded. "I'll keep the answering machine on. Good night, Charlie. I'm glad we met."

Penelope took a deep breath as Beth glided from the room, leaving her alone with Charlie. She didn't want to look at him. The apartment was reasonably spacious, but Charlie had a way of filling a room with his presence. She could practically feel him now, though her back was turned to him.

"I'm quite capable of sleeping on the floor if you think I'll roll off the sofa and wake you up with the noise," he said dryly from behind her.

"Don't be ridiculous." Penelope spoke more sharply than she'd intended, but she didn't know how to deal with any of this. Frustration ate at her insides, and fear gnawed around the edges. If she were completely rational, she might recognize that her fear was more of Charlie and her own feelings for him than of their circumstances, but she wasn't ready for rationality. She just wanted her old life back. Nothing about her life had been logical or practical since Charlie'd barged into it.

"I'm not doing this just to annoy you," he said with patience. "I got you into this mess, and I want to get you out."

She breathed again. That was the tactic. She just wanted out. Penelope turned, and the intensity of Charlie's gaze from this proximity almost knocked her over. She saw things there that terrified her. She couldn't deal with this now. Maybe never. She blinked and looked away. "If you don't think they'll come here tonight, then you don't need to act as guard dog. Take my bed. I can sleep on the sofa."

Charlie tucked his finger under her chin and urged her head

up to meet his gaze. Penelope flinched but didn't defy him. Couldn't. She liked his touch too much, needed it, and hated herself for doing so.

"We're not strangers anymore, Penny. We've managed to share a bed these last few nights without killing each other. And unless you keep rubbers in your bedside drawer, I don't dare touch you in any other way, so you're safe from me."

She heard his sincerity, ached at his words, but nodded and jerked her head away. "If I had them, they'd be expired by now," she said wryly. "Take a shower while I clean up here."

Charlie caught her arm before she escaped. "Your honesty doesn't scare me, Penny. If you want to chase me away, show me your indifference."

He brushed a kiss across her hair, dropped her arm, and stalked away before she could find an adequate response.

Her *indifference*. What a word. Charlie Smith must be reading dictionaries in his spare time. Rattled and vaguely amused, Penelope gathered dirty cups on the tray and carried them to the kitchen.

As the water pounded in the other room, an image of Charlie naked and stepping into her shower earlier that day sprang to mind. That morning. Less than twenty-four hours ago, she'd been naked and writhing in Charlie's arms. A tremor quaked through her, and she almost dropped the tray.

God, she couldn't stand it. She set the tray on the counter and buried her flushed face in her hands. Why did Charlie have to be the one who taught her to like sex? She didn't believe in fast and loose affairs. She believed in her career, first and foremost, followed by family and commitment. She couldn't have any of that with Charlie. They would kill each other before they even talked of wedding bells.

She'd just agreed to go to bed with him. Why didn't she cut her own throat and get it over with?

Wrapped in one of Penelope's generous bath towels, Charlie cautiously stepped into the room she'd indicated was hers. He heard her enter the shower he'd just vacated, so he had time to look around. The faint scent of her floral perfume wafted around him, and he felt like a trespasser in this all-feminine territory. Except it wasn't as foreign a territory as he'd assumed, he realized as he switched on the bedside lamp.

One entire wall was filled with crowded bookshelves. He scanned some of the titles with curiosity, discovering a number of the techno-thrillers he enjoyed, romance fiction he wouldn't touch, intermixed with history, biography, and even a few philosophical tomes. Admittedly, he didn't read much, but he saw dozens of books here he wouldn't mind opening on a rainy evening.

More comfortable with that discovery, he scanned the rest of the room. Instead of the pink and lace confections he'd encountered in one too many boudoirs, Penelope favored clean, modern lines and good, solid wood. He ran his fingers over the polished oak of her dresser, nudging the framed pictures of her niece and nephew that were almost the only clutter there. He suspected the silk rose in a crystal vase was a gift from someone she loved, and he hoped it was from the kids or her parents.

The bed with its high back was as sleek and elegantly designed as Penelope herself. A simple cream-colored, quilted down comforter covered the mattress, contrasting with the rich chocolate brown linens. A man could almost live with linens like that, even if—after closer investigation—they were trimmed in champagne satin ribbon. The thick feather pillows were like enormous chocolates, sinfully soft and decadent. Charlie could think of any number of tempting things he could do with those pillows and Penelope in the bed.

Except he'd told her he wouldn't.

Maybe he had time to run back to that drugstore. . . . Why the *hell* hadn't he thought of it while they were there?

He heard the shower stop. She'd be drying off now, and spraying herself with some of that oily fragrance he'd seen in the tub. She'd come out all sweet-smelling, shiny, and soft, and there wouldn't be a damned thing he could do about it. If he didn't go in there right now, she'd probably cover up all

that creamy skin with some hideous man-tailored suit of pajamas. He could imagine how her curves would push at the V
neck of the shirt and fill out the boxy trousers, making him
ache with desire.

Hell, he'd be better off on the sofa.

Snatching up a pillow and a blanket he found in the chest at
the foot of her bed, Charlie hurried toward the door. He met
Penelope coming in.

Her eyes widened at the stack in his hands, and she looked
at him questioningly. Charlie was grateful the pillows disguised his lower half. As if he weren't already aroused enough,
the appreciation he read in her gaze as it settled on his uncovered chest nearly crippled him.

"The bed isn't big enough?" she inquired with a modicum
of hurt.

He'd been almost right. Beneath the thick black spill of her
hair, she wore a tailored, silky nightshirt in baby blue instead
of pajamas. He could see the shadow between her breasts
where they rose and fell against the cloth. Charlie bit back a
moan and heroically stood steadfast against temptation.

"Not for both of us," he replied in his best John Wayne imitation. At her puzzlement, he caved. "I'm not holding this
pillow because I have a lust for chickens," he admitted. "Go
on to bed, get some rest. I'll sleep a hell of a lot better on the
sofa."

She was a little slow on the uptake. Miss Penelope Albright
apparently wasn't too bright in recognizing her attraction to
the opposite sex. How she could be so blind to her abundant
charms mystified him, but Charlie liked the way she tilted her
head and looked at him as if he were the only man in the
world.

That realization floored him. She'd not once looked at another man since he'd met her. Not once. Most beautiful
women were relentless flirts. Penelope, however, hadn't even
smiled at the worldly Roger Henwood, or tried to wrap the
pilot around her little finger, or played games with any of the
men they'd encountered these last few days. Hell, he knew

women who would have flirted with the drugstore clerk. Not Penelope. She didn't even acknowledge their existence. But she was acknowledging his now.

He detected a distinct gleam of satisfaction in her eyes as she realized why he was running from her bed. If she had feathers, she'd be preening them. Charlie considered dropping the damned pillow, grabbing her, and to hell with the consequences. Only, those consequences had wreaked havoc with his mind all day. He couldn't risk an instant replay.

"I'd hate to be the reason for a gallant gentleman fleeing from the scene of battle," she said mischievously, touching her upper lip with the seductive tip of her tongue. "I've never terrified a man that badly before." She trailed a neatly manicured fingertip down the valley between his pectorals.

That did it. He'd never left a challenge unanswered, and he wasn't about to start now, even if his opponent was female. Dropping the pillow, letting the towel slide away with it, Charlie grabbed his daredevil hostess by her baby blue silk waist and hauled her from the floor.

"Charlie!" She whispered the cry near his ear as he kicked the pillow and blanket out of his way and carried her to the bed.

"I'm not one of your wimpy pussycats," he growled as he fell on top of her. "And I'm not too dumb to know there are ways of making love without making babies. Let's work out a few more of these differences between us."

Her fingers dug deeply into his shoulders as he pressed her into the comforter and covered her mouth with his, but her protest died the instant their breaths mingled and their tongues touched. If she'd left him any shred of ego at all, he'd believe she'd goaded him into this on purpose.

A moment later, as her knowing fingers wrapped around his arousal and her lips fastened on his nipple, Charlie knew he'd been had, and the pleasure coursing through him mixed with heady triumph. Sinking his hands in silken hair, he took her with him as he rolled over on his back and settled her on top of him. This time, Miss Penelope would have to admit that she was the one who needed this.

He gasped with pleasure at her nipping teeth, and his whole body bucked with the powerful desire to bury himself inside her. Hell, at this rate, she would turn him into that whimpering pussycat. . . .

And he'd die happy.

Before her tempting mouth could slide lower, Charlie rolled Penelope on her back, and, unbuttoning her shirt, applied the same principle she'd used against him. Her suppressed cry of joy relieved any anxiety he might have felt about the equality of this battle of the sexes. The lust was mutual.

With that in mind and her breasts firmly in hand, he slid down her perfumed body until he reached the nub they both wanted him to touch.

He'd gladly writhe beneath her as she did beneath him now. He just wanted to do it to her first.

❧ TWENTY-THREE ❧

"I hate you," Penelope murmured against the sweaty salt of Charlie's shoulder as dawn worked its way through the bedroom window.

"Ummm, I hate you too." He wrapped his hand in her hair where it spilled across his chest. "I always hate women who give me great sex."

Great sex. Of course. That's all it was. He was a blatantly physical man. To him, this was just a physical encounter, a release of pent-up hormones, a venting of frustrated testosterone. Really great sex. Nothing more. Oddly, a modicum of relief seeped through her at that realization. Sex, maybe she could handle. Nothing deeper. Her life was too complicated as it was without entangling it more.

Penelope twirled a hair on his chest, and Charlie tucked her more comfortably into the curve of his arm and shoulder. She'd never had great sex before. Why shouldn't she look at it the same way he did? It wasn't as if they had a meeting of minds and souls and hearts or anything. She'd given up on that fairy tale crap back in college. She'd thought for a while that Beth might have found it, but even that brief storybook romance blew up in everyone's face. So, that kind of relationship didn't exist, not in the world she knew. Not between two intelligent people who knew better.

So, why shouldn't she enjoy great sex while it lasted, like

men did? It wasn't as if she was in danger of losing her heart. Disillusionment had broken that long ago.

Smiling in satisfaction, Penelope draped her bare leg across Charlie's. His hand slid over the curve of her hip to cup her buttock.

Just as she decided they needed to make a trip to the drugstore after they got dressed, her mind hit the hurdle that her senses had obscured.

She couldn't have great sex with Charlie Damned Smith because he thought that gave him a right to tell her what to do.

Punching him in the ribs, she shoved away his arm and leapt from the bed. "I'm going to work."

She gave him credit for not bellowing and waking Beth. Locking the bathroom door and stepping into the shower, she waited for Charlie to batter the door down. The door remained ominously silent. Penelope regarded it warily by the time she stepped out of the shower. She wrapped a towel around her and wondered if he could blockade her in here.

She dried off and pulled on her warmest, fluffiest robe. Charlie had a way of making her forget her intentions, and she didn't want any distractions when she walked out. She knew what she was doing. She couldn't let him divert her for his own nefarious purposes any longer. So, maybe they could enjoy some kind of affair after he got his business sorted out. That didn't mean she had to give up her career.

He wasn't in the bedroom. His clothes were gone. Had he left without saying good-bye? Had she just been a means to an end, and now that she wasn't cooperating anymore, he'd taken off? If so, she'd kill the bastard. He'd left her to deal with protecting Beth, and maybe even Tammy. She couldn't believe he'd do that to her.

That thought startled the hell out of her. Men *always* did things like that to her. Why in the name of heaven would she think Charlie was different?

As she pulled on a navy cashmere suit and a silk shell, Penelope fought an internal battle. What in the world would make her think Charlie was different from any other man she'd known? Just because she'd actually been dumb enough to go to bed with him didn't make him the kind of man who stuck around when things went wrong.

But Charlie had. He hadn't left her behind when the dead body turned up on the beach. Another man would have thought of his own neck first and run like hell. Another man might have dumped her on his family and sneaked off into the jungle. Maybe Charlie thought she had her uses, but even that was unusual for most men. The ones she knew always thought they could handle things themselves, without her help.

She was actually making excuses for the wretch. He'd probably cost her her job, maybe her career, and dragged her and Beth into a dangerous situation, and she was thinking he wasn't such a bad guy after all. Where were her brains?

Still, somewhere in the back of her rebellious mind, she hoped she'd walk out of this bedroom and discover Charlie had solved all their problems. She'd never known sex could rot the brain.

She found Charlie charming Beth over coffee and muffins in the kitchen. He'd apparently retrieved his backpack from the car and actually wore a regular button-down shirt for a change, although it was work-shirt blue and worn over a slightly tattered black T-shirt. She certainly couldn't accuse him of being a clotheshorse as so many men with his looks were. Or maybe he knew work clothes enhanced his rugged handsomeness.

He stood up as she entered the room and, without the slightest hint of embarrassment, caught her waist and brushed a kiss across her forehead. "Cool suit, but I like the braid and baseball cap better."

He was entirely too cheerful. Penny regarded him suspiciously as she poured her coffee. Kisses and hugs at this hour had her totally disoriented. "Have you two been entertaining each other this morning?"

"Charlie said he could partition those cabinets so I can sort things and find them easier. Do you think the complex will let him do it?" Beth removed a platter of eggs and bacon from the warming oven. "I told him he might as well go ahead and eat these because you wouldn't, but he insisted on waiting."

"I'll have a bite of the eggs, but I've really got to get to the office. I've got a lot of explaining to do." Penelope poured juice into Charlie's glass, all too aware of his masculine bulk as she leaned over his shoulder to reach the table. Every nerve stretched tight as he gave her his best little-boy smile. He was up to something.

"Oh, you don't have to worry about that St. Lucia client," Beth said disingenuously as she spread jam across a muffin. "Charlie's already called the resort and explained the dangerous situation and that he thought you would be safer back in the States until the criminals are caught. They understand perfectly. They've packed up your clothes and are holding them until you come back." She shot Penelope a startling smile. "He told them he was your husband. Isn't that cute?"

Shocked that he'd so casually removed her from her job, Penelope set the pitcher down and stared at the two of them. "You did *what*?"

"Sit, Penny. Eat," Charlie ordered. "We've got a day at the office ahead. You've just acquired a new client."

She sat, but she didn't eat. She stared at Charlie, wondering if she could see into his head if she looked hard enough. "What new client?" she finally asked. Hell, he must have been one adorable little boy. She could see the gleam in his eyes even now. He had *criminals* after him, for pity's sake, and he sat there as if he'd just offered her Christmas.

"Me. Smith and Son Construction. We're entering the computer age with your help. You can take me to work with you."

She didn't know whether to cry or shoot him. She took a bite of her muffin and thought about it. "I'm taking you to work as a new client," she said calmly, or she thought she said it calmly. She hadn't decided whether to get hysterical or not. She could imagine introducing Charlie in his work shirt and jeans to the pinstripe suits at the office. Maybe he had a point.

She could go out and get hog farmers as clients next. Start a whole new field of endeavor for PC&M. The place could use some new perspectives.

"You got it." He smiled meltingly at Beth even though she couldn't see him. "These are the best eggs I've ever eaten. I don't suppose you've taught Penelope how to make them?"

Not hysterics, Penelope decided, a baseball bat. She'd take a bat upside his head. "I don't cook," she enunciated clearly. "I don't clean house. I'm a software expert. I install computers and software that meet your business needs. Do you need inventory software, Charlie? Accounts receivable? A complete package, perhaps? I don't come cheap."

"Didn't think you did, sweetheart." Charlie's eyes gleamed as he met the dangerous sparkle in hers, but he didn't carry the innuendo further. "Your company handles Jacobsen's accounts, don't they? I'm bigger than he is."

Penelope eyed his broad shoulders and nodded. "Yeah, I'd say you are. You're bigger than most people. What's that got to do with it? Jacobsen goes to our tax specialist. Want me to send you to him?"

"Nope, I want that software package. Inventory. I've always wanted to know how much inventory I have."

Before she could respond appropriately to that, a frantic pounding at the front door intruded.

Charlie was on his feet and at the door in seconds. Penelope had never seen a man that large move so quickly. She would lay wagers he'd been a quarterback. After checking the peephole, he jerked the door open and immediately slammed it behind the pair of intruders after they tumbled in.

"Tammy!" Penelope leapt up to greet Charlie's sister and the tall, slender man accompanying her.

"I think they saw us. I didn't know the place was being watched. Is there a back way out of here?" The slender man with the light olive complexion, who Penelope assumed was Raul, cursorily inspected their surroundings, keeping the protective shield of his arm around Tammy's frail shoulders.

Charlie cursed and turned expectantly to Penelope.

"The tunnel into the medical center." She'd blown her chance for indulging in hysterics. Now was the time for concentration. "How do you know they're watching?"

Tammy answered first. "Black Cadillac, tinted windows, engine running, parked by the Dumpsters. Limo service, maybe?" she asked hopefully.

"Not here," Beth practically snorted. "The complex is for the physically challenged, not the wealthy."

As Charlie secured the door lock, Penelope thought quickly. "Beth, get the cell phone. Call John and have him bring the van to the medical center. I'll pack what you need for a few days."

"There isn't time—" Raul started to protest as Beth grabbed the phone and punched in numbers.

"Whoever's out there will have to call and ask what they should do next." Charlie spoke over Beth's quiet conversation. "Then they've got to figure out the best way of getting in here. Unless they followed you up, they may not even know which apartment we're in." Charlie threw his backpack at his friend and grabbed Penelope's bag from where they'd dropped it the night before. "How about cash? Is there an ATM at the medical center?"

"Probably." Pocketing the phone Beth handed her, Penelope left her twin hastily cleaning off the table, scraping eggs into the disposal, and stacking dishes in the dishwasher, while she hurried into Beth's room and pulled out dresser drawers. "Where do we go from here?" she shouted. And why did she think Charlie would already have the answer? She had fallen into the habit of relying on him on the island, where she knew nothing. She was on home territory now. She should be thinking for herself.

"The most public place you can think of. Get them out in crowds, in a place that can't be identified with any of us."

"Disney World," Penelope replied as she returned carrying Beth's overnight bag.

"Disney World," Beth said in unison, dropping her dish towel on the rack.

Charlie offered a harried grin. "You've been practicing."

He glanced back to his sister's pale face. "You up to it, midget?"

Tammy straightened her shoulders and glared at him. "You bet I am. I want to see it *all*." She hesitated, then added, "Isn't Disney kind of far from here?"

"That's the best part." Charlie shouldered Beth's bag and grabbed her by the elbow. "Did you reach John?"

"Paged and left a message. Do you think we could take the kids?" Beth asked wistfully as Raul opened the door and checked the hallway.

"Have them skip school? What kind of mother are you?" Charlie chided, steering her out the door at Raul's gesture to go ahead. "Why not?"

Penelope could think of half a dozen reasons why not, but then, she could think of several more that said it would be better if John had the whole family in his company. Six of one, half a dozen of the other. Might as well go for the gusto. She was beginning to sound like a beer commercial.

They took the elevator down to the basement without seeing another soul. Penelope watched the two lovebirds with surreptitious interest, but they didn't appear very loving. Raul stood stiffly at the back of the elevator, on Tammy's right should she falter, but he didn't touch her otherwise. Tammy clenched her cane like a weapon, scarcely leaning on it. They didn't even look at each other. But something in the tension between them warned they were intensely aware of each other's presence.

She threw Charlie a quick look, but he avoided her eyes. Guiding Beth into the basement hallway as the elevator doors opened, he hurried them down echoing corridors into the antiseptic smell of the clinic.

She wouldn't tease him. Poor guy, he was having a hard time dealing with the knowledge that his little sister was old enough to fall in love. Add danger into the equation, and he had his hands full. She was beginning to understand that Charlie was the kind of man who accepted his responsibilities and took them seriously. She really hadn't given him enough credit, probably because he damned well annoyed the devil out of her when he assumed she was one more of his duties.

"All right, is there a lounge or somewhere we can wait and watch until John shows up?" Charlie demanded as they reached the carpeted hallway of the clinic's main entrance. "I don't want to sit in front of all this glass like a sitting duck."

"Upstairs, second floor," Beth ordered. "There's an employee lounge. I've been helping out where I can. It's early. I don't think anyone will complain."

Everyone's nerves hung by a fine thread, but they all remained calm and polite as they maneuvered in the elevators, looking like an abandoned tribe of nomads with all their belongings on their backs. No one seemed to pay them much mind.

"They probably think we're all from the mental hospital and you're our administrator," Charlie whispered, falling back to Penelope's side as Beth took command and led the expedition forward.

"I feel more like one of the inmates." She'd forgotten she wore her best suit while everyone else was in jeans. "Are you sure Raul isn't just a little on the paranoid side?"

"More than a little. It's how he's survived all these years. He's nearly always right." Charlie stepped forward to hold the lounge door open so Beth and Tammy could pass. He stuck his hand out and halted Raul before he could follow. "You and me are gonna have a talk, buddy."

Raul looked guilty, but his glance darted to Penelope and back. "Not now, all right? Later."

"I think we'd better stick to the problem at hand, Charlie. You can give your morality lecture later, not that you have much in the way of morals to brag about," Penelope reminded him.

Charlie scowled at her. "If we send them to Orlando, they'll have to stay up there. The resort has a suite at one of the hotels for the company's use, but I'll be damned . . ."

"I won't touch her, all right?" Raul said in a low voice, glancing toward the door Charlie had allowed to close. "I want what's best for her. I can't believe you let her come here like this."

"*Let* her? Like I had a choice." Still scowling, he shoved open the door and transferred his frown to Penelope. "We're staying here. I'm still your client, got it?"

Penelope studied his expression, saw what he didn't say, and nodded. "I've got it."

He was telling her they would act as the decoys so the others could get away.

Penelope shivered and wondered if she really wanted to share that much responsibility.

❧ TWENTY-FOUR ❧

As he traversed the hushed, carpeted halls of one of Miami's many glass-enclosed office buildings, Charlie wondered if helping Penelope keep her job and letting her run his campaign against evildoers counted as a valentine present.

He wished he knew what the hell else he thought he was doing. There had to be ten thousand other ways of handling Jacobsen besides walking next to this elegant woman in her sophisticated suit through the halls of the enemy. Charlie didn't fool himself. These were definitely the halls of the enemy. Jacobsen wore fancy suits like the insects scrambling up and down these corridors, throwing them curious looks. Jacobsen was the one who rubbed shoulders with the bigwigs behind those closed doors, the one who partied with men like Emile. Not Charlie. Smith and Son got its clients the old-fashioned way, by hard work, quality results, word of mouth, and the best bids. And he and his employees did it wearing work shirts instead of Italian suits, and driving pickups instead of BMWs.

So what the hell was he doing here?

As he watched Penelope stride confidently through the corridors, nodding curtly at acquaintances, he knew he was here because of her alone. He should be worrying about Raul and Tammy, looking after business, tracking Jacobsen down in his lair and pounding him against a wall.

Penelope shoved open a glass door and entered a reception area like a general marching to war. Aware that his rumpled work clothes attracted stares, Charlie wondered if he was embarrassing her, but Miss Penny seemed well above that mundane human emotion. He kind of liked that about her.

"Rachel, this is Charles Smith of Smith and Son Construction. Start a new client file if you would." For the first time since they'd entered the building, she glanced at him. "Would you care for some coffee, Mr. Smith?"

All right, two could play this game. As much as he would like to plant a big one on her right now—she looked so cute with her forehead wrinkled in that officious frown—Charlie gallantly resisted. He'd wager she was treating him just as if he were a multimillion-dollar client. "Black, please."

Penelope nodded, Rachel made a note and scurried away, and they advanced down more hallways.

Charlie shook hands as she introduced him to a few termites scurrying out of the walls waving papers in Penelope's direction. He frowned at the bespectacled nerd who dared halt her to talk about a golf date. The man got the message and hastily departed. Charlie wondered if it was his imagination or if mouths were gaping as he passed by. The bull-in-a-china-shop neurosis returned, but instead of wanting to run, he was beginning to enjoy himself. He suspected half the stares they attracted were pure speculation about his relationship to the gorgeous woman at his side. He'd bet good money that she'd ignored most of the men in the company and rejected the rest. He considered placing a proprietary arm around Penelope's shoulders just to watch her coworkers go ballistic, but he had the feeling Penelope would blast his arm off first.

Charlie noted with appropriate appreciation that she had an office with a bank of windows to herself. As soon as she shut the door behind them, he shared his appreciation by catching her starchy suit by the waist and pulling her into his arms.

She struggled briefly, but even in the rarefied air of this environment, the electricity between them ignited fires. Charlie sighed with delight as her lips softened beneath his and the sweetness of her breath invaded his mouth.

"Charlie," she whispered, embarrassed, as he relented slightly and released her mouth. She'd caught her fingers in the faded fabric of his work shirt, and he could feel the heat of them against his chest. Maybe he should start wearing the shirt unbuttoned.

"I don't know what's going on here," Charlie murmured as he slid his hands under her jacket to stroke the silk beneath, "but I'm about ready to admit that it's more than sex. How about you?"

"Impossible." She struggled to free herself, and Charlie let her go. Her hand flew up to check the tight knot of her hair and adjust her glasses. She gestured helplessly with her other hand. "You said you wanted to be a client."

He hadn't imagined how much that one little word, *impossible*, could hurt. He'd thought she was enjoying this as much as he was. Maybe he was wrong. Maybe he'd just embarrassed the hell out of her. "Right," he ground out between clenched teeth as he shoved his hands in his pockets. "Impossible to imagine anything between a clown and Miss Junior League. What was I thinking?"

She flung the papers in her hands onto her desk and retreated to her office chair. "That's an insult to clowns and probably to the Junior League. I'm a little too bossy for the tea-and-garden-party set. Now, what is it we're supposed to be doing?"

Charlie relaxed a fraction as he settled into a rolling leather chair. He'd flustered her, he could tell. She wouldn't look him in the eye. "Okay, if we're not clown and Junior League, what are we, then? Oil and water? Is it so impossible to think maybe we've got something going between us?"

She ran her long, slender hands up and down her face. "Don't do this to me, Charlie. I'm scared to death about Beth, I'm worried about my job, about this whole blasted mess. I can't even think straight anymore. Just tell me what we're supposed to be doing here besides providing entertainment for the rest of the firm."

So, she'd noticed it too. Charlie relaxed and hid a smile. "I'll come back next time in my best funeral suit. We'll see if they like that any better."

A faint smile curled the corner of her mouth. "Wear it with muddy boots. Then they can have the cleaning crew follow us around." She shook her head and finally met his gaze. "Charlie, I'm real good at games. Don't make me play them. You can come in here wearing a clown suit for all I care, but let's do it some other time. I want to get this over with and get on with my life."

She said that as if she expected the rest of her life not to include him. He'd correct that impression later. He could be just as stubborn as she could. Charlie leaned forward and confiscated her desk phone. "I've got to call my lawyer and start working on the bank account problems. You need to find those Jacobsen files and tell me anything that's open for public record. Look for new companies."

She seemed relieved to be treading familiar ground. "Let me check my messages first. Believe it or not, I do have real clients."

Charlie relinquished the phone. "Are there rules against having an affair with clients?" he asked innocently.

"Why ask?" She pushed a stray hair from her face as she hit her message button. "You'd break them anyway."

She didn't appear too worried about that. She seemed completely cool about the whole thing. Charlie admired her professional attitude as she jotted notes and ignored him. He had tidal heat waves surging through him just looking at her. She hid anything she felt behind her demure demeanor. Knowing her that intimately reassured him.

He enjoyed it even more when a starched rump in an Italian suit and impeccably styled silver hair rapped on the door, walked in, and raised an eyebrow as he took in Charlie's appearance. Deliberately not rising, Charlie stretched his Nike-clad size-fifteens out in front of him.

"Miss Albright, if I might have a word with you . . ." the rump said icily.

Penelope clicked off her machine and nodded. "Mr. Poindexter, this is Charles Smith, of Smith and Son Construction, a new client." She turned to Charlie. "If you don't mind, Mr. Smith?"

Charlie waved his hand magnanimously. "Not at all." He turned his gaze back to the Italian suit. "Miss Albright was generous enough to show me how her software could help my St. Lucia project. If this works out, I'm recommending her to St. Philippe and his cronies back on the island. The Foundation's accounting system could use updating."

Charlie watched Poindexter's spine stiffen, his eyes narrow, and his gaze shoot obliquely to Penelope as she emerged from behind her desk. He couldn't tell if it was guilt or greed causing the reaction, but the old goat recognized Emile's name.

Poindexter managed a nod of acknowledgment. "Miss Albright is one of our best." He held up his hand to Penelope. "Don't let me interrupt. I'll come back later. I simply wanted to remind you that we have the quality-control team in next week. Your time sheet will need to be on my desk first thing Wednesday morning. It was good meeting you, Mr. Smith." He strolled out, leaving Penny gaping after him.

She turned her amazed gaze to Charlie and he shrugged. "I'm good at games too. The old competitive instinct kicks in. If I bring in Emile's account, do you think Poindexter will invite me to the office Christmas party?"

"*I'll* invite you to the office Christmas party," she muttered, returning to her chair. "The phone's all yours. I'll call up the file on the computer and work from there." She rubbed her hand over her wrinkled brow. "What the *hell* am I going to put on my time sheet?"

Figuring that was a rhetorical question, Charlie copped the phone. He had employees to pay. Their groceries were more important than Penelope's time sheet.

He called his office and listened to Sherry pour out the list of problems stacking up on his desk. He called his lawyer and left a message. As he worked, he watched Penelope frown over her computer screen, pound away at the keys, and print out stacks of material. She didn't seem conscious of his presence. Accustomed to the kind of women who clung to his arms and hung on his every word, Charlie decided he could learn to enjoy the freedom Penelope's independence gave him almost as much as he enjoyed watching her full lips pucker thoughtfully as she frowned at her screen.

Penelope shoved her chair back and rose just as he hung up the telephone after leaving another message for his lawyer. "I'm looking for Jacobsen's file. What I want doesn't seem to be in the computer."

She stalked out without giving him a chance to reply. Okay, so maybe he had to teach her to share a little better. He could live with that. Charlie reached for the phone book. Now was the time for a few more interesting calls.

By the time Penelope returned to her office, Charlie was apparently speaking with Raul. Figuring Raul must be using Beth's cell phone, Penelope flipped through the pages of the file she'd found, seeking the information she needed while listening to Charlie's end of the conversation with half an ear. Charlie had puckered his forehead in thought, but he didn't seem in any panic, so she assumed the van was safely on its way to Disney World without incident.

With delight, she discovered a list of Jacobsen's interconnected corporations and began jotting notes. The man had his fingers in almost every development pie on the south coast. And Charlie thought his corporation was bigger? He must be dreaming.

"Shit." Charlie slammed the phone down and glared at it.

Penelope's stomach did a nervous jig as she looked up at him. "Are they all right?"

Startled as if he'd forgotten he wasn't alone, he glanced up and attempted a smile. "The kids are bouncing up and down, your brother-in-law is barking commands, and Tammy isn't speaking to Raul, if that counts for anything."

"And Beth's singing," she finished wryly. "It's how she deals with stress."

"I think I heard 'I Will Survive' in the background," he admitted with a slightly bigger grin as the tune registered.

"But something's wrong," she prompted him.

He raked his hand through his disheveled hair. "The office trailer on the island was ransacked several times while Raul was in town. Or with Tammy, more likely," he admitted grimly. "When he took to sleeping in the trailer with a shotgun, someone tried to set fire to it—while he was inside. They sabotaged his truck and piped raw sewage into the drinking water. His watch and the cash drawer were stolen on one of the nights the trailer was ransacked. He wasn't aware the bank account had been emptied, but he figures the thief must have taken blank checks at the same time."

"How did his watch end up on a body in his hut or tree house or whatever you called it?"

Charlie's shoulders slumped. "That's where the story gets sticky. Raul's positive Emile found out about him and Tammy. It got so Tammy couldn't leave the house without someone with her. When she did slip away, she thought she was being followed. After the fire at the trailer, Raul didn't dare meet her in the jungle again for fear she would get hurt. He didn't know the tree house had been burned, but it's obvious the same thief who ransacked the trailer and stole his watch had to be the one who died in the fire. He may have been lying in wait for them. Besides Tammy, the only people who knew about the place had to be whoever was following Tammy and whoever hired him. Since Emile is the only person with a reason or the resources to have Tammy followed . . ."

"That connects Emile with the thief and the sabotage," Penelope finished with a sigh. "Not good."

The intercom buzzed and they both jumped. Chuckling nervously, Penelope hit the button.

"You have a delivery, Miss Albright," the receptionist announced. "I can't get away from my desk right now."

"I'll be out in a minute, Rachel." Penelope sat back in her chair and watched the man across from her with sympathy. Betrayal by family had to hurt the most. She tried to distract him with what she hoped was a more cheerful topic. "Did you get the bank account situation straightened out yet?"

Charlie's jaw muscles tightened more. "I can't reach my lawyer. He isn't returning my messages." He stood up. "I'll go get your delivery. I've got some thinking to do anyway."

Penelope's eyes widened as Charlie strode out as if he owned the place. Clients didn't *do* that, not unless they were powerful men accustomed to running whatever office they entered. And then they didn't go pick up deliveries for the peons working for them.

She was engrossed in note-taking when Charlie returned. She could almost sense his lighter step as he shut the door and crossed the room, but she didn't look up from her task until he leaned over and kissed the top of her head. In surprise, she lifted her eyes and encountered a crystal vase glittering in the sunlight streaming through the windows. Spilling from the vase were a dozen perfect sweetheart roses in an assortment of colors. She dropped her mechanical pencil in astonishment.

"Happy Valentine's Day," Charlie whispered from somewhere beside her, but she could scarcely tear her gaze from the roses.

She'd received dozens of bouquets during high school and college and her modeling career. Men flashed them like diamonds, expecting a lot in return. Red hothouse roses had the same hard, scentless uselessness as diamonds. The perfumed fragrance of the roses in front of her filled the room, and rainbows danced with the light through the crystal. This bouquet was *alive* with color and light and scent. She'd never seen anything so perfect in her life.

"It's okay if you don't like them," Charlie said flatly, moving away. "It was the best I could do at the last minute. The florists were sold out days ago. I had a friend with a nursery put these together, but they're scarcely those big things the florists have. Sorry." He dropped into his leather chair and reached for the phone again.

Penelope choked on any reply she could have made. She couldn't remember anyone actually *caring* whether she liked her roses or not. They just expected her to jump with joy because they'd spent a lot of money. Gently, she touched a velvet yellow petal. She must be out of her mind to get weepy and sentimental over a stupid rose.

"They're the most gorgeous roses I've ever seen, Charlie," she finally whispered as he punched the buttons of her phone as if it were his personal enemy. He'd wear the numbers right off if he hit them any harder.

He flashed her a bleak smile and shrugged as the person on the other end apparently answered.

She'd *hurt* him, actually hurt this arrogant man who had pushed her around for days. She'd insulted him, dumped fish bait over his head, smacked him, and heaven only knew what else, and he'd cheerfully proceeded without complaint. But he hadn't been able to offer her a flashy present, so he thought her silence meant she was rejecting his meager gift. Stupid man.

She hadn't realized it was Valentine's Day. She hadn't received a Valentine's gift in years. It was one more holiday she'd written off her list and pretended didn't exist. She wished she had something to give Charlie in return. The roses had melted a great big puddle in the vicinity of her long-absent heart, and she ought to return the favor.

What the hell was she thinking? Penelope closed her eyes and took a deep breath. She wanted to express affection for this man who had turned her life upside down and inside out? Was she mad? She could be unemployed shortly if she had to turn in a time sheet with no billable hours. Charlie's grand gesture only delayed the inevitable.

She opened her eyes again, and a tiny rainbow danced across her desk blotter.

"Penelope." Charlie's voice was almost apologetic as he hung up the phone. "I'm going to have to leave. I've got to pay my employees somehow and I'm not making any progress from here."

Steeling herself as best as she could, she looked up and met Charlie's eyes. She saw regret there, and she didn't like it. She didn't want him thinking she was ungrateful for the flowers, and she owed him a favor in return.

She pointed at the chair from which he was rising. "Sit. Give me your bank account numbers and your lawyer's name."

A wrinkle appeared between his eyes as he reluctantly withdrew account cards from his wallet and handed them over. "There's a lien on them. You can't take anything out. What are you going to do?"

"Give your employees a Valentine's present," she announced sweetly, reaching for the phone.

She jerked it from his hand as he tried to take it away and continued hitting buttons. As the person on the other end answered, she turned away from Charlie. "Hi, Celia, put me through to Marshall, would you?"

She sensed Charlie warily sitting back in the chair. She couldn't very well admit she was doing this for him. She didn't want to admit he was getting to her. She couldn't afford any kind of relationship right now, and certainly not one with a man like Charlie. But she wanted to do this anyway. Idly, she stroked a fragile yellow petal as she waited for someone to pick up the phone on the other end.

"Hi, Marshall, how's Gloria? How did you place in the tournament?" She hated these little social games, but they worked. Besides, she liked Marshall and Gloria, even if they were golf nuts. She grimaced at the news that they'd placed out of the running, offered sympathetic noises, then finally launched into her reason for calling.

"I've got a client who's run into a little problem with bank liens, and his attorney is out of town. If we don't get it untangled today, his employees won't get paid. We could probably do a personal loan and open a new account, but the IRS gets a little antsy when we play around like that. If I fax the info over to you, could you take care of it for me?"

She smiled as she hung up. Charlie still eyed her suspiciously, but he waited instead of commenting.

"Have your secretary fax the lien documents to this number." She pushed the card from her Rolodex across the desk. "Marshall knows all the nooks and crannies at the courthouse. He'll shove those spurious liens down someone's throat before the day's over."

Charlie reached for the phone with a smile of admiration. "You play this game well, don't you? Golf?" This last he asked with a quirk at the corner of his lips.

Penelope shrugged. "If that's what it takes."

"How good are you?" Catching Sherry on the first ring, he gave her the fax number and repeated Penelope's orders.

Penelope waited until he hung up to reply. "Not bad. It's a silly game, but I've got a good eye."

"Football's more fun," he said hopefully.

"Football's cold." She didn't have any intention of elaborating, but before Charlie could argue, the phone rang and she grabbed for it. The voice asking for Charlie sounded panicky.

Charlie took the receiver when she handed it over, frowned at what he heard, and pinched the bridge of his nose. "Tell him I'm on-site and you left a message. Send him to the hotel project if he persists."

Penelope waited patiently as he hung up and said nothing.

With a grimace, he threw back his shoulders and glared out the window. "That was Sherry again. Emile just arrived at my office."

❧ TWENTY-FIVE ❧

"He could just be looking for Tammy," Penelope reminded him.

"*That's* supposed to make me feel better?"

There was a knock on the door, and Rachel stuck her head in.

She smiled dreamily at Charlie as she handed Penelope a parcel. "This just came by special messenger. Could I bring you more coffee, Mr. Smith?"

"This is fine, thanks." He nodded at the cup he'd scarcely touched since Rachel brought it in earlier.

"You didn't play with the Dolphins at any time, did you?"

"*Rachel,*" Penelope cut in, lifting her eyebrow pointedly.

"Sorry." With a decidedly unapologetic smile, she retreated.

She shouldn't be so irritated with the receptionist's blatant admiration of Charlie. Rachel flirted with all the good-looking men who passed her desk. Penelope had always laughed at her before. She wasn't laughing now as she tore into the package.

Charlie got up and stalked the room. His restlessness was beginning to rub off on her. She could hope Beth and the kids were safe, but she didn't *know* it. For all she knew, Jacobsen had located the suite Charlie's company used in Orlando, and he was waiting for them. Or Emile could have brought his hired thugs with him and could be even now tracking them down. Men who murdered to get what they wanted could have more contacts than she knew. What the devil did she know about murderers anyway?

The brown paper finally fell away and Penelope gasped in surprise at the familiar gold box inside. "Godivas! Who on earth would send me Godivas?" A box this large would require a bank loan to buy and a detox center to recover from.

"There should be a card," Charlie muttered. "It's not as imaginative as getting the liens off my account, but it's the best I could do at short notice."

Penelope flipped open the gold card. *Don't eat them all in one place. Love, Charlie.* Love, Charlie. It was just a cliché he'd thought necessary for a valentine gift, but she was still amazed that he'd remembered the day at all. His generosity overwhelmed her. Flowers *and* candy.

"It's the spirit of competition, isn't it?" she asked thoughtfully, lifting the lid and selecting her favorite truffle. It melted deliciously in rivers of raspberry and dark chocolate on her tongue as Charlie turned and glared at her.

"What's the spirit of competition?" he demanded.

"If I do something for you, you've got to do something better. That's what we have in common."

He opened his mouth to reply, shut it again as he watched her savor the chocolate, then reluctantly grinned. "Okay, maybe. Now can we get out of here?"

"Out of here? Where to? And why?" She offered him the chocolates, trying to behave as if this were a normal business conference. But Charlie's restlessness was rasping against her already ragged nerves.

"My stepfather knows who you are. Jacobsen must know you work here. Sooner or later, one of them is going to show up, and I don't want you around when they do." He tore the wrapping off a plain chocolate.

Penelope figured he didn't have an answer to the "where to?" or the "how?" that was forming on the tip of her tongue, so she didn't waste her breath. "You don't really think they're inclined to come in here and mow us down with machine guns, do you?"

"I believe the term is semiautomatic weapons, and no, I don't see that scenario. I can, however, see Jacobsen calling Poindexter with some fraudulent charge and demanding your instant removal. We can worry about the semiautomatics as we're tossed out on the street."

This still didn't feel really real to her. She hadn't seen Michel's body or the skeleton in Raul's hut. She hadn't seen the ransacked cottage. She'd been in an auto accident before. They happened without rhyme or reason. She had no way of knowing if that ravine was intended for them. For all she knew, Charlie was as paranoid as Raul. The paper trail to the possible Russian Mafia worried her though. Still, that didn't mean—

Charlie slapped both hands on the desk in front of her and leaned over until they were practically eye to eye. "Did you find any new companies in Jacobsen's file?" he demanded.

The harshness of his gaze froze her. She almost wished for his mirrored sunglasses back. "He just incorporated a new construction firm under the name of St. Lucia Productions. The Russians are on the stated board of directors. So is Emile."

He muttered a foul expletive, straightened, and plowed his fingers through his hair. "The last time I looked, Jacobsen's corporate office was closed and up for sale. I don't suppose you can give me the address of the new company?"

"He's incorporating in Delaware and lists a Delaware attorney as his agent of record. But the mailing address is St. Lucia." Penelope held her breath and waited for the explosion.

His shoulders hunched. He turned his back toward her, so she couldn't see his expression, but she could see his fingers form fists. He didn't know what to do with her, she realized. He wanted to find Jacobsen, but he didn't dare leave her alone. She didn't know how she felt about that. Glancing at the rainbow of roses in the crystal vase, she decided it was best not to ponder too deeply on how she felt about anything.

Emotions only confused matters. Logic and concentration, on the other hand, could put together pretty clear pictures.

"The company uses a rental car agency down the street. They'll deliver a car to the parking garage attendant. I can tell Rachel we're heading out for an early lunch and then to your office for the afternoon. She'll accept that. I can't set up a system without examining your books." She bounced her pencil on the desk and eyed the Godivas longingly. She really *needed* chocolate right now. "If you think there's any danger, you may want to tell your office staff to clear out."

He seemed to take a deep breath but didn't turn. "I think, at this point," he replied slowly, as if thinking aloud, "they're after us and your computer. There wouldn't be a lot of point in drawing attention to themselves by terrorizing anyone else, unless they figure my staff has access to the information."

"Why don't we just let the FBI handle this?" she asked softly. "Tammy and Raul are safe. Your employees will get paid. We can just hide away somewhere until this is over."

Charlie turned, and the heated look in his eyes almost blew her away. He acknowledged her reaction with a wry grin that didn't reduce the smolder. "Someplace with hot springs and big beds?" he suggested. "I might take you up on that offer."

Oh my. Oh double my. Just like the Wicked Witch of the West, she melted into a puddle at his feet. She should have been wearing her ruby slippers. Even with her limited imagination Penelope could see them both naked in some bubbling jungle spring. To hell with the real world. She wanted the promise she read in Charlie's eyes.

She called the rental car company. They'd arrived by taxi, leaving the Escort and her car at the apartment to confuse anyone following them. A rental car in the company name should be equally untraceable.

Charlie nodded approvingly, then returned to pacing. He spoke as soon as she hung up. "If they've got any brains at all, they'll know about my plane by now. We can't use that. I'll call a 'copter company and have them deliver you to Orlando. You can have a good time with the kids."

You? He was sending *her* to Orlando? The morning's tension hit an outlet and erupted. Penelope heaved the box of chocolates at him. Silver and gold foil, white and dark chocolates exploded across the room as the shiny box bounced off Charlie's huge shoulders. She could scarcely miss a target as broad as any barn.

"You bastard!" She would have shouted, but that would only bring the curiosity seekers running. She seethed too much to desire an audience. He'd conned her with warm looks and pretty flowers, made her think he was actually listening to her excellent advice, and then he dumped her on family. She would kill him for building her hopes so high.

Charlie stood amid the sea of expensive chocolates and glared at her. "That's a nasty right arm you've got there. Throw the roses too, if it'll make you feel better. It won't change my mind. You're home and you're safe and I want it to stay that way. You can help your brother-in-law look after Tammy and Raul."

"*Ex*–brother-in-law," she reminded him. "And just what do you think you'll be doing? Taking Emile out to dinner and explaining all the reasons why he can't marry his daughter off to Russian Mafia or European nobility or whatever? Or maybe you thought you'd single-handedly take on Jacobsen and his thugs and blow them off the map? What the *hell* do you think you can do that the FBI can't?"

He shrugged his big shoulders. "I don't know, but I'll do it a lot easier knowing you're safe."

Men! More exasperated than outraged now, Penelope returned to bouncing her pencil on the desk. "I haven't given you Jacobsen's address yet," she pointed out. "You can't just attack him without any evidence."

He hadn't really thought about it. Watching the glossy knot of Penelope's black hair in the sunshine from the window, Charlie couldn't think of much at all except keeping that slender neck out of trouble. She kept stroking the rose petals and moving the crystal to catch the sun when she thought he wasn't looking. A woman like Penelope, one who acknowledged she'd once been a fashion model, must have received hundreds of roses in her lifetime, but he thought maybe she fancied his offering a little. He wanted her safe until he could come back and take her out properly. Maybe he'd even escort her to the symphony or something, so he could prove he wasn't a complete hick.

"Let's just get out of here, all right?" he suggested. "If you're not here, your boss can't fire you. Bill all your time to my account. That's what my accountant does anyway. How long before the car arrives?"

She shrugged and looked regretfully at the flowers. "Not long. I guess it would look kind of odd to take these with me."

"I'll buy you more. I'll buy entire bushes. C'mon, let's go. The longer I stay in this place, the more nervous I get." Scraping a path through the chocolates with his foot, Charlie pulled her from the chair.

She reached over and captured a fragile peach-colored bud from the vase, then scooped up a handful of the foil-wrapped chocolates from the floor. "Rachel will think we had a food fight."

The longer she dragged this out, the more nervous he got. He wanted to throw her over his shoulder and bodily carry her to safety. Charlie figured she was making him crazy on purpose. He rescued the box and dumped a handful of truffles into it. "Everyone has to eat a bit of dirt in their lifetime. Here, take this."

She carefully reattached the lid and tucked the box and his note into the bulging leather satchel containing her laptop. Then she jerked open a desk drawer and removed a compact cell phone. "I hate these things, but it might be helpful. Surely Jacobsen can't trace calls?"

"Hell if I know." Catching her elbow, he dragged her toward the door. "Can you throw basketballs as well as you throw candy?" he demanded as they hurried down the silent, carpeted corridor. He had to keep her busy mind occupied.

"I was a cheerleader, remember? Didn't have time for bas-ketball." Her long strides matched his easily.

"Bet you would have been good," he muttered as they reached the lobby. Charlie grimaced as still another mes-senger appeared outside the glass enclosure. One of these days he'd learn not to go overboard.

The gray-capped delivery man entered bearing a giant white teddy bear cuddling a shiny red cardboard heart-shaped box. Rachel looked up at it, grinned, and turned a speculative gaze to them as Charlie tried to push Penelope out the door.

"Better wait a second, Miss Albright. Looks like another special delivery."

Penelope had donned her horn-rimmed glasses sometime during their flight down the hall. With her hair jerked back in its tight knot and wearing her straitlaced, no-nonsense suit, she had reverted to the iron robot Charlie had first seen at the airport. But he knew her better now, knew the passionate woman who could make love to him in a Jacuzzi, dump fish bait over his head when angered, and love her family to the point of working herself to death for them. That woman gazed longingly at the giant white teddy bear.

Penelope hesitated just long enough for Rachel to sign the messenger's receipt and glance at the delivery name. When the receptionist didn't stop her, she started to turn and follow the messenger out the door.

"For you, Miss Albright," Rachel called brightly.

"Damn you, Charlie Smith," Penelope murmured beneath her breath. "I'm going to hate you forever for this."

Charlie speculated on the nature of love/hate relation-ships as she took a deep breath, straightened her shoul-ders, and swung around to act totally surprised for Rachel's benefit.

"For me? Beth must have found a bargain on stuffed ani-mals somewhere. Thank you." She gingerly lifted the mam-moth animal with her free arm. Charlie tried to relieve her of the laptop so she could hold the bear more comfortably, but she clung to it as she would to a lifeline.

"Aren't you going to look at the card?" Rachel called after her as Penelope strode hurriedly for the door.

"I'll look at it later. It's probably for the kids." Breezily, she swept out of the office, leaving Charlie to catch up.

"Damn you, damn you, damn you," she muttered as she hurried down the stairs rather than waiting for the elevator.

"How do you know it's from me?" Charlie demanded as he raced down the dark stairwell after her. He'd never met so perverse a woman in his entire life. Try to make her smile, and she cursed. Still, he'd seen her eyes when that bear arrived, and he could hear the tears in her voice now. She was on the verge of breaking down. He was starting to understand that Miss Penny didn't like losing control.

"Nobody sends me stuffed animals," she practically sobbed as she shoved at the heavy metal door to the parking garage. "Do I look like a stuffed animal kind of person?"

"You look like a woman who would have a houseful of dogs and cats, given the opportunity," Charlie declared boldly. "I would have given you a puppy if I'd thought the complex would allow it." He couldn't believe he saw her so well, but he did, as if a giant lightbulb had turned on and illuminated her soul. She was as soft and squishy inside as those candies she'd shoved into her briefcase, but this damned job and her responsibilities were drying her out and making her as hard as her exterior disguise.

"I—" She halted abruptly in front of him, and Charlie nearly plowed into her.

Righting himself, he glanced over her shoulder at the two men in dark raincoats blocking their path to the garage. One aimed what Charlie could only assume was the semi-automatic rifle they'd discussed earlier. Behind them waited the black Cadillac with tinted windows.

Cursing under his breath, Charlie bumped his hip into the elevator button in the concrete wall. Then he prayed.

"The briefcase, Miss Albright," the tall gunman demanded.

Penelope hesitated. Charlie's heart nearly stopped. "Give it to him," he all but shouted. He sure as hell didn't intend to lose her over a blasted computer.

With obvious reluctance, she slipped the heavy strap from her shoulder. She juggled the bear and the bag with suspicious awkwardness. Charlie had never seen her make an awkward move. Just as he realized what she intended, she swung the bag—hard.

Oh, hell.

The taller man screamed in pain as the heavy briefcase connected squarely with his groin.

As the elevator door slowly opened, Charlie shoved the red fire-alarm button, jerked Penelope to the ground, and rolled into the elevator just as bullets pelted over their heads. The fire alarm screeched and echoed through the hollow cement walls of the garage. The elevator doors slammed closed.

Gunfire shot through the doors as the elevator plunged downward.

❦ TWENTY-SIX ❦

"Damn you, why couldn't you just give him the damned computer!" Charlie raged as the elevator hit bottom and the doors didn't open.

"You were supposed to knock the other guy over, not get us locked in a stupid elevator!" she screamed back, standing and pounding the emergency button.

She still clung to the bear. From the looks of the mangled box in the bear's arms, the animal had taken the brunt of her fall. Charlie swallowed a small gulp of relief. He'd never tackled a woman before. He'd been afraid he'd broken every bone in her body.

"Just like the TV movies, I suppose," he said derisively. "I should have tackled him, torn the gun from his hands, and sprayed them with lead. Right, I'll remember that next time," he shouted. He was still shaken. He didn't mean to yell at her like that.

The elevator door sprang open and Penelope all but fell out onto the pavement. The wail of the fire alarm pounded against Charlie's eardrums as he caught her and steered her toward what he thought should be the entrance. From a distance, he could hear the scream of sirens. That ought to give the two goons pause.

"I suppose the rental car is upstairs," he grumbled, finally taking her briefcase away and slinging it over his shoulder.

"Yeah, but the elevators lock, and if anyone pays attention to fire alarms, the entire building should be emptying down those stairs by now." She clutched her bear with both arms and let Charlie drag her toward the entrance ramp.

Deciding she was already scared enough without him yelling, Charlie shut his mouth. Even if crowds of people poured into the streets, he and Penelope couldn't lose themselves in the mix. They might enjoy the protection of police and fire crews for a while, but the goons could still see them. He had to think of a way out of here without being seen.

"Back entrance, Penelope," he demanded, stopping short, holding her elbow. "The bastards will run out the front with everyone else. They can't be everywhere at once."

She hesitated, then turned back toward the concrete blocks of the stairs. Charlie followed. He didn't think returning upstairs was such a hot idea—he'd seen entirely too many movies where someone got trapped on the roof because they were too stupid to run down instead of up—but he didn't know this building as she did. He'd have to trust her.

She skirted around the concrete blocks to the back part of the garage. A low wall separated the parking spaces from an oleander foundation hedge outside the garage. With only a moment's hesitation, she scanned the hedge, found the weakest spot, and determinedly strode toward it.

A parking lot full of interested sightseers waited beyond. He and Penelope would have to take their chances that the gunmen were still at the front end of the building, waiting for them to come out the ramps. Charlie dropped Penelope's arm, parted the hedge as best as he could, and lifted her up to step over the wall first. He followed, leaving a gaping hole of broken branches. If anyone cared to look, they would know how they'd escaped. He prayed he and Penelope would be well on their way before anyone figured it out.

The sightseers hurried over to talk to them, but Penelope just vaguely waved toward the front of the building. "It's up there. Flames all over. I couldn't breathe." She talked as she walked, pushing people aside and aiming for the street without giving anyone a chance to stop her.

Charlie loved the way she did that. She sailed past men and women alike, as if she were a queen with more important places to be. He'd admired her style from the first moment he'd seen her.

That didn't mean he wasn't still furious at her for risking her damned life. Hailing a taxi slowing down to watch the spectacle, Charlie jerked her toward the road.

"Got a fire?" the driver asked laconically as Charlie opened the door and all but shoved Penelope in, bear and all.

"False alarm," he asserted coldly. "We're late for a meeting." He gave the driver the address of the hotel his crew was working on near the airport. Then he turned to Penelope and held out his hand. "Give me the phone."

She rummaged in her briefcase and produced the compact phone. "You wouldn't have it if I'd given them the bag," she reminded him.

"I wouldn't need it if you'd given them the bag," he retorted. Then, after pounding in the numbers for his office, he barked orders at Sherry.

In the corner of the backseat, Penelope hugged her bear and looked out the window. They were back to square one.

"We don't *need* a map, John," Beth said patiently, trying not to hold her hand to her pounding head, praying the pain would go away so she could think clearly. "There are signs right on the highway. All you have to do is follow them."

In the backseat, Tammy was halfheartedly singing the alphabet song with the kids. The two runaway lovers had been remarkably unloverlike all the way up here. Beth could have told Charlie's little sister that men didn't like women running after them, but she guessed people had to learn for themselves. Of course, if Raul had just been playing with Tammy and hadn't meant anything serious, Beth suspected Charlie would rip his friend's head off.

None of that was her problem. Her problem, as always, was

the obstinate jerk in the driver's seat. Most men wouldn't stop for directions, but John was insistent on finding a map. How in the world anyone could get lost looking for the state's biggest tourist attraction was beyond her.

She rubbed the heel of her palm against her aching forehead. Of course. John had something he wanted to do before he got to the park. Police work, without a doubt. Even if he'd changed from lawyer to cop, he hadn't changed his work-obsessed mentality. How could she have forgotten?

"Fine. Watch for one of those tourist stands. We'll pick up maps. The kids can use the rest room. Take all the time you want," she said pointedly.

He squeezed her hand with what she assumed was gratitude. "Thanks. Tammy can help you handle the kids, can't she?"

"I don't need help handling the kids." This was an old argument, the one that had ultimately led to the destruction of their marriage. He'd wanted to treat her like a damned helpless invalid. She might as well have had a giant billboard pasted to her face, saying OUT OF ORDER.

Wisely, he didn't argue. He pulled into a parking lot, shut off the car engine, and announced break time.

She might boldly proclaim her independence, but the truth was, in unfamiliar territory, she was lost. Grasping her stick, she climbed from the van on her own, then listened for the sound of voices. John and Raul had stepped behind the van to talk. Gratefully, she heard Tammy limping toward her with the kids chattering beside her.

With shouts, the kids raced toward the rest rooms. They could read the signs, and Sean stopped outside the men's rest room, waiting for his father.

"Come along, Sean. We'll go in here. Your father's asking directions to the park."

Sean dragged behind, probably throwing anxious glances to his father, but Tammy shooed him in after his sister.

"What do you think they're talking about?" Tammy asked

as they waited outside the rest room stalls the kids were using.

"I'm not certain I even want to know." Emerging from the stall, Sean fought off Beth's efforts to help and strolled to the sink on his own.

"Raul's furious with me," Tammy admitted. "I think he's paranoid. My father wouldn't hurt him."

Beth assumed the girl was looking for reassurance. Well, she had news for her—she wasn't getting any. "John says the situation is dangerous. I don't know anything about your father, but John doesn't worry over nothing. I wish Penny had come with us."

Tammy sounded guilty. "Do you think she's in trouble because of me? Charlie will take care of her."

Beth uttered a mental groan at the self-centeredness of youth, then debated the wisdom of correcting it as she helped Deedee dry her hands. If Tammy was ever going to grow up, she had to be told the truth.

Chasing the children out toward the van and their father, Beth followed slowly so she could speak with Tammy without being overheard. "We're not doing this just to hide you from your father," she warned. "We're talking about the possible involvement of some very dangerous criminals who want your brother's land. They've already murdered two men on the island, and from what I overheard Raul say, they've probably tried to murder him. *That's* what Charlie and Penny are trying to protect us from."

She waited out Tammy's silence as the girl recognized what Beth had understood from the start. Beth hadn't objected to Charlie and Penny's plans, couldn't. She had to protect her children. But she was worrying herself sick about her twin every minute they didn't hear from her.

"They're in serious danger, aren't they?" Tammy whispered as they slowly approached the van.

"Yeah, and if my ears aren't deceiving me, our two heroes are fighting over which one of them is going back to the rescue. I'd commend their bravery," Beth said wryly, "if I didn't think they were driven to escape a day in Mickey Mouse land."

Tammy's tone was grim. "All right. I've been stupid long enough. I'll take care of the problem." She touched Beth's arm. "Your children need their father. I am quite capable of dealing with my father without anyone's help. If he's involved, it's better that I be there. He and Charlie have never agreed on anything, but I swear to you, my father is not a bad man."

Beth listened with interest. Her pain seemed to be easing. Maybe the first doctor was right and it was all in her head. That was a lot better than imagining her brain exploding from the pressure. "What are you saying?"

"I'm saying Raul and I will go back to Miami. I have no reason to fear my father, and if Raul is in danger, then he should not be near your children."

Beth tilted her head thoughtfully as she contemplated the girl limping along beside her. Charlie and Penelope wouldn't appreciate this. She was being selfish considering it. But she knew from the argument ahead that at least one of the men would make a break for it, and she'd rather it be Raul than John. She hadn't rationalized why just yet, but she knew it in her bones.

"I think maybe it would be better if you let Raul go on his own," she answered as she considered all the angles.

Tammy's voice contained a streak of stubbornness. "Penelope didn't let Charlie go on his own. Would you let John go?"

"I think Penelope took off on her own and Charlie just followed her." Beth hadn't missed the way Tammy's big brother and Penelope struck sparks every time they touched. Considering Penelope's antagonism toward men, and athletes in particular, Beth had to wonder about the odds of success between them. "And John and I are divorced. I'm blind, remember? I couldn't follow him anywhere."

Tammy snorted. "But he followed you to Disney, with two kids and two strangers in tow. Men will follow you and your sister anywhere. It's not the same for me. I've got to learn what you already know. I have to make Raul see me as a woman."

"He's going to look at you as a darned nuisance," Beth warned.

"Fine. Then I'll be a darned nuisance. How much do you want to bet they've just called a rental car company?" Tammy commented as John spoke into the cell phone.

Who was she to argue with a woman in love? It had been two years since the accident, a year since their divorce, and Beth still couldn't get John out of her heart. She might as well let Tammy learn the ugly truth about love all on her own.

Beth just prayed Raul and Tammy could make a difference and help Charlie and Penelope out of whatever trouble they were causing now, because she knew as sure as she knew the names of her children that they were up to their ears in it.

"All right, I give up," Penelope said shakily as the taxi stopped in front of the girder frame of a sprawling building under construction. "Why are we meeting Emile here?"

"If nothing else, to hold him hostage against any further attacks." Charlie peeled off a handful of bills and handed them to the driver.

Penelope eyed the roll of money and wondered if he'd emptied his personal account. She didn't think the paperwork could have been handled yet on his business accounts. "What if Jacobsen was the one who sent the gunmen?"

"Then we can only hope we can brainwash Emile into joining our side." Charlie caught her elbow and helped her around a pile of trash inside the chain-link fence.

She was feeling rattled enough to appreciate the support, she decided, as he led her toward the trailer office. Maybe she hadn't felt danger before. Maybe she'd thought Charlie was paranoid. Not anymore. The gunfire still pounded in her ears. Two men with an ugly gun had *shot* at them. She couldn't absorb it entirely. It was too unreal. Didn't one call the police when shot at?

Charlie opened the trailer door and all but shoved her in. Maybe she'd been right from the first, and Charlie was the bad guy in this equation. She hugged the bear and rejected that notion completely. He'd looked like Mafia in that scruffy mustache and shades when she'd first met him, but he'd behaved more like a teddy bear ever since. A surly teddy bear, maybe, but not evil.

She didn't want to believe Charlie was the bad guy because she was falling for the lout, she realized. Eyes widening as he helped her to his desk chair, Penelope watched Charlie turn to confront the silver-haired man waiting for him. Every muscle in Charlie's body tensed as Emile stood up. Sympathy for Charlie's plight washed over her. This cold man had raised Charlie through his teenage years, he was married to Charlie's mother, was father to Tammy, and now Charlie had to accuse him of the worst sort of treachery and murder. She would have run first, let someone else handle it.

"Where is my daughter?" Emile demanded.

"Where you and Jacobsen and your goons can't harm her," Charlie countered.

"Jacobsen!" Emile shouted. "What the hell does Jacobsen have to do with this? I want my daughter back. I'll go to the police if I have to."

"She's of legal age. The police would laugh in your face. But they won't laugh so hard when I point out the bullet holes in the elevator door where Penny and I were nearly killed an hour ago. Where's Jacobsen? I want his head in a noose."

Charlie carefully positioned himself between Penelope and his stepfather, but she eased to one side and watched Emile's face. The man's eyes widened in astonishment at the mention of bullet holes, but he was too angry to fully comprehend Charlie's accusations. The twitch Tammy had mentioned jerked rapidly in the corner of his eye. Penelope glanced out the trailer windows to make certain they weren't surrounded by tall men in raincoats, carrying semiautomatic weapons.

She raised her eyebrows. Men in yellow hard hats gathered

along the fence, leaned against stacks of steel, and rested on the seats of idling bulldozers. Even without seeing out both sides of the trailer, she'd wager the hard hats had surrounded them. Charlie had arranged a circle of safety for this confrontation. If Emile had brought any goons with guns, they wouldn't make it past the first barrier alive.

"What the hell does Jacobsen have to do with anything!" Emile flung his elegantly tailored arm upward in impatience. "He's slime, but his projects make money. I don't have to entertain the man. I just want my daughter back."

"His projects make money," Charlie repeated derisively. "You want to know why his projects make money? I'll show you why." He reached over and pulled a fat manila envelope from his desk drawer and slammed it into Emile's hands. "I'll explain what you're looking at as we go."

He jerked open the trailer door, reached down to pull Penelope to her feet, and nodded at Emile to precede him.

Just like that, he commanded the troops. Penelope considered refusing, but she was too curious to let him leave her behind. Besides, she didn't feel safe anywhere except at Charlie's side. Maybe she was a slow learner, but she was beginning to realize that Charlie was a leader, a man people followed because they trusted him. The jocks she'd known in college had been too full of themselves to lead anyone anywhere.

"You could leave the bear here," Charlie offered as she carried it toward the door.

Penelope shook her head. He could have the damned laptop and the cell phone and all the technical toys. She was keeping this one, if only as a souvenir of her own stupidity.

She couldn't remember the last time anyone had given her a stuffed toy. People had never thought of her as the fluffy kind of female who collected silly toys any more than she'd thought it of herself. By covering teenage awkwardness with a modeling career, she'd distanced herself from boys her age. Outside her cheerleading activities, she never had time for them. In college, she'd chosen a career that proved she wasn't just a pretty face. Since then, she'd developed a persona that scared most men silly. No one could think of her as a foolish female who collected stuffed toys.

She wasn't a foolish female, Penelope decided defiantly as Charlie opened the door of the chauffeured limousine waiting outside the gates. Emile took the seat across from her, allowing Charlie room to slide in beside her. Charlie wasn't so dumb as to think her a silly female. He'd just given her the bear because he couldn't give her a puppy, because he wanted to give her something to hold and love. She didn't want to admit she needed something—someone—to love and hold.

Even if she did admit it, she didn't want to believe Charlie was that someone. She'd almost rather face the gunmen again.

When Charlie ordered Emile's driver to the airport, they both stared at him.

"Where are we going?" Emile demanded.

Penelope didn't bother asking. By now she knew she'd find out when she got there. Charlie wasn't much at explaining himself. Damn, but she was even beginning to understand the man.

"Look at the pictures in that envelope." Charlie nodded at the unopened file in his stepfather's hands. "Tell me that's what you want for St. Lucia. Tell me your damned bank account is more important than an entire country, than men's *lives*."

"What the hell does this have to do with Tammy?" Emile muttered, twisting open the metal clip and pulling out a stack of photos.

"It has to do with the men you're dealing with, the kind of men who would dump raw sewage in a water supply, kill innocent men, and shoot at unarmed women. If you're going to hang around men like that, then Tammy is damned well better off here where I can look after her."

Charlie sat back in the leather seat, but he didn't relax. He wrapped his arm around Penelope's shoulders, but she could feel the tension in him, in the way his muscles bunched and his fingers drummed against her arm. She thought longingly of the Jacuzzi and wondered if they'd ever be that happy again.

What was she thinking? Once he solved his problem with Jacobsen, a man like Charlie would submerge himself in his work again. She'd be lucky to see him on the few Friday nights when there wasn't a game. Once this was over, he'd have no reason to see her. Women and sex came easy for him. She was the one with the problem.

Depressed more than scared now, Penelope watched as Emile shuffled through the snapshots. Most of them appeared to be steel structures similar to the one they'd just left.

Charlie leaned over and pointed at a shot of a nearly completed building. "That's when the crack first appeared. See? Right smack down the middle, where the girders weren't properly supported." He pulled out one of the photos of the skeletal frame and pointed out the same spot in the incomplete structure.

"I'm not an architect." Emile shrugged and looked at the photo again. "I suppose you're telling me this is one of Jacobsen's projects."

"Damned right. Just one. I've got others, but this is the most obvious." He pulled another photo from the deck. "Here, see where he patched the crack?"

"Foundations shift. Patching cracks has to be expected. I trust he fixed the paint job later?"

Charlie snorted, ripped the photos from Emile's hands, and sorted through them until he found what he wanted. "Yeah, right, like paint would hold steel girders together."

Penelope glanced over his shoulder. She caught a glimpse of a sprawling flamingo-pink hotel with half its rooms crumbled into chunks of plaster and twisted steel.

"Nine people died in that collapse." Charlie sat back again, his expressive lips turned down at the corners as he glared out the tinted windows. "Twenty were injured. If the building had been fully occupied at the time, the disaster would have involved hundreds. They've found evidence of inferior steel, improperly spaced girders, and a foundation too shallow for that soil. He's not come to trial yet, but I know of inspectors he's bribed to ignore the faults. That ought to make him a real shoo-in for St. Lucia, don't you think?"

"This is ridiculous." Emile threw the photos aside. "What does this have to do with anything?"

"Maybe nothing." Charlie shrugged his massive shoulders and twisted a finger in an escaped tendril of Penelope's hair. "Jacobsen is on St. Lucia, isn't he?"

Emile nodded curtly. "I'm on a board of directors with him. We've met and discussed several projects. I have some papers of his that I'm supposed to sign."

"You really don't get it, do you?" Charlie asked with a trace of wonder. "It's all bits of paper to you. Can you even read a financial statement?"

Emile crossed his arms and glared back. "Why should I? That's what I have advisers for."

Charlie laughed bitterly under his breath as he drew Penelope closer. Some of the tension in him had dissipated, and she dared to rub his thigh under the cover of the bear in her arms. He threw her a quick glance, but maintained his concentration on his stepfather.

"And here I thought I was the ignorant nobody because I couldn't keep straight which fork was which. It just goes to show how skewed our priorities can get sometimes," Charlie said wearily.

"What the hell does that mean?" Emile asked in irritation. "I pay people to read financial statements for me."

"And you sit on boards of companies your advisers tell you make lots of money. Did it ever occur to you to ask why those companies make lots of money? Or does it even matter? Don't bother to answer. I already know. It's never mattered." He scowled and watched as the limousine rolled down the ramp to the terminal. "Just tell me where to find Jacobsen and I'll tell you where to find Tammy. I made sure she didn't stay in any place Jacobsen built."

Emile stiffened. "You're actually trying to tell me that

any project he's worked on is likely to collapse? That's preposterous."

Charlie pointed at the envelope of pictures. "That one collapsed, and it was built here in Miami, where we have building inspectors and the kind of soil with which Jacobsen ought to be familiar. What do you think will happen in St. Lucia, where materials are difficult to obtain, inspectors are easily bribed, and the soil is little more than volcanic ash?"

"The company will go bankrupt!" Emile complained.

This time, Charlie laughed out loud.

🎋 TWENTY-SEVEN 🎋

"You can't take that damned thing on an airplane," Charlie whispered as Penelope lugged the bear through the crowded corridors of Miami International.

"I can't stuff him in a locker," she retorted, jerking the bear protectively away from him. Just because the big galoot had gotten her off the hook with the resort didn't mean she had to trust him in everything. She wasn't a female James Bond. She couldn't imagine why she should be included in this little jaunt to nail Jacobsen. Or maybe she could; she just didn't want to because it meant recognizing more in Charlie's behavior than she wanted to acknowledge. She'd cling to her irritation; it was safer.

"It's a damn good thing I didn't buy a puppy." Charlie caught her elbow and steered her after Emile, who was hurrying toward the private jet he'd chartered.

"A damned good thing," she agreed vehemently.

"What are we fighting about?" he demanded as they hurried down the steps in the direction of the tarmac.

"How am I supposed to know? You never tell me anything."

Charlie grinned. It made about as much sense as anything else these days. "I can still send you to Orlando."

"Oh, yeah, I'm looking forward to that. Semiautomatics in the hands of Mickey Mouse. The possibilities are fascinating." She hurried faster. "Are you going to tell me why we're going back to St. Lucia?"

"Because Jacobsen's there."

"Right. How silly of me. One always runs *toward* danger instead of away. Why can't I remember that?"

"Because you're a woman." Charlie stayed out of the line of fire after that one, turning her over to Emile's flight attendant while he talked with the pilot.

His stepfather watched with acid resignation. It had taken Charlie all these years, but he'd finally found a level on which they could communicate: money.

By the time Charlie climbed on board, Penelope had strapped the bear into the seat beside her. Charlie unstrapped it, deposited the ungainly thing behind the seat, and strapped himself in its place. She glared and returned to watching out the window. Maybe he ought to tell her to open the bear's valentine box. Nah, she'd only crash harder.

He was up to his ears in hot shit and almost enjoying himself. He'd probably gone around the bend. If so, Penelope had driven him there. They could fight like cats and dogs, but that undercurrent between them never went away. It just grew stronger. Lust didn't have a damned thing to do with knowing she was terrified and taking her fear out on him. It wasn't lust that made him want to shake the mighty PC&M partners and throw them out the windows for not recognizing the gem right under their uplifted noses. And he had no idea why he was imagining making babies with this woman, but he'd sure as hell never considered it with any other woman before.

Hot shit might be more comfortable than what was going through his mind right now. What if she wasn't feeling what he was feeling? Worse yet—what if she was? She was precisely the kind of woman he'd vowed never to marry: an upscale, career-minded yuppie. He couldn't fit her into the mold of suburban housewife with the proper blue-collar attitude toward his bad habits.

For reassurance, Charlie appropriated Penelope's hand and squeezed it. Her fingers curled up inside of his. She was probably making a fist to sock him one, but she didn't pull away.

"It's gonna be all right, I promise." He lowered his voice so Emile, in front of them, couldn't hear. "I've got friends there, remember? Once we get Jacobsen locked up, we can take care of your little problem with your bosses. Maybe we could take a little vacation together."

She shot him a look of disbelief. "Tammy and Raul are back in the States running around together, you haven't looked after your business for a week, you probably have mountains of paperwork and problems waiting for you, and you're going to take a vacation?"

"Which are you having difficulty believing, that I'm so lazy I'd let my business go on without me, or that I would give it up to spend a week with you?"

She looked hard at him then, and the reflection in those thick-lashed eyes nearly undid him. He thought his heart stopped beating. He damned well knew he'd stopped breathing. He could see the confusion in her eyes, and knew it matched his own. They barely knew each other, but something was happening here, something pretty damned scary.

"I'm not letting you go," Charlie said recklessly, not waiting for her reply. "We've got something here, and I'm not giving it up without taking it further."

She took a deep breath, not that her boxy jacket allowed him to appreciate it. Her jaw muscles relaxed slightly, and her fingers wrapped around his. "Right," she said dryly. "I have a friend who gives me tickets to the symphony. Shall we make a date?"

"If you'll go with me to the Garth Brooks concert."

"I don't know anything about Garth Brooks."

"I don't know anything about symphonies. We'll learn." With that matter settled, Charlie leaned back in the seat and prepared to enjoy the rest of the flight. It might be the last chance he had for a while.

* * *

"Tell me again why we're doing this," Penelope sighed as she twisted her hair and attempted to pin it up with Tamara's scattered collection of hairpins.

Charlie caught her hand, untwisted the thick length of hair, and smoothed it over her shoulders. "Wear it down, for me. You've got such gorgeous hair, I don't know why you try to hide it."

She might as well wear her hair down. Charlie was wearing her down in more ways than one. She couldn't summon her protective armor when he looked at her as he was doing now. He stood behind her, but she could see his reflection in the mirror. In that tux, he took her breath away. The look in his eyes robbed her of any remaining sense.

Since that first day she'd seen him in a red muscle shirt, she'd thought him an impressive figure of a man. Now, in white coat and black tie, he encompassed every dream she'd ever had, and then some. How could a muscled jock who seldom wore more than T-shirts and jeans look like James Bond preparing for a presentation to the queen? He didn't even look the slightest bit uncomfortable in the formal silk shirt and tie.

Glancing from the mirror image of Charlie to herself, Penelope tugged uneasily at the heart-shaped red bodice of her gown. "I shouldn't have bought this," she muttered. She wasn't uncomfortable with the stares of men. She'd known them all her life. She simply didn't like being stared at as if she were a piece of meat. Once men noticed her cleavage, their minds blanked out and they never said another sensible word. She grimaced as Charlie draped the waterfall of her hair over her shoulder.

"I'm not hiding my hair," she said defensively. "It's a nuisance. If I eat or drink, I have to peel it away from my mouth. I can't keep it neat like this." Still, she didn't reach to put it up again. Charlie's fingers tugging through it held her entranced.

They'd arrived at the St. Philippe mansion late last night, and Charlie had left her alone in the bedroom his mother had assigned her. She suspected Charlie had stayed up late, conniving with his stepfather and the FBI and making telephone calls, but she'd been too worn out to care. Charlie had had a fit when he learned of Tammy and Raul's escape, but once she'd ascertained that Beth and the kids were all right, Penelope had left the men to their manipulations.

Maybe that had been a mistake. Maybe she and Charlie should have worked out a little more of this sexual tension between them so they could both think straight. She'd never had a man mess with her mind like this before. Just watching him in the mirror as he stood behind her, playing with her hair, left her breathless.

"I'll buy you some of those pretty combs for it. Doesn't Tammy have any in there?" Charlie gestured at the drawers of his half sister's vanity.

"What is the fascination men have with hair?" she asked with an irritation she really didn't feel as she searched the drawers, producing an enameled pair of combs that worked with the red of her dress.

"We envision tugging you back to the cave with it?" he asked facetiously. "I don't know. Maybe it makes you more approachable. You look like a real woman and not an automaton, dressed like this."

She ought to bust his chops for that remark. Instead, Penelope rose and wrapped her fingers in his neatly knotted bow tie. Even though she was wearing heels, Charlie still towered over her by several inches. Few men could do that. She'd planned on knocking his eyes out with one of those sexy poses she'd learned as a model. Instead, the heated blue of his gaze practically immobilized her. It scorched right through her, making her feel totally desirable and incredibly feminine, and she hadn't done a thing except touch him.

"I'm going to enjoy ripping that dress off you in a few hours," he murmured as he leaned over to brush his lips against hers.

She should complain that he'd mess her lipstick, but she didn't care. She slid her fingers into his hair and encouraged him to suck what remained of her breath from her lungs. She'd totally lost her mind, and for once, she was enjoying it.

"God," Charlie whispered worshipfully as he dragged himself away and looked down at her in wonderment. "I think I'll keep you locked in this bedroom all night. You're a walking powder keg. I'll have to beat the men off you."

"You can't," she reminded him. "You're supposed to be scaring the pants off Jacobsen instead."

"Why don't I just strangle him and leave him out in the garden for the birds to find?" he asked hopefully.

Penelope grinned, although her insides clenched as she remembered the kind of dangerous game they played. She'd never attended a party with men who hired killers before. "Don't you think I can handle those little pups out there by myself?" she teased, diverting her thoughts and his from the evening's purpose.

"I figure you could snatch them bald, turn them inside out, and stuff them up the chimney before they knew what hit them," he admitted. "But duds like these make me feel real primitive. I want to bash anyone who looks at you twice."

Penelope rolled her eyes and returned to her seat to repair the damage to her makeup. "Civilized clothing makes you feel primitive? So you're most civilized when you're naked?"

"Yeah, will you hurry it up there? I want to get this over with so I can get you into bed. These damned trousers don't leave much room for imagination. Or anything else."

Admiring the drape of expensive cloth he tried to adjust, Penelope smiled. There was something particularly satisfying in arousing a man against his will. She'd never bothered exercising her feminine power before. She thought she might enjoy it—only with Charlie, she realized.

Charlie possessed the ability to turn something on inside her, something terrifying and wonderful at the same time. He gave her the confidence she needed to be completely herself. She could be a woman and not be ashamed of it. She could let her hair down and cry and be afraid, or she could throw a tantrum and scold, or she could turn him into mush with a kiss, and he accepted all of it as part of her and wasn't in the least bit afraid or put off. That much freedom was intimidating. She'd have to take it slowly.

"You really think Emile can get Jacobsen to talk? I thought it was only in murder mysteries that the crook tells all, just before falling off the cliff or something." She applied her lipstick and wished she had some jewelry. The hasty shopping trip to Castries hadn't given her time for more than the dress and shoes and some clean underwear. Charlie had sent someone over to the resort to pick up the remainder of her things, but that didn't include any necklaces suitable for a gown like this.

"If Emile can't do it, the FBI will send one of their men in. They're experienced at interrogating. If we can just get enough on tape to justify a court order to open all his records, we should be fine."

"And you won't get involved at all?" she asked, searching through Tammy's drawers for something, anything, to relieve the bare expanse above the gown's bodice.

"What are you looking for now?" he asked impatiently. "We've got to get out there. I want you surrounded by people so Jacobsen doesn't have a chance at any more of his strong-arm tactics."

"You don't think he'll run as soon as he sees us?" She slammed the drawer. "I should have brought a scarf. I feel like a damned ostrich in this thing."

"I doubt if he'll recognize you. If he sees me, it should put his nerves on edge. If he's got any brains at all though, he'll know Emile and I hate each other's guts. He'll believe it if Emile tells him he wants to keep me out of St. Lucia." Charlie picked up the teddy bear and dumped it on her lap. "Did it ever occur to you that the stupid bear is holding that box for a reason?"

Penelope glanced at Charlie in surprise, then cuddled the bear in her arms so she could pry at the heart-shaped box. "I thought it was for looks. If it's candy, I've smushed it into fudge by now."

"I noticed the Godivas survived," he said dryly. The candy box sat on the vanity beside her.

"It will be all your fault when I gain ten pounds I can never lose again." The box finally popped open, and a tumble of velvet and something hard fell out. Penelope's heart lodged in her throat as she reached for the sparkly shimmer of gold at her feet.

"Ten pounds will just give me more to put my arms around," Charlie replied complacently, but she noticed his expression wasn't quite as serene as his words. He watched her nervously as she opened her fingers to see what she'd retrieved.

A fragile gold chain interspersed with the soft glow of pearls draped over her palm. Penelope gasped, then stroked the rainbow shimmer of the center pearl. It warmed against her hand. "Charlie!" she finally managed to murmur. "It's exquisite. And entirely too expensive." This last emerged reluctantly. She'd love to keep it, but she had a healthy awareness of the price of pearls. He could probably pay his employees for a week for the cost of this.

Gingerly, he took the delicate piece from her hand and draped it around her neck, fumbling with the snap until it caught. "I can afford it, and you're worth every penny. If I'm going to flaunt you, I might as well do it right."

"Is that what you're doing, flaunting me?" She leaned over to admire the result in the mirror, but she was watching Charlie's reflection. A man as handsome as Charlie didn't need to buy women with jewelry. He could have all he wanted for a whistle. She wondered what was buzzing around in that inscrutable mind of his now.

He caught her elbow and dragged her up. "I'm waving you in everyone's face and saying 'Nah-nah, she's mine and you can't have her,' " he said calmly, pulling her toward the door. "Isn't that what every man dreams of? You're the female version of my GTO. I've got one and no one else does."

"Macho scum," she muttered as he threw open the door. "At least this way you can safely say yours is bigger than anyone else's. I doubt there's another woman my height in the room."

Charlie chuckled. "Then we're well matched, sweetheart. And mine *is* bigger than anyone else's. You'll just have to take my word for it."

She'd bash him over the head some other time. Right now, she needed him by her side as they strode toward a room full of strangers, one of whom was probably a murderer.

❧ TWENTY-EIGHT ❧

"Charlie will rip my guts out," Raul muttered as he steered Tammy toward the hotel elevator. "I should never have let you come with me."

"I'm of age," Tammy reminded him. "And Charlie hasn't played my guardian for a decade. You're just looking for excuses."

"You don't know Charlie," he grumbled. "He thinks women are little kittens to be played with and protected. Until now, he's thought you protected. He'll cut my head off." He unlocked the door to their room and shoved her in. "I have no excuse for taking you with me instead of leaving you at Disney."

"If Charlie thinks women are kittens, he needs his head rearranged. I've a feeling Penelope will take care of that," Tammy said with satisfaction as she glanced around the inexpensive hotel room, "but first we've got to see they're safe. I want to help instead of being a burden, for a change." She'd always stayed in five-star hotels when she traveled, but this room seemed to contain the basic requirements: a bed and clean sheets.

"Penelope isn't his sister; you are, and he's expecting me to look after you, not get you in trouble." Raul stood awkwardly near the door, not touching her, barely even looking at her.

Tammy thought this nonsense had gone on long enough. She reached for the knit of his shirt and tugged it upward. "I want a reward for braving the airport alone and for finding you without anyone's help."

He caught her hand and held it away from him. His dark eyes harbored no anger, just serious concern. "You should never have done that. Miami is a dangerous place for someone with no experience in traveling alone. It is even more dangerous in my company. I want you to stay here while I go to the office. I want to see if Charlie's checked in."

Tammy let go of his shirt and limped backward. "If you don't want to be seen with me, just say so. You don't have to make up excuses."

Pain etched his wide brow as he finally looked at her, but he still kept his hands firmly at his sides. "Charlie is right. I can only hurt you, and you deserve better than that. I love you enough to want what is best for you, even if it means sending you away."

Tammy's heart skipped a beat as she searched his expression for sincerity. She'd never heard the words *I love you* directed at her before. She wasn't certain of their meaning even now. She just knew that in these last months this kind and caring man had taught her more about the meaning of life than her parents had in twenty years. She didn't want to lose him. She had too much more to learn.

"Don't you think I'm old enough to know what's best for me?" she asked quietly.

Raul closed his eyes and leaned against the door. "That's what I want to believe, but you are young and reckless. You do not know what the world is like." He opened his eyes again. "Now is not the time for this discussion. I must find out what Charlie is doing and how I can help."

Tammy nodded wisely. She knew a great deal more of the world than Raul realized. Being crippled and an object of pity and scorn taught lessons he could only imagine. But she wouldn't press the subject now. He was right. They needed to help Charlie and Penelope.

"Call the office," she offered gently. "I think we'd best stay unseen until we know what's happening."

"I already know what's happening," Raul replied gloomily. "I followed one of Jacobsen's men on the island after he tried to burn the trailer."

Tammy raised her eyebrows. "You didn't tell Charlie?"

Raul narrowed his eyes to slits. "And have him tearing in there and getting shot? Your brother doesn't know the meaning of caution."

"Or patience," Tammy agreed.

"I wanted to get back here first, where we could talk and I could prevent his doing something foolish, but I didn't dare fly off the damned island. I was afraid they'd catch me at the airport." Raul gripped his fingers tighter. "I had to sail out. If only I could have reached Charlie sooner . . ."

"You did everything possible," Tammy reassured him. "You can't blame yourself because Charlie jumped off half-cocked." Sensing his continued tension, she watched him warily. "So, what did you find out?"

"The thief led me to Jacobsen's office in Castries. I broke in and read through his contract files. Jacobsen has a major contract with a foreign company, to build a resort on St. Lucia with a completion date of next year. Jacobsen has sold shares of the project to several real estate developers, including companies your father owns. He cannot possibly finish a project of that size in time if he doesn't already own the land and have the permits."

"And he doesn't own the land," Tammy finished softly. "He's told them he owns the property you're developing. They don't know it belongs to Charlie."

Raul shrugged. "Charlie didn't want your parents to know he had any connection with the island." He hesitated before adding, "The profit would be enormous, enough for a man with few scruples to kill for."

"And Penelope and Charlie have already proved that Jacobsen's working with men of few scruples." Tammy's stomach sank to her feet as her mind slowly absorbed the seriousness of their situation.

"I think," Raul said slowly, "he must force Charlie into

signing away all the land and permits, which is why he tried closing Charlie's bank accounts, thinking Charlie's cash flow was as limited as his own. Now, he must try some other method." He shot Tammy a worried glare. "If Jacobsen had something Charlie wanted bad enough, he could force him to trade. That is why you must stay out of sight."

"What about Penelope?" Tammy whispered. "Would he know about Penelope?"

Raul moved toward the telephone. "This is what we must find out."

"I hate these monkey suits," Charlie said resignedly, grimacing at the rum punch in a crystal glass a waiter handed him. "First time I wore one, I spilled grape juice down the front and my mother didn't speak to me for a week."

"You can spill as much juice as you like now," Penelope reminded him with humor. "You're paying for it."

Charlie grinned. "You wouldn't care if I spent the rest of the evening with purple down my front?"

She shot him a look of exasperation. "Charlie, get it through your fat head—I've spent the better part of my life with people judging me on how I look and not caring who I am on the inside. Do you really think I'm so shallow as to care if you wore jeans and a clip-on tie to this thing?"

He snorted. "What do you want me to believe? You've been cutting me down for my clothes ever since we met."

Penelope had the grace to look guilty. "It's easier to dismiss someone as the clothes they wear, not the people they are, until you get to know them." She lifted her chin. "You wanted to look like a tourist. It worked, didn't it?"

Charlie narrowed his eyes and disregarded her attempt to deflect the subject. "So, now that you know who I am, you can't dismiss me because of what I wear?"

She sighed. "Now that I know who you are, you could wear a bunny suit and I couldn't dismiss you. Actually, I had a damned hard time ignoring you in a tank top."

He set the glass down and grinned with his usual arrogance. "If I sat down on one of those Louis the Whatever chairs over there and made an ass of myself crumpling it into dust, you wouldn't flinch with embarrassment and hide in the closet?"

At that picture, Penelope relaxed and eyed the gilded chairs. "Why don't you sit on one and I'll sit on your lap and we'll find out."

"I'd take you up on that, but I believe Jacobsen just walked in."

Penelope glanced in the direction of Charlie's gaze and saw the burly contractor dressed in a tux, striding purposefully into the ballroom. He looked no different from every prosperous man in here. She had difficulty believing he could hire assassins.

"I don't think a confrontation is a wise idea until the FBI gets some answers," Charlie whispered in her ear. "Let's get out of here. Dance with me." He pulled her into his arms to the musical strains of an old Beatles song and swung her toward the open patio doors.

Humid air washed over them as they stepped beyond the glass portals of the air-conditioned ballroom, into the moonlit night. Shutting out any drama about to occur in the house, Penelope closed her eyes and drank in the fragrant scents of jasmine and the earthy odors of jungle and soil. A bird called from the frangipani tree high overhead. The filtered strains of the orchestra drifted through the open doorway.

"Do you want to know a secret?" Charlie whispered in time to the tune, swinging her across the flagstone terrace.

Penelope smiled at the old refrain and enjoyed the intoxicating experience of Charlie's hands guiding her with an expertise that allowed her to sink into the song without worrying about crashing into other couples—or in this case, trees and flowerpots. She'd already noted that for a large man, he moved with grace. He also moved with the rhythm of a professional dancer. She could spend the night dancing in his arms. Or half the night, she amended. Already, she was anticipating that big bed back in her assigned room.

"I'm in love with yo-o-u. . . ."

Goose bumps shivered up and down her arms as Charlie crooned the words, even though he sang them jestingly. What would it be like loving a caveman like Charlie? With his prehistoric blue-collar attitudes, he'd expect his wife to stay home, barefoot and pregnant in the kitchen, popping popcorn while he watched football on TV. She'd grown so soft in the head, she could almost find that scenario attractive, as long as he wore his tux occasionally and took her dancing and sang to her like this.

The idea of losing her shape and control of her life to carry a man's baby had never appealed to her as it had to Beth, but she saw its temptation now. A man who loved her, who would take care of her and the baby when she couldn't handle everything herself, a man who would understand that she didn't cook and didn't want to . . .

"Shit."

Charlie's expletive shattered her daydream with alarm as he halted their seductive glide in the shadows of the shrubbery, pulling her behind him as if to protect her from some unseen danger.

"What?" Penelope demanded from behind his back. "What is it?"

"We're about to either catch a thief, or one of Jacobsen's partners. Go inside and send someone to check on Emile. This guy's coming from the study." He shoved her toward the patio door.

Penelope balked, looking over her shoulder in the direction Charlie watched. "What are you going to do?" She should know better than to ask. Cavemen didn't believe in explaining.

"Just do it." He slipped into the shrubbery and was gone before she could reply.

Irritated by his high-handedness, but understanding his fear for Emile, Penelope avoided the crowded ballroom by crossing the grass to the study window and peering in. A desk lamp illuminated an ornate ormolu table covered in business papers, but she saw no one working over them. A movement near the floor caught her eye. Emile!

Holding his hand to his head, he struggled to sit up. Heart pumping, Penelope shoved at the casement. Before she could open it, Vivian appeared in the doorway and screamed. One of the FBI men hurried in right behind her.

Inside the ballroom, the orchestra crashed to a halt. Penelope glanced quickly from the rapidly filling study to the movement of the shrubbery where Charlie had disappeared. She figured Emile was in better hands than hers. Her priority was to keep an eye on Charlie. She hurried down the garden path.

She caught him hot-wiring a Porsche on the drive. "Who taught you that?" she asked as he got the engine started.

He frowned as she climbed in the passenger side. "Emile wouldn't give me the keys when I was a teenager, so I figured out how to do it myself. I told you to get inside the house."

He eased the Porsche out of the line of cars, and without turning on the headlights, steered the car silently down the drive.

"You told me to check on Emile, and I did. Vivian and a ballroom full of people are with him. It looks as if someone hit him over the head while he was going over some papers, but he seems okay. I'm not much used to being part of the crowd, so I thought I'd stay where the action is."

"I can believe that. I bet you got the lead in all your high school plays." He gunned the accelerator as soon as they hit the open road.

Ahead of them, Penelope could see the lights of another car. He wouldn't explain and she wouldn't ask. She would just assume that was the thief out there. She shrugged at his accusation. "I played Hamlet to Beth's Ophelia, if that's what you're asking. We were both too tall to play opposite anyone but the basketball team, and they had better things to do than take drama."

Charlie sniggered. "Bet they regretted that when they saw

you two in tights. I suppose you'll always expect to be the star of the show."

He had her so rattled, she almost understood the direction of his thoughts. The direction maybe, but not the intent. She cast him a sideways glance but he concentrated on the dark road ahead. He still hadn't turned on his lights.

"I don't ever expect to be the star of the show. Beth and I just had enough modeling experience to carry off the drama better than anyone else. But I don't believe in sitting around waiting for things to happen, or waiting for someone else to do things for me, if that's what you mean. I'd rather do them myself."

Charlie wrapped both hands around the wheel as if he'd strangle it, but he nodded. "I can buy that. You'll never play second banana to a man."

"Right." Penelope crossed her arms firmly over her chest, realized she was wearing a low-cut evening gown, and grimaced. Maybe Charlie would be satisfied with trailing the suspect, and she wouldn't end up chasing through jungles in high heels. Maybe barracudas had wings. Charlie's choice of subject left her decidedly unsettled.

"I'm not used to that," he informed her as he swung the sports car around a hairpin turn with breathtaking speed. "I'm used to being the one who makes the calls."

"Well, you just go right ahead and make them." Where the hell was he going with this? And where the hell was the car ahead of them going?

Charlie chuckled. "And you'll go ahead and do what you want. I'm not totally dumb."

"As far as I can tell, you're a Neanderthal with brains," she agreed.

"All right, I'll settle for that, just as long as you don't think Neanderthals live in a matriarchal society." He swung the car up a gravel road and only slowed when the potholes had them bumping their heads into the car roof.

"Right now, I just think you're insane. Is this your means of distracting me so I won't ask where we're going?"

"I didn't know where we were going until now. This road is a dead end." He slowed as they reached a slight rise.

"And you know where we're going now?" she asked as he eased the car into the shadows of what in the moonlight looked like palmettos.

"To the volcano."

❧ TWENTY-NINE ❧

"Stay here," Charlie whispered as he stopped the car and pulled the wires. He figured it was a pretty safe bet Penelope would follow his instructions rather than sink her heels into the mud around the pit of the volcano.

He ignored her glare as he slipped from the car. The other guy was driving some small foreign job that he apparently didn't mind risking by taking it beyond the gravel of the parking area. Charlie could think of a dozen better places for a secretive meeting, but he knew the island. An outsider wouldn't. A tourist attraction like the volcano might be an obvious choice.

Who was the thief and what could he have wanted from Emile's study? It made no sense for Jacobsen to hire a thief. Emile had been on Jacobsen's side. Even if Jacobsen had discovered the FBI's involvement, why would he hire someone to hurt Emile? St. Lucia was outside the FBI's jurisdiction. Since Jacobsen was an American citizen, and they already had agents here investigating the Russians, the FBI had been willing to stretch their involvement, but Jacobsen wouldn't know that. Did someone else? Who?

Charlie knew he had little chance of walking through the parking lot without being heard. But if the thief was as much a stranger to the island as Jacobsen, he wouldn't be familiar with the sounds of the forest. Maybe he'd think Charlie's rustling through the underbrush was a jungle cat. He'd terrify the shit out of the bastard.

Having spent eight of his more adventurous years on the island, Charlie didn't hesitate to walk under the shadows of the trees. He could hear voices ahead. A little eavesdropping might be advantageous.

"Did you get the seal?" a rough voice whispered with a decidedly American twang.

Charlie didn't hear the reply, but a grunt of satisfaction followed the sound of a snap opening.

"I don't know why you have to be so damned secretive about this. You Russians suspect everyone. We don't have KGB over here. We could have met in a decent restaurant and no one would have noticed or cared," the voice grumbled.

That wasn't Jacobsen. Charlie had met the man only a couple of times, but he would have recognized the polished voice. Besides, he'd just seen Jacobsen at the party. He couldn't have arrived here ahead of him.

A heavily accented voice murmured something Charlie couldn't catch.

"You guys are gonna have to start learning to do things the American way. That machine gun shit will only get you canned. With this seal, we make it all right and tight and no one can touch us. We're a legitimate business, remember? With your cash and our connections, we can own half the Caribbean. No more Moscow winters for you."

Emile must have been keeping the corporate seal to one of his companies in his office. It should have been locked in his safe, unless he'd been using it for something this evening. Charlie just couldn't figure out how a seal would solve anyone's problems.

"Yeah, Smith and his right-hand man are a nuisance," the American replied to the Russian's heavily accented English, "but I think we've got him beat now. With Jacobsen's signature and this seal, we can probably get an easy billion out of the Foundation and leave old Emile holding the bag. Smith might hate the old man, but he won't let his mother and sister go down the drain with him. He'll have to sell to get that kind of cash."

Well, thank you very much. Not totally grasping all the ramifications of the plan but easily figuring out his place in it, Charlie rose from his crouch as the Russian muttered something quarrelsome. The Russian must be pretty damned sure of himself to argue with an arrogant ass like this guy. Charlie only wished he'd called for backup so he could catch both of them. He'd have to settle for the ass with the seal.

Gunfire erupted the instant Charlie stepped from the trees.

Oh, hell. He should have figured the Russian was packing firearms.

Grabbing the American by the throat, using him as a shield, Charlie rolled to the ground. His first thought was for Penelope. He didn't dare hope she'd know how to hot-wire the car and get the hell out of here.

Puffs of dust spat up around him as gunfire erupted again. The ass screamed in panic.

"Don't shoot! You'll hit me!"

Charlie jerked back on his captive's jaw. His opponent was a tall man, but soft. He screamed in agony and terror.

"Give me the seal, you bastard."

"I haven't got it. I swear, I haven't got it. Dmitri kept it," the man babbled.

Charlie could hear footsteps crashing through the underbrush and figured Dmitri was well on his way to safety. Cursing, he jerked at the asshole's jaw again. "I don't believe you."

"Charlie! Charlie, are you all right?"

Penelope. Groaning, Charlie slammed his fist into a square jaw. His captive slumped into unconsciousness, and hastily Charlie patted him down until he located the heavy seal.

"Charlie!" She sounded nearly hysterical. "Answer me!"

Her concern would have tickled him at another time, but not now. He wanted her out of here. "I'm fine. Don't get any closer. The volcano's right here. Don't get off the damned boardwalk." Fear laced his words, making them sharper than he'd intended.

The moonlight provided enough illumination over the stinking morass of the volcano to reveal Penelope's slender silhouette cautiously approaching. The boardwalk ended yards away from where he was concealed by the shrubbery. He didn't like her exposed like that. He couldn't be absolutely sure if the Dmitri thug had left the area yet.

The man on the ground groaned. So, he wasn't as soft as he seemed. Charlie jerked his victim's arms behind his back. "I need something to tie him with. Any ideas?"

"Your cummerbund?" she suggested dryly, from a safe distance.

Oh, hell, he'd wrecked the tux for certain. He'd had to rent this one in Castries. It was the only one they'd had in his size.

The instant he let go, the man on the ground rolled over, swung a kick at Charlie, and stumbled to his feet.

"Penny, run!" Charlie shouted, shifting to tackle position. His bad knee crumpled under him, and he missed.

"Give back the seal," a guttural voice demanded from behind him.

Oh, triple shit. Ignoring the pain shooting through his leg, Charlie crouched amid the ferns and assessed the situation. The Russian with the gun must be behind him in the trees. The American nursing his bruised jaw stood in the moonlight at the volcano's edge, holding his hand out. Somewhere just beyond the curve of the volcano, on the safety of the walkway, stood Penelope, holding her breath, Charlie suspected.

He hadn't been brought up to let the bad guys win. He still had his quarterback's passing arm. If the seal landed in one of the molten pits of the volcano, so be it. Emile could get another one.

Flinging the heavy metal object in his hand as far and wide over the American's head as he could, Charlie used his good leg to shove into a crouching tackle. To his astonishment, beyond his opponent's shoulder, the red of Penelope's elegant gown leapt high in the air, seeming to float for a moment on the breeze. The shimmering silver arcing through the moonlight landed in her hand, and she broke into a run as soon as her feet touched ground.

Damn, but she should have played football.

Screaming with fury, the American crashed to the ground a second time as Charlie slammed into him. The gun fired again, and Charlie's heart nearly stopped beating. Penelope. The Russian was after Penelope.

Without hesitation, Charlie stomped the American's soft belly as he leapt up. He'd give the damned Russian a much bigger target to cope with than Penelope.

A siren screamed in the distance as he raced toward the circular boardwalk where Penelope had stood not moments before. He could see the shimmering red of her gown darting across the paved walkway to the parking lot. To his left, a bulky shadow loped in the same direction—straight across the volcano's core.

It was possible to walk on the hardened crust, in places. But even the most experienced of guides couldn't always predict where those places were. One of the more foolhardy a few years back had jumped up and down on the crust to earn a few extra tourist dollars for his daring. He hadn't survived the burns to collect them. A man the size of the Russian probably weighed three times as much as one of the native guides.

Charlie took the long way around, dodging the American's limp body to leap up to the boardwalk. Intent on Penelope's fleeing figure in the darkness of the tree-lined road ahead, the Russian ignored him. Maybe the goon was out of bullets.

A second siren joined the first and both wailed closer. Focusing on the Russian, Charlie ignored the sound. Penelope had a head start and could probably have outraced them, if she'd been wearing something more sensible than heels. His heart caught in his throat as he watched her stumble, but she righted herself and ran on. Damn, she could run. She must have starred on the track team. No female he knew could run like that.

Charlie saw the blaze of bullets before he heard them. He howled in anguish as the red silk of Penelope's gown faltered, swayed, and toppled. Despite the shooting pain in his knee, he pumped his legs harder, praying to hold back time, to stop the action, to jump in front of bullets already fired—anything but see Penelope crumple onto the gravel of the road.

Not Penelope, he gasped as he ran, not his beautiful, hard-headed Penelope. His lungs choked on air he didn't breathe as he tried to reach her before the goon with the gun did. Please, God, keep Penelope—

An anguished scream from his left jerked Charlie's attention back to the volcano. The sulfurous fumes filled his nostrils, and he nearly choked on them as he caught his breath. In disbelief, he watched the Russian stumble, throw up his hands, and fall face forward into the heated crust of the lava.

Shutting out the horror of the sight, chest heaving as he gasped in air, running almost entirely with the thrust of one leg, Charlie rushed toward the place he'd last seen Penelope. The Russian deserved the hell of the volcano for harming his woman.

Charlie's knee collapsed under him, and he staggered as the red silk half rose from the gravel and swiveled to stare at the place where the Russian had gone down. She was alive.

Heart singing, Charlie righted himself. The piercing screams of agony from the volcano halted abruptly. Behind him, Charlie sensed the American tottering to his feet. Ahead, even Penelope halted in the sudden silence. Frozen, they all stared at the place where the Russian had been moments before.

Siren wails propelled them into action again. The American, too far away to accomplish anything, crashed into the shrubbery. Charlie briefly contemplated running after him, but he could tell by the way Penelope rose cautiously, watching the volcano, that he had more pressing problems on his hands. And the damned island police had arrived.

"Don't, Penny!" he shouted as she limped toward the boardwalk.

Charlie caught her by the shoulders and jerked her away from the sight of the steaming volcano. Flashing red lights halted in the parking lot a few yards away, and dark figures leapt out, weapons pulled.

"Let the cops do their duty." Blocking the volcano with his bulk, he ran his hands up and down her, searching for damage, his heart pounding so erratically he thought it might explode. "Are you hurt? Tell me where he hit you."

"I fell. The damned heel broke on my shoe." With disgust, Penelope leaned against him to examine the damage. "I think I twisted my ankle."

All the air flew out of him. Head spinning in relief, Charlie steered her away from the volcano edge, into the deeper darkness of the trees, where the flashing lights didn't reach. "How the hell did the cops know where to find us?"

"I found a cell phone in the car."

She shivered despite the humid heat, and Charlie hugged her tighter. She was always so strong and courageous, he'd forgotten how slender she was. He could wrap his fingers around both her wrists and have room to spare. Her vulnerability terrified him. He could have lost her. He could have woken up to a world with no Penelope in it, no long legs and biting wit. No soul-searing kisses or clever tongue. No wide brown eyes shimmering with tears over a damned teddy bear. A world without all that wasn't worth living in.

Charlie wanted to haul her into his arms, howl "I love you" at the stars, and smother her with kisses until her senses got the better of her brains and she agreed to anything he asked. Instead, he held her tightly against him as one of the cops approached.

In native patois, he identified himself and warned of the body in the volcano. The cop shouted over his shoulder, and the rest of the night's ordeal began.

* * *

"There's still no proof Jacobsen's involved," Emile argued from his bed, where he sat with his head bandaged and his dislocated arm in a sling. "He was talking to your mother when that criminal broke in and stole the seal right from my hands. He wasn't anywhere near my study."

"And what the hell were you doing with the seal out?" Charlie asked angrily.

"I got Jacobsen here as you requested so he could sign those papers. I didn't see any reason to waste my time and his if this was all a misunderstanding. I wanted the papers ready for Jacobsen to take with him when he left."

"Papers he'd asked for in the first place? Ones that had to have your seal?" Charlie pointed out. He couldn't believe Emile was still vacillating over Jacobsen's guilt. Obviously, Emile was accustomed to dealing with crooks. He just didn't like being around ones who might get caught.

"That doesn't mean anything." Emile slammed his coffee cup on the tray.

"Well, fine, don't listen to me then, but if you don't call the rest of the Foundation's board and have him voted out, I won't bail you out when it sinks like a stone." Charlie paced the bedroom floor restlessly. He'd grabbed a few hours' sleep after the cops brought them home and before Emile woke, but he was operating on pure adrenaline. He needed to talk with Penelope, find out where the devil Raul had taken Tammy, and get home to his business. He didn't need his stepfather's bullheadedness.

"I scarcely have all my funds tied up in one company," Emile replied dryly. "No matter what your opinion of me, I'm not a fool."

"And I'm no accountant, but I've got a good grasp of borrowing power. What will the banks here loan? Two, three times the Foundation's assets? And Jacobsen could lay his hands on all that money with a signature and a seal?" Charlie clenched his fists and glanced at the door. Penelope would still be sleeping. She'd had a long, exhausting twenty-four hours. He needed to figure out what to say to her when she woke.

"I'll have the board change the bylaws to require three signatures for loans, then I'll look for a buyer for my share of the company," Emile compromised.

"Fine. Whatever." Charlie forced his attention back to the bed. "Has anyone heard from Raul or Tammy?"

"I'll not let that colored son of a—"

Charlie cut him off. "With that attitude, you'll drive Tammy right into his arms, and damned if I'll stop them. Raul's a good man. She could do far worse. I just want to make certain Jacobsen hasn't found some way to get at them."

"You have no proof—" Emile began again when a knock at the door interrupted him.

Vivian stuck her head in. Finding her son, she breathed a sigh of relief. "Penelope just left in a cab. I thought you should know."

Oh, hell, he'd waited too long. That overworked brain of hers had kicked in again, and she was running like the sensible woman she was. Only this time, Charlie had more sense than to believe he could let her go.

Penelope stood in the broiling humidity of the interminable waiting line at the airport ticket counter. The lackadaisical fans overhead scarcely stirred the waves of heat pouring off the masses of humanity yearning for home.

Well, maybe she was the only one yearning. The rest of the crowd looked sun-bronzed and relaxed after days of tropical vacation. She still hadn't done more than set a toe in the surf.

She could stay, she supposed. Now that the police knew about Jacobsen and his cronies, she could stay and listen to Charlie's protestations of gratitude or concern or whatever other excuse he'd make up to keep her here while her career went down the drain.

Only the real reason for running wasn't her job, but her

damned cowardice. She'd woken up this morning with anxiety slamming into her chest like a sledgehammer. Last night had been a fantasy where they'd dressed up in party clothes, drunk champagne, and Charlie had whispered pretty words of love she wanted to hear. They'd chased bad guys and won. Reality had smacked her in the face this morning.

A man had died in a volcano and Charlie had almost been killed.

Life and death. She'd never been more shaken in her life than the moment Charlie had gone down in a hail of bullets. Only the car accident that had ended Beth's sight had ever torn her so completely from her roots, leaving her swinging in the wind. Sheer terror of a man like Charlie—a good man, a brave one who fought with everything in his power for his beliefs—dying before her eyes while she watched, helpless, had broken something inside her. She couldn't live through that again. Wouldn't.

Worse was realizing why Charlie's near death had shaken her so horribly. She couldn't face the changes inside her just yet. Things had happened too fast. She hadn't had time to adjust to these terrifying emotions he'd awakened, or to follow the logical path to where such emotions led. Maybe after life had returned to normal, she could look at this episode through clearer eyes. She'd been in love before. It had been a stupendously blinding experience. She knew better than to jump in headfirst now.

Maybe, if it hadn't been for Beth, if it hadn't been for her career, she could have loosened up and enjoyed the possibilities of Charlie's company a little longer. As it was, she was terrified that if she stayed longer, she'd never want to leave. That dance in the moonlight had shaken her to her toes. The bullets later, followed by Charlie's familiar football shoulders slamming to the ground, had cracked something wide open inside, leaving her as shaken and vulnerable as a shorn lamb. She needed time to patch herself together again, so she could be strong when she faced him. *If* she faced him.

Maybe Charlie Smith was the only man in the world who could shoot her hormones into overdrive. Maybe she cared about him enough to look past his Neanderthal attitudes to the fascinating mixture of intelligence and charm and—she sighed in exasperation—masculine arrogance that made Charlie who he was. Maybe he took her breath away with his impulsive gifts and silly songs and tender caresses. That didn't mean he was any more ready for marriage than she was. He wanted *babies*, for heaven's sake. He didn't understand her at all. She had Beth's operation to worry about. The airheaded silliness of love couldn't erase reality. They were headed in two entirely different directions.

She was almost at the front of the line. In back of her, the hordes of tourists with their stacks of suitcases stirred restlessly, murmuring louder. Children chattered, a baby cried, and a loud male voice protested something impatiently. Penelope laid her passport and credit card on the counter. She wished she was better with accents. She struggled to understand the ticket clerk's questions.

As she picked up the ticket, she thought she heard someone calling her name. Her heart stumbled and fell, but she'd been down that road before and knew better than to follow it. Ignoring the sound, she strode briskly toward the departure lounge, carrying her teddy bear and carry-on. Let Charlie figure out how to get the rest of her luggage to her. With ticket in hand, she walked through the gates without trouble.

A mob milled around her even in here. At least this part of the terminal was air-conditioned. She could wander the few stores while she waited for her flight. Where had this place been hidden while she'd been herded like so much cattle at her first arrival?

How long ago had that been? It seemed like forever, but she supposed it had been scarcely two weeks. No sane person could fall in love in two weeks. It had just been the pressure of the circumstances that had stirred her blood—and her heart, and her soul.

She wandered in and out of shops until her flight was called. If she'd thought she'd heard Charlie earlier, she must have imagined it. She despised tearful farewells. It would only be her tears anyway. Charlie would just argue until they both got angry. It was better this way. He'd have his hands full with Jacobsen and the police and whatever. He didn't need her for that.

The blast of heat off the tarmac nearly knocked her sideways as she stepped through the doors. Out of habit, she wore the business suit she'd arrived in. She should have grabbed something lighter from the luggage Charlie had retrieved from the resort. It didn't matter. The airplane would be cooler.

She filed out in line with the other passengers, following the markings on the pavement to the small airplane waiting for them. Things had certainly changed since she'd arrived here the first time, terrified of the unknown. Now she knew she could handle a great deal more than she'd ever thought possible, thanks to Charlie. Most men preferred to shake her confidence to promote their own—for good reason, she supposed. Her new confidence led her straight away from Charlie.

As she strolled toward the plane, she noticed armed soldiers casually pacing the runway. Maybe they had drug-sniffing dogs somewhere. She was going home. It didn't matter.

Uneasiness crept beneath her skin as two of the soldiers turned and consulted each other while watching her. Men often stared at her. She shouldn't worry. They were probably just exchanging dirty jokes. She'd bet Charlie would tear their heads off if he heard them. She kind of liked that Neanderthal aspect of him. She was tired of defending herself, tired of hiding behind dependable business suits. She wanted to wear red again.

When the soldiers approached and took her arm, pulling her out of the line, Penelope panicked. Terror shot through her with the speed of adrenaline. They spoke English, but her ears didn't comprehend. She tried to shake free, but they held her firmly.

When she saw the helicopter on the pad ahead, blades slowly revving, her eyes widened.

He wouldn't. He damned well wouldn't dare.

❦ THIRTY ❦

Watching as the soldiers steered Penelope away from the other passengers and across the tarmac, Charlie could see the instant her terror turned to fury. He almost relished the battle to follow.

Dammit, he'd tried to reach her in a more reasonable fashion, but she'd ignored his shouts, and hordes of people had gotten in his way, and the damned gate attendants wouldn't let him through without a ticket. She could have saved herself the price of that expensive ticket. He just didn't intend to take her where she wanted to go.

"Charlie, I swear, I'll throttle you. I've got a plane to catch. Tell these hired thugs of yours to let me go." She practically spat the words at him as she jerked out of the soldiers' grips. Carefully, they set the white teddy bear on top of her carry-on.

"Well, at least you're not afraid of them this time." Charlie grinned, handing over another stack of bills with a jest in patois as he dismissed the men. He wouldn't have her loaded on the helicopter at gunpoint, although from the looks of it, he ought to consider it. If she had a knife, she'd probably slit his throat.

"What in hell has that got to do with anything?" Released from captivity, Penelope turned on her heel and started toward the plane.

"Oh, no, you don't." Charlie grabbed her by the back of her boxy jacket, but she slipped out of it and kept marching. Thinking it was a useful maneuver to relieve her of some of that stiff clothing, he gallantly resisted grabbing the back of her silk shirt. Instead, he caught her by her model-slim waist and hauled her toward the helicopter. "This birdie cost me too much trouble to let it go without you. Behave yourself. I promise you'll get home safely."

The pilot was already loading her bear and suitcase. Dragging Penelope literally kicking and screaming, Charlie shoved her into a rear passenger seat and climbed in beside her. Calmly, he snapped her harness in place. "Show's over, Miss Penny. Your plane is taxiing down the runway. If you want off the island, it will have to be with me."

She took a deep breath and, refusing to look at him, watched through the Plexiglas as her plane disappeared. Then, crossing her arms over her silk shirt, she glared at the back of the pilot's head and said nothing.

At least she wore her hair in that luscious long braid instead of a tight knot, Charlie reflected as the pilot worked through his checklist before takeoff. That was a sign of something. And a few weeks ago she wouldn't have done anything so obvious as crossing her arms to emphasize her breasts as she was doing now. Body language was a wonderful thing. She'd left the top buttons of her shirt unfastened too. Definitely a promising signal.

"Trust me, Penelope," he yelled over the increasing racket of the rotor blades.

"In hell," she yelled back.

All right, so he deserved that, more than she realized, since he had no intention of returning her to Miami yet. He was taking a huge risk, but he'd built his business by taking risks. It wasn't in him to be cautious. He had Raul for that, and Raul wasn't here. If this risk panned out, he'd have Penelope to slow him down in the future. If his risk didn't pan out, it didn't matter what he did. He'd have no need for caution ever again. Given those choices, he figured he was safer taking a chance.

The helicopter rose at a slow angle that had them over water within minutes. Charlie watched Penelope. She stared at the landscape below. She didn't seem particularly terrified, but he'd learned Penelope hid a lot inside. He removed her hand from where she clenched it beneath her armpit and tucked it safely between his fingers. She didn't pull away.

Charlie had plenty of time to contemplate the precariousness of his situation as the 'copter flew over choppy turquoise waters. He also had time to contemplate how right it felt having Penelope sitting beside him, holding his hand. It was as if he'd been a hexagonal screw in a round hole all these years, and someone had suddenly jerked him out and installed him where he belonged. Maybe they were maple and mahogany and didn't belong together in any normal manner, but whatever they had between them worked.

He thought it did anyway. Miss Penny was obviously of a different opinion. He had this one chance to persuade her otherwise. If he let her drift back to her old world, he might never get another opportunity to make her see what they had together. It was too easy to put off voices on the other end of a phone line, to plead business, to get trapped in time warps and travel plans and the demands of daily living. Besides, he had one other excuse for his madness: Jacobsen and his Russian Mafia still needed his land. He'd talked to Raul on the phone this morning.

The noise of the helicopter prevented his telling her any of that. Instead, Charlie just held Penelope's hand and prayed as he'd never prayed before in his life.

The helicopter landed on the flat roof of a stuccoed building Penelope assumed was some isolated Caribbean resort. She could see the ocean on her right and palm trees and well-tended tropical gardens on her left, but no evidence of any other human habitation.

A golden-skinned man in white shorts and polo shirt

darted from a stairwell to take their luggage and to guide the pilot down a back way. Charlie caught her arm and prevented her from following.

"Let's go to the balcony. I called ahead and they'll have our room prepared and lunch ready, but I think a drink is called for first."

Their room. Penelope suppressed a shiver and followed Charlie across spectacular peacock blue tiles to terrace steps adorned with terra-cotta pots filled with flowering brome-liads, orchids, and bougainvillea vines that spilled down the stairs to dangle over the terrace below. The hand-painted tiles of the terrace reflected all the colors of the ocean, from sea green to midnight blue, and the walled terrace overlooked a white sand beach with gracefully waving palms. She should be furious and maybe even a little bit scared, but the setting was too stunning to do more than gape in awe.

"Charlie, I appreciate your choice of accommodations, but I—"

"Do you like it?" He swung his hand to take in the white-washed walls and the bright splashes of sea-blue shutters. "My company built it. The owner gives me use of it for sales pitches since he's seldom here. If I had a place like this, I'd never leave."

Penelope took the cushioned wrought-iron chair he offered and drank in the beauty of her surroundings. How could one man own all of this? Terra-cotta roof tiles gleamed in the sunlight. Silica had been added to the whitewash so the walls sparkled and glittered like diamonds. She supposed Charlie had little to do with the pots of plants, and perhaps the archi-tect took responsibility for the way the color and design blended so perfectly with the setting, but she'd lived in Florida long enough to know the difference between shoddy construc-tion and quality. Tropical sun and hurricane winds deterio-rated badly constructed buildings rapidly. She didn't see a single sign of chipped tile or cracking stucco or mildewing wood anywhere.

"It's gorgeous, Charlie. How long has it been here?"

He shrugged and pulled out another seat. "It was one of my first projects when I persuaded Dad to get out of home improvements and into major contracts. Friend of mine from college designed this place and told me about it. Since I know the islands pretty well, I could make a bid lower than most other offers. My father's company had a reputation for quality, so the owner took a chance. It was risky, but worth every bit. All I have to do is fly people out here and they're sold."

She wanted to be angry. There was safety in anger. She had easily scorned other men who had tried to impress her with their Jaguars and expensive condos. But Charlie wasn't trying to impress her with what he owned. He owned a damned GTO and probably had an apartment under a bridge somewhere. He was trying to impress her with what he could do. She didn't know why that made a difference. It just did.

She took the umbrella-adorned cherry-red drink a servant brought out and pressed the icy glass to her cheek. She was doing it again, falling blindly for a man who thought he could tell her what to do and expected her to gear her life toward his expectations. Men were the most aggravating, arrogant, self-centered . . .

Damn, but she loved him anyway. Charlie sat there looking vaguely uncertain of himself, waiting anxiously for her reaction. He had the audacity to kidnap her and disrupt her entire life, but he still wanted her approval. She ought to dump her daiquiri over his swollen head, but she loved that look in his eyes too much. Damn, but she was an idiot. Maybe she could try reasoning with him.

"It's magnificent, Charlie, and if you wanted to impress me, consider me overwhelmed. That doesn't change anything. I still have to get back to Beth and to work. I thought you would be working with the police and whoever, to pin down Jacobsen. Isn't that what you wanted?" She sipped the icy drink in hopes it would cool her off. Charlie looked all too appealing sitting here in all his sun-bronzed glory, chestnut hair tousled in the breeze.

"I learned a long time ago that to get what I want, I have to set priorities. I want lots of things, but I can't go after all of them at once. I've got to pick and choose. I choose you. Jacobsen can wait."

He seemed deadly serious. Penelope could only stare at him. Until this minute, their choices had been fairly limited by circumstances. They'd been thrown together by danger and desperation. They hadn't had a chance to explore a leisurely courtship where they learned about each other in a succession of civilized meetings. For a long time, she'd considered him little more than a half-cocked barbarian. Last night, he'd swept her off her feet by donning a tux and playing Prince Charming. Today, he looked the epitome of any sophisticated rich man she'd ever imagined. He was even wearing a respectable golf shirt and tailored linen shorts. She'd like to know where he'd stolen them. The man she knew lived in jeans and muscle shirts and wore mirrored sunglasses.

She reminded herself firmly of that. Charlie Smith was a construction worker who drove ancient behemoths, lived in jeans, drank beer, and watched football. She had nothing in common with a man like that.

She had nothing in common with men in pinstripe suits who drove Jaguars either. She'd just thought that was who she should marry if she wanted a comfortable, settled married life. Men who gambled and took risks like her father were dangerous. Charlie took risks and was definitely dangerous. But she'd gone to bed with Charlie and not the men in suits. She'd risked her life, her career, and her twin's health for Charlie, because he was doing the same for his sister and partner and the well-being of the unsuspecting islanders.

She loved him. She would make any excuse for the damned man. She couldn't stop herself. Despairingly, she set her drink down. "Where do we go from here?"

He reached out and brushed a tendril of hair behind her ear. "We take one step at a time. Lunch, then a swim in the ocean maybe."

"What about my job?" she whispered, desperate to accept his words but still denying the possibilities he offered.

"I keep telling you I've got friends." He caressed the tip of her nose. "You don't need those jerks. You can have your own business. You can work in mine. You can do anything you damned well want. Let go, Penny. Let them all go. Readjust your priorities and take time to explore what we have."

Definitely a dangerous man. She'd spent a lifetime plotting her career, step by step, knowing exactly where she was going, working around every obstacle thrown in her way, never losing sight of her goals. And within two short weeks he had her contemplating throwing away a lifetime of achievement and planning to start all over.

"But Beth . . ."

He handed her the daiquiri. "Will get her operation, one way or another. We can make it work. I'll put both of you on my payroll, make certain we have insurance that covers it, pay for it myself if necessary, whatever it takes. We might never have a chance like this again, Penelope. Put yourself first, just this once, and I won't ever ask it again."

What if they had this little island idyll and decided they wouldn't suit after all? What if they ended up arguing as usual and stormed back to Miami and never spoke again? She'd be out of a job, Beth would go without her operation. . . . He was asking her to take a huge risk, to trust him, to jump off a cliff without a parachute. She didn't do those things.

He wasn't asking any less of himself. He had dangerous men trying to kill him, to steal a multimillion-dollar project, to ruin his business and harm his friends and family, and he'd tucked them all away to bring her here so they could straighten out what was happening between them. He was the scariest man she'd ever met.

"Tammy and Raul?" she whispered, still looking for an out.

"I told them to take the company credit cards and get the hell out of Miami for a few days while the FBI does its job. John's taking Beth home with him. Now that we've quit meddling, they should be safe. Let the rest of the world go for a little while. Let's just concentrate on us right now. Start by admitting there's something between us."

There was a hell of a lot more than "something," and he knew it, or he wouldn't be doing this. Gulping, Penelope tilted back her head and studied the intensity of Charlie's expression, the way he looked at her as if all this magnificence around them didn't exist and they were the only two people on the planet. Her heart pounded so hard she feared he could see her chest rising and falling.

The step she took now would lead down terrifying pathways into the unknown of a future she hadn't planned. Saying the one simple word he wanted was far more terrifying than landing alone in a foreign airport in an exotic country. She'd had a right to be terrified that first time, but this man had led her out of danger unscathed. For the first time in years, she listened to the little voice inside her screaming to be free.

"Yes," she murmured.

"Thank you," he said solemnly, and then he leapt up, grabbed her out of her chair, and swung her around the terrace with wild crows of triumph.

❦ **THIRTY-ONE** ❦

The Caribbean sun disappeared behind thin layers of rainbow-painted clouds, coloring the turquoise sea with midnight blue and gold and illuminating the sky with a last green flash of brilliant light before the first star of the evening popped out.

A gentle surf lapped at their toes, indicating the tide had turned. Exhausted, skin tingling from the sun's caress, coated with layers of lotion and salt, Penelope couldn't move a contented muscle. Beside her, Charlie clasped his hand around hers. A callused finger stroked her palm, and instantly, every nerve ending in her body leapt to attention.

They wore their bathing suits, but their awareness of each other was such that they might as well have been naked. True to his word, Charlie had gone slowly, never once taking advantage of the physical need pulsing between them with every touch, every gesture, every look. They'd danced in the surf, slept in the sun, hunted for shells, and adorned themselves with orchid chains, but they'd never gone near the dim coolness of the room and bed waiting for them, although the knowledge of its presence was with them every minute of the day.

An assortment of kiwi, papaya, plantains, and other exotic fruit lay half-eaten on a platter above the cotton-covered rattan mat they lay upon. The beach was in a secluded cove out of sight of the house but within easy walking distance. They should probably roll up the mat and return for dinner, but Penelope didn't want to disturb the perfection of this moment. She watched the star rising on the horizon and curled her fingers around Charlie's broad ones. His bare foot tilted to rub against hers.

"Dinner?" he suggested lazily.

"Bath first," she decided.

"Shower?" He eased up on his elbow and gazed down at her through heavy-lidded eyes.

Her heart pumped a little faster as all that suntanned heaven of muscled shoulders and naked chest leaned within easy reach. "Jacuzzi," she countered.

A smile teased the corner of his lips. "With champagne."

She grimaced. "I don't like champagne."

He grinned wider. "Gotcha. Neither do I." His gaze dipped to the slope of her swimsuit top. "How about another swim first?"

Penelope could tell by the tone of Charlie's voice that swimming was the last thing on his mind. They'd played these word games all day, disagreeing at every turn but always finding a compromise that showed how shallow their differences actually were. He was simply letting her take the lead, because she had what he wanted. He wanted her. It was as simple as that.

Amazed that she'd never understood how easy a relationship could be, Penelope stroked the bristle of his jaw. "Naked," she whispered naughtily.

Charlie eyed her. "We could be seen."

"And?" she taunted, knowing that didn't bother him at all.

"In my current state, it could definitely be dangerous." This time, the gleam in his eye was noticeable.

"That's never bothered you before," she scoffed, trailing a finger down the sandy expanse of his chest, twirling it in a curl of dark hair.

Charlie hooked his finger in the clasp between her breasts and, with a flick, unfastened it. Penelope's breath caught as he stared at her breasts, hunger and admiration blatant in his expression. The waiting had ended, then. He wanted her, and he would do whatever she liked to have her, but this was definitely a two-way street. Desire poured like warm honey through her veins and pooled in her lower abdomen until all her muscles drew tight with expectation.

"I bother you," he amended with a note of triumph. "Cool, elegant, untouchable Penelope, hot and bothered by a dumb jock. Admit it."

"That you're a dumb jock?" she asked, lifting an eyebrow.

He stroked her erect nipple and she nearly grabbed his neck to haul him down where she could reach him, but they fought a war here, and she didn't give up easily. He had been right when he'd said they were competitive spirits. She wanted to win.

"Not so dumb, maybe," he answered more thoughtfully than she'd expected. "I've been told it often enough to believe it. Maybe I've tried living up to my reputation. But I'm smart enough to know a good thing when I see one, and I'm smart enough to go after what I want and get it. I want you, Penelope." He said it as a warning.

Before she could reply, he leaned over and licked the peak he'd caressed to screaming sensitivity, and she arched upward, digging her fingers into his thick hair as he wrapped his arm around her back and pulled her against him.

"If you want more time, you'd better tell me now," Charlie whispered, brushing kisses across her temple. "Because when I come into you this time, I'm going to make you mine. I'm going to take all this heat and electricity we're generating and pump it into you until we've welded shackles around our hearts that can never be broken. Every time I take you, I'll forge another link in the chain." His hand stroked downward, slipping beneath the elastic of her bikini bottom, pulling it over her hips so she had to wiggle out or be trapped. A sea breeze lapped at her nakedness.

Charlie's big hand covered her where she was most vulnerable, sheltering her against the breeze. "I'm a man who works with his hands, Penelope. What do you think your chances are against me?"

None, absolutely none. She should laugh at his silliness, but she knew Charlie meant every word. She should be furious at his arrogance, but she understood what drove him. She should be terrified at how swiftly she succumbed to his domination, but she knew her own power and that she could use it against him, or with him. The choice was hers. He'd opened himself entirely for her attack. His words had stripped him of shield or weapon, exposing his vulnerability, something few men dared do. And she loved him for it, loved him wholly, without question, mindlessly, insanely, hopelessly.

"I dare you," she threw at him, having no other words to express the challenge she knew they faced.

Charlie swung his leg over her hips so she lay trapped beneath him. His weight held her pinned against the mat, his breadth blocked the stars. The powerful tendons of his arms strained to hold him back. Penelope knew his expression despite the darkness. It would be taut with expectation, his eyes hot with desire, his mouth turned slightly upward, revealing the dimple that gave away his joy. Silly man, thinking he was in control here.

"This isn't a game, Penelope," he warned again, as if she hadn't taken him seriously enough. "This is for life. If I take you now, I'll want you again in the Jacuzzi, in the shower, in that bed waiting for us upstairs, all night, every night, from now until forever." He pried his knee between hers and parted her legs so she lay spread-eagled beneath the stars and the palm trees.

He was talking commitment. That scared the hell out of her. She hadn't really thought about it, although she should have. She wanted it. She just didn't know if she could handle it. Panic surged through her veins, along with the hot flood of desire. "I'm a coward, Charlie," she whispered.

He stared at her incredulously. "You? The woman who gave up her own life for her sister? The woman who risked her career for an old man she didn't even know? More people should have your kind of cowardice." With those scoffing words, he rolled off to remove his trunks.

She had an instant's reprieve while he stripped, but his words held her spellbound. He didn't think she was a coward. Could her strength really lie deeper than her career?

She didn't have longer to think than that. The moment Charlie rolled back over her and took the tip of her breast into his mouth, she was lost. His heat surrounded her, enveloped her in a raging inferno, cast her into that volcano that had smoldered at their feet all these nights. Bathed in fire, cast in the furnace, consumed, and resurrected into something shiny and new and entirely different—

Penelope's cry mixed with the call of a night bird overhead as Charlie surged into her and the fire melded them together. From the inside out, the clay became porcelain, the iron turned to steel. Neither of them shattered in the process. Stars exploded and surf pounded at their ankles. Penelope surrendered to the tide, to the moment, to the man and the elements as their separate parts bonded into one. Waiting for that surrender, Charlie joined her with a wild cry, his big body shuddering as he flooded her with all the potential he possessed and held her while she accepted the possession.

He'd done it, then, she thought idly moments later, looking up into the tropical sky as Charlie's heavy weight pressed her into the earth. He'd forged her into a crucible for his seed, molded her body into one she didn't know, linked her heart to his so they could never be fully apart again, no matter what the future would bring.

Joy flooded through her as thoroughly as the waves washing up their legs.

They sat on opposite sides of the spacious Jacuzzi, wineglasses nearly empty, skin cleansed, muscles relaxed, but Penelope thought the steam rising between them had more to do with the heat they generated than with the hot water. Charlie rested his muscular arms on the pool's edge, providing her a full view of his powerful chest and shoulders, and she didn't think she could swallow another drop.

"Dinner?" she suggested cautiously.

"We can eat anytime. Are you coming over here or do I have to go over there and get you?"

The gleam in his eyes warned that dinner would wait. Just that knowledge heated her skin and tightened her lower muscles in anticipation. She didn't understand why only Charlie could turn her on like this, but now that he had, she couldn't find any way of turning herself off. Didn't want to. Still, she made no move toward him.

Charlie took care of the matter. In a single step he was beside her, lifting her from the seat and into his arms. He was already as aroused as she was. Once on the beach wasn't enough, would probably never be enough.

"We're not using protection, Charlie," she whispered as he buried his lips against her nape and shot shivers straight down her spine.

He cupped her wet breasts and teased them tenderly. "I know."

His mouth moved to hers, and for long moments, Penelope had no other thoughts at all. The play of his hands and tongue drove her mind out the door and she was all nerve endings begging for more.

Then he lifted his head and, in the moonlight, gazed down at her. "We've wasted enough time making money. Now it's time to do something more productive."

She knew what he meant, had always known his intention. She'd just wanted it verified. The secret desire she'd hidden from herself slid open a long-buried door and peeked out with rising hope. "I'll not stay home barefoot and pregnant for any man," she warned, just so he knew he wasn't in charge here.

"I'll buy you shoes," he teased, running kisses down her throat.

How could she resist a man like this? He didn't even get angry when she argued. She spread her hands across his broad back and let him lift her high enough to suckle her breast. She gasped at the sensation shooting through her.

"I want this baby now," Charlie informed her, sliding his finger inside to encourage her. "You can decide when we have the next one."

The next one. He was already talking about two babies and she hadn't even adapted to the idea of marriage yet. Ever since she'd met this man she'd been spun around in a vortex of events that kept her from knowing where she stood, or if she stood at all. Penelope grabbed Charlie's shoulders as he carried her out of the pool and toward the bed.

Damn, but he hadn't been kidding when he said that if he wanted something, he went after it. Suddenly, it no longer mattered if she knew where she stood or not. Charlie knew, and he'd take care of her.

Free at last, Penelope wrapped her legs around Charlie's hips as he perched her on the edge of the high bed. Arching into him, she trusted him with her future. As Charlie drove into her, Penelope rose willingly to take him, visions of making babies to love and hold together cracking the final barriers to her heart.

With dinner finally consumed, they lay quietly on the cool sheets, bodies touching, listening to the roar of the waves beneath their window.

"You're the first woman I've ever known who makes me feel like Superman instead of a bull in a china shop," Charlie reflected out loud, sliding his hand over the silken skin of Penelope's thigh.

"Superman?" She propped herself on one elbow and stared down at him, her hair tumbling in a black waterfall around them.

Charlie tensed, waiting for the laughter to follow. He'd opened himself so wide this day that he couldn't stop his loose tongue from rattling. Penelope's acceptance of him as the father of her children had bowled him over more than he'd anticipated. He still couldn't believe it. He'd seldom known this kind of joy, and he waited for the next blow to fall.

From beneath the curtain of black hair falling over her shoulder and across the sculpted white of her breasts, Penelope traced her finger down his breastbone. Charlie already knew it was difficult for her to open up to him as he did for her. She'd spent years perfecting a wall of reserve not easily breached. She was so beautiful, it terrified and excited him at the same time. No one had ever dared give him anything so precious and so breakable before. He didn't want to hurt her, but he didn't know how to go about protecting delicate females. Maybe he was a damned bull in a china shop after all.

He sensed more than saw her slow smile as she digested his stupid declaration. "I suppose, if we're being honest, that you make me feel as intrepid as Lois Lane. No man has ever given me that kind of confidence before."

Charlie sighed in satisfaction and pulled her down on top of him. Instinct had told him she was the right woman for him. Time would prove it.

He caught her mouth and set about forging more heart chains.

Morning sparkled over both the balcony and the beautiful woman sipping her coffee at the table, admiring the crash of foam-capped waves below. The power of all that beauty was so sharp, it hurt, and Charlie crushed the messages in his hand as he stood inside the shadowed room, looking out. He still couldn't believe a crippled football player and ragged construction worker like himself could be so lucky, but the elegant woman sitting there was his, was waiting for him, after a night he'd remember for the rest of his life.

He could only pray that he'd forged chains of steel in the last twenty-four hours, because it looked like that was all they were going to get.

She looked up with that long, slow, inviting smile of hers as he stepped into the sunshine. Charlie supposed, if he was being objective, that her mouth was too wide for her narrow, elegant face, but she had lush, rosy lips that begged to be kissed, and he didn't give a damn for proportions. He leaned over and kissed them.

She tasted of coffee and smelled of him. The sensual combination intoxicated him, but he knew he couldn't delay the news any longer.

He laid the scribbled messages on the table. "Raul called. I told him how to find us in case of emergency."

Instantly, alarm leapt to her face, and she grabbed the messages. "What's happened?"

The pink slips had no more than phone numbers and times on them. Charlie took the chair beside her. "The helicopter will take us over to Puerto Rico. My plane will meet us there. We'll be in Miami in a few hours. She's in good hands, Penelope. There isn't anything you can do but be there."

She found the slip with John's name and stared at him in horror. "Beth? Something's happened to Beth?"

"Raul doesn't know the details. John simply asked how to reach you, said he'd taken Beth to the hospital. They're operating on her this afternoon."

She turned so pale, Charlie thought she'd faint. He didn't know what else to do besides what he'd already done. "I'll get you home, Penny," he assured her.

Wide-eyed, she gulped, nodded, and looked away. He could feel her pulse pounding beneath his hand. He hadn't entirely understood what the kind of relationship he wanted meant until now. It wasn't just sandy beaches, steamy sex, and making babies. It was helping each other through the bad times, feeling each other's pain, being there when they'd rather be anywhere else. He scarcely knew Beth, but he knew Penelope's twin was more a part of her life than he could ever be.

"The helicopter is ready anytime you are," he whispered.

❧ THIRTY-TWO ❧

Penelope gazed out the window of Charlie's plane and sought some relief from the panic jumbling her thoughts into incoherence. Charlie's bulk filling the seat beside her both reassured and confused her more. She felt as if she were splitting into two people: the old Penelope who strode firmly toward her goals and held her sister's well-being in her hands, and the strange new Penny who had recklessly turned down a path committing herself to a lifetime with a virtual stranger, leaving Beth behind. She was more familiar with the old self and sought the security of the known.

"I don't know what I could have been thinking of," she muttered. "The sun must have baked my head."

Charlie reached over and swallowed her hand in his. "Don't, Penelope. Don't blame yourself."

Out of habit, she wanted to jerk her hand away, but the new Penny wanted the sharing touch. Still, her old self had control of her mind, what was left of it. "I'm not blaming myself for Beth," she explained curtly. "I'm blaming myself for not being there, for not returning to my job, for not sticking to my goals. What if they've fired me? Beth's insurance is limited. She can't support herself. And here I am, letting you talk me into having *babies*, for heaven's sake!"

"Beth has children," he pointed out. "She can't deny you that right."

"*Me?* It never occurred to me. This is entirely your bright idea. More babies is the last thing this world needs."

"We have every right to want children of our own, Penelope," Charlie said calmly.

"You're just being selfish." The calmer he got, the more irritated she became.

"Nobody says I'm not. I'm entirely human." Complacently, he draped his arm over the back of her seat, enfolding her in the circle of his protection.

"Bringing a child into this world is a selfish act of ignorance," she insisted as he hugged her closer.

"I figure we've got more to offer than most." Unperturbed by her diatribe, he tickled her shoulder. "Why shouldn't we give it a try? Maybe we'll have the kid who grows up to be the president who brings world peace."

"You're not dealing with reality here!" she practically screamed in frustration. "Reality is drugs and war and poverty and prejudice."

He rubbed her arm soothingly. "So, I'm dreaming. When I dream, I dream big. It doesn't hurt. Try it sometime."

"How can you dream when reality is all around you? Look at the divorce rate! The number of kids who die in car accidents. AIDS! Why would you want to bring up a kid in a world like that?" She knew she was being irrational, but she couldn't help it. Terror screamed through her veins, and she had no means of controlling it. She couldn't control anything that was happening to her these days. Even her own body betrayed her. It could be growing a child inside even now, a child that would fill her womb and dominate the rest of her life. A child that could die or be maimed in the blink of an eye, like Beth. She wasn't prepared for this. She couldn't handle it.

"You would prefer it if only drug addicts had children?" he asked irrelevantly. "Stop beating up on yourself. I love you, Beth loves you, and any child we might have will love you. You can cry and scream and get angry, and we'll all still love you. Life happens. You don't have to be in control of it every minute."

Penelope broke down and cried then, pressing her face into Charlie's broad shoulder and sobbing out her fear and terror until she couldn't sob anymore, while he hugged her close, unafraid of her outburst. She hiccuped and curled her fingers into his shirt and continued hiding against his chest after the tears were spent. She'd never broken down like that before, not in front of anyone. She'd cried more tears into her pillow than she could count, but she'd always stayed calm in the presence of others. Why did she accept Charlie with the same intimacy as part of herself? She didn't know who she was anymore.

He'd said he loved her.

She'd never thought herself lovable.

"Close your eyes, Penny. Rest. It's gonna be a long day." Charlie cupped his hand over the back of her head and cradled her against him.

"I can't rest. I want to explode. I want to be there right now." Her words were muffled and she didn't know if he heard them. Better if he didn't. Superman might decide to fly the plane. She hiccuped on a giggle and decided she was hysterical.

"Then think about something else. Where would you like to live?" He didn't wait for her answer. "I've always imagined getting married and living in the suburbs and playing football in the front yard with the kids, but I've always kind of had this dream of designing my own house too."

So, she wasn't the only one who harbored hidden dreams. She'd been so damned selfish, she really hadn't taken Charlie's feelings into consideration. She'd spent her life protecting herself against invasion. Beth was the only person she'd ever let beyond those barriers. Now there was Charlie. Oh, God, how there was Charlie. He'd more than slipped beyond barriers. He'd been inside her and knew what made her tick. Sometimes, he ticked for her.

She dried her tears on his shirt but still didn't look up. She was a mess. She didn't cry prettily. "I like space," she whispered. "Lots of space. And light."

"I can't afford my own island yet," he teased softly.

"There are some lovely places on the Carolina shore." She remembered happier days, before her family fell apart, days on the beaches with the grasses and the herons. She'd been a child then. She could be carrying a child now. She wanted her child to have that happiness.

"Carolinas, huh? We could work up to that. Most of my contacts are here in Miami, but I can branch out. What about Beth? She'll want to be here, with her kids."

Penelope shook her head against his chest. "It's just a silly dream."

"Whoever told you that you can't have your dreams? We'll need a big sunny playroom for the kids. Are there jobs up there for you, or shall I make you my chief financial officer?"

She knew he was teasing, but his voice soothed the pain and confusion inside her head and heart. "Computer experts are needed everywhere," she answered airily. "Even pregnant ones," she finished with decided dryness.

Charlie chuckled, and the sound felt good rumbling against her ear. "Well, we may be rushing our boats a little. The chances of your walking down the aisle with rounded belly are probably pretty slim at this point."

Considering all the times she'd had unprotected sex with Zack without result, Penelope had to agree with him. To her surprise, the realization hurt.

To distract her thoughts from further pain, she finally looked at him, knowing her nose was red and runny and her eyes were probably black with mascara. "You haven't even asked me to marry you," she accused.

Charlie grinned and rubbed at the mascara beneath her damp eyes. "Did anyone ever tell you that your eyes sparkle like diamonds when you cry? I didn't ask because I didn't want you telling me no. We're just going to wind up standing before a preacher one of these days, and you'll never know how you got there."

The way things were going, the damned man was probably right.

They rushed into the hospital just after noon. By the time they located Beth's floor, she had already been wheeled into the operating room.

They found John pacing the crowded waiting area, the kids playing quietly nearby. He looked up at their entrance, but his stony face held no expression.

"She was in pain," he blurted, as if he had to defend himself.

"What did the doctor say?" Shivering inside, grateful for Charlie's strong hand on her shoulder, Penelope waited. She wouldn't think about Beth's panic as she was taken away in the hands of strangers. She'd always been there for her, and this separation from her twin ripped at her. Maybe Charlie was right; maybe she needed to let go more often.

"He said the nerve has been deteriorating under pressure from a clot, that she'd needed the operation for some time. He doesn't know if he can fix it." Pain etched John's face. "Why didn't she tell me?"

Penelope shook her head. "Why should she? You couldn't do any more than I could. The insurance won't pay for experimental surgery."

"It's not experimental, dammit! She was in pain! You didn't see her faint like I did. She scared the damned shit out of me." John turned and stalked away.

The children sat on the floor, staring at him, tears streaking their cheeks, worry puckering their brows.

Charlie crossed the lobby, scooped them up, whispered in their ears, and when they nodded, carried them out. Penelope blessed his heart and loved him even more. When she turned back to John, he must have seen what was written on her face.

"Don't let what happened to us happen to you," he said quietly.

"Life happens." Irritated to hear herself repeating Charlie, Penelope dropped down in one of the hideously hard plastic chairs. "In your case, you happened. You broke her heart and tore it into tiny little pieces. She was just getting over it. I should never have called you in."

"Beth would never have called me in," he agreed, flinging his long frame into another chair. "She froze me out as soon as she learned she'd never see again. She didn't want my help or my sympathy or anything to do with me. I didn't break her heart. She tore it up and threw it away herself."

"Oh, listen to the big tough guy," Penelope taunted. "Her entire life fell apart, and what did you do? Threw away your job, moved to Florida, and took the kids with you. That really helped a lot."

John slapped his hands on the chair arms. "What the hell was I supposed to do? She went home to your mother. She wouldn't let me near her. I was damned if I was going to let your mother take over my kids too. The woman has a heart of stone. All she was ever interested in was how much money I made. I swear, she wouldn't let Beth marry me unless I promised to join that damned law firm. How do you think I felt? My wife was blinded for life, she wouldn't let me near her, and your damned mother wanted to steal my kids. I had to stand up for myself somehow. And I didn't take the Florida job until she mentioned moving down here to be with you. I figured it would inspire her to get away from the witch."

He slumped in the chair and buried his face in his hands. "What the hell difference does any of it make now? I can't make her better. I can't make anything better."

Penelope bit her lip and wished Charlie were back here again. She didn't know what to say. She'd spent a lifetime bottling things up inside of her. Her parents had fought constantly, and she'd thought hiding her feelings would help. So she'd tiptoed around them all her life, and continued tiptoeing even after she'd grown up and moved on. But she couldn't tiptoe around this problem now. Beth wasn't the only one hurting. Her children and this man crumpled in the chair were suffering. Penelope had little experience at healing hurts.

"I don't suppose you ever asked why Beth wouldn't let you near her?" she asked tentatively.

John shrugged. "Said she didn't like pity. What the hell was I supposed to feel? She was in pain, she couldn't do any of the things she used to do. I wanted to help, but she wouldn't let me."

Penelope repressed an urge to speak sharply. "Did it ever occur to you that she was ashamed of herself? Beth has always taken pride in her appearance, but after the accident, she couldn't tell a red dress from a black one, or how bad the scars looked. She knew she was a good wife, and she took pride in that too, until you started treating her like cotton candy instead of a desirable woman. She thought maybe she could handle the kids, but you took them away from her. You left her nothing."

John's big shoulders sagged. "I couldn't bear seeing her pain," he whispered. "I couldn't even look at her," he said with anguish indicating he'd never admitted this to anyone. "I didn't realize she knew. . . ."

A tear slid down Penelope's cheek. She remembered that period too well. They'd all had an awful time adjusting to Beth's scarred beauty and blank stare. "It wasn't just you," she answered softly, haltingly. "Beth should have made you look at her, got up in your face and told you how she felt, instead of running home to Mother. You're right, you both had too little experience at handling the downside of life." Penelope's fingernails bit into her palms as she realized her words spoke for herself too. She and Zack had been much too young to stand up for themselves. She and Charlie weren't. The knowledge opened new vistas.

"And maybe, if she'll admit it, Beth needed to learn to stand on her own," she added with new insight. "She's always had someone looking out for her. Maybe I hurt instead of helped in that respect."

John rubbed the heels of his palms into his eyes. "I adored Beth from the moment I first laid eyes on her, wanted to take care of her, and didn't want to lose her. When your parents broke up, I used that as an excuse to marry before we gradu- ated. I tried to be what she wanted, tried to support us like she expected, but I hated that law firm; I hated getting criminals out on technicalities. I was turning into a fungus like all those other toadstools in there."

He raised his head and reached blindly for his cold cup of coffee. "But I would have done it, for Beth. After the acci- dent, when she wouldn't even talk to me, I just kind of lost it. I had some funny idea that maybe I'd have more time for her and the kids if I quit the firm, that maybe then I could figure out how to talk to her, but it never happened."

Penelope twisted her hands together. She'd always held John up as an example of how love failed, but love hadn't failed. Communication had, maybe, but the love was still there. Life happened, as Charlie said. Had she ever told Charlie she loved him?

Terrified that she never had, that life was so unpredictable she might never have the chance, Penelope stared longingly at the doorway through which Charlie had departed. Here was a prime example of what happened when someone didn't reveal their feelings. She could end up like John, hurt and all alone, maiming the person she loved. She didn't want that. She wanted Charlie filled with joy, as he'd been yesterday. If she could give him that joy, she'd gladly throw away her job and take her chances on the strange new future opening be- fore her.

"Tell her you love her, John," she said firmly. "The only thing it can hurt is your pride. Tell her you love her and that she's a wonderful mother and you want her for a wife. She has rocks for brains sometimes, but you can turn them to mush if you try."

John was silent, and she didn't have time to turn and study his expression. Tammy appeared in the doorway, and Pe- nelope knew instantly that something was wrong.

She rose slowly to her feet, the question she couldn't ask in her eyes. Beside her, John stood up too.

"We stopped to get Beth's things, like John asked," Tammy

whispered, fear widening her eyes as she held out the suitcase. "Someone followed us when we left. We tried to lose them, but when we got here, Raul thought he saw the other car again. He sent me up here and he's heading for the cafeteria, hoping we could distract them by splitting up. He wants to talk to Charlie. Is he here?"

"The kids," Penelope whispered. "Charlie's with the kids."

"Where would he take them?" John demanded.

"I don't know. The gift shop?" Penelope looked up at her brother-in-law and saw the same terror reflected in his face that she knew was on hers. "The cafeteria?"

"Stay here with Tammy," John said brusquely, pulling out a battered notebook and handing her a sheet of paper with numbers on it. "Call these guys. They're the ones working on the case."

They stood in a waiting room full of people, some watching them curiously, most absorbed in their own worries and grief. Surely a place like this was safe. Penelope took the paper and handed it to Tammy. "Be our communication central. I'll help John look."

She ignored John's protests and strode for the door. "You take the gift shop, I'll take the cafeteria. If either of us finds Charlie or Raul, we'll send them up here. What about hospital security?"

"I'll take care of them. Penelope, dammit . . ." John hurried after her. "Stay up here where it's safe. Beth will need you."

"I know all about this operation, John," she informed him as they aimed for the elevators. "It takes hours. And I'll be damned if I'll let anything happen to Charlie before I tell him I love him."

Or before anything could happen to the kids. Surely no one would harm innocent children. . . .

❧ **THIRTY-THREE** ❧

As Penelope entered the cafeteria, Raul was gesticulating vociferously at Charlie. Charlie wore no expression at all, although she detected a flicker of something—worry, relief?—as she walked in. In a room full of people, he spotted her instantly. Her gaze dropped to the kids noisily slurping chocolate milk at the table beside the men, and she breathed a little easier. Maybe it was all a false alarm.

The instant she saw the man in the trench coat hovering at the back of the crowded room, she lost that hope. Charlie must have seen her fear, for he tensed and gripped Raul's arm, whispering something hastily in his ear, but he didn't turn.

Penelope approached with caution. She tried to think of something intelligent to do—pretend she hadn't seen them and leave? Look for John? Scream bloody murder? But she could see only two curly heads and the man she loved. No way in this world could she walk away and leave them. Her cowardice and fear of risks disappeared.

Charlie didn't greet her as she walked up. He merely tousled Deedee's curly head and nodded in the direction of the two uniformed policemen eating doughnuts at a corner table.

"Take the kids over there," he said quietly, "sit down, and explain what's happening. Raul and I will take care of our Russian friend."

She wanted to argue. Charlie could see it in her expressive

face. Penelope never trusted, never accepted without explanation. He tensed, preparing for the fight, but it didn't come.

"I love you, Charlie," she said softly but distinctly, and then with a smile to the children, she helped them out of their seats and drew them toward the safety of the far corner of the crowded room.

Her actions screamed far louder than her words in Charlie's heart. She trusted him to do what was best. She was making him feel like a damned Superman again, but she was a sight smarter than stupid Lois Lane. A rush of love had him smiling at the comparison, but remembering the confrontation ahead, he jerked his head toward the back of the room.

"You want to go with me or go find Tammy?"

"We're in this together," Raul replied stiffly.

They had a few issues to fight out when this was over, Charlie figured, but he couldn't think of a better man to have at his back than Raul. "I don't know if the goon back there has called in reinforcements yet. Let's take him by surprise before they arrive."

Raul nodded, and as one, they swung around and stalked across the room in the direction of the Russian in the trench coat. Charlie calculated the man would have at least one hand-weapon on him, but he'd have some difficulty using it if his hands were otherwise occupied.

Before Trench Coat could decide whether to run or pull a gun, Charlie had one of his arms in a no-nonsense grip, and Raul had the other. Without a word, they lifted him from his feet and carried him into the relatively deserted corridor outside the cafeteria.

"Now, we're going to have a little talk," Charlie said coldly.

The man burst into an excited, unintelligible spurt of Russian.

Charlie waited calmly until he finished, then with his spare fist around his captive's throat, pounded him against the wall. "Look for his gun, Raul."

Raul checked the coat, located a small-caliber pistol, then, searching his suit, uncovered a Magnum in a holster. He stepped back, holding the Magnum professionally. "I've got him covered, Charlie."

"Good." Charlie rapped the man's head against the concrete-block wall again. "Now, we can stand here all day until you remember how to speak English, or I can just pound the memory out of you and make it faster. How would you like it?"

The stranger fought then, kicking at Charlie and twisting at his arms. Charlie kneed him in the groin and tightened his grip on his throat. Gasping in pain, the Russian collapsed against the wall.

"He's turning blue, Charlie. You might want to loosen up."

He'd rather strangle the bastard. There wasn't a doubt in Charlie's mind that this was one of the goons who had tried to machine-gun Penelope at her office. But strangling him wouldn't help. He eased his grip enough for his captive to breathe.

"You speaking English yet, friend?" Charlie asked with as much coolness as he could muster.

"*Nyet.* I no speak. I want lawyer."

"Charlie."

Charlie's head jerked up. That couldn't be Penelope's voice quavering behind him. He'd left her with a damned cop.

"We got company, Charlie."

Reacting to the wariness in Raul's tone, Charlie tightened his grip on the Russian's throat and slowly turned to face the corridor.

Jacobsen. With a gun at Penelope's back.

"It was me or the kids, Charlie," she said apologetically, her eyes wide with fear.

"I'll let her go if you come quietly."

Jacobsen spoke calmly, but only a desperate man would risk this kind of public confrontation. Charlie didn't trust him to do as promised. He glanced at Raul holding the Magnum, but Jacobsen used Penelope like a shield. Her height effectively blocked Jacobsen from an inexpert marksman like Raul.

Charlie had no choice. Behind Jacobsen, the police were hurriedly emptying the cafeteria full of people out the far entrance. The kids were safe.

Taking a deep breath, Charlie started to release his hold on the Russian. If he could just separate Jacobsen from Penelope . . .

"No, Charlie!" Penelope screamed in warning as Jacobsen trained his gun on Charlie. In the same breath, she jerked her head backward, smashing the contractor's nose, slammed her heel into his polished loafer, and, taking advantage of Jacobsen's loosened grip, threw herself sideways.

Raul fired.

Charlie nearly broke the Russian's neck as Penelope screamed and fell. He couldn't move fast enough, couldn't reach her soon enough. . . . Flinging the Russian aside, he raced to catch her, hold her, reassure himself that she breathed, that her heart still pounded in tandem with his. He sucked in drafts of air as he folded onto the floor, and she reached for him.

"I think we got reinforcements, Charlie," Raul said tiredly, standing over Jacobsen's prostrate form and holding the Magnum trained on the Russian.

With Penelope's fingers clutching his shirt, her soft sobs wrenching against his chest, Charlie glanced over her shoulder. He recognized Penelope's ex–brother-in-law and assumed the men with him were plainclothes officers. The two uniformed officers he'd left Penelope with now stood in the doorway of the cafeteria, guns drawn. From a back hall, two uniformed security guards approached. The whole damned circus had arrived.

"It would have been simpler if you'd let me get a confession first," Charlie griped as John pushed past Raul and clapped handcuffs on Jacobsen. The man still breathed.

"But not legal. This family needs only one cop, all right?" John snapped the other cuff closed while his fellow officers handcuffed the Russian and a medic ran up to check Jacobsen's shoulder wound.

"I thought they'd banished you from the family," Charlie

commented idly to John as Raul handed the deadly weapons over to one of the policemen. Penelope was surreptitiously wiping her eyes, but he wasn't letting her out of his arms.

"I've decided not to stay banished," John replied curtly. "I'm going back upstairs. The FBI has enough evidence on Jacobsen and his cohorts to keep them occupied for quite a while. They've caught the guy you tackled at the volcano. He's got a few broken ribs and he's squealing like a pig. You won't have to worry about them again."

Charlie nodded. He didn't care about Jacobsen or the FBI or anything else but the woman in his arms, love and pride glowing in her eyes. He hadn't done a damned thing, but she looked at him as if he'd hung the moon. A guy could get used to that kind of admiration. She made him feel as if he deserved a woman like her, that his job and his background and all that other superficial stuff had no relevance at all. Hell, maybe she'd even forgive him football and the GTO.

As the crowd dissipated, Charlie didn't bother to see where everyone went. He simply stood up without letting her go.

Her arms slid around him, her hair brushed his chin, and he rested his head against hers. "Say it again, Penny," he whispered.

She didn't even hesitate. "I love you, Charlie. Will you marry me?"

He laughed. He roared out loud, causing several of the departing crowd to turn and gape. He caught her up and lifted her from her feet, dangling her above him, no mean feat since his Penelope was nearly as tall as he was. She propped her hands on his shoulders and grinned. Grinned. He'd made Hard-hearted Miss Albright smile.

"Where's the chapel? Call the preacher. There's always one of them hanging around places like this."

"I think you need a license," she reminded him politely. "And I want Beth beside me. You'll have to wait."

He lowered her carefully. "Not long," he threatened.

She sighed and rolled her eyes. "I know, we've waited long

enough, life happens, you believe in doing not talking, and I suppose there's no time like the present."

Charlie steered her down the corridor toward the bank of elevators. He couldn't hurry Beth's operation. They couldn't possibly do anything today, but he had this urge to rush, as if she'd change her mind if he didn't. "Damned right. We'll have it in your sister's hospital room. If you want a fancy wedding, we can repeat it again later. I'll not have you accepting a better offer. I want this contract signed, sealed, and delivered."

"Charlie, this isn't a business. . . ."

She was still protesting as he hauled her into an empty elevator and kissed her even before the doors closed.

"I believe the operation went reasonably well," the doctor intoned. "We removed the clot causing the pain. You do understand her eyesight will never return to normal," he warned them, directing his attention particularly to John. "There may be some degree of light and dark, but no more than that."

"But no pain, and no more danger to her health?" John asked anxiously.

"None that we can foresee."

Penelope watched as John took a deep breath of relief and jabbed his fingers into his hair with the look of a man reprieved from death. Instead of condemning him as she had in the past, she would have to sing his praises to her twin. They deserved a second chance.

She slid her fingers around Charlie's sturdy arm and leaned her head against his shoulder. Beth would be all right. That's all they could ask for now.

"Tammy and Raul took the kids back to your place, Penny. Somebody ought to go back and relieve them," Charlie reminded her. "Want me to go while you wait for your sister to wake?"

John's head jerked up. He focused a determined glare on Penelope. "She's my wife. Leave me with her."

Penelope heard the warning in his voice and smiled. "Ex-wife," she reminded him gently. "And I'm not our mother, John. I won't take her away. But I won't let anyone hurt her either."

He looked momentarily uncertain, then nodded. "I won't hurt her. I just want her to know I'll be there for her, okay?"

"Tell her I'll look after the kids until she's ready." With a shrug, she added, "I don't think I'll be going back into work anyway."

John didn't even question her. He hurried down the hall to the room where Beth slept. Penelope endured the tearing pain of separation from her twin, but it was time to let go. Beth had to put her own life together.

Charlie clasped her shoulders and gently led her away, but he hadn't missed her comment at all. "You talked to your boss?"

She shrugged again. "Checked my voice mail. Jacobsen got to him. I've been fired. They're sending my personal effects by courier."

"I can get you the job back, if you want it," he assured her.

She threw him a curious glance. "I don't particularly want it, but I don't know how much of this operation Beth's insurance will cover. John's salary certainly won't handle it. As much as I'd like to take your suggestion and start my own company, it's not a wise idea to start a new business while thousands in debt. I've had offers from other firms. I'll be all right."

"I got you into this; I'll take care of it," he said firmly.

"Poindexter?" Holding the phone close to his ear, Charlie could still hear the kids screaming with laughter in the front room of Penelope's apartment. They'd sent Tammy and Raul back to his place last night, and he and Penelope had stayed here, waiting for word on Beth. The general cheer in the other room now was mostly relief at Beth's phone call this morning. She'd promised them she'd be home soon to teach the kids how to tickle their father.

At the sound of Penelope's employer's voice on the other end of the line, Charlie returned his attention to the matter at hand. "Poindexter, this is Charles Smith of Smith and Son Construction. We met last week. I understand Miss Albright is no longer with your firm. I want to cancel my account with you. Send me a finalized bill. My stepfather will be withdrawing his proposal for the Foundation's account as well, so you may as well get that one together also."

Charlie listened briefly to the older man's prolific excuses and offers of better personnel, but he didn't have the patience for more and cut him off. "You don't understand, Poindexter. Miss Albright was the only reason we even considered a stagnating firm like yours. Now that Jacobsen and his companies are being indicted for fraud, corruption, and a list of charges longer than my arm, I don't want my companies to have any association with a firm that harbors criminals." Charlie smiled into the stunned silence and threw the final blow. "I've warned the builders associations, Poindexter. Mine won't be the only company taking a long hard look at the way your firm does business. I hope you enjoy your association with Jacobsen. Expect to spend the next few months in court. Have a good day." Gently, he returned the receiver to its cradle.

Charlie looked up to find Penelope standing in the bedroom doorway, watching him. He didn't know how much she'd heard, but it didn't embarrass him. He crossed the room and kissed her. "You've got Cheerios in your hair," he whispered in her ear.

She crushed her fingers into his shirt as if to hold him off but he had full confidence in the ties binding them now. She wouldn't kill him for having a little fun.

"That was getting my job back?" she asked mockingly. "Did he have a heart attack?"

"Probably," he said cheerfully. "He was sputtering pretty good there at the end." He retrieved the Cheerio and handed it to her. "I'm not done yet though. I know ten contractors right off the top of my head who've told me they've been thinking

about setting up better computer systems. Corporations can
have different divisions, can't they?"

She looked at him through eyes narrowed with suspicion.
"Of course. Why?"

He wrapped his arms around her waist and pulled her
closer. Her hips rubbed his, but she held him off with her
hands so she could watch him.

Charlie smiled. "I'm thinking if I put you on my payroll,
we can cut out all that extra tax business and insurance you'd
have if you started your own shop, and you can head up some
kind of financial division of my company, specializing in
construction software."

She stared at him. "Charles Maximillian Smith, you've already planned a wedding, two babies, and a house. Now you
want to take over my career?"

He glared at her. "Who told you about that Maximillian
part?"

"Did you think you'd hide it from me forever? Your mother
and I had a long talk." Grinning, she slid her hands from his
chest to circle his waist. Then she wiggled her hips against
his. His response must have been pretty obvious, because she
giggled and pressed herself closer. "Can't, not now. We've
got kids, remember?"

"We'll hire a nanny," he growled. At a shriek from the far
room, he grimaced. "Maybe two."

❧ EPILOGUE ❧

Beth adjusted the wide-brimmed lacy concoction of her hat at a jaunty angle. "No one can see I look like warmed-over death, can they?" she asked anxiously.

Penelope kissed her sister's cheek. "You're so radiant, they'll think you're the bride."

"Oh, Pen, I wish I could see you. I bet you look gorgeous." She fingered Penelope's silk brocade. "I'm glad Mother could be here to see you in her gown."

"Umm, well, it's a good thing she was pregnant with us when she got married or my waist would never fit in it," Penelope replied with a sniff, adjusting the circlet of flowers holding back her hair.

"Penelope! That's a terrible thing to say. You have a lovely waistline. Mother was only eighteen when she married. We were a lot skinnier at that age too. The gown fits just fine."

"Ladies, I suggest you hurry. The groom's threatening to come after you." John appeared in the doorway of the reception room they were using for last-minute preparations. He'd taken the day off from his new job at the DA's office, where his legal background had proved invaluable in tracking all the evidence for the Jacobsen case.

"Well, tell him to hold on to his cummerbund; we'll get there when we're ready," Penelope said acerbically. "He's the one who decided to make a production of this."

Beth shook her head at John. "She's just nervous; ignore her. We'll be right out. Tell the piano player to get ready."

Penelope could see him standing there stubbornly, waiting for Beth. It was a damned good thing this was a casual affair. The argument over whether Beth could walk the aisle alone had been an ongoing one from the very start. The small garden beside the apartment complex had a path accessible to all its physically challenged occupants. Beth could maneuver it with a cane, but she'd been hesitant about using one and ruining the look of the wedding. Penelope hadn't objected, but John had insisted that he could rent a tux and walk beside her. After that, Penelope had just stayed out of the way.

The first strains of the wedding march rang through the open doorway, carried on the same breeze as a strong scent of gardenias. A tear crept from the corner of Penelope's eye as Beth hesitated, then slowly accepted the offer of John's arm. They looked wonderful together. She'd not lied earlier. Beth looked so radiant, people would mistake her for the bride, and John just beamed with happiness. To heck with formality, this was what weddings were all about—love.

She gulped nervously as her turn came to walk down the aisle. Her father had stayed home, probably too broke to afford airfare or too ashamed to face them, so she had to walk the aisle alone. She didn't mind. She'd walked alone for years. It was just the principle of the thing right now. If a love like Beth and John's, or her mother and father's, could go so far wrong so easily, what were her chances of succeeding?

Remembering she had already made that decision, that it was far too late to turn coward now, she took a deep breath and stepped out.

One look at Charlie's face at the far end of the aisle provided all the reassurance she needed. He broadcast his love and happiness with his smile, in the pride with which he followed her progress, in the eagerness with which he reached for her. A breeze rippled his thick chestnut hair, and impatiently, he shoved a blunt hand through newly shorn locks. He was probably the most impatient man alive, but Penelope understood his eagerness to grasp life. For too long, she'd been afraid to grasp anything. She took his hand proudly now.

She scarcely noticed Charlie's best man until the minister said the words and Raul handed Charlie the rings. Charlie's mother and stepfather were here somewhere, and Tammy was with them, for now. That was another battle that had raged these past weeks, with no winner. Tammy would be staying in Miami and attending the university. Penelope would wager the chance of the love between Tammy and Raul surviving was even slimmer than the chances she'd given herself and Charlie. Still, here they were, standing before the minister, exchanging vows, sliding on the visible symbols of the chains of love they'd forged together. With love, anything was possible.

The crowd cheered and blew clouds of rainbow-prismed bubbles over their heads as Charlie kissed her, and they turned to meet their audience as husband and wife. Sunlight sparkled through the bubbles, in the tears of the women watching, on the roses bobbing on the trellis overhead. Joy filled Penelope's heart as Charlie took her hand and proudly paraded her down the path.

They'd scarcely had time for each other in these last frantic days of preparation. He'd had lawyers and accountants lined up putting together the new division of his company. He'd testified against Jacobsen and his firm. He'd had Raul back in St. Lucia, finally getting the project under way. And he still had his other projects to oversee.

He'd left Penelope to help with Beth's children while Beth recuperated, and to organize the wedding on her own. He hadn't wasted any time in talking to his fellow builders about her software, and in between the kids and the wedding, she'd been putting together proposal packages and interviewing with prospective clients. She had no fear of being a burden on Charlie's income. With all these new clients, she could pay for Beth's operation on her own. Not that she had anything to fear about bankrupting Charlie. She'd discovered Charlie really hadn't been bragging when he'd said his company was larger than Jacobsen's. Her muscle-bound, T-shirted construction worker had more money tucked away than he knew what to do with.

Actually, he knew what to do with it. He just hadn't bothered until now. They'd already hired the architect for the house they were planning to build together. Penelope smiled up at him as Charlie drew her onto the dance floor of the reception room with the first beat of the Beatles tune they'd last danced together. Ridiculous wedding song, she knew, but she loved him for the choice.

"Do you want to know a secret?" she whispered in Charlie's ear as he drew her up against him.

Charlie pulled her closer until her breasts crushed against his chest and some of his workers cheered in the background. "I don't think it's a secret anymore," he whispered back. "I think they've guessed."

Shocked, she pulled back to stare up at him. "How could they? I just found out myself."

It was his turn to look surprised. "Found out what?"

Embarrassed, Penelope realized they were talking about two different things. She tried to shake her head and wave it away, but the band changed their tune, and the floor filled with eager guests. Charlie waltzed her toward the edge of the floor.

"What secret?" he demanded. "We just stood before this crowd and vowed to love and honor for all the world to hear, so you can't renege on that one now."

She played nervously with his tie. "You know how I said we had nothing at all in common?"

Impatiently, he stopped her hand by holding it against his chest. "Yeah, but that was all superficial stuff. I thought I proved that. So I like beer and you like wine. I watch football and you watch opera. That stuff doesn't count if I'm willing to try wine and opera and you're willing to learn about football."

"Symphonies, not opera. I don't like opera either," she

stalled. "And I used to be a cheerleader, remember? I know all about football."

He brightened. "That's right. I won't have to teach you. I've got season tickets. Now I won't have to cancel them."

She grinned. It took so damned little to make him happy. "You were planning on canceling your tickets for me?" she asked in astonishment.

"Well, maybe I would have shared them with others more often," he answered grudgingly. "We could go just once in a while." His eyes narrowed again. "You still haven't told me your secret."

"You weren't planning on canceling the tickets," she accused.

"We could get season tickets to the symphony too," he compromised, tugging her toward the door.

"We can't leave yet," she protested as they slipped into the garden. Their guests were still occupied with the music and the freely flowing liquor. "I haven't thrown my bouquet. I want Beth to catch it."

"Do you have any idea how many women are in there waiting to catch that damned thing? You'd have to throw each flower individually before she'd have a chance." He drew her into the shadows of the arbor and kissed her nape. "Now spill it."

Shivers flew up and down Penelope's spine at his kisses. She wouldn't be coherent much longer, and she had so much to say. Only silliness seemed able to escape her lips. "Beth will catch it. We've worked out a signal."

Charlie groaned and lifted his head to stare down at her. "There isn't any secret, is there? You're just trying to make me crazy. What signal?"

"The same one we used when we were playing softball. Drove the other teams crazy. She'll know it's coming to her when I whistle."

"Softball? You played softball?" Bewildered, bemused, and utterly bewitched, Charlie shook his head. "When were you planning on telling me you played softball?"

She shot him an impatient look. "We couldn't play basketball or football because we were on the cheerleading squad. Pay attention, Charlie. So we played softball. We took the team to the top two years in a row."

He bent his head so his brow rested against hers. "Tell me you were the umpire."

"Of course I wasn't the umpire. Don't be ridiculous. I was the pitcher. That's how I know Beth will catch the bouquet." Her heart thumped harder. Charlie's head might be resting against hers, but she didn't think he had his eyes closed. The low-cut bodice of her mother's gown strained a bit too tightly across her breasts.

"My wife the athlete, and here I thought I would be the only dumb jock in this family. We'll have a family of Neanderthals. Do you think we could teach them football and softball both?" His hands crept up to rest just below her breasts.

Breathless at this proximity, Penelope tried to respond sensibly. She should have waited until tonight, until they were alone, but she'd wanted to share this gift with him for hours. She'd wanted to share it that morning, when she'd found out. So, maybe impatience was another trait they shared.

"Well, twins run in the family. We could eventually have enough to make an entire team."

Charlie's hands stopped their slow upward movement, and he lifted his head enough to watch her face instead of her breasts. She could almost see the blue of the tropical skies in his eyes.

"Twins usually skip a generation," he said carefully.

Penelope shrugged. "Twins run on *both* sides of our family. My grandfather had a twin brother."

"Beth and John didn't have twins," he pointed out, a shade nervously.

"John doesn't have twins in his family. Your mother said your father had uncles who were triplets." She figured her pulse had reached rocket proportions. How dense could one man be?

"Triplets," he repeated flatly. "We could have triplets." Grasping her shoulders firmly, Charlie filled his chest deep with air and asked, "How soon?"

It was a good thing Charlie's hands were holding her up or she might have collapsed with sheer relief at not having to actually say the words. "By my inexpert calculations," Penelope whispered, "in seven months."

He dropped to the arbor bench with a puff of exhaled air. The bench cracked with the weight of the blow. Charlie didn't seem to notice. He caught her hips between his big hands and pulled her toward him, studying her flat belly intently. "Seven months?"

She nodded, although she doubted he saw her.

"A baby?" He looked up hopefully, this time watching her face.

"No, a rocket ship," she said dryly. "Or triplets. What's the difference?"

"Or triplets. My God." Stunned, he sat there a moment longer, absorbing the information. "I think I'll have that champagne now."

"You don't like champagne," she reminded him.

"That's all right. I'll take a magnum of it anyway." Lumbering to his feet, towering over her, his barrel-wide chest and shoulders powerful enough to support a small car, Charlie swayed like a leaf on the wind.

He stared down at the waistline he'd studied moments before, and Penelope could swear he turned gray.

"Triplets?" he inquired weakly.

"Three dozen dirty diapers a day," she replied wickedly. "Three mouths screaming at midnight. Why, you could have a whole *team* of football players in a few years."

"You'd do that to me, wouldn't you?" he demanded, recovering enough of his equilibrium to push her toward the reception hall. "You'd do it to me just to get even with me for getting you pregnant."

"If that could be arranged," she agreed as they stepped into the crowded room. As he grabbed a bottle of champagne from a passing waiter, she stood on tiptoe and whispered in his ear, "I think it was the Jacuzzi. The *first* one."

His hand jerked, and the champagne cork hit the ceiling.

Foam fizzed and spurted across the room, drawing all stares in their direction. Waving the foaming bottle at his audience, Charlie shouted at the top of his lungs, "We're going to have a *Jacuzzi*!"

Laughter erupted and rolled around the room until Penelope's ears turned red and she pounded Charlie's wide chest in embarrassment. He merely lifted her from her feet and swung her in circles, swigging the champagne straight from the bottle, spilling half of it down his tux and her gown.

"Hey, John," he shouted again, spotting a tower of flowers on the table with their untouched wedding cake. Grabbing a bouquet, he swung around until he found Beth's ex standing in a far corner, watching the scene with amusement. "She says it's your turn next. Catch!"

The bouquet flew swiftly and accurately straight into the hands of its intended target. John stared at the flowers in puzzlement.

"We're gonna have us a football team! You'd better start teaching your kids."

With that rollicking cry, Charlie swept Penelope off her feet and into his arms, and proceeded out the door.

No one tried to stop him. Not even Penelope.

And not once did she ever mention his rude, uncouth, Neanderthal behavior, except maybe a few times amid a litany of more explicit curses during the interminable hours of labor seven months later. But that was to be expected of a mother of five-and-a-half-pound twins.

Charlie bought them Dolphins helmets. One had a pink bow.

The national bestseller

BLUE CLOUDS
by Patricia Rice

Around the small California town where Pippa Cochran has fled to escape an abusive boyfriend, Seth Wyatt is called the Grim Reaper—and not just because he is a bestselling author of horror novels. He's an imposing presence, battling more inner demons than even an indefatigable woman like Pippa can handle. Yet, while in his employ, she can't resist the emotional pull of his damaged son or the chance to hide in the fortress he calls a home.

Then Pippa's amazing gifts begin to alter their world in ways none of them could have imagined. But soon something goes wrong. Dangerous "accidents" occur, threatening to destroy the tremulous new love that Pippa and Seth have dared to discover.

New in hardcover . . .

THE WILD CHILD

by Mary Jo Putney

author of the

New York Times bestseller

One Perfect Rose

Published by Ballantine Books.

THE WILD CHILD

Dominic Renbourne agrees to take his twin brother
Kyle's place at Warfield Manor, where he is to pay
gentlemanly court to Lady Meriel Grahame, the
orphaned and extravagantly wealthy heiress Kyle
intends to marry. The last thing Dominic expects is
to be entranced by a silent woman whose ethereal
beauty is as stunning as her mystical relationship to
the intoxicating flowers and trees that surround her.
But will Meriel forgive his deceit once she learns he
is not Kyle? And will their passion endure the rift
that will divide the two brothers?

MIDNIGHT ON JULIA STREET

by Ciji Ware

The sultry allure of New Orleans comes to dazzling life in this enthralling tale of romance and mystery that sweeps from the modern heart of the Big Easy back to the shimmering city of a century past. Reporter Corlis McCullough's search for the truth drives her to chase a story involving historical preservationist King Duvallon, an adversary from her college years. After a decade, he still manages to incite her fury—and worse: a growing attraction as strong and unstoppable as the tides along the Delta.

Published by Fawcett Books.
Available in bookstores everywhere.